Fiercely, Cain pulled her into his arms
and silenced her words with his mouth
against hers. Elizabeth tried to pull away,
but he was too strong. Her struggles went
unheeded as Cain seared her lips with a
fiery all-consuming kiss of unleashed barbaric passion. Then, as suddenly as he had
begun his assault, he released her.

"Look into your heart, English woman,"
he said huskily.

Elizabeth swallowed hard. Her pulse
was racing and her knees were too weak
to stand. Tentatively, she touched her
lower lip with the tip of her tongue, remembering the feel of his hard mouth on
hers, savoring the bittersweet pangs of
sensual longing. Why? an inner voice
cried. Why did this savage affect her this
way?

LOVESTORM

JUDITH E. FRENCH

AVON BOOKS ◆ NEW YORK

AVON BOOKS
A division of
The Hearst Corporation
105 Madison Avenue
New York, New York 10016

Copyright © 1990 by Judith E. French
Inside cover author photograph by Susan Gregg
Published by arrangement with the author
Library of Congress Catalog Card Number: 89-91929
ISBN: 0-380-75553-X

First Avon Books Printing: February 1990

AVON TRADEMARK REG. U.S. PAT. OFF. AND IN OTHER COUNTRIES, MARCA REGISTRADA, HECHO EN U.S.A.

Printed in the U.S.A.

RA 10 9 8 7 6 5 4 3 2 1

For my tough, beautiful baby sister, Valerie Bennett Donahue, ever my faithful sidekick. At the beginning, when no one else would, she listened to all my stirring tales of high adventure and never, ever laughed when they weren't supposed to be funny.

This night of no moon
There is no way to meet him
I rise in longing—
My breast pounds, a leaping flame,
My heart is consumed in fire.

Ono no Komachi

Part One

Chapter 1

The Virginia Coast
April 1664

The square-rigged barkentine pitched and rolled in the savage seas like an untamed horse. Gale-force winds ripped at her yards and topsails, tearing at the sailors high in the rigging, carrying away sections of her port rails and binnacle, shredding sails and sending yards and widow makers plunging to the deck.

Lady Elizabeth Sommersett fought her way up the ladder in pitch darkness and threw her weight against the hatch. A gust of wind seized the wooden door and wrenched it from its hinges. Elizabeth clung to the side of the hatchway and stared into the mouth of hell.

Waves crashed over the slanting deck, and human screams mingled with those of the horses trapped below deck. Not six paces from where she stood, Elizabeth could see the bare feet and legs of a man protruding from a shapeless heap of tangled sailcloth and rope. The bosun's whistle sounded over and over, the shrill notes distorted and carried away by the relentless wind.

Elizabeth threw up a hand to shield her face

3

from the driving rain and salt spray as a sailor
staggered past her with an axe and began to hack
at the mainsail. She stared in disbelief, too
shocked by the fury of the storm to utter a sound.
We're going to sink, she thought. We're all going
to die.

Suddenly, the ship's captain materialized out
of the darkness and seized Elizabeth's arm. Leaning close, the man shouted into her ear. "To the
longboat, m'lady! Her back's broken! We're aban-
doning ship!" Without waiting for an answer, he
began to drag her across the deck.

Elizabeth shut her eyes against the force of the
wind and rain, only half aware of the weeping
girl who grabbed on to her free hand.

"Are we goin' t' dee?"

Elizabeth turned to see little Betty, her aunt's
scullery maid, clinging to her. Barely eleven and
thin as a rail, the child was in real danger of being
washed overboard by the force of the wind and
water. "Hold tight to me!" Elizabeth commanded, locking her fingers around Betty's wrist.
"I won't let you die."

"Quick now, Lady Elizabeth!" the captain interrupted. "The longboat's full! We've no time
for—"

"But what of my aunt and uncle!" she cried.
But he couldn't hear. Her words were lost in the
wind. Seconds later, Elizabeth spied her aunt and
uncle huddled in the small boat with a half dozen
other passengers and several seamen. Four sailors
were in the process of lowering the boat from
davits into the angry sea.

Her aunt caught sight of her and screamed.
"Elizabeth!"

"Hurry!" the captain insisted, shoving Elizabeth toward the longboat. "They've only room for one more!"

Betty's face whitened, and she clung to Elizabeth, screaming. "Don't leave me here t' dee! M'lady! Please don't leave me!"

"Elizabeth!" her uncle called. One end of the boat tilted violently.

Elizabeth steadied herself against the port rail. "Can't we take the girl?" she asked the captain. "She's small. She won't—"

"No! The boat is overloaded as it—"

"Is there another longboat?" she demanded.

"Yes, on the starboard side. But—"

Elizabeth spun Betty around and shoved her toward the boat. Betty's knee struck the gunnel, and she tumbled screaming into the midst of the passengers. The sailors released the ropes, dropping the longboat into the waves below.

"You fool!" the captain cried. Taking Elizabeth's arm roughly, he pushed her toward the far side of the ship.

A wave swept over the deck, soaking her to mid-thigh and nearly knocking her off her feet. Elizabeth covered her head with her hands as a heavy weight fell from above to glance off one shoulder. A splinter of wood ripped through her gown and cut a gash across her back. She cried out, falling forward into the captain's arms, and he steadied her, pointing ahead to the outline of another longboat.

They stumbled toward the starboard rail together. The first officer was alone in the longboat; the bosun and the ship's carpenter manned the davits. "No more of your nonsense, woman," the captain shouted. "In you go." Catching Elizabeth around the waist, he lifted her into the stern of the longboat with the first officer. Other passengers and sailors pressed closely about them. "Hold!" the captain ordered. "We'll use the Jacob's ladder."

A grinding crash shook the ship as the mainsail fell. Instantly, the ship began to tilt, lifting the longboat even higher from the surface of the sea. Elizabeth clung to rough boards of the seat, trying to extricate her ankle from the tangle of line in the bottom of the boat.

"She's taking water!" a man screamed.

Two seaman lunged for the rail, and Elizabeth caught the gleam of steel as the captain's sword flashed. Someone screamed, and a widow maker thrashed back and forth, knocking the carpenter over the side. Without warning, before anyone else could get in, the bow of the longboat plunged down toward the water, and the first officer fell headlong into the sea.

Elizabeth dangled head down in the swaying boat, one foot caught by the coil of rope. She cried out in pain and fear as her head slammed against the side of the longboat. Beneath her, she could see the white turbulent water.

"Cut the rope!" a man shouted.

Elizabeth's head struck the side of the boat again, and her world dissolved into soft blackness.

Shivering, Elizabeth raised her head and stared into the emptiness of the gray morning. As far as she could see, there was nothing but whitecaps and rolling waves. The rain was cold on her face and arms; her feet and hands were too numb to feel anything. She was alone in the Atlantic, marooned on a fragile scrap of worm-riddled wood that bobbed to and fro at the mercy of the wind and tide. Elizabeth had seen nothing, heard nothing but the ceaseless wind, the waves, and the constant drumming of the icy rain. No screaming gulls, no white-patched petrels skimming over the gray-green surface of the angry sea . . . no sign of land.

Elizabeth cupped her hands to catch the cold rain. It tasted of salt, but she didn't care. She was thirsty—so thirsty that she couldn't seem to ease her parched throat no matter how much she lapped at the salty rainwater.

She wondered how far the boat had drifted in the storm. At first light, she'd strained her eyes to see the outline of the *Speedwell*, or some bobbing speck against the horizon that might be the other longboat. Common sense had told her that the *Speedwell* had gone to the bottom, and the other boat, if it had not sunk, would be leagues away. But she had hoped and stared until her eyes ached, and she had seen nothing but rain and water and gray sky.

She laughed, a lonely sound in the little boat. She had always prided herself on being a realist. The *Speedwell* was gone; her aunt and uncle and the others in the first longboat might well be dead—even whining little Betty with her grubby bare feet and close-bitten fingernails. She hoped not. They'd had a chance, surely. Her aunt's boat had oars and seamen to man them.

Elizabeth had no idea how far they were off the Virginia Coast. Thirty leagues? Sixty? The captain himself might not have known exactly where they were when the ship began to break up.

Storms had plagued the *Speedwell* from the time it had left the West Indies. The ship had been traveling in company with another vessel, the *Fruitful Merchant*, which had turned back to the Indies when sickness had broken out aboard. Her aunt had begged the captain of the *Speedwell* to return with the other ship to the port in the islands where they had anchored for fresh water and supplies, but he had laughed at her fears. There had been a few days of brisk sailing before they had reached Cape Hatteras, then the weather had turned foul. Near hurricane winds had battered the ship northward for days, culminating in the squall that had brought disaster to crew and passengers alike.

Elizabeth's heart was heavy as she remembered the screams of the horses trapped in the hold. Her own mare, Sarah, and the bay stallion she was bringing Edward as a wedding gift were probably as dead as the rest. Such a terrible waste! Sarah was dear to her, and the stallion probably would have sired finer colts and fillies than any now cropping the green grass of the Virginia Colony.

She laughed again, ruefully. Her mother had accused her of being shallow and godless. Perhaps Mother had been right. What kind of woman would regret the loss of a pet horse when her aunt and uncle, and some thirty other souls, all lay at the bottom of the sea?

Elizabeth sighed and buried her face in her hands. She had not loved her aunt and uncle, but she was fond of them. Her aunt was a silly woman, all flutter and show—too lazy to be unkind and too stupid to ever have an original thought of her own. Her uncle John had no lack of brains, but they had been wasted in the foolish pursuit of loose women, as his ample inheritance had been squandered at the gaming tables. Elizabeth had learned early that it was best to stay clear of Uncle John when he was in his cups. His hands had a habit of straying where they should not, even if the object of his attention was a twelve-year-old niece. Yet, despite their faults, Elizabeth would not have wished her aunt and uncle dead. Guiltily, she offered a murmured prayer for their safety and wondered if they believed her lost forever.

The sky was so gray she couldn't see the sun. Was her boat drifting farther out to sea or toward the Virginia coast? There was no way to tell. If she didn't wash up on land, or if she wasn't picked up by a passing ship, she would either drown or starve to death. Elizabeth shuddered.

Nonsense! She was too young to die. And certainly too young to die in an absurd accident at sea! "If I were going to drown, I would have done it by now," she declared, spreading her hands out in front of her. Her fingers were puckered, her palms raw. She wondered why her hands were scraped and bruised, and supposed it must be from clutching the rough sides of the boat.

Her rings hung loose on her fingers—the pearl her father had given her for her sixteenth birthday, the ruby she had inherited from her dead Scottish grandmother, and the heavy gold and emerald betrothal ring. If she drifted to shore, perhaps she could trade the jewelry for food or safe passage to Jamestown. Would her betrothed begrudge her trading an emerald ring that had been a gift to one of his ancestors from Henry VIII, to some painted savage for a meal?

There was a loud *whoosh*, and something huge surfaced beside the longboat. For an instant, Elizabeth stared into a round, black eye, and then the creature vanished beneath the waves. "Oh!" Elizabeth let out a long shuddering breath. She clamped her chattering teeth together and stared at the spot where the beast had been. Before her heartbeat had slowed to normal, the waves parted on the far side of the boat, and a pair of dolphins gazed curiously at her.

"Oh, my," she managed. "Oh!" They were enormous, with dark, sleek bodies and intelligent eyes. She had no doubt that the dolphins could swamp her boat if they wanted to, but Elizabeth was oddly without fear. "Oh," she repeated softly, "you beautiful things."

As if sensing her admiration, the larger of the two mammals dove straight into the air, giving a spinning twist as it plunged into the sea. The second followed suit, then both returned to the surface near the spot she had first caught sight of them.

For nearly an hour, the dolphins swam and played beside the boat, then as suddenly as they had come, they disappeared. Elizabeth watched and waited for a long time, and a heavy sadness settled over her as she realized once more how truly alone she was.

Her head ached. The rain had long since washed away the blood from the cut on her head, but her ruined gown was stained with ugly brown patches. A lump the size of a pullet egg swelled just above her left ear, and her back stung where salt water soaked into the gash she had gotten on the ship. Her honey-blond hair hung in sodden ropes, and she realized with ironic amusement that she was wearing only one shoe.

"The Lady Elizabeth Anne Sommersett," she proclaimed mockingly. "Lady Elizabeth wishes coffee and sweets served to her guests in the orangery." Tears welled up in her green eyes, and she ripped off the single shoe and flung it as far as she could into the ocean.

The rise and fall of the boat knotted her stom-

ach into spasms. Her weakness shamed her. She
had always been a good sailor; even as a child
when she'd crossed the Channel to France or gone
to Ireland with her father. If only she wasn't so
damned cold. If only the dolphins would come
back . . .

Shaakhan Kihittuun's muscles rippled beneath
his bronzed skin as he thrust the hickory paddle
deep into the blue-green water and parted the
waves in a tireless rhythm. The dugout skimmed
over the surface of the sea, responding to his
commands as though it were an extension of his
sleek, powerful body. Even the color of the cy-
press wood blended with his copper skin and
glossy, sable-brown hair, making it difficult to see
where the man left off and the boat began.

The sea was an angry gray, the whitecaps divided by swirling eddies of frothy green and dirty
brown, legacy of the storm that had assaulted the
beach and surrounding forests for three days and
nights. The clouds hung low over the water,
pierced by the hungry cries of seagulls. The birds
wheeled and swooped overhead, occasionally
diving into the sea and emerging with a squirming fish trapped in their beaks.

Shaakhan loved the sea in all her moods. When
the sun shone and bits of light danced across the
surface of the water, he would paddle his dugout
far to the east out of sight of land, sometimes to
fish, and sometimes just to become a part of the
magic of water and sky that stretched on beyond
a man's imagination. He knew the creatures of
the sea—the mighty whales and the enigmatic
rays, the fish and the dolphins—as well as he knew
the animals and birds of the forest. Those days

were good, when the weather was fair and the great salt water rocked his dugout in her arms as gently as a mother might rock her child.

But Shaakhan knew the sea was as changeable as a woman. He loved her still when her winds blew and her waves rose and fell in crashing fury. Sometimes, he thought he loved the sea best when she battled with the shoreline and tore away whole sections of beach, threatening the boundaries of the forest. And when the worst of the storm had passed, he never failed to launch his boat into the surf and challenge her undaunted spirit.

His dark, almond-shaped eyes narrowed as he fixed his gaze on an unfamiliar object bobbing on the waves far out on the sea. He had glimpsed it before, then lost sight of it. It was foreign to the sea and sky, and Shaakhan grew curious. What was this thing cradled on the breast of the great salt water, and where had it come from?

Shaakhan hesitated, his paddle poised in midair while silvery drops of water dripped off the blade. Then the waves parted and a dolphin leaped out of the depths and flew over the dugout. Before Shaakhan could do more than gasp in wonder, a smaller dolphin repeated the performance.

The man smiled. "Ah, my friends," he called to the dolphins. "It is good to see you again."

Immediately, the larger creature rose out of the water and bounced across the surface on the tip of his tail. The smaller, a young female, contented herself with several excited jumps and a wide-mouthed hissing.

"What is it?" Shaakhan eased the paddle into the dugout slowly and laid it across his lap. "Do you wish to tell me something?"

The male disappeared beneath the surface of the water and came up beside the female. For a moment, they lingered within arm's length of Shaakhan, then both turned and made a final twisting leap before diving out of sight. When they surfaced again to breathe, it was nearly a bowshot away. Shaakhan saw only a flash of white, and then the dolphins were gone.

Just beyond the point where the dolphins went under bobbed the strange object. Shaakhan lifted his paddle and turned the dugout in that direction. As he narrowed the distance between them, he realized it was some sort of canoe.

Elizabeth lay on her back in the bottom of the longboat. She was no longer conscious of time or of being cold. In fact, she was hot; her face and arms, the surface of her skin, seemed to be burning up. Her mouth was parched, her lips swollen and cracked. Her eyes ached so badly that it hurt to try to open them.

She knew the rain had ceased because she was so thirsty. She missed the sound of the drops hitting the wooden vessel. Now there was nothing but the rise and fall of the waves and the *whoosh* of water against the hull. Up and down . . . up and down . . . She threw an arm over her eyes and thought of ripe strawberries. Strawberries with fresh cream.

The memory was so pleasant that she didn't hear the scrape of wood as the two boats brushed against each other. She was unaware of the man binding the two crafts together with a bit of bark fishing line and climbing in beside her.

"Hokkuaa?"

Elizabeth moaned deep in her throat and tossed her head. An arm slipped under her shoulder and lifted her up. "What?" She blinked as a man's tanned face came into focus. "Where am I?" she gasped.

"*Mumaane*. Drink . . . drink this."

A few drops of sweet water trickled between her lips, and Elizabeth clutched at the gourd container.

"No, just a little," the man cautioned in husky, precise English.

She gulped at the precious liquid until he pulled it away. "Do I know you?" Her voice was cracked and weak. Was this real or a dream? Elizabeth willed her mind to function. "Who are you?"

He smiled, his large, dark eyes kind in his bronzed face. "I am Cain," he said. "Do not have fear. I will not harm you."

"A ship?" Elizabeth reached for the water gourd again. "Do you have a ship?" He let her have another sip of the water, and she closed her eyes in weariness. He looks like a pirate, she thought, but a gentle pirate. It was impossible to be afraid of those huge, liquid eyes.

"You are . . . on the great . . . great salt water," he said. "I take you to land. Be not afraid."

She knew when he lifted her, but she was powerless to help or to resist him. He laid her on her side and removed his doeskin vest, covering her face with the soft garment.

"To stop the burn," he said.

The movement of the waves was different. When Elizabeth pushed away the covering and forced her eyes open, she saw the outline of the man above her, bare-chested, dark against the sky. "Who are you?" she asked again.

He laughed softly. "I told you," he said. "I am Cain."

"But . . ." Her mind hovered between light and darkness. "Do I know you?"

"You know me," he replied. "You have always known me."

Chapter 2

Elizabeth gradually became aware that there was no movement beneath her. The steady swish of the water was absent; she heard nothing but the sound of her own breathing. Hesitantly, she opened her eyes and found she was in a small, shadowy room that smelled of pine boughs. She raised her right hand; it brushed against a rough, sloping wall. Bewildered, she tried to sit up.

"Lie still," a masculine voice commanded. "You are safe."

Elizabeth sighed and laid her head back as she recognized the voice of the man who had taken her from the longboat. Wherever she was, she had not been robbed or ravished. Her rings still hung heavy on her fingers.

"Wh-where am I?" Her throat hurt, and she sounded like an ancient crone. "Is this land?"

The man chuckled. "Unless the sea decides to claim it again." He squatted beside her and held out a bowl. "Have you hunger?"

Elizabeth moistened her cracked lips with her tongue and tried to gather her wits. She was warm, her eyes caught the flicker of a small fire, and the bed beneath her was soft. When she shifted her weight on the mattress, the odor of pine became stronger. She blinked, adjusting her vision to the dim light of the fire. This is not a room in a house, she thought. It is some primitive hut. In the center of the low roof was an opening. "Stars," she said, half to herself. "It's night."

"Yes," her companion agreed. "Yesterday, I take you from the sea. You have fever. You sleep long time."

She tried to place his accent. *Yorkshire?* His speech was oddly old-fashioned but perfectly comprehensible. Elizabeth put a hand to her hair. It was neatly brushed and bound into braids. It felt damp. She was wearing a crude skin tunic. Whoever did my hair must have changed my clothing, Elizabeth thought. She fixed her gaze on the man once more. "You are . . ." She struggled to remember his name. "Cain?"

"Cain Dare."

"Yes." She caught a whiff of what was in the bowl and was suddenly ravenous. "Is that soup?"

"Good."

He grinned broadly, and she noticed that his dark hair was cut off square at the shoulder. He was wearing a sleeveless leather vest, open in the front; beneath the garment his muscular chest was bare. A wide copper bracelet encircled the bulging biceps of one brawny, hairless arm. A pirate! She remembered her earlier impression with a shiver of excitement. I've been captured by a pirate!

"It is good that you hunger," he continued. "Food and rest will make you strong." He set the bowl on the floor and lifted her to a half-sitting position, adjusting a wooden backrest behind her. "There," he said. "Now you eat."

Elizabeth started at his touch. There was nothing lewd or familiar about the man's manner, but the heat of his arm burned through her rough garment like fire. He lifted her as easily as though she were a child. She drew in a ragged breath. "Oh."

Sensing her fear, he withdrew a short distance away and crouched motionless. "You have no danger," he repeated. "I am friend." He held out the steaming bowl of soup. "Eat."

"I have not thanked you for saving me," Elizabeth said shakily. "I am the Lady Elizabeth Anne Sommersett. I am betrothed to Edward Lindsey, son of the earl of Dunmore. If you take me to Jamestown, or inform my family that I am here, you will be richly rewarded."

"Eat the soup while it has hot."

"Don't you understand?" Elizabeth grew imperious. "I am a person of great importance. Do you know where Jamestown is?"

"I know." He rose to his feet.

Elizabeth felt her cheeks grow hot. The man was wearing little but an apron of skin about his loins. Hastily, she averted her eyes. Even a pirate would be civilized enough to wear breeches! Was she being held prisoner by a madman? "I insist that you contact my betrothed at once," she sputtered.

"This one hears you. Do you always talk so loud?"

Torn between the desire to put this ruffian in his place and to fill the aching void in her stomach, Elizabeth allowed herself a haughty sniff. "Send me a serving woman," she commanded. "I want my own clothes. I cannot wear this . . . this thing." She fingered the buckskin tunic distastefully.

Cain folded his arms across his chest and stared

down at her. "I do not understand what is *serving woman*," he said.

"The woman who removed my garments, who braided my hair. Send her to me at once!" Elizabeth reached for the bowl of soup and the horn spoon, and took a tentative sip. The broth was delicious! Eagerly, she spooned the rich mixture into her mouth. Even the seasoning was delicate, she was glad to discover—in her experience, cooks tried to cover the taste of spoiled meat with heavy spices.

The man's amused chuckle brought her to an abrupt halt. She glared at him fiercely. "I am not accustomed to asking twice for what I want," she said.

"I can see that."

Elizabeth felt her temper rising. "Well?"

"There is no woman here."

"No woman? Nonsense," she retorted. "If there's no woman, then who . . . Oh." Her cheeks burned with embarrassment. "You . . ."

"You were wet and cold," he explained. "I did not want you to have sick." He shrugged. "There is no need for shame. Your body is lovely, but you be not the first woman I have seen without her clothes."

"Oh!" Angrily, Elizabeth threw her bare feet over the edge of the bed and stood up shakily. Cain made no move to stop her as she staggered toward the open doorway. Shoving aside a skin curtain, she stepped out into a warm spring night.

In panic, Elizabeth stared around her. There were no other houses, no people, no lights except the stars. The only sign of human habitation was this small hut beneath the trees. Heart pounding, she held her breath and listened. From far off, she heard the sound of the surf. "Where am I?" she cried out. "What godforsaken place is this?"

"This is my home. If I told you name, you still not know where you be."

Elizabeth shrank back. She was tall for a woman, but this man loomed over her. His shoulders were as broad as a blacksmith's; his sinewy naked thighs gleamed in the moonlight like those of some pagan gladiator.

"You have fear."

"I'm not afraid of you," she lied.

He sniffed disbelievingly. "Your tongue say one thing, but body say another. You tremble as a doe before the hunter's arrow."

"You're not English," Elizabeth exclaimed suddenly. "Who and what are you?"

"I am warrior of the Lenni-Lenape. Clan of Munsee—the wolf."

She shook her head in disbelief. "An Indian? You're an Indian?"

"India be far away." He waved his hands expressively. "Farther even than the kingdom of the Virgin Queen. This one has told you, I am Lenni-Lenape. Among my people, I am Shaakhan Kihittuun—in your tongue, Wind from the Sea."

"But you lied to me! You said your name was Cain." Elizabeth backed away until she bumped into a tree trunk. "You told me—"

"I do not lie. My grandmother shares your blood. It was she who gave me my English name."

"What are you going to do with me?"

"I take you back to the wigwam. If you run about the night with nothing on your feet, you will take again the fever and die."

Elizabeth swallowed hard. Cain's soft voice had taken on an edge of steel. "And if I refuse?"

"You cannot. You are a gift from the sea."

She scanned the ground at her feet for a rock, a stick, anything to defend herself from this savage, but there was nothing.

As if reading her mind, Cain sighed in exasperation. "If you run, I run faster. If you strike me, can you know I will not strike harder? Stop acting like spoiled child and return to house. Your soup will be cold."

"How dare you give me orders!" she said. "What right do you have to—"

"I have every right," he replied. "You belong to me."

Fear trickled down Elizabeth's spine like icy water. The man was mad! Her great-uncle Stephen's wife had been taken with fits of madness. Everyone in the household had taken pains not to alarm her for fear of her violent rages. "Pretend to agree with her," Grandmother had said. "Be ever wary with the insane." Grandmother's advice echoed in her mind as Elizabeth forced herself to stand motionless when every instinct bade her flee this crazed savage.

"Come back to the fire," Cain urged gently. "I do not hurt you."

Silently, she nodded. For now, there was nothing else she could do. Trembling, she allowed him to lead her back inside the hut.

"Will you sup?" he asked.

"No." She retreated to the bed and pulled the deerskin covering over her head. Her hunger was gone, driven back by fear. In a futile act of defiance, she turned her back on him and clenched her eyes shut.

Chuckling softly, Cain lay down on the far side of the fire and instantly went to sleep. Elizabeth lay awake until the stars began to fade from the sky.

When Elizabeth opened her eyes again, sunlight poured through the roof hole and spilled across the floor of the hut. She was alone in the room.

After a few minutes, she rose from the bed and glanced cautiously out the doorway. There was no sign of Cain. Nothing moved but a half-grown rabbit. The creature sat up on its hind legs and stared at her, twitching both ears in curiosity.

Elizabeth turned back toward the firepit; only a few coals remained, but beside it was a large clam shell containing some kind of porridge. She dipped a finger in the mush and tasted it. It was unfamiliar but delicious. Quickly, she devoured the porridge, two round cakes of unleavened bread, and a smoked fish, washing it down with water she found in a gourd container.

Her hunger satisfied, she looked around the hut more carefully. The roof was sloping, high in the center coming down to low sides. The walls were covered with bark over woven branches. Baskets and bowls hung from the ceiling supports; tanned skins covered the floor. Fishhooks and line were neatly coiled around pegs; dried corn and fish hung from strings against the far wall. What Elizabeth assumed were changes of clothing were carefully folded and stacked on a narrow platform near the entranceway. There was nothing in the hut that could be construed as a weapon, unless she counted the clay bowl of arrowheads beside her bed.

Sinking down again on the pine-bough mattress, Elizabeth tried to still her panic long enough to reason clearly. She was alone, a prisoner of a red Indian, somewhere on the coast of America. She had no way of knowing if anyone else had survived the shipwreck, but if they had, they undoubtedly believed her drowned.

All her life, she had been protected from the world by her birth and position. Her father was a powerful earl with connections to all the great houses of Europe. Since childhood, she had been cosseted and fawned over. Servants had helped to dress her, to prepare her bath and do her hair. She had never gone without a meal, or been cold, or lacked shoes.

Elizabeth stared at her scratched and swollen bare feet in disgust. How many pairs of shoes had she brought with her in her trousseau? Twenty? Thirty? She had no idea. Elizabeth's shoes were not her concern. A maid had always seen that proper attire was laid out for each occasion. Elizabeth sighed. Her shoes had gone to the bottom of the sea with all her lovely gowns, her precious books, and her jewelry. She wiggled her bare toes against the animal skin on the floor.

"You were right, Bridget," she murmured sulkily. "I should have deserted with you."

Bridget had been her maid since Elizabeth was ten years old. The black-haired Irish girl was supposed to come to the Virginia Colony with her, along with the undermaid, Nan. But Bridget had been terrified of crossing the ocean. When it came time for the ship to sail, Bridget was nowhere to be found.

Elizabeth laughed. "I called her a traitor, but she was the wise one."

Her maid Nan had sickened and died two weeks out of Bristol. Her body had been consigned to the sea long before the *Speedwell* reached the West Indies, and for the rest of the voyage,

Elizabeth had had to make do with the aid of her aunt's two French maids and useless little Betty. The French girls hadn't been in the boat with her aunt. She was afraid they had died horribly when the ship went down.

Elizabeth rubbed her face with her hands. There was no one to help her. If she was to survive this ordeal, it must be by her own wits, her own determination. She was, after all, a Sommersett, and the Sommersetts had a proud tradition of fortitude stretching back to the ancestor who had come ashore with William the Conqueror. No true Sommersett would allow himself to be intimidated or bested by a mere savage.

This barbarian might be used to dealing with simple native girls, but he had never been confronted with an English noblewoman. This whole situation was obviously a gross misunderstanding due to Cain's ignorance of the workings of the civilized world. Once he was able to comprehend Elizabeth's true station in life and her father's importance, it would be simple to insist that he transport her to the nearest English colony without delay.

Elizabeth sighed with relief. She had been foolish to panic last night when she found out the man was an Indian. He hadn't hurt her in any way—he had rescued her from the sea. She'd not been raped or abused. Cain was not dangerous, despite his misguided delusion that she *belonged* to him.

Actually, the savage had treated her quite well. He had provided food and water and a shelter from the elements, regardless of how crude. Elizabeth glanced about the hut and permitted herself a condescending smile. Except that it was so clean, the hut might have served as a henhouse on one of her father's country estates.

Feeling greatly relieved, Elizabeth left the hut and followed the sound of the waves down to the water's edge. She stopped and looked around her, taking deep breaths of the invigorating, salt-tinged air. A white sand beach stretched in either direction as far as the eye could see. The blue-green sea was calm beneath a glowing sun, and the surf rolled in gentle waves against the damp sand. It was a beautiful spring day, and the air was full of the scents and sounds of an untouched paradise.

Seagulls and shore birds of many kinds strutted along the surf line, or swooped and dove in the sky overhead. Elizabeth laughed as a crab scuttled around her feet, dragging a lacy bit of green seaweed like a ribbon behind it. "You remind me of an overaged maiden dancing around the May-pole," she said.

The crab reared up on its back fins, waved one claw in the air, and fled toward the safety of the water, still dragging the seaweed behind it.

"Coward," she taunted. She crouched down to inspect a tiny hole in the sand, when suddenly a man's head and torso surfaced above the waves directly in front of her. Startled, she jumped and fell on her backside. A rushing wave surged around her, wetting her deerskin tunic to the waist.

Cain threw back his head and laughed. He stood waist-deep in the water and held up a spear. A large fish wiggled on the end of it. "I catch our midday meal," he called. Still grinning, he pointed to the sun. "Are you always so lazy?"

He waded toward her, and Elizabeth leaped to her feet, staring in disbelief. The man was totally nude. Sparkling drops of water ran down his powerful chest and narrow waist. His hips and loins were as smooth as marble, his belly taut above his exposed male organ.

Elizabeth swallowed hard, unaware of Cain's amused scrutiny. She had seen forbidden books, and once a Greek statue, but never had she gazed upon a naked adult male. An unfamiliar tingling in her midsection caused her breath to quicken, and she took a step backward. He's beautiful, she thought.

"Are there no men in your country?"

Cain's question brought Elizabeth instantly to her senses. Her cheeks flamed as she realized she had been staring at his unclad body and thoroughly enjoying the sight.

"I do not mind if you look."

"Where are your clothes?" she flared. "You're indecent!"

He motioned to where his loincloth and leather vest lay on the sand a few yards behind her, then ran a hand through his wet hair. "Do the English always say one thing and think another?" he asked, tossing down the spear. "I will dress if it pleases you, but only a fool would spear fish in buckskins."

Trembling, she turned away, mentally cringing under waves of shame. How could she have done such a thing? Now he might think she . . . Elizabeth bit her lower lip. He couldn't believe she found his primitive charms attractive. *Liar!* an inner voice cried. It had not been mere curiosity that had caused her to stare at him. Indian or not, Cain was an extremely virile man. There was a sensual magnetism about him that transcended race and culture. Shaken by her own realization,

Elizabeth began to walk swiftly away down the beach.

"Where are you going?" he demanded, sprinting after her.

She stiffened her shoulders and lengthened her stride. "I'm going to Jamestown," she said. "If you won't take me, I'll find it myself."

"Very well," he answered solemnly, "but there is something you should know."

She whirled to face him, fists clenched at her sides, green eyes flashing with sparks of iridescent gold. "And just what is that?"

"You're going the wrong way."

Chapter 3

Elizabeth's eyes narrowed with suspicion, and she shook her head forcefully. "I don't believe you!"

"Shaakhan Kihittuun does not lie."

She began walking again.

"Eliz-a-beth."

The sound of her name on his tongue was oddly disturbing. It was soft—almost a caress. No one had ever said her name in quite that way. She stopped and took a deep breath, trying to force herself to gain control of her own emotions. At least he had tied that skin apron around his waist again. Attempting to converse with a naked savage was must unnerving!

"You will tire yourself," he persisted. "You are still weak. You have . . ." He struggled for an unfamiliar English word. ". . . your back. I have medicine to make healing."

Tears welled up in Elizabeth's eyes and she blinked them away. Her back did hurt. Vaguely, she remembered being struck by something before she reached the longboat on the *Speedwell*. "I want to go back to my own people," she said stubbornly.

Cain stepped in front of her, blocking her path with his solid, muscular body. "You must forget them," he said gently.

"You're crazy!" She turned away from him and looked out over the rolling surf. Her hands were trembling and she balled them into tight fists at her sides again. "They will think I'm dead."

"Yes."

"You don't understand."

"It is you who not understand. Many years I wait for you."

It was hard to think when he was standing so close to her. She couldn't get her breath, and she felt dizzy. The air between them seemed to crackle with strange energy. "Nonsense!" she stammered. "You couldn't have been waiting for me. You didn't even know I was alive until you found me in the boat." Elizabeth kicked at the damp sand with her bare foot, trying to ignore the fluttering sensations in the pit of her stomach.

"I go back to wigwam now. Cook fish. Eliz-a-beth come when tears stop." It was more of a question than an order.

"I'm not crying," she lied, dashing away the betraying moisture with the back of a hand.

"The sea brought you to me as my vision promised. To fight against the will of Manito is useless." He moved closer. "You are very beautiful, Eliz-a-beth. This one does not think your mind is as empty as *honneek* the squirrel. Accept what must be."

Unable to respond, Elizabeth stood rigidly staring at the water. It was minutes before she suspected he was gone. When she could stand it no

longer and turned her head to look, Cain was
trotting down the beach, back the way they had
come. "Damn you," she whispered. Trembling,
she sank down onto the warm sand, stretching
her legs out in front of her.

"Why?" she asked.

There was no answer. The deserted beach
seemed to stretch on forever on either side. The
sky overhead was a brilliant blue, the sun hotter
than any sun she remembered in England.
"Maybe this is all a dream," she murmured. But
she knew that it wasn't—it was all too real.

Nothing in her twenty-two years had prepared
her for the sinking of the *Speedwell* and the events
that followed. Adversity had never threatened her
gilded world; certainly she had never been in
physical danger before. Even Cromwell's iron rule
of England had had little effect on her sheltered
childhood.

Sighing, Elizabeth picked up an empty shell
and tossed it into the water. Her family had always had the cunning to be on the winning side
of any political dispute, even those that dislodged
kings and destroyed other noble houses.

Her great-grandfather, the sixth earl of Sommersett, had been a devout Catholic and a strong
supporter of Charles I. When the King was de-
feated, the wily old earl transferred all his wealth
and lands to his oldest son, Elizabeth's paternal
grandfather, a professed Roundhead and Protes-
tant convert.

The family had maintained their estates under
Cromwell, paying lip service to the attempted
army-controlled republic and secretly supporting
the royalist cause by sending money to Charles II
abroad. Elizabeth had been eight years old when

her father, Roger, took part in the ill-timed Presbyterian rising in 1650 and became part of Charles's court in exile.

Although she had not seen him again until the King's restoration in 1660, her life was little changed by his absence. It was the Sommersetts' custom to raise their children on country estates, far from the bustle of London and court affairs. Even before her father's exile, she saw her parents only once or twice a year. Elizabeth, her brothers and sisters, and an assortment of Sommersett cousins had been cared for by an ever-changing staff of servants.

When her father fled the country, Elizabeth's grandfather, the earl, disowned his son Roger and denied any responsibility for his treason, thus keeping the Sommersetts in favor until Cromwell's death in 1658. When King Charles took the throne, Roger, now earl of Sommersett due to the old earl's death, received a favored position at court and huge grants of virgin land in the Virginia Colony. He had quickly decided that this thickly forested land halfway across the world would be an adequate dowry for his younger daughter, instead of the Hampshire estate he had originally promised her.

"It's all the fault of that damned Virginia land," she muttered. The family had arranged her betrothal to fifteen-year-old Edward Lindsey when she was only nine. Edward, the second son of a powerful earl, was considered a good catch for a second daughter. Even if he had little hope of inheriting his father's title, he was financially secure.

With King Charles's restoration and her own father's subsequent popularity, she, her sisters

Alice and Ann, and her brothers had at last gone to court. Elizabeth had quickly been caught up in the color and excitement of the seemingly nonstop masked balls, fêtes, and theater performances. She had been surrounded by ardent gentlemen paying her excessive compliments, writing poetry in her honor, pressing her into dark corners, and singing tearful romantic ballads in an effort to gain her favor.

Her betrothed, Edward Lindsey, was conspicuously absent from this crowd of admirers. Rumor had it that his father, the earl of Dunmore, had sent Edward to the Virginia Colony to keep him from wasting any more of his inheritance. To Elizabeth's delight, her parents had postponed plans for her marriage to Edward, hoping to replace him with a more advantageous match. Finally, after three years' delay, Dunmore complained to King Charles, demanding that Elizabeth follow Edward to Virginia to fulfill the contract.

Elizabeth threw another shell into the water. Would that her parents had broken the betrothal agreement! Then she would have been safe at court instead of stranded in this wilderness. She hadn't wanted to come to America, and she certainly hadn't wanted to marry Edward Lindsey.

Now, Edward seemed the lesser of two evils. "Doubtless his complexion has cleared in the years since I last saw him," she said wryly. Wrinkling her nose at the thought of that last awful meeting, Elizabeth stood up and brushed the loose sand off her legs.

Cain had insisted that she was walking the wrong way down the beach. Did that mean that Jamestown was south? She tried to remember the maps of the American coast she had seen. Far to the north was the Massachusetts Colony. What was between Virginia and Massachusetts? Was Cain telling the truth about where she was?

Elizabeth sighed and pursed her lips. There was no way to be certain. She could walk a hundred leagues north or south and find nothing but wilderness. She knew she couldn't survive alone on so long a journey; she would starve or be devoured by wild beasts. As distressful as the solution was, she would have to stay with Cain until she could persuade him to take her to the English, or until someone else came to help her. Resolutely, she began to follow his tracks back toward the hut.

Elizabeth smelled the fish before she saw it broiling over the flames. Cain had built a fire outside the hut and was crouched beside it, naked to the waist, arranging clams on a slab of wood. She paused, gathering her courage, then cautiously approached, being careful to keep the firepit between them.

He glanced up at her and smiled, his large dark eyes concealing none of the satisfaction she supposed he was feeling at her return.

"Don't look so smug!" she snapped. "Did you expect me to stay on the beach and die of exposure?"

The corners of his mouth twitched with amusement. "On such a hot day? That would be irrlogical," he answered.

"*Illogical!*" she corrected. "The word is *illogical*. Your English is atrocious."

Cain moved to turn the fish, and his back muscles rippled beneath his skin in a way that made

Elizabeth's heart seem to rise in her throat. Her breath quickened, and she became aware of the strangest sensation between her thighs. Suddenly weak, she sat down on the ground and tried to catch her breath.

"Il-log-i-cal," he repeated, carefully mimicking her pronunciation. "I must remember. It is a good word, and my grandmother will want to know that she is saying it wrong all these years."

"I . . . I think my fever has come back," Elizabeth ventured. She did feel overly warm. Surely, an April day couldn't be this warm—even in America.

"That would not be il-logical," Cain said, savoring the taste of the English word on his tongue. He rose to his feet and came toward her.

Elizabeth threw up a hand. "No . . . I . . ." she stammered. "Don't . . ."

He dropped to his knees before her and laid a broad palm on her forehead.

His face was inches from her own, his hand touching her familiarly. "No!" she said, shoving his hand away. "Don't touch me." His eyes held hers; she was unable to tear her gaze away. "Please . . ." she said.

Cain shook his head. "I feel no fever," he said gently. "But if you have sick you must rest." Ignoring her protests, he swept her up in his arms and carried her toward the hut.

"Put me down!" Elizabeth cried. "I said *put me down!*" Her mouth tasted of ashes, and the sudden knowledge that she was afraid turned her fear into white-hot anger. "Release me at once, you . . . you red savage!" Balling her right hand into a fist, she struck him as hard as she could on the side of the face.

Cain gasped, and Elizabeth felt his muscles tense. *"Tshingue,"* he muttered between clenched teeth.

She raised her fist to strike him again.

"Do not," he warned softly.

His stride quickened. They were past the hut and moving swiftly toward the beach.

"Where are you taking me?" she demanded as the sound of the ocean grew louder. "Cain!" Her voice took on a shrill edge. "Cain!"

"You want down," he said. "You get down."

"Cain, no!"

Water splashed around his ankles.

"Cain!"

"If you have fever, cool."

Without warning, Elizabeth was in the air. Before she could catch her breath, she plunged into the icy water of the Atlantic. "Ohhh!" Coughing and sputtering, she struggled to get her feet under her. An incoming wave tripped her, and before she could recover her balance, an iron hand closed around hers and dragged her back to the beach.

She sank down on the warm ground, spitting out sand and salt water. "Damn you," she choked. "You tried to drown me."

Cain's answering chuckle was almost more than she could bear.

"You're inhuman!"

"This one does not know this word *inhuman,*" he said solemnly.

"Stop it! Stop taunting me. I hate you!" she cried.

He dropped to the sand beside her. "I do not think you hate me."

"I do! I—"

Fiercely, Cain pulled her into his arms and silenced her words with his mouth against hers. Elizabeth tried to pull away, but he was too strong. Her struggles went unheeded as Cain seared her lips with a fiery, all-consuming kiss. Then, as suddenly as he had begun his assault, he released her.

"Look into your heart, Englishwoman," he said huskily. "Wipe the salt from your eyes and truly look. Tell me then if it is hate you feel for Shaa-khan Kihittuun."

Before she could reply, he was gone, walking back toward the hut.

Shaken by his kiss, Elizabeth wrapped her arms around herself and rocked in trembling silence. Her bruised lips tingled, her thoughts were in turmoil. *Why?* an inner voice cried. *Why does this savage affect me this way?*

She was not new to the art of kissing. Men and boys had kissed her since she was twelve. Many had tried to take greater liberties. She had kept herself pure, despite the surroundings of the decadent Stuart court, but she could not deny that she had allowed herself to be fondled by ardent swains. She had known physical desire before . . . or what she had believed was desire. But there had never been anything like this raw aching that swept over her at Cain's touch.

Elizabeth swallowed hard. Her pulse was racing, and her knees were too weak to stand. Tentatively, she touched her lower lip with the tip of her tongue, remembering the feel of his hard mouth on hers, savoring the bittersweet pangs of sensual longing.

"I don't hate him," she whispered. "God help me, I don't."

For nearly an hour, Elizabeth sat on the beach,

not knowing what to do. Then she heard Cain call her name.

"Eliz-a-beth." He came toward her carrying a bowl of food.

She got to her feet and faced him, unsure of what to say or do.

Cain stopped a few yards away and held out a carved wooden bowl containing fish and clams and some sort of green leaves. His wide brow furrowed with concern. "I have great shame," he admitted. "I am sorry. I have anger at you for hitting me, and so I kiss you." He took another step closer. "I bring you food. You must eat and come out of the sun. *Kiisku* will burn your pale skin."

Elizabeth's temper flared. "You threw me into the ocean! You tried to drown me, then you assaulted me, and now you come with a plate of clams, say you're sorry, and prattle on about the sun?"

"I have said it."

"Why should I believe you? Why would I trust you again?" she challenged. She knew she was being unfair, knew she had goaded him with her own foolish actions, but she didn't care. Blaming him was easier than blaming herself for what had happened between them.

Cain sighed deeply. "I give you my word, word of Lenni-Lenape warrior. I do not throw you into the sea again. I do not kiss you again . . . unless you ask for kiss."

"There's not much chance of that, is there?"

He shrugged.

"What kind of man are you? To force yourself on me because you were angry? No English gentleman would do such a thing." Elizabeth's cheeks colored. She knew the words were a lie as soon as they slipped from her lips. There were many gentlemen who would dare as much—and more—if they thought they could get away with it.

"I did not mean to frighten you," Cain said. "It is not the way of my people for men to—"

"To attack women? To bully them?"

"No. I was wrong."

"I'm glad you realize it. I'm not used to being mauled." She motioned for him to come closer. "I will forgive you this time, but it must never happen again," she warned. "My father is a very powerful man. He could have you put into prison—hanged—and he would if he thought for a moment that you had laid hands on me." She tried to keep from trembling as she reached for the food he carried.

Cain gave it to her with the grace of a French courtier. "I want to be your friend," he said.

"Then you must remember your place." Elizabeth scrutinized the bowl of food; the clams and the fish she was familiar with, but she wasn't certain what the green leaves were. "What's that?" she demanded.

"I do not know English word, but is good to eat."

She brushed the leaves off into the sand. "I am not accustomed to eating grass," she said. "The fish and clams will do. But I am thirsty. Do you have ale or . . . I don't suppose you have any decent claret."

Cain shook his head. "I do not know these things. We drink only water."

Elizabeth sat cross-legged on the sand. "Very well then, bring me water to drink with my meal."

His eyes narrowed. "There is water in wig-wam."

She took a bite of the broiled fish. It was seasoned and cooked to perfection. "Fetch it then," she ordered.

"I catch the fish for you. I cook it," Cain answered slowly. "I will show you where *mimipeek*—fresh water pond—be. I will not carry water for you."

"You can't expect me to carry water!"

"Why I cannot?"

"I told you. I am Lady Elizabeth Anne Sommersett. I am an English noblewoman."

Cain smiled and nodded.

"Well?"

He folded his muscular arms over his bare chest. "I am Shaakhan Kihittuun. I tell you I do not carry water for healthy woman. If you have thirst, carry."

Elizabeth sprang to her feet and threw the bowl into the sand. "How dare you speak to me like that?" she demanded. "You haven't understood a word I've said to you."

A slow smile spread over Cain's face. "Do you have husband?" he asked.

She blinked. "What?"

"Are your ears full of salt too? I ask you, Englishwoman, do you have husband?"

"I told you before, I am betrothed to Edward Lindsey, son of the earl of Dunmore. I am going to Jamestown to be married."

Cain's smile became a grin. "Good."

"What are you smirking about?" Elizabeth braced her fists against her hips and glared at him. "You're infuriating," she sputtered. "You're crude and barbaric and—"

"And I will be your husband," he said.

For seconds, Elizabeth stared at him, too shocked to speak. "What did you say?" she managed.

"I take you from the sea," Cain said, "and I mean to have you for my wife."

Chapter 4

"**Y**ou think I'd marry you? A savage?" Elizabeth stiffened with indignant fury. "I'd sooner wed a dancing bear!"

Cain chuckled as he placed the remainder of the fish and clams into his own food bowl and kicked sand onto the small campfire. "A wise hunter knows that the woman bear has sharper teeth than the man bear," he said. Ducking into the wigwam, he returned with his bow and quiver of arrows slung over his shoulder.

"Where are you going?" she demanded.

"To sup in quiet."

Elizabeth flushed and looked down at her fish and clams laying in the sand. "And me? What am I supposed to eat?"

He shrugged. "What you catch." He turned away and walked inland toward the trees.

"When will you be back?" she called after him. "Cain!"

He kept walking, giving no indication that he heard her.

"Damn you," she muttered, kicking at her ruined dinner. "It would serve you right if I starved to death."

For a few seconds, Elizabeth considered gath-

41

ering up the clams and washing them in the
ocean. She got as far as retrieving one and holding it at arm's length, but immediately wrinkled
her nose in disgust. "I'm not that hungry," she
declared. "I'd never be that hungry."

Yet, even as she tossed the shriveled clam away
and brushed the sand off her garment, she remembered the terror of being in the longboat. She
had suffered terribly from hunger and thirst; she
would have eaten a raw fish or even a bird if
she could have caught one. If I was marooned on
an island, I might eat it, she admitted to herself,
but I'm not that hungry now.

She remembered seeing cornmeal in a container in the hut. Eat whatever she could catch
indeed! She'd simply take Cain's flour and prepare some kind of coarse bread. She'd never actually done any baking, but she'd played in the
great estate kitchen as a child. She'd seen the
cooks bake dozens of kinds of breads and pastries. How difficult could making cornbread possibly be?

Picking up a stick, she dug the coals out of the
sand, knelt, and blew on them. The ashes glowed
red, and she patiently fed small twigs into the
coals until they flared into flame. Then, satisfied
that she had resurrected Cain's cooking fire, she
went into the wigwam for the corn flour.

As she rummaged through the woven contain-
ers, she noticed a gourd hanging at eye level. She
took it down, unstoppered the wooden plug, and
poured a little of the pale golden contents into the
palm of her hand. To her delight, it was honey,
sweet and delicate—as delicious as any she had
ever tasted at home.

"Just the thing to have with my cornbread,"
she murmured. She found an empty clay bowl

that seemed clean and scooped several cups of cornmeal into it. There was no milk or butter to go into the dough. "I'll use water instead." There was salt in a tiny bowl. How much do I need? she wondered. Alfreda the cook had often declared that bread without salt was like a man without a wife. "Salt, surely," Elizabeth mused, "but how much?"

She dropped to her knees on the deerskin rug. She'd watched Alfreda mixing and kneading bread, but the exact measurements of the ingredients had never seemed important. Alfreda had made ten loaves at a time, so it was difficult to imagine how to make enough for only one person. After pondering awhile, she decided that the best thing to do would to be to simply use salt water from the ocean for her dough. "It's bound to be cleaner than that stagnant pond Cain wanted to send me to," she reasoned.

Taking the gourd of honey, a wooden spoon, and her bowl with the cornmeal, she went back outside. She left the honey by the fire and walked down to the ocean's edge, and mixed a little of the cold sea water into her meal. She stirred until the mixture was smooth, then sampled it. She wrinkled her nose as the tasteless goo coated her tongue and stuck to the roof of her mouth.

Sighing, she walked back toward the wigwam. Sea salt obviously wasn't enough. She'd have to add real salt, and then, when the batter was right, she'd think of some way to bake it. She'd be damned if that heathen savage would get the best of her. It would serve him right to come back and find her dining on bread and honey!

An hour later, Elizabeth was in tears. She had burned two fingers, scorched the side of Cain's boat paddle, and lost half of her flat, hard biscuits in the sand. In any case, what was left of her baking was inedible to anything but a seagull. "Even a pig wouldn't eat this slop," she wailed, spitting what was left in her mouth into the fire. "Ugh!" Shuddering, she cleaned her mouth with the back of her hand.

Sinking onto the ground, Elizabeth buried her face in her hands and wept, not only for her ruined dinner, but also for the disaster that had separated her from her own people and left her to the mercy of a heathen savage.

Gradually, the tears slowed and she regained control. "Bawling like a kitchen slut over burned biscuits," she sniffed, wiping her nose. "A Sommersett." The hot New World sun must have baked her brain!

She got to her feet and looked around the clearing. She needed fresh water to rinse her face and wash the bite of salt from her mouth. The pond Cain spoke of must be nearby. Taking his dugout paddle for protection against wild animals, she set off in the direction he had indicated earlier.

The pond was only a few hundred yards inland from the campsite, hidden by low trees and shrubs. A sloping bank led down to the water. Cautiously, Elizabeth approached and crouched down to splash some of the cool water on her face, then she cupped her hands and drank. Despite the brown color, the water was sweet and clean tasting. Gratefully, she drank mouthful after mouthful, unable to get enough of the cool liquid.

At last, when her thirst was satisfied, she lay on her stomach propped up on her elbows and stared at her reflection in the water. The sunburned face that peered back at her was almost unrecognizable. Shocked, Elizabeth realized that the braided hair and deerskin shift made her look like a kitchen wench rather than an English lady.

"This is all a nightmare," she whispered into the still afternoon. "I'll wake and find myself on the ship bound for Jamestown . . . or better still, I'll wake in Father's London house."

A scarlet-hued bird lit on a branch not an arm's length away and trilled loudly as if to mock her.

Elizabeth smiled at the insolence of the little creature. The bird hopped closer, fluffed up its feathers, and stared at her with round, coal-black eyes. "Hello," she said softly. "Are you an Indian too? You've the feathers for it."

The bird twisted to tuck in a stray wing feather, then fluttered away into a tree top. "Goodbye," Elizabeth called after it. "Come see me again."

The air was still so warm that she decided to wash her hair. It felt sticky from the salt water, and the plaits banged against her sunburned neck like tar ropes when she walked. She would wash it and brush it out, then try and arrange it in some sort of order. "Bridget always parted my hair in the middle and dressed it into deep side ringlets." Her hair was so thick that her maid never needed to pad it with false hair like most women were forced to do. But Bridget was far away in England. "I'll have to do the best I can."

Hair still damp and tangled, Elizabeth returned to the wigwam to find her fire had burned out. There was no sign of Cain. Nervously, she entered the hut and sat down to wait.

The minutes passed slowly into hours. Darkness settled over the land, and the day sounds were replaced with strange rustlings and weird, echoing cries. Elizabeth huddled beneath a deerskin robe, straining her ears for human footsteps and hoping desperately that Cain would come back. Eventually, fatigue overcame fear, and she fell into a restless sleep.

The sun was well up over the eastern horizon when Elizabeth ventured from the door of the wigwam. She paused outside and straightened, looking up and down the beach for any signs of movement.

The pristine sand stretched as far as her eyes could see in either direction, bordered on one side by the rolling blue-gray sea and on the other by stunted forest and dark green shrubs. There were seagulls wheeling and dipping over the surf, and several strutting pompously down the beach, but nothing large enough to be a man.

"Where are you?" she shouted. "Cain?" The only sound was the crash of the surf and the cries of two quarreling gulls.

"Damn you," she said as she turned in the direction of the pond. She'd been so certain he would come back to the wigwam in the night. What if he never came back? What if she were truly alone in the wilderness?

She kicked at a weathered clam shell with her bare foot. The edge of the shell cut her big toe, and she winced. "If he doesn't come back, I'll take food and supplies and walk down the beach until I come to a settlement. If he said that way was wrong"—she glanced north—"then I'll just go the other way. I'm bound to find Jamestown sooner or later." She grimaced. Brave words—but utterly ridiculous. Without a guide, she could never find Jamestown. She would starve, or die of thirst, or be eaten by wild animals. "I'll have to stay here with Cain until I can convince him to take me to Jamestown," she murmured, "even if it takes weeks."

The ground was cool beneath her feet this

morning, but the air was fresh and invigorating.
She breathed deeply, taking note of how new
leaves were forming on the trees and everything
was turning green. There was a primitive beauty
to this land, she admitted. The sky seemed bigger, the clouds whiter, and the vegetation more
vivid in color. It wasn't anything like the ordered
landscape at home, but she could understand why
some Englishmen called America the new Eden.

The pond seemed exactly as she had left it the
night before, except that this morning the surface
of the water had become a shining mirror sparkling in the sunshine. A pair of ducks paddled
lazily near the far bank, and birds called to one
another from the branches of a graceful cedar
swaying overhead. Eagerly, Elizabeth dropped
onto her knees and reached down to scoop up a
handful of water.

Suddenly, a hairy gray beast with gleaming
sharp teeth sprang snarling at her from the
bushes. "Wolf!" Elizabeth screamed and fell
backward, slipping down the bank into the waist-
deep icy water. She caught a glimpse of two
bloodred eyes as the creature leaped past her and
vanished in the bushes. Still screaming, Elizabeth
scrambled up the muddy bank and fled toward
the wigwam.

She looked back over her shoulder as she ran,
to see if the wolf was chasing her, and slammed
with full force into an immovable object. Stunned,
Elizabeth staggered and would have fallen if two
sinewy arms hadn't closed about her.

"What is it?" Cain demanded. "What is
wrong?"

Weeping hysterically, Elizabeth slumped
against his chest, unable to convey more than the
single word, "W-wolf."

"Speak slowly," he instructed. "I can't understand you." He gathered her up in his strong arms and carried her back toward the campsite. "Are you hurt?"

She shook her head and sobbed against his bare chest. "It . . . it tried . . . tried to . . ." She sniffed and attempted to wipe her runny nose, an impossible feat when both arms were clutched around Cain's neck in a viselike grip. ". . . snarled . . ." She shuddered, remembering the fierce expression in the wolf's eyes. "I jumped . . . into the pond," she managed. "The wolf . . . wanted . . . to eat me."

"*N'tschutti*, beloved, I should not have left you alone so long," he soothed, kissing the top of her honey-gold hair. "Are you certain it was a wolf?" He looked down into her tearstained eyes. "*Munsee* has much shy."

She nodded. "A wolf. It was gray and big with long, white teeth and horrible eyes."

Cain reached the clearing beside the wigwam. Clearly, Eliz-a-beth was safe now from whatever had frightened her so badly, but it was pleasant to hold her thus, and even more pleasant to feel her warm breasts pressed against his body. "I do not know why a wolf would do as you say," he stalled. "It is the way of their clan to run from the smell of man."

She pressed her face into the hollow of his throat, and he felt a warm tightness growing in his loins. He had not shared his blanket with a woman since the moon of snapping branches, and desire was thick in his blood. Reluctantly, he lowered Elizabeth to the ground. Whatever might bond them in the seasons to come was not yet. He knew instinctively that to rush her would be to lose her trust forever.

"Wait here in the wigwam," he said. "I will hunt out this wolf."

"It might be gone by now," she said nervously. She glanced toward the trees. "Or it might come while you're—"

"You will be safe," he promised, giving her hand a final squeeze. "I will not go far."

She nodded, wiping her eyes. "Be careful."

"The wolf is my totem. I speak his tongue. I do not think *munsee* will harm me."

Elizabeth smiled at him weakly. "Maybe . . . maybe I frightened it away with my screaming." She shivered in the salt breeze that blew from the sea.

"Take off your wet garment," he said. "Wrap yourself in skins. This one does not wish you to have fever." Dismissing her with a nod, he turned toward the fresh water pond. If a wolf had attacked Eliz-a-beth, it must be sick. He would have to track and kill it—a terrible crime against one of his own totem—before it could make other animals sick.

As Cain covered the short distance between the wigwam and the pond, he freed his mind of Eliz-a-beth and all other thoughts but the hunt. He reached deep within his being, allying himself with the men of his father's blood, with the Lenni-Lenape, stretching back until the dawn of time. Cain Dare, the Englishman, fell away, leaving the white-hot core of Shaakhan Kihittuun, a man as much a part of this sand and forest as the gray wolf itself.

A few minutes later, kneeling by the river bank, he realized he need not have bothered.

"Inu-msi-ila-fe-wanu," he said softly, "this is a good joke on your child." Chuckling, he rose to his feet and wondered how he would explain the truth about this *wolf* to Eliz-a-beth without making her lose face.

The tenseness eased from his muscles and he followed the spoor of the animal for several yards through the beach plums and pine. When he was satisfied, Cain turned back toward the camp.

"Eliz-a-beth," he called at the wigwam entrance. "Are you covered?" He knew that as much as he would like to see her unclad body, it would cause her shame if he entered unannounced. "I come."

"All right." Her reply was weak, unlike her usual bold manner.

Cain paused inside, letting his eyes adjust to the dim interior of the wigwam. Eliz-a-beth was on her sleeping platform, wrapped in a deerskin.

"Did you kill the wolf?"

He shook his head. "No. It ran away from the pond." That much was true. He looked at her more closely, noting her tangled hair and scratched face. "I should not have left you alone so long," he said. "I wounded a deer and had to follow until I brought him down. We will have fresh venison."

Elizabeth burst into tears again.

He covered the distance between them in one leap. "What is wrong?"

She reddened and turned her face away. "Nothing," she protested. "I . . . I'm hungry. I made bread and it—"

Cain turned away and hung his bow on a rack above the entrance. It would not do to let her see the amusement in his eyes. "You have not cooked on Lenni-Lenape fire before," he said noncommittally.

"I have not cooked at all," she admitted.

"This one will teach you." He picked up her

wet dress from the floor. "I will lay this in the sun to dry. Then I must work it, to keep leather soft." He glanced at her. "It is best not to wear doeskin to swim."

Elizabeth's face darkened like a thundercloud. "I wasn't swimming. I told you, I only jumped into the water to get away from the wolf." She brushed a damp lock of hair out of her face. "You'll have to braid my hair again. I tried to do it last night and I couldn't. I've always had a maid to do my hair."

Cain made a sympathetic sound in his throat. "I have sadness for you, Eliz-a-beth, that you had no mother to teach you the things a woman should know."

"I have a mother," she answered sharply, "and she has never neglected her duties to me. I explained before. We are of very high status in England—nobility. It is not necessary for me to know how to cook or dress my own hair."

"It seems necessary to me."

She sighed impatiently. "That is because you are an ignorant savage." Settling back against her sleeping platform, Elizabeth pulled the deerskin up high around her neck. Because she had been grateful to see him was no reason for Cain to feel he could take liberties.

"This one is an ig-nor-anne savage?"

She nodded. "Yes. I don't mean to insult you, but it's true."

He crossed his arms over his chest and stared down at her. "You cannot cook, even to keep from starve. You cannot brush and care for your own hair. These things are true."

Elizabeth averted her eyes. "Yes."

"Can you sew?"

"I can embroider," she said proudly. "If I have

silk thread, and linen, and the proper needles."
It was a skill she had acquired quite young. She
had made a pillow cover for her mother's last
birthday. "Ladies do not need to sew or weave
cloth. Fine embroidery is considered an art."

"You can skin game and make hides into clothing?"

"No." She grimaced. "Of course not. Game is
dressed by huntsmen."

"Can you build a wigwam of poles and bark?"

"This is ridiculous," she protested. "We do not
have wigwams in England."

"Ah, then you can build an English house."

"No."

"You cannot cook, or sew, or dress skins. You
cannot build a shelter, cannot find food or water
when they are all about you, and I am the ig-nor-
anne savage?"

"Ignorant," she corrected.

"Yes," he agreed. "That is what you are, Englishwoman. You are ignorant, and only a very
brave and wise warrior could make you into a
proper wife."

"How dare you insult me!" she flared. Her eyes
narrowed as she regarded him with unconcealed
ire. "You are wrong," she said haughtily. "I am
not ignorant. I have been educated to be the perfect wife for a British nobleman. We are nothing
alike, you and I. Nothing you could ever do
would make you a suitable husband for me. It
would please me if you didn't speak of marrying
me again."

Eliz-a-beth's words would have angered Cain if
he had not noticed the quiver of her lower lip. It
was plain to him that she was afraid, and that she
hid that fear with brave words. He remembered
how good she felt lying close against him, her

arms around his neck and her breath warm on his face. He desired her as he had never desired another woman, but he wanted her to come to him of her own free will. "This one would never do you harm," he said.

"I am your prisoner, but you don't own me," she flung at him.

"No, *dah-quel-e-mah*. I am the prisoner." He stopped by the entranceway and looked back at her. "I will not speak of marriage again. You, Eliz-a-beth, you must look into your own heart and see what is true and what has not truth." He smiled. "This night, when the moon rises, we will hunt your wolf together."

"No, we won't! You're crazy if you think I'm going to put myself within reach of that wild beast again!"

"We hunt."

"Savage!" Elizabeth swore an oath and reached for the nearest object, a carved cedar bowl. Laughing, Cain ducked outside, and the bowl bounced harmlessly against the wooden frame of the wigwam.

"Don't come then," he teased, "but if you do not, then this one make you cook your own supper!"

Chapter 5

Elizabeth lay flat on her stomach in the low grass. Cain stretched close beside her, one hand resting on her arm. She wasn't sure how long they had been here without moving or talking; it seemed like hours. She wiggled her toes in the soft deerskin moccasins, glad for their warmth and doubly glad for the leggings he had insisted she wear under her doeskin dress.

The full moon had risen over the sea, a shimmering disk of iridescent silver casting an enchanted light over the hushed forest and the pond. The night was warm; the slight breeze came from the land, not the cold, rolling waters of the ocean. Cain had explained that the direction of the wind would hide their scent from their quarry. If the breeze had been off the salt water, they would have had to circle around the pond and come up to it from the far side.

Elizabeth turned her head slightly to look at Cain. He was so still that if she hadn't heard his breathing, she would have believed him made of stone. His boldly sculptured face was in shadow, but the moonlight glistened off his naked shoulders, bathing his thick, dark hair in radiance.

His solid presence was oddly comforting. Al-

though she had protested loudly, Elizabeth was
not sorry she had come on this unlikely adventure. If any of her friends had suggested she
would be hunting wolves beside a red savage in
America, she would have verbally consigned them
to Bedlam. But the truth was, she was enjoying
the expedition.

Her eyes sparkled as a bubble of excitement rose
in her throat. Once I am safely at Jamestown, she
decided, I'll have an unbelievable tale to relate.
No one will have an after-dinner story to match
this!

Her left arm began to cramp, and she leaned
her weight on the right and sighed. Cain's fingers
tightened warningly on her arm. The pressure
wasn't enough to cause her pain, only enough to
let her know that he had noticed her restlessness.
"Patience," his touch urged. If he had spoken,
his meaning could not have been clearer. Elizabeth stifled the urge to give him a piece of her
mind and lay still, straining her eyes to see any
movement in the bushes around them.

She felt strangely alive. The sharp odors of the
sand and grass, of the cedar and pine, and the
unmistakable scent of the ocean filled her nostrils.
She was intensely aware of the texture of the earth
beneath her body and the star-strewn sky above.
And—more than she cared to admit—she was
conscious of the man beside her.

She knew she should have felt anger for the
liberties Cain assumed. But then, nothing in her
upbringing or past experiences had prepared her
for Cain Dare, and she was at a loss to find the
right way to deal with him.

Across the pond, an owl hooted, and an answering call came from the forest. Elizabeth didn't

flinch. She knew an owl when she heard one, and she certainly wasn't afraid.

Frogs peeped and croaked from the pond, and there was an occasional splash of water. Once, she caught sight of a furry head breaking the surface of the pond. Then, a graceful animal moved from the shadows into the moonlight, followed by a tinier replica. To Elizabeth's delight, a doe and fawn walked toward the water's edge. Nervously, the mother deer lowered her head to drink while the baby butted and frolicked around her.

Elizabeth blinked her eyes and the deer were gone. Had she fallen asleep? She wasn't certain. She tried to look up to gauge the position of the moon, but Cain squeezed her arm once more. Before she could respond, a twig snapped a few yards away and she tensed as she remembered the fierce beast they had come to hunt.

Cain leaned close to her ear and whispered. "Shhh, *oopus* comes."

Elizabeth gasped as a doglike animal trotted into the moonlit clearing. The creature paused and raised its head, sniffing the air, then gave a sharp whine. "The wolf," she murmured softly. The breeze brought a light musty scent, and her eyes widened as she realized that it was the beast she smelled.

"Watch," Cain ordered. His voice was so low, Elizabeth wasn't certain if she heard him with her ears or with her mind.

In the bright patch of moonlight, the shaggy gray animal cocked its head as though it were listening. The pointed ears twitched, and it dropped to a sitting position and emitted another high-pitched whimper. Immediately, four pups bounded from the darkness, launched themselves onto their mother, and began to nurse.

Elizabeth let out a muffled gasp. "Oh. That's my wolf," she whispered, "but it looks smaller now."

Cain's hair brushed her cheek, and a little shiver passed through her. "Not *tumme* the wolf," he corrected. *"Oopus* the fox."

She stared at the vixen and her cubs, suddenly aware of what must have happened when she believed she was under attack by a ravaging wolf. Even her father's hounds would growl if a stranger came near their pups. "A gray fox," she uttered softly. "Not a wolf, but a vixen."

"You learn," Cain replied gently.

The animals gave no indication that they were aware of human presence, and Elizabeth realized that the noises the young foxes made prevented the bitch from taking alarm. One of the pups had left off nursing and was tugging at the mother's tail; another burrowed under the vixen's neck.

Elizabeth was fascinated by the scene. An accomplished horsewoman, she had always been fond of animals. As a child, she had loved an odd assortment of kittens and dogs; once she had even kept a mouse hidden from her nurse for weeks. But never before had she seen a wild creature so close.

"Shall I slay her for you?" Cain asked.

"No!"

The vixen's head snapped up and she gave a warning yip. Before Elizabeth's eyes, mother and cubs vanished into the darkness.

"Oh," she protested, scrambling to her feet. "I didn't mean to—"

Cain stood up and smiled at her.

"You wouldn't have hurt the fox, would you?"

He shook his head.

"But you thought I wanted it dead?"

He chuckled. "No, brave hunter of wolves. I knew you did not. This one only wish to hear you say so."

Perplexed, she opened her mouth to reply, then closed it when she realized she was at a loss. She averted her eyes to keep him from reading what was on her mind.

"You hide a woman's heart, Eliz-a-beth," he chided gently.

"You knew it wasn't a wolf, didn't you?"

He nodded. "The tracks tell me."

"Why did you let me go on believing—"

He reached for her hand. Trembling, she let him take it. "Would you accept my word?"

"No." Elizabeth's mouth felt dry and her knees weak. "No," she admitted. The touch of his hand sent tremors up her arm, but she had no desire to pull free. "I was convinced I had been attacked by a wolf."

"And now?" He moved a step closer.

She swayed in the moonlight. "Thank you for the foxes," she murmured. "They . . . they were beautiful."

"It is not wrong to stand firm," he teased, "if such a one does not stand on a thin branch." He took another step.

A flush of heat coursed through her as she tilted her face to stare into his eyes. Unconsciously, she moistened her lips with the tip of her tongue. "I'm cold," she said. Her voice sounded strained and far away.

He opened his arms. "I will warm you, Eliz-a-beth."

Against her will, she moved into those arms and laid her face against his chest. His heart beat strongly, and he smelled of pine and tobacco. "I don't know why I'm doing this," she protested.

His hand stroked her hair. "Hush," he soothed. "Hush."

Somehow, her lips were touching his—hesitantly at first, and then with a growing intensity. His mouth was firm and tasted of honey as he returned the kiss. Elizabeth's pulse quickened and the confusion in the pit of her stomach returned full force. Breathless, she pulled away. "I . . . I'm sorry," she stammered. "I didn't mean . . ."

Cain's eyes reflected the moonlight. "Do the English always say what they do not mean?" he asked. "It is something my *cocumtha* did not tell me."

Elizabeth swallowed hard, unaware that she had brushed her tingling lips with the tip of a finger. "It . . . it was my fault," she corrected. "You didn't take advantage of me."

Cain's deep laugh blended with the boom of the surf. "I did not," he agreed. "But it was a pleasant kiss—was it not?"

She felt herself blushing.

"Truth."

She darted off toward the beach. She'd not gone more than five yards when her toe caught in a root and she went sprawling into a beach plum bush. As she struggled to get up, she tangled her other leg and went down again. "Just don't stand there laughing like a fool," she cried. "Help me."

"Does English custom allow ignorant savage to help a lady out of a bush?"

"If it doesn't," she replied, "it should."

He put his arms around her waist and tried to pull her up. She freed one ankle and hooked it over his, so that he fell on top of her.

Elizabeth twisted and wrapped her arms around his neck. "Now!" she declared. "You are my

prisoner.'' She brought her face close to his.
''That's what you get for . . .'' Her teasing words
trailed off unfinished as a surge of overwhelming
desire flooded through her.

''I see it is the custom of the English to torture
prisoners,'' he answered hoarsely. He lowered his
head to capture her parted lips.

She met his caress willingly, touching her
tongue against his in a tender, lingering kiss of
exploration that left them both trembling. ''Cain,''
she whispered. Her voice was strained and
throaty.

His hand spanned her hip as he shifted his
weight to press full-length against her. *''N'ma-
mentschi.''* His lips brushed her throat. *''N'dellennowi.''*

The soft words were strangely exciting as he
nuzzled her neck and let his fingers slide up to
cup her breast. The fluttering sensations in her
stomach escalated to a sweet ache as their lips
met again in a searing kiss of uncontrolled passion. The length of his hard body burned against
hers, and she felt the unmistakable proof of his
rising desire.

With a cry, Elizabeth broke off. ''Please,'' she
begged. ''No more. I—'' Confusion brought tears
to her eyes, and she blinked them back. ''Cain,
please.''

She heard his sharp intake of breath as he rolled
away. For an instant, regret knifed through her,
and she felt a sense of tremendous loss. She
brought her hand to her mouth and bit down hard
on one finger in an attempt to regain her shattered control.

His breathing slowed to normal, and when he
offered her his hand, it was the hand of a friend.

"Come, little one," he said. "I will not harm you."

Shaken, wide-eyed, Elizabeth stumbled to her feet. Shame flooded over her. Am I a wanton? Never had she allowed a man to go so far, and never had she wanted him to go even farther. "Cain . . ."

He turned his back on her and began to walk toward the wigwam with long, even strides. Suddenly chilled by the April night, Elizabeth hurried to keep up. How quietly he moves, she thought. The deer made more noise than Cain did.

The throbbing in her stomach had turned to a heavy, sinking feeling. How will I sleep in the same room with him? she thought. How will I face him in the firelight?

He waited for her by the door of the wigwam. "I will keep the fire this night," he said, "in case of wolves."

Unable to speak, she ducked past him and into the hut. She crawled fully dressed beneath the deerskin on her sleeping platform and pulled the skin blanket over her head. What came over me? she cried inwardly. Why did I let him kiss me like that? Touch me?

Memories of Cain's burning kisses returned to taunt her. The fresh taste of his mouth, the texture of his tongue, the waves of intense yearning . . . He was a man of another race, another class, and she had welcomed his ardent lovemaking like some jaded court whore. "What have I done?" she whispered into her clasped hands.

She was no prude. Any female over the age of five in Stuart England knew about life. Charles's court was as debauched as any Turkish sultan's palace, and the King's own behavior would shame many a courtier. Still, she was a Sommersett, and she had been brought up properly. No Sommersett bride had ever gone soiled to her husband's marriage bed, and none had disgraced her husband by taking a lover since the time of Henry VIII.

She had done her share of flirting; she had even allowed King Charles to sneak a kiss in a quiet corner of the orangery, but it was all in fun. It had been clearly understood that Elizabeth Anne Sommersett was a sensible young woman. She would do nothing to shame her family.

What she had done with Cain Dare went beyond flirting. It was dangerous, and it frightened her because for the first time she had been overwhelmed by feelings of carnal desire she had only suspected were buried deep within her. Cain was no polished English gentlemen; he was an Indian savage. Rules of proper conduct would mean nothing to him. If he had ravished her on the spot, she would have been in no position to condemn him for his actions.

Too hot beneath the deerskin, Elizabeth rolled over onto her back and stared up at the low ceiling. What if he had not stopped when she'd begged him? What if Cain had taken her maidenhead? What would it have felt like?

As the forbidden questions rose in her mind, she felt a return of the warm ache in her loins. She stirred restlessly, trying to push away the provocative thoughts—thoughts she had no right to dwell on. Her throat tightened and she squirmed, pushing back the blanket. Savage or not, Cain Dare was a man unlike any she had ever met before.

She tried to banish Cain's image by reminding herself of her intended, Edward Lindsey. She had not seen him since he was a youth. She remembered his blond hair, clear blue eyes, and fair skin. Edward had been slight rather than sturdy, but he had looked like a proper Englishman.

It might take weeks, even months, but eventually she would be found and taken to the English colony. Her marriage with Edward would go forward as planned. If they had little in common, it would not matter. They would return to England; she would have the governing of some great house and Edward would be about his own business. Once she had given him an heir, they might not even share a bed.

She sighed deeply. Her future was carved in stone. It had been decided at the moment of her birth when the midwife had declared that she was a jill. She was not her father's firstborn; he already had a healthy son and daughter. Even if she had been a boy, she would not have been his heir. As a male child, she would have been educated in the church or the military; as a female, she was destined to wed wherever it would increase the Sommersett fortunes.

Her destiny had never troubled her. She had accepted it with the same ease that she accepted her own physical beauty. Her honey-blond hair had framed a face that would have commanded attention even in a girl without her family's wealth and position. She had inherited her fair looks from a grandmother and had never been particularly vain about them. She had known, of course, that her physical charms enhanced her value in her father's eyes, and she had taken a most unmaidenly pleasure in the fact that her older sister Alice had a nose too long to be considered attractive.

Alice had wed the widowed earl of Trusberry two years before and had flaunted her new title, reminding Elizabeth that Edward Lindsey had small chance of ever coming to his father's title. "I shall take precedence over you when we are presented at court," she had said mockingly.

Elizabeth had only laughed. Alice's earl was in his dotage and as bald as a pigeon egg. Edward might have an unpleasant disposition, but at least his flanks wouldn't be as thin as bed slats.

The high tones of a flute snatched her from her reverie. The haunting refrain came from just outside the wigwam. Cain, she thought. It must be Cain! Unable to resist the lure of the music, she rose from her bed and left the wigwam.

When she got outside, he was gone. The notes faded into the night, leaving only the sound of the wind and the waves. "Did I dream it?" she whispered.

The fire had burned low. She knelt beside it, holding out her hands to the warmth. Minutes passed, and then he was there sitting beside her.

"How do you do that?" she demanded.

"Do what?"

"Come and go without my seeing or hearing you. That was you playing the flute, wasn't it?"

He shrugged. His face was immobile, revealing nothing. "Perhaps you heard the dolphins. They sing at night."

"Do they?" She inhaled shakily. "I would like to hear them sometime. There were dolphins when I was alone in the boat on the sea. They kept me company for a while." One hand dropped to her side; idly she sifted sand through her fingers. "That was no dolphin I heard before. Where is your flute?"

"Do you wish to see the dolphins now?" Catching her hand, he pulled her up on her feet and began to run down the beach. When they reached his dugout, Cain pointed to a place in the bow. "Sit there," he ordered.

"Now? We're going out on the ocean now?"

"You said you would see the dolphins. I do not know if they will sing tonight, but they will swim in the moonlight. Will you come, Eliz-a-beth?"

Nodding, she climbed into the boat. For the first time, she realized that she had seen nothing of the longboat since he had brought her ashore. "What did you do with the boat I was in?" she asked.

"Burned it for firewood." The muscles on his back and shoulders rippled as he began to push the dugout down the sand to the water. Elizabeth clung to the sides with both hands. With a shout, he splashed into the low rolling surf and shoved the boat toward an outgoing wave. When he was almost chest-deep in water, Cain heaved himself over the side, seized his paddle, and guided the dugout through the waves.

In minutes, they were beyond the surf. Cain chanted as he drove the paddle into the sea in a steady, rhythmic pattern. Elizabeth couldn't understand the words of his song, but she found herself humming along.

Gliding along the surface of the dark water seemed almost like flying. As the moonlight frosted the waves with silver, Elizabeth hugged herself to prove she wasn't dreaming. The spray was cold against her face, but she didn't care. The night was one of wild enchantment, and she meant to savor every bit of it. She glanced back at Cain, and her heart thudded in her chest so loudly she was certain he must hear it.

"You promised me dolphins," she reminded him.

In answer, he raised the tip of his paddle and

pointed. From the east, a dark form rose in the water and emitted a shrill cry.

"Oh," Elizabeth murmured as the second dolphin broke the surface of the sea. "They're coming. They're really coming."

He nodded. "They come, and if the wind is kind, perhaps they will sing to you of deep water and far-off shores . . . or perhaps they will sing you a tale of the dolphin people who live beneath the sea."

"Perhaps they will," she agreed with shining eyes. "After this, I'd believe anything."

Chapter 6

The sweet, poignant song of the dolphins echoed in Elizabeth's head in the days and weeks that followed. There was no repeat of the intimate kiss she and Cain had shared that night they watched the vixen and her cubs, but she knew that a bond was forming between them. "Our souls have touched," Cain had said. Elizabeth wondered if, in his primitive way, he was right.

Although they lived together in his wigwam, shared their meals, slept within arm's reach, and spent most of their waking hours together, both were careful not to touch. No maiden aunt could have been treated with more courtesy; no cloistered nun could have expected more respect from a man. Yet no hour passed without Elizabeth being intensely aware of Cain's masculinity or the fact that he was courting her.

Each morning when she awoke, she found a gift beside her sleeping platform: a polished conch shell, a string of copper beads, a comb of honey, a scarlet feather. Once there was a slate-colored stone, weathered and beaten by the ocean, twisted by nature into the form of a dolphin. Using only beach sand and reeds, Cain had painstakingly drilled a hole through the top so that the amulet could be worn on a braided leather cord.

At night, Elizabeth fell asleep to the sounds of an eagle-bone flute and to the muted cries of owls and nighthawks. Her dreams were always of Cain, and in the misty world of her dreams he did not keep his distance. Time after time, she woke at first light still feeling the warmth of his touch, the thrill of his impassioned embrace.

With May came the buzz of honeybees and the heady scents of wildflowers. Never had she seen or smelled such a profusion of plants and flowers, spilling across the earth in every color of the rainbow. She gathered handfuls of blossoms, laced them in her hair, and filled the wigwam and campsite with fragrant bouquets.

The warm weather brought other changes to the beach. Birds and ducks and geese filled the skies, and the soft spring air rang with their melodious calls of mating. Cain pointed out the different types of shore birds, patiently identifying them in his own language. Gradually, Elizabeth began to sort out their colors and sizes, finding immense delight in matching the Lenni-Lenape words to the right bird.

Cain taught her to weave a fish net and carve a fish spear. At night they would go out in the dugout beyond the surf. She would hold a torch over the water, and he would spear the fish attracted by the light. Together, they dug clams and netted crabs in a shallow bay to the west.

Always, Cain took exactly what they needed and no more. "To waste is against the ways of Inu-msi-ila-fe-wanu, the Great Spirit," he explained gently. "It is a great wrong."

"Like a sin, you mean?" she had answered.

"A mortal sin," he agreed.

"Then this Inu-msi is your god. I thought his name was Wishemenetoo."

Cain had frowned, searching for the right words to explain something he obviously believed even a child should know. "No. They are not the same. Inu-msi-ila-fe-wanu is the Great Spirit, a grandmother. Wishemenetoo is the Great Good Spirit. Wishemenetoo is a male spirit."

"You told me you believed in one God, as I do," she had reminded him. "Now you say there are two Indian gods."

He had sighed and shook his head. "One Creator, one over all. We do not speak His name." He stared at her shrewdly. "And the English have more than one god."

"We do not."

"Father, Son, and Holy Spirit," Cain retorted. "Three."

"It isn't the same."

"The same."

"You are a pagan. I don't expect you to understand."

He had laughed. "Who made the sea, the earth, and the heavens?"

"God."

"What is His name?"

"Just God. He has no other name."

"Ah hah! One Creator. I know His name, but I will not tell you."

"We have no female gods."

Cain's eyes narrowed mischievously. "Mary."

"She is the mother of our Lord, but she isn't a god."

"You pray to her. This one has heard you. 'Holy Mary,' you say. 'Cede for me.' "

"It isn't the same."

"Same."

Elizabeth had decided it wasn't worth discussing theology with an Indian. He didn't realize when he was being blasphemous, and he took the entire subject too lightly.

Late one afternoon, Elizabeth returned from the pond with water for cooking. Cain had taken his bow and arrows and left camp after the midday meal, promising to bring home a turkey. Spending part of the day alone was no longer frightening for her. In all of her time on the beach, the only dangerous creature she had seen was a shark, and that had been caught on one of Cain's fishing lines. She had begun to think of the wilderness not as an enemy, but as her friend. The forest gives us food and drink and shelter, she thought. I'd be foolish to go on being afraid of my own shadow.

The day was so warm that she had cast aside her moccasins, running about in bare feet as she had done on carefree afternoons in her childhood. She'd just entered the camp when she saw two human figures coming down the beach and was so startled that she dropped the water jug. The clay bowl broke as it struck the ground and water sprayed in all directions, but Elizabeth didn't notice. She stood frozen to the spot, staring at the advancing men.

The strangers were too far away for her to tell if they were red or white, but the men carried a large bundle between them, swinging from two poles. Seizing a fish spear that stuck upright in the sand, Elizabeth ran toward the advancing party. "Hello!" she cried. "Hello, there! Are you English?"

Her heart pounded as she ran. Had the men come to rescue her? Had they been searching since the shipwreck? She strained her eyes in the bright sunlight, trying to make out their features.

The figures stopped and pointed in her direction, then quickened their pace. The lead man waved and called out, but Elizabeth couldn't hear what he was saying.

"Hallo! I'm Elizabeth Sommersett!" she shouted. Her bare feet sank into the hot sand. "Hallo! Hallo!" Her breath came in great gulps, and she was dizzy with excitement. The running soon tired her, and she slowed to a trot and finally a walk. The men were much closer now, almost close enough to . . .

Elizabeth stopped, swallowing a lump in her throat. The men were copper-colored, not white, and the first man wore his black hair in a high stiff comb, shaved on either side. His face was painted with yellow streaks, and his legs were bare beneath a short loincloth. The second man was older, with streaks of gray in his long hair.

She leaned on the fish spear, trying to catch her breath and regain her composure as they approached.

"*Ta koom?*" the man with the shaved head called.

"*A Lenni-Lenape?*" his companion asked.

"*Mata. Quanna eet auween gatta napenalgun.*" Both men laughed.

Elizabeth stiffened. *Lenni-Lenape*, she understood, and the word *mata*. Cain used it for *no*. "I am Elizabeth Sommersett," she replied formally. "I am English."

"*Englishhokkuaa?*" came a muffled voice from inside the large skin bag. "You are English?" The tone was high and reedy, the accent strangely like Cain's.

Hair rose on the back of Elizabeth's neck, and her mouth dropped open in astonishment.

The men came closer, and a shriveled hand appeared through a hole in the bundle, pushing aside the flap. Two faded blue eyes peered at Elizabeth from a tiny, wrinkled face. "Good morrow, Mistress Eliz-a-beth," came the stilted greeting from the bright-eyed elf. "I am verra pleased to make your 'quaintance. I be Mistress Virginia Dare."

Elizabeth blinked twice and backed away. "But you can't be," she protested. "Virginia Dare has been dead for nearly a hundred years. She was massacred with Sir Walter Raleigh's lost colony."

The second man said something in the Indian tongue that sounded like a question, and the elf answered. Again, both men laughed.

Elizabeth felt her face flush. "I'm not a fool," she said, feeling like one. "Who are you, and what do you want?"

The little old woman chuckled, a sound like dry cornhusks rubbing together. "I have told you, child. I am Virginia Dare, the daughter of Ananias and Eleanor White Dare. I was born on August 18, in the year of our Lord, 1587. That hardly makes me one hundred years old, even if I be poorly at sums."

"What . . . what do you want here?" Elizabeth stammered.

"I come to see my grandson, Cain." Her face dissolved into a mass of wrinkles as she smiled, revealing a mouthful of pearly white teeth. "Are you Shaakhan's woman? Have you broken the marriage cake together?"

"No. *Mata!*" Elizabeth cried. "I am not his wife. I was on a ship bound for Jamestown and we were wrecked at sea. He rescued—"

The old woman laughed again. "He plucked you from the sea?" She clapped her hands together. "He said it! He said you would be a gift from the sea." She flung out her hands. "Come close, *daanus*. Come here, daughter, and greet your grandmother. I have waited so long to see you."

"No." Elizabeth backed away. "You aren't my grandmother, and you aren't Virginia Dare."

The older brave shifted one pole a few inches to ease his shoulder, and pointed north along the forest's edge. *"Pennau!"*

Elizabeth glanced over her shoulder and gave a sigh of relief as Cain came striding across the beach. The two men waved and called a greeting; the elf waited in silence for Cain to draw near.

"Ili keheleche?" Cain said formally. "Grandmother, do you still draw breath?"

"N'leheleche," the old woman replied. "Yes, I still draw breath."

Cain flashed a smile at Elizabeth, then dropped to his knees and extended his hands to the little woman. "My heart is glad to see you again, *Cocumtha*. It has been too long."

"It eases these old eyes to see you again," she answered, hugging him. "We see you find that which you seek." Mistress Dare released him and looked pointedly at Elizabeth. "Did I not tell you that Englishwomen have hair like autumn grass?" She chuckled. "Did I not say that I had such hair in my day?"

Cain rose to his feet and went back to Elizabeth, catching her by the hand. "You have met my dear grandmother," he said. "You must say to her a good greeting in English."

Feeling awkward, Elizabeth executed the most graceful curtsy possible in a short deerskin dress.

"I am most pleased to make your acquaintance, Mistress Dare," she said.

Cain nodded his approval. "This is my uncle, M'biak," he explained, "and this is H'kah-nih Elene, Bone Man." Cain grinned. "H'kah-nih Elene is a Shawnee and very fierce."

The crested warrior said something in his own tongue and smiled broadly at Elizabeth.

"He does not speak English," Cain continued, "but he understands a little. He has been to trade with the white men at their settlement, and he says they called him Harry. He says you may call him Harry also, so that you do not make a mock of his true name."

At the mention of the English settlement, Elizabeth felt a rush of excitement. If Harry had been there, perhaps she could persuade him to take her. Calmly, hiding her thoughts from Cain, she curtsied once more. "M'biak, Harry," she said graciously. "Good morrow, sirs."

Harry spoke again, and M'biak pursed his lips to keep from laughing. Elizabeth looked expectantly at Cain.

"He says your manners are much better than those of Englishmen. He says they behave like overfed toads in a muddy pond."

"Did you come from Jamestown?" Elizabeth asked Harry. "Jamestown?"

Cain's grandmother chuckled. "Mosquito Town," she corrected in her thin wavering voice. "These English build on swamp. I think wigwams sink into mud before many seasons pass." She scratched the top of her head. "Are we to stand here all afternoon?" she demanded peevishly. "I am hot in this bag, and my belly growls with hunger. Will my grandson invite us to his campfire before the snow flies?"

"Yes, Grandmother," Cain replied with affection. "I have the manners of an Englishman. Come. There is a basket of oysters cooling in the pond and a turkey for the spit." He motioned toward the campsite. "We will sit in the shade and you will tell me all the gossip."

"This one does not gossip," Mistress Dare protested. "But I do have news of your cousin, Aman. He has taken Yapewi's young wife. Between them, they have made a scandal."

"I knew you would have something interesting to tell me." Cain winked at Elizabeth. "Grandmother forgets that she once caused the greatest scandal of all."

Laughing and talking together in the Indian tongue, the group moved up the beach to Cain's camp. Mistress Dare swung gently to and fro in her skin litter as her bearers trotted along. Elizabeth trailed after them, trying to sort out truth from nonsense. Obviously, the old woman was Cain's grandmother. Could she possibly be Virginia Dare—the first English child born in America—or was this all some monstrous jest?

When they reached the wigwam, Cain helped his grandmother from her strange conveyance. To Elizabeth's relief, the white-haired woman was not crippled and was quite able to walk under her own power.

Elizabeth tried not to stare at her strange apparel. The old lady wore a long skirt of the finest white doeskin that reached the tips of her tiny quill-worked moccasins. The skirt was topped with a tightly laced vest, worn over a full-sleeved bodice with wide, beaded cuffs. Around her neck was a ruffled collar consisting of hundreds of russet and white feathers, and on the back of her head she wore a matching feather cap that tied under her chin. Her hair, what there was of it, was tucked under the cap. Large pearls in an old-fashioned silver setting dangled from her tiny pierced ears. Elizabeth could have sworn the earrings were of English design.

Cain brought a deerskin robe from the hut and folded it to make a seat for his grandmother, then produced a backrest of woven willow branches for her to lean on. M'biak went to the pond for fresh water to quench her thirst, and the Shawnee searched through a pack to find a goose-feather fan.

Mistress Dare beckoned Elizabeth to sit beside her as the men hastened to open the oysters and pluck the turkey. "Come, come, child," she cried. "I want to speak with you. Tell me of the Queen. Is she well?"

"Queen Catherine?"

"Catherine? I know nothing of this Catherine," Mistress Dare insisted. "I would know of England's good Queen Bess."

"Catherine of Braganza is queen, madam. The old queen has been dead for many years."

"Are you certain?"

Elizabeth nodded. "My cousin is lady-in-waiting to her majesty. I have been presented to her several times myself."

"Aiiee," Mistress Dare groaned. "Cain said it must be so, but this one did not want to believe. When I heard your name, I was sure you were named to honor her majesty." The faded blue eyes took on a faraway look. "My mother said Elizabeth had always been queen and always would be. I knew she was a silly woman, my mother." She folded her knotted hands and rocked back and forth. "She was a good woman, but foolish at times." Her head snapped up, and she fixed Elizabeth with a piercing stare. "I suppose Raleigh is dead too."

"Yes."

"This Catherine of Braganza—she is good queen?"

Elizabeth paused for a moment and considered her answer. "It is said that she is a kind and just lady, but many would think better of her if she could give King Charles a son."

"Char-les." The name on Mistress Dare's lips was softly accented and foreign. "King Char-les." She shook her head as though unconvinced. "Good Queen Bess was the Virgin Queen. She had no man to rule beside her."

"True. But she left no heir either. James of Scotland ascended the throne of England, then his son Charles." Elizabeth watched the old woman intently to see if she was able to comprehend.

"Then this Char-les is a Scot." Mistress Dare's eyes were nearly lost in wrinkles when she smiled. "My father said the Scots were savage warriors."

"There has been war in England, madam," Elizabeth explained. "Terrible war. That Charles died horribly, and his son, also named Charles, now rules."

Mistress Dare made a clicking sound with her tongue. "Ah," she exclaimed. "Then that is why my grandfather did not come for us as he promised. My mother did not know why. All her life she watched the sea for a ship."

The men had cleaned the turkey and washed it in the sea. Cain was making a spit to hold the bird over the fire. He caught Elizabeth's eye and smiled at her.

"Are we to eat today?" his grandmother demanded. "I was promised oysters."

"And you shall have them," Cain promised. "They are roasting in the coals."

She wrinkled her nose. "They are probably as small as wren's eggs," she grumbled.

"For you, Grandmother," he teased, "I cook only those as large as pumpkins."

"Hmmph!" Mistress Dare clapped her hands and M'biak brought her a pipe of shiny green stone. Carefully, he packed it with tobacco, lit it with a coal from the fire, and handed it to her. The old lady drew a long puff and blew smoke into the air.

"What was your grandfather's name?" Elizabeth asked. When she was a child, her grandfather had read her the story of Raleigh's lost colony. She knew that after establishing a settlement on Roanoke Island in Virginia, the leader of the expedition had sailed back to England for much-needed supplies, leaving his daughter and newborn granddaughter, Virginia Dare, on the island. When he returned, three years to the day later, all trace of the English were gone. Although it was commonly believed that the settlers had perished at the hands of hostile Indians, the mystery had never been solved.

Mistress Dare chuckled. "You think I have forgotten? I have not. His English name was Gover Norwhite." She took another long draw on the pipe. "I think it is best he did not come for my mother. The Lenni-Lenape follow the peace trail. Grass grows on the path of war, and babies with empty bellies do not weep for dead fathers." Suddenly she reached out and seized Elizabeth's hand. "You do not believe me, do you?"

Elizabeth tried to pull free, but the old woman's

grip was like iron. "Please . . . madam," she stammered. "I do not—"

"Hah!" Mistress Dare released her and laughed. "It does not matter, for this one be not sure she believes you. The English speak with tongue of *hahees*—the crow. Good Queen Bess may still sit on the throne of England!"

Chapter 7

By the time Cain announced that the meal was ready, evening shadows were beginning to spill across the campsite. The five gathered near the low fire and shared the bounty of the land and sea. Although Elizabeth had lived with Cain for weeks, she still marveled at the variety of delicious food he and the men produced without a proper kitchen.

There were oysters and tiny clams, some raw and others steamed in their shells, and a rich soup of crab and fish, seasoned with wild onions and herbs. The turkey had been divided in two; part was grilled over the fire and part wrapped in a casing of mud and baked in the hot coals. There was a dish of pale green seaweed that Mistress Dare declared delicious, and steamed cattail shoots, along with pumpkin and squash, flavored with honey. Dried, crushed berries added to the taste of flat corn cakes—cakes that bore no resemblance to Elizabeth's earlier inadequate attempt at baking.

To Elizabeth's surprise, Cain apologized to his grandmother for the poor quality of his feast. "If you had sent a runner, Grandmother, I could have offered you better food."

"Hmmph," she muttered. "Or perhaps you might have hidden this good turkey and offered me cold fish." The three men laughed.

The meal went on for hours, and it became clear to Elizabeth that much of Mistress Dare's grumbling was only done in jest. All of the men obviously regarded her with great respect and affection. Cain was careful to offer each new dish to his grandmother first and then to Elizabeth. Cain and Mistress Dare spoke in a mixture of softly slurred English and Indian; often Cain made a point of translating something that was said in Algonquian.

As the others talked and joked with each other, Elizabeth watched. She was not yet convinced that Cain's grandmother was who she said she was. The leader of the lost colony and the grandfather of the real Virginia Dare had been the artist John White. Was it possible that she had merely forgotten her grandfather's name? Regardless of who she was, it was obvious that the old woman had had a great deal of contact with the English. If Mistress Dare could be persuaded to help, Elizabeth was certain she would be reunited with her people.

Her opportunity came when the three men announced that they would walk down the beach in search of sea turtles. Elizabeth and Mistress Dare were left alone together. As soon as the men were out of hearing range, Elizabeth moved close to the old woman.

"If you are English, you must help me," she whispered urgently. "Your grandson is holding me captive."

The corners of Mistress Dare's mouth turned up in a sly smile. "You do not look like any prisoner I have seen, Eliz-a-beth," she said. She took a sip of water from her painted water jug and looked at Elizabeth quizzically. "Has Cain beaten you? Does he force you to carry water and cook for him?"

"No, but—"

"Ah." She held up a finger for silence. "I did not see you prepare this meal." She extended both hands and waited expectantly.

An owl hooted from the direction of the pond. Elizabeth trembled, despite the warmth of the fire and the mildness of the evening. Reluctantly, she put her hands in Mistress Dare's.

Nodding approval, the old lady turned Elizabeth's hands over, examining her palms by firelight. For long minutes, she stared, saying nothing. Finally, she raised her eyes to meet Elizabeth's. "These are not slave hands," she pronounced in her lilting, high voice. "Too soft, like hands of a babe." She arched one snow-white eyebrow. "I see you watching my grandson. You do not watch with the eyes of a captive."

Elizabeth pulled her hands away. "That's not true!" she protested. "I want to go to Jamestown. I must! The man I will marry is there."

"The lines of your hand say he is not there," Mistress Dare intoned softly. "Your hand says you will bear strong sons and daughters for my grandson."

"No!" Elizabeth moved to the other side of the fire. The owl hooted again, closer, and a queer prickling sensation rose in Elizabeth's throat. "You can't read the future," she cried. "That's witchcraft."

The old woman chuckled. "A witch now, am I? I have been called many things, but never witch. Aiiee." She rocked back, and mischief twinkled in the faded blue eyes. "No, no, child, you need not fear me. Think you I can fly up into that tree? Turn into a owl?''

Elizabeth shivered as icy fear rose within her. Was the woman a witch? Elizabeth had always scoffed at those who ranted of demons and black magic, but what if it were all true? Her mouth went dry as sand, and she felt her pulse pounding as she looked about for a weapon to defend herself.

"Shhh," Mistress Dare soothed. "I have never harmed a child in all my life. What I see in your palm is not sorcery. It is written here plain for any to read. Each life has a destiny." She closed her eyes and rocked slowly to and fro. "Three times you will cross the sea," she murmured, "and three times you will wed." She took a long breath. "Three but only two, and of the two, only one."

"Stop," Elizabeth said. "No more, I beg of you. All I want is your help to get to Jamestown. I'll take you with me, if you wish. I'll see you get safely home to England."

Mistress Dare chuckled. "Home? Home to England? England is not home."

"It is for me."

"Is it?" Mistress Dare closed her eyes.

Minutes passed, and Elizabeth realized the old woman had fallen asleep. Her breathing was so light that only the faint stir of her feather ruff gave any indication that she was alive.

What am I doing here? Elizabeth cried inwardly. Why me? I should have gone with my aunt instead of pushing that stupid chit into the boat in my place. At least if the boat went down, we would have drowned together.

"No," she murmured, as shame replaced self-pity. I'm not sorry for what I did, and I'm not sorry I'm alive. Elizabeth chuckled wryly. I'm not even sorry I left England. If I had stayed safely at home, I'd never have glimpsed this strange New World. I'd never have known Cain.

Elizabeth jumped as a hand descended on her shoulder. "Oh!" She whirled to see Cain standing behind her. "I didn't hear you come back."

"I did not wish to frighten you, Eliz-a-beth. We find a turtle. She comes to lay her eggs in the sand. Do you wish to look upon her?"

"A sea turtle?" Unconsciously, she twisted the fringe of her skirt in her fingers; her breathing quickened and she averted her eyes. The heavy night air seemed charged with expectancy, and the man she felt she knew was suddenly a mysterious stranger. "On the beach?"

"Yes." He fixed her with an unwavering gaze.

His impassive face gleamed in the flickering firelight; his copper-hued shoulders seemed to Elizabeth too broad, too perfect to belong to a living, breathing man.

The tightness in her throat spread down her chest, making her breasts swell and tingle. Her nipples rubbed against the inside of her leather dress with every breath. Nervously, she smoothed her hair. "Your . . . your grandmother," she stammered. "Will she—"

"She sleeps," he said.

Elizabeth moistened her dry lips. "Harry . . . M'biak." It seemed important she not be alone with Cain on the beach tonight. Not with the luminous moon hanging like a great golden crescent among the clouds . . . not with the scent of beach plum blossoms wafting so sweetly in the air. "Where are they?"

"They wait and watch." With tantalizing slowness, he captured her hand and raised it to his lips, placing a lingering kiss on the sensitive under-side of her wrist. "You have beauty, Eliz-a-beth," he said in his soft, husky cadence. *"Nibeeshu*, the moon, has not your beauty."

Her heart fluttered wildly in her breast as she leaned against him, letting her lips brush the satin of his skin. The tip of her tongue flicked against the hollow of his throat; he tasted of salt and pine needles. "Cain," she whispered. "Cain."

Across the fire, Mistress Dare's faded eyes opened a crack, and a smile tugged at the wrinkled creases of her mouth. She coughed and jerked upright with a snort, as though waking from a dream. Cain and Elizabeth jumped apart. "Hmmph." Mistress Dare rubbed at her face and called sleepily in English. "Grandson? Are you here?"

"I am here, Grandmother."

"We are both here, madam," Elizabeth said, too loudly. "Are you well?"

"M'biak? Where is M'biak?" the old woman demanded testily.

"N'dapi, onna," came M'biak's reply. He and Harry entered the firelight and sat down on the sand.

"This one is hungry," Mistress Dare complained. "Am I such a poor guest that my belly is to shrivel like an empty waterbag? I suppose there are no corn cakes left."

Cain chuckled indulgently. "There are corn cakes, *Cocumtha.*" He glanced at Elizabeth, and she picked up a bowl and handed it to him.

The old woman took a cake and nibbled at it. "Am I to eat alone?" she said.

"Mata," Cain replied. He took a portion of the flat cake and broke it in two, offering half to Elizabeth. M'biak and Harry exchanged glances, then

they too helped themselves to the crumbly bread as Cain ate his.

Elizabeth bit off a piece of the cake, then gratefully sipped from the water jar Cain passed to her.

"Grandson," Mistress Dare cried. "Do you care for this woman?"

"I have given her bread and water."

The old woman wiped the crumbs from her mouth and sighed. "You, Eliz-a-beth."

"Madam?"

"My grandson pulled you from the sea?"

Puzzled, Elizabeth nodded. "Yes, madam. I told you so before."

"He is your friend?" Mistress Dare persisted. "You trust him?"

Embarrassed, Elizabeth nodded and mumbled something incoherent.

"Yes or no?" the old woman demanded. "You care for him?"

"Yes . . . of course," Elizabeth answered, "but I—"

"Is enough," Mistress Dare declared. "So be it." Chuckling, she clapped her hands. "Does the moon sleep in the west? Are you men or suckling babes?" She grinned at her own joke. "Let our hearts be warm on this night. Let us laugh and tell wonderful stories."

M'biak said something in the Indian tongue and slapped Cain on the back. Harry passed Mistress Dare a turkey wing, and the old woman began to chew on it greedily. M'biak got to his feet and spread his arms over his head.

"M'biak will tell the first story," Cain explained in English. The older man began to speak, and Cain and Mistress Dare took turns translating.

"Long ago, when the world was young and the animals could talk . . ."

The story went on and on until Elizabeth could no longer keep her eyes open. Vaguely, she was aware when her head drooped and someone put a deerskin over her. Then, the firelight and the droning voices blurred together and she was no longer aware of anything.

When she opened her eyes again, the sun was rising over the rim of misty blue-green sea. The fire had burned to ashes, and she was alone with Cain. With a start, she sat bolt upright and looked around. There was no sign of M'biak, or Harry, or Mistress Dare.

She rubbed the crick in her neck and yawned. Cain smiled at her. "Where are they?" she asked. She had the strangest notion that it had all been a dream, that the old grandmother and the others had only existed in her mind.

"*Cocumtha* never visit long," he said. "She is on way to make visit of my cousin at the Place of the Bubbling Spring. My cousin, Okottimaang, has a new baby girl. Grandmother will give the baby a name." He grinned. "She says she will name the baby Eliz-a-beth."

Elizabeth rubbed her eyes and pulled the robe around her against the damp morning air. "Do you always eat so much?"

"Sometimes."

She stood up, and something tumbled into the sand at her feet. She bent and picked it up. It was a locket of tarnished silver, surrounded with a circle of seed pearls. "What is this?" she asked. "Did Mistress Dare lose this?"

Cain shook his head. "Open it."

Her fingers found the minute catch, and the lid snapped open. Inside was a painted miniature of the old queen, Elizabeth. "Oh." She stared down at the lovely painting. "Oh," she repeated. "You must run after your grandmother. This must be very precious to her."

"She did not lose it. She left it for you, Eliz-a-beth."

"A present? For me?" Her forehead creased in a frown. "But why?"

Cain chuckled. "It is her marriage gift to you."

"Marriage?" Elizabeth's mouth dropped open in surprise. "But I'm not—"

"You are. Last night . . . when we broke the corn and drank of the same jug. We are wed, *ki-te-hi*. In the eyes of the Great Spirit and of my people, you are my wife."

Elizabeth shook her head in disbelief. "You're lying. I'm not your wife! I can't be."

"It is not good for man and woman to share wigwam when they be not one. Unless . . ." He looked at her questioningly. "You be not widow, be you?"

Her balled fists dropped to rest on her hips and she glared at him. "Widow? Widow?" she cried. "I'm not even a wife."

"A bride without spirit is like cold soup." He grinned wryly. "This one does not think he has taken such a woman."

"We are not married," she insisted. "Your corn and water mean nothing to me. I am a Christian."

"We trick you, but you say the words. *Cocum-tha* gives the blessing. English, Lenni-Lenape, does not matter. We be man and woman. Water and corn taste the same no matter what the tongue speaks."

"You've taken leave of whatever sense you ever had!" Elizabeth flung back. "I'll not be bullied by

you or your crazy grandmother." Angrily, she
spun around and stalked off toward the wigwam.
"If you come in here," she threatened, "come at
your own risk."

Cain watched her until she ducked inside the
skin entrance flap of the wigwam. He had known
Eliz-a-beth would be angry when she found out
she was his wife. He hoped that anger would cool
in the days and nights to come.

The rays of the rising sun warmed his back.
Taking a deep breath, he walked to the water's
edge and raised his arms in silent prayer, giving
thanks to the Creator for a new day. When the
familiar ritual was complete, he cast aside his
loincloth and waded out into the rolling surf.

The ocean water was cold and invigorating.
Scooping up handfuls of sand, Cain scrubbed his
chest and arms until they tingled. Salty foam
lapped about his thighs as he walked out into
deeper water. The sea floor was smooth sand,
gently tapering to a dropoff beyond the breaking
waves.

The high, shrill hunting cry of an osprey
sounded above the raucous clamor of the gulls,
and Cain paused to stare up at the majestic bird
swooping low over the water. It was a mighty sea
hawk with a wingspread of six feet and gleaming
white talons.

"Greeting, brother," Cain called to the huge
black and white bird.

The hawk dipped one wing, as if in salute, then
dove and plucked a wiggling fish from the water.
Clutching the fish, the bird rose into the air and
flew inland, toward the shallow bay.

Cain took a deep breath and plunged into the
blue-green water. He opened his eyes, despite the
salt sting, and swam a long way before surfac-

ing. Then he floated on his back, letting his mind dwell on the foreign woman he had just taken as his wife.

To trick Eliz-a-beth was wrong, but to take her without benefit of a marriage ceremony would be a greater wrong. There was no doubt in his mind that this was the woman promised to him by his spirit guide, and nothing would convince him that she did not return his love for her. It might be weeks or months before another of his people came to the beach—too long to wait for a proper wedding.

The Lenni-Lenape code was rigid. A man might lie with a willing widow or a divorced woman. Those women were free to do as they chose without reproach. But for one such as Eliz-a-beth—a virgin—it was different. A man of honor could make love to a maid only if he made her his wife. That Eliz-a-beth was English made no difference. He was Lenni-Lenape; he was bound by the law.

When Cain's first wife and small daughters had died of the white man's measles, he had wanted to follow them to the dream land. For many turns of the moon he had mourned them with a heavy heart. Then his grandmother had summoned him and bade him seek a vision. That vision had brought him here to the edge of the sea, had brought laughter back to his heart—and had prepared him for this woman with hair like autumn grass.

The wait had been a long one. Twice, the time of snow and ice had come and gone. Twice, he had watched the pale green of new grass break through the sleeping earth. And then, when he was beginning to doubt the wisdom of his lonely vigil, the dolphins had led him to Eliz-a-beth.

Even so, he had been patient, teaching her the

ways of the people and letting her come to trust
him. Night after night, he had lain awake listening to her soft breathing with the blood running
hot in his veins. His desire for this Englishwoman
was great, but he knew she must come to him of
her own will.

The night they had watched the gray vixen and
her cubs, all was changed. Eliz-a-beth had come
into his arms. He had seen the longing for him in
her eyes, eyes the color of a stormy sea. He had
wanted her as badly as he had ever wanted anything in his life, wanted to carry her to his sleeping platform and share the joys of the mat with
her.

Cain dove again, swimming with powerful
thrusts of his legs to the bottom of the sea. A
school of fish swam around him, moving with in-
finite grace. A larger shadow, perhaps a skate,
hovered close to the sand. Cain swam until it felt
as though his lungs were bursting, then at last he
broke the surface and sucked in great mouthfuls
of air.

"I have waited long for you, Eliz-a-beth," he
shouted above the crash of the surf. "Now I have
made you my wife, and I will wait no longer!"

Chapter 8

"**E**liz-a-beth." Cain crouched to enter the wigwam a short time later. "We must talk."

She raised her head and stared at him. "Yes. We must." She swung her feet off the edge of her sleeping platform and sat up; her eyes were swollen and red with weeping, and her hair was plaited in one untidy braid that hung over her left shoulder.

Cain smiled as he thought how beautiful she was. "You look like a sleepy child."

"Stop it! Don't try to charm me. What you did was wrong. Don't you realize that?" Her eyes darkened with anger. "You can't force me to become your wife."

Cain took a few steps toward her and she stiffened. Immediately, he crouched down. "Be it wrong to love you, Eliz-a-beth?"

"Yes, if it makes you hold me prisoner and try to trick me into marriage." She rose to her feet. "I'm not an animal, Cain. You can't trap me and hold me against my will."

His voice deepened. "You were promised to me in a vision. I took you from the sea."

"It was your vision—not mine!" She drew in a

shuddering breath. "You treat your grandmother with honor, but what about me?"

Cain winced at her harsh words. "You do not understand. I would never force—"

"You're forcing me now! I'm English, can't you get that through your thick head?" Angry tears gathered in the corners of her eyes and she blinked them away. "I'm not an Indian, and you aren't English."

"*Cocumtha* was born white, but she became one of the true people."

"If she is the real Virginia Dare, she was a baby when she went to live with the Indians. She never knew any other life. I have! Don't you understand?"

He swallowed, struggling for composure. This wasn't the way it was supposed to be. They were wed. Eliz-a-beth was supposed to throw herself into his arms, to let him touch her in the ways of a man and woman, to touch him. "You would have me take you to Jamestown so you might join with another man?"

"You must. If you hold me here, I will hate you for the rest of my life."

Cain's vision blurred as he turned away and left the wigwam. His stride lengthened, and he broke into a run, inhaling deep breaths as his feet flew over the hard-packed sand at the ocean's edge.

She is mine! I cannot give her up! He continued to run, staring with unseeing eyes at the beach ahead of him. Sweat beaded on his forehead and chest; the sinews in his powerful legs ached with the strain.

Tawny sandpipers fluttered up in alarm as the man raced past them, and gulls screamed and wheeled over his head. He ran on, welcoming the pain of tired muscles, glad for anything that would distract him from the anguish in his heart.

At last he slowed and sank down on the warm sand. The sound of the surf was loud in his ears as the image of Eliz-a-beth's tearstained face rose to haunt him. *I will hate you for the rest of my life*, she had said.

"*K'dalhole*, Eliz-a-beth," he whispered hoarsely. "I love you." He choked back the sadness that threatened to overwhelm him. "I love you . . . but it is not enough."

For long moments he sat there, letting handfuls of sand run through his fingers. Then he stood up and began to retrace his steps.

The sun was directly overhead when Cain reached the campsite. Elizabeth was waiting for him by the water's edge, watching with reproachful eyes as he drew near.

"I take you back to your people on the next tide," he told her.

Her eyes widened in astonishment. "You'll take me?"

"I have said it."

"Oh. I—"

Cain silenced her with a fierce look. "I take you to Jamestown. See this Englishman you wish to have as husband. Search his soul and your own. For the time of one turning of the moon I leave you to him, then I come again. The choice be yours, Eliz-a-beth."

Her face lit with joy as she took a hesitant step toward him. "Thank you, Cain."

"Do not thank me. I was wrong. Only a woman free to follow her own heart can be true wife to Shaakhan Kihittuun."

* * *

For five days, Cain paddled the small boat along the coast. Elizabeth sat in front of him, watching the sea birds and the passing shoreline, lost in her own thoughts. Cain seldom spoke to her, and he never sang as he had done on their earlier ventures at sea.

They rode the tides southward, paddling for six hours, then pulling the dugout onto the sand to wait for the change of tide in another six hours. Elizabeth slept in fits and snatches—Cain seemed to never sleep. Although they saw no sign of human life, he grew more vigilant with each day's passing.

The weather remained fair, so they could camp on the beach at night with only the overturned boat as shelter. After the first three days, Cain refused to light a fire. They survived on dried fish, corn cakes, and a chewy mixture of dried meat, bear fat, and berries that he called *pemmican*. Twice, he left her alone while he went inland to find fresh water.

The third time Cain went in search of water it was late at night, and they had beached the dugout on a small, wooded island. Elizabeth curled up in her deerskin and closed her eyes. If she slept, she wouldn't hear the night noises or stare fearfully out into the darkness. This time, however, sleep wouldn't come.

Her initial excitement at the prospect of returning to her own world had dampened with each league they'd traveled. She had to admit to herself that she felt some regret in leaving the Eden she'd shared with Cain. She wondered what it would be like to rise to the clamor of bustling servants and be cinched into tight garments each morning, rather than awakening to birdsong and slipping a single loose dress over her head.

Reaching Jamestown would mean the end of a freedom she had experienced in the wilderness but had never known in England. A lady of her station had a certain position to maintain. If she wished to keep her respectability, she must establish a staff of chaste female servants and wellborn ladies-in-waiting. She would spend her days surrounded by other people. Each hour of her day would be filled with routine activity—instructing the cook and housemaids, entertaining, being fitted for gowns by the mantuamaker, having her hair styled, and attending church services. There would be no leisurely walks alone on a pristine beach, no nights sitting before a flickering fire with the echoes of an eagle-bone flute wafting on the salt air.

Doubtless, she and her betrothed would be wed as soon as the banns could be cried. She would be the subject of rampant gossip because she had spent weeks in the company of a red savage. It would be necessary to begin her life as wife and mistress of Edward Lindsey with as much decorum as possible in this uncivilized colony. Any doubts Edward had about her morals would be soothed as soon as they bedded. Her maidenhead was intact, and he would be the one to part it. As long as her husband believed she was pure, it wouldn't matter what others speculated.

Elizabeth's maid, Bridget, had told her before she left England that even virgin brides didn't always bleed enough to please jealous bridegrooms. With a little coaxing, the sassy wench had passed on a trick that she'd claimed Irish colleens had used for time out of time.

"Not that I'd be suggestin' ye would ha' need o' such a scheme yerself, m'lady," Bridget had exclaimed with an exaggerated wink. " 'Tis just a bit o' blarney." She'd grinned broadly, exposing a missing tooth. "But they do say a lady should go nowhere wi'out her sewin' bag—not even to her marriage bed."

Elizabeth opened her eyes and stared up at the myriad of twinkling lights that spilled across the heavens. Often on clear nights, Cain had pointed out groups of stars and told her stories about them—the rabbit, a pair of twin hunters, an eagle, and a throwing stick. She would miss their evenings together—she would miss Cain. She was going back to a life he could have no part of, but she knew that he would be hard to forget.

They had come close to being much more than captor and captive; they had nearly become lovers. For a minute, Elizabeth let herself wonder *what if*. What if Cain had never agreed to return her to Jamestown? What if she had remained with him and become his wife?

She exhaled sharply and shook her head. The shock of the shipwreck and her ordeal in the longboat had doubtlessly addled her brain. She'd been confused and ill, unable to reason. The physical attraction she'd felt for Cain must have been the result of that emotional turmoil. They were as unsuited to each other as a wolf would be to one of King Charles's spaniels.

She wiggled to get comfortable on the sand and noticed a star low in the east. Puzzled, she peered through the darkness at the unusually bright flicker and sat up. The star seemed so close. No, it's not a star, it's a light, she thought. "A boat lantern!"

Suddenly, Cain materialized beside her. "Shhh," he warned. "Make no sound."

"But it looks like—"

"Shhh," he ordered sternly. "Danger."

The strains of human voices echoed across the water, but it was too great a distance for Elizabeth to understand what they were saying.

"It is a boat," she whispered, shivering with excitement.

Cain caught her wrist. "Come!" Pulling her along, he hurried toward the low shrub pines at the center of the island. "Trust me, Eliz-a-beth."

Once they reached the first trees, Cain began to run, dragging her after him. Bushes scratched her face and arms and caught in her hair. Finally, when she stumbled on the uneven ground, he slowed his pace. Elizabeth was breathing hard when he finally stopped beside a fallen cedar tree.

Quickly, he tore aside the branches. "In here. Hide," he commanded.

"Why? They may be Englishmen."

"Or Spaniards." He shoved her into the hole and piled the branches on top of her. "Ships come to this place for water. Stay here and make no sound."

"You're leaving me alone?"

"I must move the dugout."

Elizabeth felt something alive walking on the back of her neck. She stifled the urge to scream and swatted at it. She looked back at Cain, but he was gone, as elusive as the pale sliver of moonlight that pierced her hiding place.

She squirmed trying to find a comfortable spot, and the creature resumed its maddening march down her spine. "Ugh," she exclaimed, rubbing her back against the log. The prickly sensation stopped, and she concentrated on the mosquito buzzing dangerously close to her nose.

This is ridiculous, she thought. If that is a ship out there, what makes him think they're Spaniards? Why not Dutch or English? She made a tiny sound of disgust. I'm probably hiding like a rat in a hole from my own rescuers.

A branch snapped to her left, and gooseflesh rose on her arms. The mosquito bit her cheek, but she was afraid to move to brush it away. Something rustled in the underbrush, and without warning a huge flapping shape descended toward the ground. An animal squealed and Elizabeth's teeth clamped shut, catching a bit of flesh on the inside of her lip. She tasted the salty bite of blood as her eyes locked on the thrashing shadows.

Then a man's voice rang out of the darkness. Elizabeth couldn't understand what he was saying, but she recognized the words as Spanish.

Almost at once, a second man answered. She made out the word *agua*—which she knew meant water—and the name Manuel. Their voices rose, and they seemed to be arguing.

Elizabeth gasped as an enormous white bird fluttered up, still clutching its prey. For a few seconds, the creature lit on a branch overhead and was silhouetted against the moon. Then it stretched its wings and glided off as silently as a ghost.

The silence was broken by male laughter and the low murmur of conversation.

Another mosquito drilled into Elizabeth's shoulder, but she was too frightened to move a muscle. Spaniards this far north of the Caribbean could only be pirates or privateers. If they found her hiding place, she'd probably be raped and murdered. Sweat trickled down the back of her neck, and her legs cramped as she strained to hear the men.

To her relief, their voices grew fainter and then faded. The only sounds she could hear were the drone of insects and the low rumble of the surf.

Elizabeth felt brave enough to smack the next mosquito that landed on her arm.

"Eliz-a-beth."

She started, clamping a hand over her mouth to keep from crying out as a man's form dropped from a tree branch a few yards away.

"Shhh." Cain pushed aside the brush and climbed into the hole beside her. "This one believes they are gone," he whispered. "We wait." He put an arm around her and leaned back against the tree trunk, positioning his bow carefully across his lap.

"They were Spaniards. I heard them."

"So."

Elizabeth's heartbeat slowed to normal. "How did you know they weren't English?"

"The English fear the night. Bad men fear day."

"Will they find our dugout?"

"*Mata.*"

She tucked her hand into his. "I was afraid. How long were you hiding in the tree?"

"Shhh. I keep you safe, Eliz-a-beth."

They waited in the darkness. Once the silence was broken by the muffled boom of a cannon and then a single musket shot. Cain's arm tightened around her shoulders when they heard the shooting.

Elizabeth's eyelids grew heavy, and she let her head rest against Cain's shoulder.

Someone was shaking her. Elizabeth groaned and tried to ignore them. She was dreaming of the grand ball at Lady Upton's country house. Two gentlemen of the King's bedchamber were—

"Eliz-a-beth!"

She opened her eyes and stared into Cain's face. It was broad daylight. "Oh. I . . ."

He smiled. "Come. The ship is gone. We go."

Elizabeth stretched and sat up, realizing for the first time that she had been sleeping on a deerskin. A short distance away was the dugout, and beyond that, the water. "How did I get here?" She rubbed her eyes. "I thought—"

"I carried you." Cain pointed west across the water. "We are on the far side of the island." He handed her a waterskin and two corn cakes. "Eat. The tide turns, and we have far to go."

His fingers brushed hers, and she pulled back as though she had been burned. In the night, she had welcomed his touch; now it was disturbing. She knew she must distance herself from Cain emotionally, but it wasn't easy. She concentrated on eating the corn cakes, keeping her eyes lowered and hidden from him. If he looked into them, she was afraid he would read the confusion and longing she felt.

I am a sensible person, she thought. My life is mapped in indelible ink. There is no place for Cain in my future.

He motioned toward the dugout, and she nodded. The sooner they reached Jamestown and her betrothed, the better. Elizabeth swallowed, trying to dispel the thick lump in her throat. I will miss you, she whispered silently. I will do as my position requires, but I will never forget or stop wishing that it could have been.

She took her place in the boat, and he quickly loaded their belongings and pushed off. Within an hour, they had reached the sea again and were moving south with the tide. As Cain had assured her, there was no sign of the Spaniards or their ship.

Elizabeth's attempts at conversation were met with stoic silence, and she soon gave up the attempt. Whatever closeness they had shared during the danger was gone. Lulled by the easy motion of the boat and the rhythmic splash of waves against the hull, she closed her eyes and dozed.

By midafternoon of the third day after they had seen the Spaniards, gray, heavy rain clouds hung low over the sea, and the waves became short and choppy. For the first time, Elizabeth noticed that they were out of sight of land. "Are you certain you know where you're going?" she demanded. He shrugged and continued to paddle without answering.

After a long time, Elizabeth caught sight of a line of trees ahead of them. This time when Cain paddled ashore, he covered the dugout with branches and led her inland. There he built a fire and left her alone while he went to spear fish for their evening meal.

As the fish grilled on green sticks, Cain fashioned a tiny shelter of live pine trees and a bearskin. Elizabeth was barely seated inside when it began to rain. The deluge drowned the fire and chilled the air, making her glad for the wrap Cain dropped about her shoulders.

"Thank you," she said.

"At least you have begun to learn some manners."

She bristled. "The Queen found no fault with my demeanor."

"De-meanor I do not know." He finished the last morsel of his fish and tossed the bones away. "But your tongue is like the blue jay. It is your nature to argue."

Elizabeth's eyes darkened with anger. "My *nature* is none of your concern."

Ignoring her reply, he continued. "I think you

be also slow to learn. Your hair looks like the nest of *honneek* the squirrel.''

She felt her cheeks grow hot with shame. The shelter was so small that if she put out her hand, it would have been drenched by the pouring rain. It was impossible to put any distance between her and Cain, and it took all her self-control to keep from smacking him. ''You're insufferable.''

''You make a good teacher, Eliz-a-beth. There are many new English words to learn from you.'' He took the end of her braid and began to unfasten it. ''Soon you will be with your people. I do not wish them to laugh at you.''

She slapped his hand away. ''I'll comb my own hair, thank you.''

He chuckled and held out a carved ivory comb. It was the one he always used to dress her hair, but she stared at it with sudden comprehension. ''Take it. It is a present.''

''That's ivory,'' she said. ''How could you—''

''My grandmother gave it to me. It was a birth gift to her from her grandfather, Gover Norwhite.''

Elizabeth blinked as her fingers closed around the precious comb. ''Gover Norwhite,'' she repeated, ''Governor White.'' Her mouth felt suddenly dry. ''It's true then—she is Virginia Dare.''

''Why would she lie?'' Cain's gaze locked with hers. ''Tomorrow we reach Jamestown.''

''Tomorrow,'' she echoed. They had traveled for so many days that their destination seemed hazy.

Suddenly, his arms closed around her and he crushed her against him. His mouth covered hers in a brief, passionate caress. Before she could summon her wits to protest, Cain released her and ducked out into the rain.

"Cain! Don't . . ."

But he was gone, and she was alone with only the sound of the rain beating on the hide roof to soothe her shattered emotions.

Sunlight pierced the lush canopy of spring leaves and set the raindrops to sparkling like myriads of diamonds in the small clearing. Elizabeth stretched and rubbed her stiff back. It was early morning—she could tell by the location of the rising sun—but there was no sign of Cain. She wiggled her toes in her damp moccasins and ran a hand through her tangled hair. The comb lay forgotten on the leaves beside her.

"Cain?" she called. Had he stayed out all night in the rain?

There was no answer. As she listened, she realized the clearing was strangely quiet. No squirrel scampered along a limb over her; no bird chirped a merry song. A faint sense of uneasiness washed through her as she crawled out of the shelter and stood up. "Cain?"

Twigs snapped and branches parted at the far end of the clearing. To Elizabeth's surprise, a tall, red-bearded man appeared, followed by three other white men.

The redbeard's eyes widened as he caught sight of Elizabeth, and he lowered his musket. "Halt!" he called.

A shorter man in an old-fashioned round helmet put up his hand and called a greeting in a language Elizabeth assumed to be Indian. She didn't understand a word of what he said.

"Be careful. There may be others," one of the party warned.

The leader took a few steps forward. He was wearing a leather breastplate and a wide-brimmed feathered hat. "She's no Indian. She's got yellow hair. She's a white woman."

Elizabeth's shoulders stiffened and her chin went up. "Are you English?" she demanded. "State your name and rank."

"In God's name," the bearded man cried. "She's an Englishwoman." He ran toward her. "I'm Captain William Trent of the Jamestown Colony."

Elizabeth waited until he was close enough for her to see the blue of his eyes. "I am the Lady Elizabeth Anne Sommersett," she declared. "And it would please me greatly if you would lower those guns and receive me in a manner fitting my station."

The man's sunburned and peeling face turned a freckled puce. "You're Elizabeth Sommersett?"

"Who else would I be? Good Queen Bess?"

Chapter 9

Jamestown, Virginia
June 1664

Elizabeth crossed the bedchamber, pushed open the diamond-panel casement window, and leaned out to catch a breath of fresh air. Ignoring the hungry mosquitoes, she raised the heavy curls at the back of her neck and let the river breeze caress her damp skin.

Pale moonlight illuminated the muddy street and the wooden story-and-a-half houses on the far side. Elizabeth could barely contain a chuckle. Jamestown was the home of the royal governor and capital of the Virginia Colony, but in England, Jamestown would be considered no more than a rustic country village. She hadn't expected the town to be a sophisticated city, but this insect-infested swamp was far worse than she had imagined.

She glanced back at the sparsely furnished bedchamber. She was standing in the best room in one of the finest homes in Jamestown. Her host, Sir Thomas Baldwin, was a member of Governor Berkeley's council. Sir Thomas and his wife were exceedingly proud of their newly completed brick

home and had insisted that she take their own
chamber while she was a guest.

Elizabeth wrinkled her nose. The Baldwins had
been exceedingly kind, and she hated to criticize.
But in truth, the room and furnishings were plain,
the pine floorboards were bare, and the walls
lacked any paintings or wall hangings.

Laughter and the murmur of male voices floated
up from the hall below. Although she had excused herself when the ladies had withdrawn to
the parlor after the evening meal, she knew the
gentlemen were engaged in a lively game of
whist.

A light tap at the door drew Elizabeth's attention. "Yes?"

Lady Baldwin pushed open the door. "Are you
well, child?" Her eyes widened as she caught
sight of the open window. "Let me perish!" The
stout, gray-haired matron hurried to the window
as fast as her too-tight kid slippers would permit,
pulled the casement shut, and locked it securely.
"The night air here is known for carrying all manner of illness. You mustn't put yourself at risk,
Lady Elizabeth, not after all you've been
through."

Elizabeth allowed herself to be led to the imposing poster bed. In the two weeks that she had
been in Lady Baldwin's home, she had learned
that feigned compliance was the easiest course of
action.

The older woman laid her palm on Elizabeth's
forehead. "You're overwarm, child," she fussed.
"I'll send Betty up to help you off with your gown
and tuck you into bed. Cook can mash some onions and make them into a poultice. There's nothing like an onion poultice to ward off the ague."

"I'm fine, really," Elizabeth lied. In truth, her

head had been aching all day, and she'd had no appetite at supper.

"You'd best heed me, my dear. I've raised four children, six if you count the two that lay in the churchyard." Lady Baldwin stepped out into the hall. "Betty! Betty!" she called. "Where is that featherheaded drozel? Betty!"

Hasty footfalls pounded up the stairs. "Yes'm?"

"Mercy me, girl! Why the Lady Elizabeth would want to train you as chambermaid is beyond me. Where were you? No. Never mind. I've no time for your excuses. Her ladyship is not well. Help her make ready for bed."

"Yes'm."

Lady Baldwin popped back into the room. "Would you like me to sit with you awhile, child?" she soothed. "My guests can simply—"

"No," Elizabeth interrupted. "I'll be fine. I'm just tired. I insist you return to your friends."

Betty's thin freckled face was anxious. "I kin build a fire fer ye, yer ladyship. Be ye wantin'—"

"No! No fire." Elizabeth felt like someone was driving a hot needle through her head. She desperately wanted to crawl between the linen sheets and be left alone.

Betty began to undo Elizabeth's borrowed damask silk gown as Lady Baldwin left the room. "Don't hesitate to call if you need me," Lady Baldwin said. "I'll put Cook to work on the onion poultice at once."

Betty was awkward but blessedly silent as she helped Elizabeth out of her petticoats and brushed out her hair. "Ye want I should blow out the candle?" she asked when Elizabeth was undressed and tucked into bed.

"No, leave it, and open that window. It's stifling in here."

"Ye wants the window open, m'lady?"

"I just said so, didn't I?"

Betty's lower lip quivered. "Mistress Baldwin says—"

"I want the window open, if you please. I'll risk the ague rather than suffocate in here."

The girl did as she was told, then bobbed a hasty curtsy. "Be that all, m'lady?"

"Yes. No. When Cook gives you that onion poultice, sneak it outside and throw it on the kitchen midden."

"Ye wants me t' throw out the poultice and not let nobody see me doin' it? M'lady," she added hastily.

"Tell Cook to give you an apple pastie and a mug of goat's milk."

Betty grinned. "Ye wants me t' bring that up t' ye."

Elizabeth forced herself to remain patient with the child. Betty was willing and good-natured, but none too bright. "No, I want you to tell Cook that it's for me and then I want *you* to eat the pastie and drink the milk yourself. You're much too thin, Betty. After that, you're to go directly to bed. You can bring me my coffee in the morning."

"Yes'm. Thank ye, m'lady." She closed the door quietly behind her.

Elizabeth blew out the candle, rolled over onto her back, and rubbed her aching head. For an instant she found herself wishing she was back on the beach with Cain. Nothing about her arrival at Jamestown had gone as she had supposed it would. Nothing.

Her first shock had been when Governor Berkeley had told her that her betrothed was no longer in the Colonies. He explained that Edward Lindsey's father and older brother had been tragically killed in a coach accident on route to a remote Welsh estate. Edward, now earl of Dunmore, had returned to England on the first departing vessel to be with his grieving mother and to assume the duties of his title.

Secondly, the governor explained that her aunt and uncle had not drowned as she had feared. They and all the members of the first lifeboat, including little Betty, had reached the coast of Virginia safely. Believing Elizabeth lost and having no wish to stay on in such a barbarous land, her aunt and uncle had left Jamestown on the same ship as Edward.

Elizabeth had come to the English settlement expecting a joyous welcome and a wedding. Instead, she had found a community of total strangers. Time and time again, she was questioned at length about the Indian she claimed had saved her life. The governor and his councilors wanted to know exactly where she had come ashore, how many Indians she had seen, and whether they had seemed hostile.

Although she was treated with the utmost respect by Sir William Berkeley, Elizabeth was not certain he believed her tale of kind treatment by Cain. When she mentioned meeting Mistress Dare, the governor could not suppress a chuckle.

"You've been through an ordeal," he soothed. "It's only natural that your mind would play tricks on you." The other gentlemen had all smiled condescendingly and nodded.

"Rest is what she needs," a burgess had pronounced solemnly. "Rest and the gentle ministrations of Lady Baldwin."

"As soon as you are strong enough, we'll put

you on the first ship for home," the governor promised. "You're safe now, and that's all that matters."

Elizabeth had been so annoyed by their patronizing behavior that she had pleaded weariness and refused to answer any more questions.

She was so hungry for a familiar face that when she had spied Betty on the street as they returned from Governor Berkeley's mansion, she had asked Lady Baldwin to procure the girl's services for her.

Elizabeth's aunt had been unwilling to pay the maid's passage back to England, and so the child had been bound out to a tanner's family. Lady Baldwin had purchased Betty's indenture in Elizabeth's name and brought the girl into her home as a servant.

Betty, who had wept with joy when she saw Elizabeth alive and well, had been beside herself when she realized her good fortune.

"Be a good girl and learn your duties as chambermaid, and I'll take you back with me to England," Elizabeth had promised her.

"Bless ye, m'lady," Betty had cried dramatically. "I'd rather cross the sea again than rot in this place. If there's another storm and we sinks, fer certain, hell can't be no worse."

Silly little Betty was no substitute for Edward Lindsey or for Elizabeth's aunt and uncle, but she was a link, however tenuous, to Elizabeth's former life, and Elizabeth welcomed the girl's company. Betty was as loyal as a sheep dog, and she did whatever was asked of her with good humor. Having one friend in Jamestown seemed important to Elizabeth.

As she had expected, the town gossips, male and female, had had a fair day with her return and the story of her escapades since the *Speedwell* had gone down. She could not enter a room without hearing the whispers or carry on a conversation about the weather without fending off insinuations about her questionable morality.

Most would not dare to insult her to her face, but she was nevertheless well aware of general opinion. Earlier, after supper, when Elizabeth had excused herself from the ladies' company, she had paused in the hall and listened to the hushed voices.

"She puts on airs, but Dunmore could hardly be expected to marry her now," one goodwife had hissed.

"What if she's carrying a red bastard?" another had chimed in.

"Ladies, please," her hostess had protested. "I won't have you going on so about a guest in my home. The child is blameless. Surely you cannot place guilt on her, regardless of what she may have suffered."

"She wouldn't let the governor send soldiers after that savage, would she? Where there's a stench, there's sour milk, I say."

Elizabeth sighed and tossed off the damp sheet. The heat in Virginia was oppressive, and this was only June. Men and women dressed here in the fashion of home, and England was never so warm. After the freedom of the deerskin dress, she was very aware of the scratchy clinging of wool garments and the odor of silk bodices too infrequently washed.

Odors seemed to trouble her more than they ever had before. Cain had bathed several times a day in the sea, and she had adopted the unnatural habit. In truth, most of these Jamestown matrons could stand a bath. One woman at dinner had reeked of onion. Elizabeth wondered if she was wearing an onion poultice as protection against fever.

Elizabeth's mouth was dry. She got up and poured herself a cup of water from the pitcher on the table. The water tasted muddy, but at least it was wet. She drank the whole cup and then another.

She returned to the window and rubbed her eyes, trying to ease the throbbing behind them. She wondered where Cain was tonight. Had he returned to his home on the beach . . . or was he out there, somewhere, in the all-encompassing forest?

"I miss you," she whispered. "I do."

She felt light-headed and a little scared. Was it possible she was ill? Everyone swore that the night air carried disease. But if that was true, why hadn't she gotten ill on the beach?

Elizabeth took a few wobbly steps toward the bed. The pain in her head made it hard to think. She was thirsty again and . . . Soft blackness enveloped her. She didn't even feel the floor when she fell.

Dr. Rupert Montgomery stepped into the narrow hallway outside Elizabeth's bedchamber and deliberately removed his spectacles to polish the thick lenses with the hem of his velvet doublet. The physician was nearly bald, and he affected the speech and mannerisms of a much older man. "Lady Elizabeth's condition is very grave," he said. "I see no improvement."

Betty sniffed loudly and wiped her nose on her sleeve as the doctor pulled the door shut behind him. Undaunted, the girl pressed her ear against the inside of the door and listened.

"But she has lain like this for two weeks." Lady Baldwin's voice wavered. "Surely there is something you can—"

"Lady Elizabeth has taken an ague," the physician continued. "I explained that when you first called me to her bedside. My potions and repeated bleedings have done nothing to lower her fever or to bind her bowels. She is in God's hands. There is nothing more I can do."

No wonder, Betty thought, scowling. A hound couldn't keep that nasty brown stuff down. As fast as I spoon it in her, it comes back up.

"Poor child," Lady Baldwin murmured. "I warned her about night sickness, but she left her windows open anyway."

"Then 'tis a lack of common sense that has brought her to the brink of an early grave, not your tender care." The physician's words grew fainter as their footsteps moved toward the stairs. "Be certain the girl keeps that fire going in her room. Lady Elizabeth may have a chance if we can sweat out the fever. I'll come again . . ."

The rest of their conversation was lost as Lady Baldwin and the physician descended the stairs. Betty sighed and turned back to her patient.

When she had first found Lady Elizabeth unconscious on the floor, Betty had been terrified, afraid that Elizabeth was dead. When Lady Baldwin assured her that her lady was only ill, Betty had been certain she would die soon.

Betty pushed up her sleeves and wiped the sweat from her forehead. The bedchamber was as hot as an oven. How her lady could have a fever in all this heat was beyond her.

She crossed to the bed and took the rag off Elizabeth's head, replacing the cloth with a wet one. Elizabeth moaned and tossed her head.

"It's jest me, m'lady," Betty said. She slipped a hand under Elizabeth to be certain her bedclothes were still dry. For days, her bowels had run like water, and she had been unable to take food without throwing up.

Betty tucked the blanket under Elizabeth's chin. She didn't mind sick people, as long as they weren't dead. Lord knows she had seen enough of them in her short lifetime. She'd watched both her mam and da die, spitting up their lungs in bloody clots. Then she'd fetched and carried for an ailing grandmother, too feeble to rise from her bed for the last two years of her life. No, the sick didn't bother her. As long as Elizabeth kept breathing, Betty would gladly wash and feed her and try to follow the doctor's orders.

The Lady Elizabeth had been kinder to Betty than anyone she could remember. She had saved her life when the ship went down. No one else would have cared if Betty had gotten in a lifeboat or not. Without her lady, she would have been drowned before her twelfth birthday.

Betty stroked Elizabeth's hair with a thin hand. "Ye got t' get better, m'lady," she whispered. "Ye got t'."

Rain beat against the diamond-paned windows, and the yellow candle flame flickered as gusts of wind tore at the house. An occasional rumble of thunder sounded above the downpour, and lightning bolts streaked across the sky. Betty shivered despite the stifling heat. She didn't like thunderstorms. They made her think of ghosts and other frightening apparitions.

Elizabeth opened her eyes and tried to focus. The flashes of brilliant light made it hard to see. "Betty," she murmured. Her lips felt dry and cracked, and her mouth tasted like ashes. "Betty."

"Yes, m'lady?" The child hovered over her.

"I'm thirsty. Could I have some wine?" Her voice sounded to her like an old woman's.

"They's water here. Would ye like—"

Elizabeth tossed her head petulantly. "No, no water. I want wine. Get me some wine."

"Be ye hungry? I could fetch ye—"

"Just the wine, Betty." Elizabeth pushed back the quilt. "It's so hot in here."

"Ye got t' keep warm. Ye been awful sick, m'lady, wi' the fever."

Elizabeth's head hurt, but her body felt light. She rubbed her eyes. "Is it night? What day is this?"

"It's June, m'lady . . . or maybe July. Ye been sick a fortnight." Betty tucked the covers under Elizabeth's chin again. This wasn't the first time her lady had been awake. Each time, she asked the same questions, as though she couldn't remember anything. It seemed important to Elizabeth to know what day it was.

"Where is the moon?"

"Ain't no moon tonight."

"But is it waning? If you could see it, would it be a crescent?"

"It's been rainin' fierce. Can't see no moon. Couldn't see one last night or the night before."

"Has anyone been here . . . asking for me?"

"Lots o' folks. The governor hisself—"

"No. Not Governor Berkeley. Someone . . ." Elizabeth trailed off. "Fetch me the wine."

"Dr. Montgomery left medicine fer ye t' take. Could ye swallow a little?" Betty went to the hearth and returned with an earthenware cup of brown liquid. "He says it will bind yer—"

The odor made Elizabeth gag. "No." She pushed the medicine away. "It's foul."

" 'Twill make ye better."

Elizabeth grimaced. "It's probably made of rat's droppings and toad skin. Throw it into the chamberpot."

"But, m'lady," Betty protested. "You've got t'—"

"I won't have it." She tried to sit up, then fell back weakly against the pillow. Betty's eyes looked large and frightened in the firelight. "Did the doctor say I was dying, girl?"

"No!" Betty cried. "He din't say that. Grave was what he said. He said ye was grave."

"I'll be in my grave if I swallow any more of that slime." She shook her head. "Take it away."

Tears slipped down Betty's cheeks. "I dasn't throw it in the chamber pot. What if someone sees? They'd blame me if ye did dee, m'lady. Ye know my kind always gets the blame. They'd hang me certain."

"Throw it out the window then. I don't care. Just get it away from me."

Timidly, Betty ventured to the window and unfastened the latch. Opening it only a little way, she poured the physician's potion over the sill and yanked the window shut. "It's no night out fer man nor beast," she said. The wind had extinguished the candle, and she took it to the hearth to relight it.

Gratefully, Elizabeth breathed in the fresh air. "This room stinks," she said. "I'm sorry—"

"No need t' thank me," Betty said. "I'm that glad t' do fer ye. Ye been good t' me, m'lady, better'n anybody ever was. I'll fetch the wine fer ye now, do ye think ye can keep it down."

Elizabeth nodded. "Thank you."

Betty scurried from the room, closing the door behind her. Elizabeth threw off the covers. Her linen shift was damp with perspiration, and the air felt cool against her skin. Once again, she attempted to sit up.

Waves of dizziness assailed her, but she persisted, swinging her feet over the edge of the high bed. The rain beat a steady cadence against the window. If I laid my cheek against the panes, Elizabeth thought, the glass would be cool. If I opened the window, the rain would run down my face.

The room seemed to spin as she slid off the bed onto her bare feet. Elizabeth clung to the bedpost and fought for consciousness. "The window," she murmured, childlike. "If I can just reach the—"

Suddenly, the window swung open and a man's silhouette appeared against a flash of lightning. The candle was blown out by the wind, leaving the room in semidarkness.

Elizabeth blinked, not certain if she had really seen the man or not. "Is someone there?"

"Eliz-a-beth."

A shadow detached itself from the darkness and moved toward her.

Her heartbeat quickened. "Cain?"

"I told you I would come for you, Eliz-a-beth."

She let go of the bedpost and reached out to him.

Chapter 10

"**E**liz-a-beth! What be they do to you?" Cain gathered her in his arms and crushed her against his wet chest. "You have fever," he exclaimed as he laid her back against the pillows.

She opened her eyes and managed a weak smile. "I was sick . . . but . . ." She glanced toward the door. "You shouldn't be here. If they find you in my room . . ." She gripped his hand tightly. "It's dangerous. These Englishmen have no love for your people, Cain."

He shrugged. "You are my wife, Eliz-a-beth. I said I would come for you in the turning of a moon." He took her other hand and leaned over her, his eyes burning into hers like glowing coals. "Have you taken another husband? Do you lie beside your Edward now?"

She closed her eyes and tried to ignore the sweet joy of seeing him again, of touching him. "You don't understand," she murmured. "Everything is changed."

How out of place he looks in this room, she thought. Cain was naked except for a scant vest and loincloth; his hair and clothing dripped water onto the wide board floor. His feet were bare, and his long dark hair was bound with a leather thong. Copper earrings gleamed in the firelight, adding a savage splendor to his proud bearing.

He took her face between his palms. "This one has not changed. Look at me, woman," he ordered.

Trembling, she turned her face away, refusing to meet his gaze. "Go, before they find you and kill you," she whispered. "Please."

"You have taken an Englishman to your bed?"

"No . . . but . . ."

He released her. "Why, Eliz-a-beth?"

"I told you that you wouldn't understand." She slid to the far side of the bed, away from his touch. He wants to kiss me, she thought. He wants to kiss me—and God help me, I want him to. Everything was so confusing. Was it the fever or her own uncertain feelings? "Edward isn't here," she said. "He had to return to England."

"He went without you."

"Yes, but he thought I was dead."

"Good. To him you are dead. Come with me, Eliz-a-beth, and be my wife in truth. The fox cubs are learning to hunt, and the dolphins watch for you." He raised her hand and turned it over to brush the pulse at her wrist with a gentle kiss. "Lie beside me, *dah-quel-e-mah*, and we will make beautiful babies with eyes as black as a crow's wing and hair the color of autumn grass."

For an instant, she let herself believe that it might be so—that she could go with Cain into the storm and forget who she was and what she was meant to do. She could leave Elizabeth Sommersett behind in this room and become a Lenni-Lenape woman, as free as the dolphin to follow her mate. For a heartbeat she let the image of the moonlit beach rise before her. In the recesses of her mind, she heard the sound of the surf and the cry of the osprey.

Go with him, an inner voice urged. *If you don't, you'll never know such happiness again.*

Betty's shrill voice came from the top of the stairs. "Yes, ma'am. I'll tend t' it soon as . . ."

"Someone's coming!" Elizabeth warned Cain. "You've got to go."

"You must choose," he reminded her sternly.

"Yes, ma'am. I put the herbs on . . ."

Elizabeth grabbed his arm. "Cain, please!"

"Come with me. It is not safe for you with these stupid Englishmen who build their houses in a swamp. I know the medicine to make you strong again. I will care for you and let no harm come to you. This I swear."

"I can't. I've got to follow Edward to England." How could she make him understand that she wasn't free to follow her heart? She was an Englishwoman with responsibilities to her family. "It would never work between us," she cried. "I do love you, Cain, but we are of different worlds. Go back to your forest and forget you ever saw me."

He reached the window in three strides. "The fever speaks for you, Eliz-a-beth, not your heart. I cannot take you into the rain when you have fever. But I will come again. In three nights. Meet me by the willow trees behind the house when the moon is high."

"No," she protested. "I can't go with you. Don't ask it of me."

"When the moon is high, Eliz-a-beth, I will wait for you beneath the willows. Come to me, or follow this Edward back across the great salt sea. The choice is yours."

"Go!" she cried in desperation. "In Christ's name go and leave me in peace!"

Without another word, he opened the window and swung out into the pouring rain. The window banged back and forth in the wind, and water soaked the pine floor.

Elizabeth turned on her side and buried her face in the pillow. Her fingers knotted into the linen sheets and she moaned deep in her throat. "Cain," she whispered, "Cain. I'm so sorry."

Outside the bedchamber door, little Betty dropped to her knees, covered her face with her dirty apron, and rocked to and fro in silent misery. She had heard the man's strangely accented voice in her lady's room, threatening her mistress.

The Lady Elizabeth had called the man Cain, and that was the Indian's name. Betty remembered Lady Elizabeth telling Sir Thomas so. Now the same savage had returned to try and take her away again. Betty knew that her lady was afraid of Cain. Hadn't she begged him in Christ's name to leave her in peace?

What am I t' do? Betty agonized. Should I tell Lady Elizabeth what I heard? What if he comes back? I'd be scalped and murdered fer certain.

The pewter goblet Betty had been bringing to her mistress lay unheeded where it had fallen from her numb fingers; the red wine spread across the wide boards like a pool of blood.

Tears streaked the child's face when she gathered her courage enough to stand. She put a trembling hand on Elizabeth's chamber door, then backed away and fled in search of Lady Baldwin.

Elizabeth's fever rose again the following day, and for a time she wasn't certain if Cain had really come to her room or if it had all been a dream. She was so weak that she could hardly raise her head or swallow the egg and wine mixture that Lady Baldwin spooned into her. Then she saw the water stain on the floor before the window, and she knew that Cain had kept his promise.

When Lady Baldwin's servants came to change her linen or to bring her wood for the fire, she asked about Betty and was told that the girl had been sent on an errand to Governor Berkeley's plantation outside of town. The girl didn't come to her chamber all day, and Elizabeth began to believe that they were lying to her.

The second day, Lady Baldwin admitted that Betty had taken ill. "Nothing for you to worry about. The girl just has a cough, but Dr. Montgomery said she is not to come near you until she is over it."

"Are you sure she's all right?" Elizabeth had insisted.

"Right enough to hoe weeds in the kitchen garden."

"But I—"

"Hush now, you need to save your strength. Drink this." Lady Baldwin held a cup of bitter herb tea to Elizabeth's lips. "Drink it all, child. It will help you sleep."

Elizabeth didn't want to sleep. She wanted to think about Cain and to find out what had happened to little Betty. But warm darkness descended over her mind, and she slept to wake fitfully and sleep again.

Lady Baldwin came again with the herb tea, but Elizabeth wasn't sure if it was the same day or another. Her eyelids felt so heavy . . . so very heavy. It was easier not to fight the weariness, easier to drift on a soft cloud of sleep.

* * *

Elizabeth sat bolt upright in bed. It was Sunday. She knew that it was Sunday morning when she heard the church bells ringing. She tried to count the nights since Cain had climbed through her window, since she had last seen Betty, but thinking was like trying to walk in molasses. It's the fever affecting my mind, she thought. But she felt different than she had when she'd been so sick and thought she was going to die. She wasn't soiling her sheets like a babe anymore, and the tea and egg posset stayed in her stomach.

Why do I feel so strange? she wondered. And the thought came to her that Lady Baldwin could be drugging her. "That's absurd," she murmured. Why would she do such a thing? I've lain here so long in this bed that my brain has turned to corn mush.

She forced herself to fight the torpor. The fire had gone out in the fireplace, and the room was blessedly cooler. Outside the window, she heard the trill of a mockingbird. Below, the house was quiet.

"It is Sunday," she said. "Sunday, and they've all gone to church."

She slid from the bed and made her way unsteadily toward the door. Once she swayed and would have fallen, but she caught herself on the candle stand. Clinging to the door jamb, she pushed open the door and listened. Still nothing.

The stairs were more difficult to navigate than she believed possible, but just being out of the sickroom gave her strength. Downstairs, she inched her way along the hall and into the winter kitchen.

The family had taken their morning meal in one of the formal rooms, but the remains of breakfast

sat on a tray waiting to be carried back to the
summer kitchen a short distance behind the
house. The back door stood open, and Elizabeth
heard a woman singing. The cook, she knew, was
a slave woman, and she often sang as she went
about her duties.

Satisfied that no one was around to stop her,
Elizabeth scooped up several scones and a dish of
preserves. A mug of ale stood beside the pewter
plate of fried fish. She picked up the ale and drank
deeply, trying not to think who might have already sipped from the cup that morning.

"Here's the scallions ye asked fer." It was Betty's voice.

Elizabeth wiped the foam off her mouth and
licked her lips. Betty's all right, she thought, just
as Lady Baldwin said. Surely it's the fever that
makes me think she might try to drug me. She
finished the rest of the ale and started back toward the stairs carrying the scones. Still, it might
be better if no one knows I'm on my feet . . . not
even Betty.

When she got back to her room, she nibbled
one of the scones, then hid the rest under the
bed. She was as tired as though she had walked
all day, and she curled up on the feather mattress
and slept.

After church services, Lady Baldwin came up
to visit, bringing another cup of herb tea. When
she reached out to take the tea, Elizabeth deliberately spilled it.

"I'm sorry," she said. "I thought I . . ."

"Not to worry, child. I'll bring you more,"
Lady Baldwin assured her. "You look so much
better today. We'll have you on your feet in no
time."

"Please," Elizabeth asked sleepily. "Could I have a little milk?"

"If you wish, but the tea is better for you."

"The milk first, and then I'll drink every drop of your brew." She offered a faint smile. "I promise." They can't drug my milk; I'd be able to taste anything added to it. "I am feeling stronger. Please, could you open the window? It's so stuffy in here."

"We can't have you taking a chill, can we? You just lie back and rest. I'll be back in a few moments, my dear."

When Lady Baldwin returned, Elizabeth pretended she was asleep. Lady Baldwin called Elizabeth's name several times, then put the cup of tea and a small pitcher of milk on the butterfly table beside the bed and went away.

Elizabeth waited until she was certain her hostess was gone, then got out of bed and dumped the tea in the chamber pot. Retrieving the scones from her hiding place, she dipped them in the jam and ate two, then quenched her thirst with the cool milk.

As she licked the crumbs off her fingers, she tried to decide what to do about Cain. If she did nothing, if she remained here in her bed when the moon rose, he would know that she had chosen a life with her own people. Surely, that would be best.

There was nothing to be gained by meeting him tonight by the willows. Doing as he asked was out of the question.

If she had been a kitchen wench or a miller's daughter, then perhaps . . . Elizabeth sighed and shook her head. If she were a miller's daughter, she would still be a Christian. Not even an Englishwoman of common birth could forsake her heritage and her faith to run off and live in the wilderness with a red savage.

How could she explain to him that marriage had nothing to do with love? Marriage was an agreement between families. A woman of gentle blood married the man her father or guardian chose for her. Land and property rights were the first consideration; security for a woman and her children were the second.

Elizabeth ran her fingers through her hair. There was no way to make a man like Cain understand hundreds of years of tradition. It was her duty to marry Edward Lindsey and to bear his children. As a Sommersett, she could do nothing less.

She did not deceive herself. If she were fortunate, she and Edward would live amiably together. They might even develop a fondness for each other over the years. He would protect her and provide for her the standard of living she was accustomed to; she would give him nominal obedience, respect, and the use of her body when he demanded it.

"Don't you see, Cain?" she whispered into the still summer afternoon. "I can't go with you." It was madness to consider such a thing . . . utter madness.

At twilight, Betty came to Elizabeth's room with soup and a mug of apple cider. "I'm that glad t' see ye, m'lady. I was so afeared thet ye might . . . might dee." She stumbled as she made a clumsy curtsy. "Cook killed a rooster special fer the broth and let me help make it." She put the tray on the bedside table and popped her thumb in her mouth to suck off the spilled soup.

"Thank you," Elizabeth replied. "I'm glad to

see you too. Lady Baldwin said that you were sick.''

Betty cleared her throat loudly and stared at the floor. "It's nothin'." She rubbed her hands on her apron. "Be ye be wantin' anythin' else, m'lady?" Spots of bright color rose on her cheeks as she backed toward the door. "Cook said I was t' come right back. She said she'd save some soup fer me, do I help her wi' the evenin' chores.''

"Do they treat you well here, girl?"

"Here?" Betty chewed at her lower lip and stared with calf eyes.

"Is Cook kind to you? Do they give you enough to eat and a safe place to sleep?"

The child nodded. "Oh, yes, m'lady. This is a fine house. I even gets meat on the Sabbath. Cook says I ain't stupid. She's teachin' me how t' make bread." She glanced toward the door. "Kin I go?"

Elizabeth nodded, and Betty scurried from the room. Feeling foolish because of her earlier suspicions, Elizabeth turned to her supper and cautiously tasted the chicken soup. To her surprise, it was delicious, and she soon finished every drop. The cider was cool and refreshing.

Gradually, the evening shadows lengthened and gave way to night. Several hours passed, and then Betty appeared with a candle in one hand and a pewter goblet in the other. "Be ye be wantin' anythin' else before I go t' bed, m'lady?" she asked. "Cook said t' bring ye some herb tea, but I know ye favor the wine, so I brung it instead.''

"Good girl." Elizabeth smiled her approval as she took the wine. "You were right. I'd much rather have this.''

Betty beamed. "Yes, m'lady. Have a good night's sleep.''

"The same to you.''

Betty bobbed a quick curtsy and was gone.

Elizabeth chuckled. If Lady Baldwin had planned to drug her, the child had outwitted her. She put the goblet on the table and went to the foot of her bed. With trembling hands, she opened a large chest and removed a pair of stockings, a linen shift, petticoats, and a blue camlet gown. Dressing as quickly as she could without a maid to help her, she brushed her hair and tied it back with a silk ribbon, then thrust her feet into sturdy leather shoes.

When she was ready, Elizabeth sat on the bed and waited until the normal household sounds below had ceased. The candle burned lower and lower, and as the pale lemon flame began to flicker before it went out, she noticed the forgotten wine goblet. She reached for the glass just as the room was swallowed in darkness.

Elizabeth sipped the last of the wine as moonlight spilled across the pine floor. She had been too frightened to think about what she was doing; she had deliberately taken one step at a time. Now there could be no more denial.

Her mouth was dry and her heart pounded as she tiptoed toward the bedroom door with her shoes in her hand. She was glad that the room was in shadow; it made it easier to walk away, to leave everything behind.

The hallway was quiet; the only sound was the purring of a cat sleeping on the top step. At the bottom of the stairs, two candles burned in a wrought-iron stand. Elizabeth took a tight grip on the walnut balustrade. She was so scared that her knees felt weak, and she paused to take a deep breath.

"Lady Elizabeth."

She gasped in alarm as she saw Sir Thomas standing at the bottom of the steep stairs.

"You shouldn't be out of bed. You're much too ill," he said, coming up the steps toward her.

Elizabeth shook her head. "No." Suddenly, her legs went limp and she sank to a sitting position beside the cat. "I have to . . ." she began. Was she dreaming? "Cain," she whispered thickly. "I have to meet—"

Sir Thomas caught her around the waist and lifted her up. "You're ill. You mustn't be out here."

She struggled weakly. "No . . . no," she protested. "I . . ."

Lady Baldwin appeared and took her by the arm. Together they half carried, half dragged her back into the room. "Poor child," the older woman murmured. "The fever's come back."

Elizabeth tried to explain, tried to tell them that she couldn't stay, that she had to go outside. Then the dream dissolved and sleep claimed her. It was a sleep so deep that she merely flinched when the muffled report of a musket shot echoed through the open window.

Chapter 11

The musket ball missed Cain's head by the width of a spear blade and smashed into the trunk of the willow tree behind the Baldwin house. He whirled to face the half dozen Englishmen who ran across the grassy yard from the stable. Another musket roared from the left, and two more figures appeared beside the grapevine, moonlight gleaming off their round steel helmets.

Raising his bow, Cain plucked three bone-tipped arrows from his quiver. He dropped to one knee, pulled the bowstring to his ear, and let the first arrow fly. With an agonized cry, the closest soldier crumpled to his knees. The man behind him raised his musket, but the second arrow found his throat before he could fire.

Cain spun left and sent the third arrow into the exposed leg of a cuirass-clad Englishman. The man dropped his musket and fell to the grass, clutching the protruding feathered shaft. Another musket roared, but a shriek from one of the Englishmen in the first group gave evidence that his aim was poor.

"Swords, you fools! Surround him!" a gruff voice shouted. "James! Your pike!"

From the corner of his eye, Cain caught sight

of more men coming from the road. He shot off two more arrows before the first man reached him. One bolt went wild in the darkness, but the other produced a satisfying groan.

Cursing, a burly Englishman slashed at Cain with his sword. Cain threw up the bow to protect himself, and the steel cut through the seasoned hickory like kindling. Another soldier hacked at Cain's thigh, but Cain twisted aside and wrenched the weapon from his hands and jabbed it into the burly man's knee.

"Aiiee!" Cain backed against the tree and cut a swath of steel around him as the Englishmen closed in. Sweat ran down his back, and his breath came in ragged gulps. "Is it a good night to die?" he taunted in English.

"Roy!" Two helmeted soldiers broke from the pack and advanced with drawn swords. The others drew back to safety beyond the reach of Cain's twisting blade.

Cain fixed his gaze on the tall bearded man shouting orders. That one, he reasoned, must be the leader.

"Lay down your weapon and surrender in the name of the King!" the tall man shouted.

Cain smiled. "Come and get it."

"You speak English? Good. I'm Captain William Trent. Surrender, and we'll spare your life." He drew closer, keeping his sword poised to strike. "Do you understand?"

"Ah," Cain said softly. "You let me go free."

"Yes."

Cain chuckled. They did take him for a fool. "And tomorrow you make me king of the English."

The captain frowned. "Who are you? What do you want here?"

"I am Shaakhan Kihittuun."

"Are you a Rappahannock?"

"Enough talk," Cain replied. "You have come to kill me without knowing my name. You do not need to know my tribe."

"You are here for Lady Elizabeth Sommersett, aren't you? You may as well admit it. The girl told us you threatened to come here and carry her away." The redbearded captain hawked and spat on the ground near Cain's feet. "You should have known we'd not allow that to happen. You'll not get your filthy hands on an Englishwoman again."

Pain as sharp as a shark's tooth knifed through Cain, and he fought to keep his features expressionless. If Elizabeth had betrayed him to the soldiers, then she truly had no love for him. If she had not come to meet him, he would have understood, but this treachery was bitter. These English warriors sought his life. They had forced him to shed their blood, and they would show him no mercy. "I be not your enemy," Cain answered, "but I give you warning. If this one dies, he does not die alone."

"Drop the sword, or I'll order my men to shoot," Trent said.

Cain stared at the captain's face for the space of a dozen heartbeats, then with a shrug, he cast aside the English sword. Before the bearded soldier could react, Cain feinted left, pulled a knife from the sheath at his waist, and lunged to the right.

Trent gasped as Cain dodged beneath his sword, grabbed his head, and yanked it backward. The Englishman froze as he felt the Indian's steel blade pressed against his throat.

"Move," Cain threatened, "and your women

will weep." He glared at the surrounding men.
"Back!" Knocking aside Trent's conical helmet,
Cain wound his fingers in the man's curly hair.
"We go," he said to the captain. "That way, to-
ward the forest."

"Hold your fire," Trent called. "Stand away."

Step by step, Cain moved across the lawn,
holding the captain as a shield. They were no
more than a hundred yards from the edge of the
forest when a soldier cursed and lunged at Cain
with an iron-tipped pike.

For an instant, regret flashed across Cain's
mind. As he stared into the hooded face of death,
his first instinct was to fulfill his promise and cut
the English leader's throat. Instead, he shoved the
man away and hurled his knife at the charging
pikeman.

The blade plowed a bloody furrow across his
assailant's cheek and spoiled his aim. It did not
slow the others. Yelling triumphantly, the English
soldiers came at him from all sides, and he went
down under their numbers, battered and slashed
into insensibility.

Sometime later—how much time had passed he
had no way of knowing—he became aware of intense pain. The throbbing which seemed to con-
sume every inch of his body drove him from the
twilight of semiconsciousness into total comprehension.

He tried to open his eyes, but they were swollen shut. From the coolness of the air on his bare
skin, he perceived that it was still night, and by
the rhythmic sway of his body, he decided he was
being carried over rough ground. Attempts to
move his hands and feet were futile; they were
too numb for him to know if they worked or not.

I'm trussed like a slaughtered doe, he thought.

And the feast I'm being delivered to is not one I'd willingly attend. The next image that rose in his muddled brain was Elizabeth's face. Had she betrayed him to these men? The aching of his flesh was agony, but the idea that the woman he loved beyond all else desired his death was worse. He shut his mind against the English captain's words, but they returned again and again to haunt him. *The girl told us . . . The girl told us . . .*

Cain tried to shake away the memory, and the Englishman's voice sounded harsh in his ears.

"Take him to the river's edge and kill him."

"Ye want us to shoot him?"

"No. No shots. Hang him."

Cain ground his teeth together as waves of fury assailed him. A man should not die like a snared rabbit in a trap.

Another spoke. The words were strangely accented and hard for Cain to understand. "I dinna ken your reasonin', captain. The council will nay be pleased. We should be tryin' the savage in full view o' the town, not sneakin' him off in the night. 'Tis nay like that skirmish can be kept secret—nay wi' Tom Potter and Robert Allen layin' dead from his heathen arrows."

"I don't make orders, Angus; I only carry them out. See him hanged and buried before the sun comes up over the river."

"Ay, sir, but the trouble be on your own head, nay mine, nor James's, nor Roy's."

Cain heard one man's footsteps fade away. The others continued on, still carrying him. He surmised that his wrists and ankles were fastened to a pole, but he couldn't get his eyelids apart far enough to see.

After traveling for some time through the forest, his captors came to a halt, and Cain was dropped roughly onto the ground. The shock stunned him momentarily, and he gasped for breath.

"He ain't dead yet, Angus. I tole you that."

"I never thought the mon was. Savage he may be, but that one's a bonnie fighter. 'Twill take more than that to send him to hell."

A third man spoke up. "Seems a waste t' me, killin' him."

"Ye heard the captain."

"Aye. Orders are orders, Roy."

"But a waste jest the same. Word is that the captain of the *Lady Jane* was hunting fer a savage t' take back wi' him. He set a bag o' silver on the table at Jenkins's ordinary. A bounty, he called it, on a red skin. Thing was, he wanted the animal t' be alive."

"Nay, Roy, ye'll see the lot o' us in stocks or worse. The captain bid us put him in the ground, and I fer one intend t' do as I was told."

"Silver, man. Is yer Scottish pate so thick ye cannot think what we could do wi' that much money? Even split three ways 'tis more than I'd see in two years of carryin' a pike. We've got to look out fer ourselves, Angus. Ye think them high-nosed burgesses care a ha'penny fer us?"

"He's tied tighter 'n a Christmas puddin'. All we got to do is carry him t' the *Lady Jane*."

"And if we're caught?"

"We won't get caught. The ship sails in a week."

Angus cleared his throat. "James?"

"I'm wi' Roy. Alice's father has forbid me t' set foot in his house. If I'm t' wed her before he signs a marriage contract wi' another, I have t' come up wi' hard coin."

A heavy foot drove into Cain's side, and he groaned.

"He cut my face, he did," James continued. "I'd rather see him hang than any o' ye, but if his hide will get me Alice Tucker as a wife, I'm game."

"Agreed then," Roy said. "We take him t' the captain."

"Aye," Angus said reluctantly. "And I hope we dinna all live t' regret it."

The Virginia Coast
July 17, 1664

Lady Elizabeth Sommersett stood at the rail of the ship and stared at the tree-lined shore of Virginia until it vanished on the horizon. The late morning sun was hot on her face, but the air was cooler on the water than it had been in Jamestown. The stiff breeze that filled the sails and sent the merchant vessel skimming along the surface of the sea smelled strongly of pine trees. Elizabeth wondered how long it would be before the scent of pine ceased to remind her of Cain.

The sickness that had gripped her for so many days and nights had passed, leaving her weary but clear of mind. Her appetite was returning little by little, and she felt almost as strong as she had when Cain had escorted her to Jamestown.

Lady Baldwin had been concerned that Elizabeth might not be ready to endure the hardships of an ocean voyage, but Elizabeth had insisted that she was fit.

"If I don't sail with Captain Douglas, it may be months before I can find another passage. I must return home to England as soon as possible."

Traveling with Elizabeth and Betty was a recent widow, Mildred Wright, and her four-year-old son Robin. The prospect of sharing a cramped cabin with Mistress Wright and her whining child for six weeks or more was not a pleasant one, but Elizabeth knew all too well the discomforts of crossing the Atlantic. Already, Mistress Wright was complaining of seasickness, and Betty was below scrubbing the cabin floor with vinegar to kill the stench of former passengers.

If I had my way, she thought, I'd spend the entire trip on deck. Coming from England, the *Speedwell* had carried horses, cows, and an assortment of other livestock. The cargo this time was tobacco, lumber, and animal skins. She hoped that the hold would be neither as noisy nor as smelly as it had been on the *Speedwell*.

She shaded her eyes with her hand and gazed out over the blue-green water. She would not admit, even to herself, that she was looking for dolphins or for some dot on the waves that might be a dugout.

Her memories of Jamestown were confused, as intangible as morning fog. Against her better reason, she clung to the notion that Cain had come to her bedchamber one night and that it had been raining. She distinctly remembered the rolling crash of thunder and a puddle of rainwater on the wide plank floor.

"He did come, and he begged me to go away with him," she murmured.

Just beyond the wake of the ship, seagulls wheeled and screeched, diving into the foam for tiny fish. Their raucous cries filled Elizabeth's ears and drowned out her whisper. Above her, sails snapped in the wind; the deck beneath her feet sighed and moaned like a living creature. The acrid scent of tar-soaked lines and spars mingled with the sharp bite of gunpowder and salt water.

Elizabeth broke a biscuit into pieces and tossed it to the seagulls. *Was I truly so far gone with fever that I thought to go with him?* She sighed and blinked back the moisture that clouded her eyes. For three nights she had gone to the willow behind the house and waited until the first coral shades of dawn had tinted the eastern sky.

I waited for you, Cain, but you didn't come.

One gull seized a bit of the bread, but the rest was lost in the tumbling waves. Elizabeth rubbed her hands together to rid them of the crumbs.

Dreams had plagued her illness, some so vivid that she ceased to differentiate between what was real and what was imagined. At one time, she had conceived the idea that someone was trying to poison her. Lady Baldwin told her that they had summoned the physician in the middle of the night to calm her hysterical outburst.

"Fever heats the brain, child," the older woman had said. "You were near death. We cannot blame you for the madness of fever."

Returning to England and to her betrothed was the only sensible thing to do. Elizabeth knew it, and she knew that if Cain had come for her and they had run off into the wilderness together, she would have regretted it for the rest of her life.

"But I waited for you anyway," she said softly. "I wanted—"

"M'lady," Betty interrupted. "I did as ye bid me. I scrubbed ever' inch o' that nasty little cabin wi' vinegar, but Mistress Wright is upchuckin' all over the floor again." The girl grimaced. "Her youngun is howlin' his head off, and she says she's gonna dee."

Elizabeth stared back at the calm water and

shuddered. If Mistress Wright was seasick barely out of sight of land, on water as flat as a bathtub, what would she be like when they hit rough weather?

"Ask her if you can bring the child up on deck. She's probably scaring him into a tantrum."

Betty shook her head. "I asked her could I bring him up, m'lady. He ain't a biddable lad, but he ain't no bigger 'an a duck. I'm stronger 'an him. I'll take Master Robin fer ye, I says. But she says I'll lose him over the side, and she's a poor widder wi'out nothin' but one chile, an' they both started in again."

Betty shrugged one shoulder and waited, her face as bland as corn pudding.

Elizabeth smiled at her, glad she had brought the wench along. Skinny and slow of wit, Betty was a good-hearted soul with no sign of seasickness. As far as Elizabeth knew, the girl had never been ill or complained once on the voyage from England to Virginia.

Betty's too-large cap was pulled down over her ears and tied tightly beneath her chin. Her stained and patched apron enveloped the once-blue bodice and tattered homespun skirt, drooping to cover the toes of sturdy, leather boy's shoes. A pointed chin and upturned nose gave Betty the look of a starving fox, but there was no mistaking the contentment in her eyes. She was as happy to be going home to London as if she had had good sense, and no one, not even Mistress Wright, would diminish Betty's excitement one bit.

"There's no need for you to trouble yourself with Mistress Wright anymore," Elizabeth said. "Let her servant Walter come up from the men's quarters and scrub her vomit. You may stay here with me if you can remain quiet."

"Yes, m'lady." Betty nodded vigorously. "I kin. I kin be quiet as a mouse." She plopped down on a coil of rope. "Ye won't know I'm here, I promise."

Elizabeth gazed back at the spot where she had last glimpsed land. Goodbye, Cain, she cried silently. I'm glad I knew you.

In the bowels of the ship a man lay, wrist and ankle chained to damp timbers in the malodorous darkness. The heavy irons cut cruelly into his raw flesh and prevented him from changing position. Cramps wracked his legs and arms and made it hard for him to sleep.

There was little to do but sleep in this foul pit. He hadn't been given drinking water in days, and the water that sloshed around over his back and lower body was little more than green slime. He would have to suffer far more thirst before he would consider drinking that.

When Cain had realized that his captors meant to sell him to another Englishman, rather than murder him as their captain had ordered, he had been relieved. Now he wondered if a quick death might not have been easier to bear.

No one had explained why the man Douglas wanted a prisoner or what he meant to do with him. The Englishmen had treated Cain with no more respect than they would a horse. They had forced him to his knees in a room full of men and laid hands upon his person. He had not been able to see, but his ears were open, and his heart felt shame.

"He's no good to me," Captain Douglas had

proclaimed. "Look at him. You've beat him to death."

"Nay," Angus had replied. "Hard as oak, this one. All the blood deceives ye, but some is English. He's in his prime and strong enough t' lift an ox."

"He's quiet enough now. Are ye certain he's not dim-witted?"

"Ask about, sir. Any what was there will tell ye this is one fightin' son-of-a-bitch. He's dangerous, I'll gie ye that, but there's nothin' wrong wi' his brain."

"Unless you've stove it in. I make no profit on ruined goods."

"No disrespect meant, captain, but did ye expect to buy a full-grown redman wi'out a mark on him? They's savages, sir, wild as any woods' boar."

Cain had knelt where they'd shoved him and pretended he was as empty as a conch shell. When the transaction was completed, other hands had dragged him out of the building and onto what he supposed was an English ship.

Here he had been chained, and for all he knew, forgotten.

In the hours and days that had passed since the battle beneath the willow, Cain had withdrawn deep within his inner self. There he did not hear the white men's scorn or feel the pain of his untended lacerations. There he waited and cradled the spark of his wounded spirit.

When the ship moved away from the shore and Cain heard the waves slapping against the hull, he came close to letting go of the thin thread that held him to sanity. They are taking me away, he thought. They are taking me across the ocean, away from my homeland.

It came to him that he could follow the example of injured animals and escape this horror in the easiest way—he would simply stop breathing. To die would be to get the best of this English captain who had paid silver for his living body. Death would be a welcome comrade. Cain knew he had only to beckon and the dark warrior would claim him.

But he did not give the signal. Instead, he let the pain and terror cleanse his blood as a hot flame burns the evil from a festering wound. *"N'dellennowi*, I am a man," he said in the tongue of his father's people.

"Lehelechejane, n'matschi. I draw breath, and I will come home again." He swallowed, trying to draw moisture from his parched mouth, and kicked futilely at a rat that scurried across his bare legs. "On the love I once bore for Eliz-a-beth, I swear it."

Chapter 12

Because of dependable winds, the eastward crossing from Virginia to England was much shorter and safer than the route to the American Colonies. The *Lady Jane* was a stout ship with an experienced captain and crew, and the voyage was blessed with fair weather. Elizabeth was well aware of her good fortune on all these counts, but it did little to lighten her mood.

Her cabin mate, Mistress Wright, continued to be seasick, so that she was rarely a guest at the captain's table during the first two weeks of the trip. She, Elizabeth, and Betty were the only females on the ship except for Mistress Maude Pierce, the wife of an official returning to England after a two-year stay in Jamestown.

Elizabeth and Mistress Pierce customarily took meals with Captain Douglas and four gentlemen passengers in the captain's cabin. Since Maude Pierce was sixty-two years of age and hard of hearing, Elizabeth found little enjoyment in her company. Samuel Pierce, Maude's husband, was somewhat younger but equally boring.

Captain Douglas was a man of indeterminate years with the speech and manners of a gentleman. A proclaimed bachelor, the captain made no secret of his admiration for Elizabeth.

"You have made this voyage a delight, if I may say so, Lady Elizabeth," he said as they sat down to a late-evening supper of roast duck and pickled tongue. The cabin boy poured the captain a goblet of wine, and Captain Douglas raised it gallantly. "To the loveliest and most gracious lady it has ever been my fortune to convey."

Elizabeth smiled at him. "Thank you, sir. You are too kind."

"Not at all," Samuel Pierce chimed in, helping himself to a generous portion of eel pie. " 'Tis but the truth, Lady Elizabeth."

Mistress Pierce glanced up from her plate. "Eh? What did he say, Samuel?"

"Yes, yes, indeed." Samuel patted his wife's hand. She looked around absently, then began anew to chew her food.

Elizabeth wondered for the hundredth time how she would survive the voyage with such company. Bored, she let her gaze wander around the cabin.

Despite the rich paneling and the stained-glass window, the captain's quarters were cramped. A built-in bunk and an inlaid walnut writing cabinet were the only furniture, save for the table and chairs. The master's elaborate oak armchair was bolted to the floor at the head of the table in the same manner as the writing cabinet. One whale-oil lamp hung over the table, and its twin gave light to the desk. The floors were bare, and the bed linens worn thin. The cabin smelled of rum, tobacco, and musty wool.

"Doubtless Lady Elizabeth will be a welcome visitor at court," Robert Hammond said. Hammond was the eldest son of a wealthy London merchant, traveling on business for his father. Although he wore a long, curled, black horsehair wig and affected the latest fashions in dress, Hammond was obviously a raw boy overcome by the opportunity to sit at the same table with an earl's daughter.

The captain passed a dish of dried peas to Elizabeth and let his glance linger on her bosom. "Have you been a guest at Whitehall already, m'lady?"

"Yes, I have," she replied, ignoring his lecherous appraisal.

She was accustomed to such behavior from men. As long as he did nothing but look, and offered no disrespect by word or action, she would not take offense. It was common knowledge that all mariners had a reputation for being rakehells among the ladies—except for those who favored their own kind. Since the *Lady Jane*'s cabin boy was buck-toothed and popeyed, Elizabeth felt certain Captain Douglas was free from that proclivity.

The boy shoved the plate of roast duck under her nose. She accepted several small slices and a wedge of cheese. Shipboard food was not to her liking.

"You've been presented to King Charles?" Robert Hammond asked.

"I've had the pleasure of meeting their highnesses several times," Elizabeth replied.

"Have you seen the South Sea Islanders?" Hammond's pale eyes widened with excitement and he leaned forward over his plate. "I've heard that Lord Walston has a splendid matched pair of natives and brings them to suppers at Whitehall."

"I've heard that too," Elizabeth said, "but I've not seen them."

"Their skins are lighter in color than a blackamoor's," Captain Douglas explained.

Samuel wiped his mouth with a napkin. "You sailed the Pacific, captain?"

"What?" Mistress Pierce inquired loudly. "A blackamoor, did he say? Plenty of them in the Colonies."

The captain shook his head. "My experience has been on the Atlantic and the Mediterranean, but I saw several South Sea Islanders two years ago in Venice. They were huge men, over six feet tall."

The ship rocked and Elizabeth captured her goblet before more than a few drops of wine escaped. She was well aware that King Charles's court considered the natives to be a rare oddity, but the idea that men could be owned and exhibited as animals had always been repugnant to her. She always felt uneasy around slaves. She had never believed herself particularly devout in religious matters, but surely even the least of humans had souls. And if they had souls, it must be a sin to treat them as beasts.

"Lady Elizabeth." The captain turned toward her. "In your stay in Jamestown, did you see any savages?"

She stiffened. Hadn't Captain Douglas heard of her shipwreck?

"Why, the Lady Elizabeth—" Samuel halted in midsentence as Elizabeth shot him a withering glance.

"I was a guest of a councilman, sir," Elizabeth replied lightly. "One does not meet too many redmen in the governor's circle of acquaintances."

"Then perhaps you would enjoy seeing one close up." The captain smiled triumphantly and rose to his feet. "It happens that I am transporting a redman on this ship."

"Upon my word!" Samuel said. "Are you serious?"

"God's wounds!" Hammond cried. "I never thought to lay eyes on one. Is he alive?"

Captain Douglas beamed. "I should hope so, as much as I paid for him. I'm transporting the creature for a gentleman, and likely he intends to exhibit him at Whitehall. I see no reason why you may not all take a look beforehand." He looked down his long nose at Robert Hammond and cleared his throat. "In case you should be forced to miss the court appearance."

Elizabeth shook her head. "I don't believe I—"

"Nonsense, there's no danger. You'll all be perfectly safe, I assure you." The captain waved to the cabin boy. "Tell Mr. Quinn I wish to see him at once."

"What's amiss?" Samuel's wife demanded.

"Nothing wrong, dear," her husband assured her. "The captain has an Indian on board."

"Bored? Utter nonsense." Mistress Pierce smiled, revealing broken, discolored teeth, and tapped the captain's wrist with her fan. "The duck was excellent. I'd like to have the receipt for our cook."

Samuel rolled his eyes in exasperation. "You'll have to forgive my wife. She has a slight problem with her hearing."

"No need to apologize, sir," Captain Douglas said, rising. "My own mother suffered from the same affliction. Deaf as a post, she was, from childhood on."

Excusing himself, he stepped out of the cabin

for a minute, then returned to his seat. "Jack has an excellent plum flummery for us. Then after supper, we'll all go out on deck and take a look at the savage. Mr. Quinn is going to wash him down, out of consideration to the ladies." He chucked. "Mr. Quinn tells me that the hold stinks like a pig sty."

Elizabeth tried to suppress a shudder. Whoever the prisoner was, he would be better off throwing himself over the side of the ship into the sea. Indians carried to England almost invariably died of disease within months. They seemed to have no resistance to measles, smallpox, or cholera. A quick death by drowning would be kinder than a slow, agonizing one from illness.

"I believe I will go and see how Mistress Wright fares," Elizabeth said. "I really don't want to see—"

"I insist," Captain Douglas said. "To view a creature such as this one at close distance is an experience of a lifetime. I won't let you miss it."

Samuel Pierce offered Elizabeth his arm as she stepped from the hatchway onto the moonlit deck. Just ahead of them Hammond carried a lantern and the captain guided Mistress Pierce. Captain Douglas was shouting something into her ear.

Elizabeth paused and tightened her grip on Samuel's sleeve. "Sir," she said softly. "I know that you are aware of the tragedy that befell me in the Colonies."

"Of course, but—"

She raised her finger to her lips for silence. "The Sommersett family and my betrothed, Lord Dunmore, would consider it a great personal favor if the unfortunate tale remained in Virginia."

"Certainly, m'lady," Samuel replied. "I had no idea—"

"I knew you would understand," Elizabeth continued with gentle relentlessness. "You are too wise a man to make powerful enemies for the sake of common gossip."

"I'fecks! I should think not." He glanced after the others. "You need have no worry on Maude's account," Samuel assured her. "She hears little of goss—" He broke off sharply and cleared his throat. "Er, what I meant was that Maude keeps to her own house and never converses idly with the servants."

"You are most kind, Master Pierce," she murmured. "A gentleman in the true sense."

"Pierce! Lady Elizabeth!" Hammond called. "You must see this. He's magnificent."

Elizabeth took a deep breath of the salt air and started toward the swaying lantern. The seas were calm tonight, and the swish of water against the hull was pleasant. I will take a quick look at Douglas's unfortunate prisoner and return to my cabin, she thought. I've no wish to be party to a spectacle.

As she and Pierce neared the others, the captain stepped aside to allow them a clear view of the captive. The man was bound upright to a mast, his arms tied behind him. On either side of the savage stood a hard-faced seamen. Ahead and to the left was the second officer, Mr. Quinn, a worn cat-o'-nine-tails coiled in his hand.

"He gave us trouble, sir," Quinn explained to the captain. "When he was loosed from the timber, the Indian attacked Gibbons with his manacles and broke his arm. Then he grabbed Witt and threw him halfway across the hold. He's dangerous, cap'n."

"Is he securely tied?" Captain Douglas asked.

"Yes, sir."

"Then I hardly believe he's a danger now." The captain motioned to Hammond. "Bring that lantern closer."

Elizabeth stared at the nearly naked prisoner, and her breath caught in her throat. His flesh was bruised and broken; fresh whip marks scored his arms and chest. But there was something familiar about that proud stance, those rippling muscles beneath a honey-hued skin, that sleek sable-brown hair. A sick feeling began in the pit of Elizabeth's stomach and flooded upward. *It can't be you,* she cried silently. *It can't!*

The officer stepped back and grabbed the Indian's hair and pulled his face up so that the light shone directly into it. Almond-shaped eyes, as black as jet, glared at them so fiercely that even the captain took an involuntary step backward.

Hammond gasped as the lantern fell from his hand. "God's bowels!" Quinn lunged forward and caught the brass handle before the lamp could strike the deck.

"Whoreson savage," Samuel muttered. Mistress Pierce began to whimper.

" 'Ads-blood," Hammond managed hoarsely. "He's not human."

Cain stared past him, searching, until his gaze locked with Elizabeth's. She gave a muffled cry and turned away.

"Too much excitement for the ladies," the captain said. "Come back to my cabin, and we'll have a nightcap." He glanced back at the second officer. "Give him twenty lashes and take him to the hold. No water tonight or tomorrow."

"Yes, sir."

Elizabeth blinked back tears and held out her

hand to the captain. "I am most surprised, sir," she said. "Commanding a ship is so different from commanding a household."

Douglas looked down at her quizzically. "Why is that, Lady Elizabeth?"

She sniffed haughtily. "If my father, the earl, had a valuable horse and the grooms mishandled it as badly as that beast has been, he'd have the grooms beaten—not the horse."

"It's purely discipline, m'lady. I cannot have a man on my ship who will not obey orders."

"Exactly my point." She laughed. "A man, captain . . . a man who will not obey your orders." She looked back over her shoulder. "That creature is no more a man than a ravenous wolf. He cannot possibly have a soul or intelligence as we know it." She fluttered her lashes and smiled at him. "The man is at fault, not the wild beast."

Captain Douglas chuckled. "Indeed. You may be right. Teach those slovenly sailors a thing or two about handling prisoners, won't it."

"No matter, really. If it dies under the lash, you'll be relieved of the burden of caging it. Besides, I . . ." She sighed and cast her eyes down modestly. "Forgive me, sir, I'm only a silly woman. I misunderstood you earlier." Elizabeth covered her mouth with her hand and tittered. "I thought you said the Indian was valuable."

"He is. I stand to make quite a profit when I deliver him to the factor in London who placed the order for an unidentified buyer."

"Then you don't know who wants him?"

"No, I don't. But the factor hinted that it was someone very high placed, a nobleman. Doubtless, he wants to create a splash at Whitehall with him."

She sighed again, hoping she was not going too

far with her performance. "A pity to mar his skin with scars. You don't suppose it will lower his worth? Of course, if he dies . . ."

"Hmm. I hadn't thought of that. Hammond! Hammond!" the captain called. "Kindly escort Lady Elizabeth to my cabin. I'll be just a moment."

As Hammond led her away, Elizabeth heard Douglas rescinding the orders to have Cain lashed.

"See that his wounds are properly treated," the captain commanded. "He's worth more alive than any two of you, and I mean to collect my fee in gold coin."

In the darkest hour of the night, Elizabeth crept from her cabin and made her way down the narrow passageway. Shielded under her cloak was a tiny lamp, but she dared not risk using its light until she had reached the lowest level of the ship. Looped around her left wrist was the string of a bag containing a bottle of wine and roast duck she had stolen from the captain's cabin earlier.

Loud snores came from the Pierces' cabin, causing Elizabeth to wonder which one was the culprit, Maude or Samuel. The last room off the passageway, the quarters Robert Hammond shared with the first and second officer, was quiet. Just beyond that was a hatch, and a steep staircase leading down.

Elizabeth forced back her fear and descended into the dank, evil-smelling blackness, one step at a time. If this ship was laid out in the same way as the *Speedwell* that had carried her to Virginia, she expected to find Cain in the hold on the starboard side. A groom had taken her below to see to the well-being of her horse on the outward voyage. This ship carried no animals, but if it had, that's where they would be. A hatchway on the deck led down to the hold, but that would be for lowering cargo by ropes and pulleys. There had to be another way into the hold, and she hoped this was it.

At the bottom of the ladder, she raised her lamp. The faint circle of light illuminated the shadowy passageway. Elizabeth clutched at the wall as waves of panic assaulted her. She had always been afraid of the dark.

The sea was very close here. She could hear it below her, feel the weight of the water pressing against the sides of the frail ship. She shivered, pulling her cloak closer against the dank, motionless air. Something squeaked, and Elizabeth heard the rustle of claws against wood. "Ugh!" *Rats. I hate rats.*

When she was a child in her father's country house, rats had killed two of her father's newborn hound pups. She had gone into the stable to cuddle the puppies and found the rats in the act of eating them. She'd been only seven, but she had been so angry that she'd killed one of the vicious creatures with a pitchfork. The blood and gore had made her sick, and she'd thrown up all over her new gown—but she'd saved the rest of the litter. She had cried until Beorn, the huntsman, took the mother and the surviving pups into his hut.

Elizabeth wished she had another weapon besides her eating knife. She supposed the tiny blade would be useless against a rat or a menacing sailor, but it was all she had. She pulled it from the embroidered sheath at her waist and held it out in front of her.

Halfway down the passage she found the hatch

she was looking for. She slipped the wooden bolt and cautiously pushed the door open. "Cain?" she called. There was no answer. "Cain, are you in here? Can you hear me?"

She had come too far to turn back now. Stepping over the ledge, she entered the cavernous hold.

"Eliz-a-beth."

"Cain! I'm here. Where are you?" She raised the lantern higher, letting the light shine over the kegs, and crates, and bales of tobacco.

"Ickalli aal!"

Elizabeth turned toward the sound of his voice. What had he said? Something abut wanting her to go away. "Cain, it's me, Elizabeth," she repeated. "I've come to help you."

"This one wants no more of your help!"

She rounded a bale of tobacco and caught sight of him, chained against the ribs of the ship. "Oh," she cried, hurrying toward him.

His tangled hair hung loose over his face. His arms were bare, but his body was wrapped in a blanket. As she drew near, he rose scowling to his feet and warded her off with manacled hands. "Mata! I do not want you here."

"Cain, please." His dirty hands were balled into fists, and his eyes gleamed with a feral flame.

"You betrayed me, woman," he said. "Now you come to taunt the wolf in his trap."

She stopped and shook her head. "No, Cain. I didn't. I didn't know you were on the ship until—"

"I came to the willows, Eliz-a-beth," he said coldly. "I waited for you. But you did not come."

"I tried. I was sick, but I—"

"Your soldiers came for me. Who told them I was waiting for you? No one else can know if you do not tell them. Pah!'' He spat on the floor and glared at her with contempt.

"It wasn't me. You've got to believe me.'' She took a step toward him. "I've brought you wine and some meat.''

Cain turned his face away. "I want nothing from you.''

"I can help you. My father is a very powerful man . . . very wealthy. I can have him buy you from—''

"Buy me?'' The cords on his neck stood out as his muscles tensed in barely contained fury. His voice dropped until his words were barely audible. "Shaakhan Kihittuun. A warrior of the Lenni-Lenape.''

"Please . . .'' Elizabeth held out her hand.

"Mata! Come closer and I might wrap these chains around your soft English neck.''

She drew back, frightened. This was a side of Cain she had never seen. "You wouldn't hurt me,'' she said.

"Do not tempt me.''

Frost leaped from his eyes, sending shivers down her back. "It wasn't me,'' she protested.

"Then who? Who knew this one had promised to come for you?''

"No one.'' She shook her head. "I don't know, but . . . maybe they found you by chance. Maybe—''

"Mata. The soldiers say you tell them.'' He smiled at her fiercely. "Be you take me for fool, Eliz-a-beth? A savage, mayhap—but no fool.''

With shaking hands, she drew the bottle of wine from her bag and held it out. "Drink this. I can't stay long, and I can't leave the bottle. I—''

"Who goes there?''

The harsh voice of a man behind her caused Elizabeth to spin around and face the hatchway.

"Who is it? Are you mad, woman?" Mr. Quinn cried. "Come away from that savage."

"Oh," Elizabeth cried. "I just wanted to—"

"Save your excuses for the captain, m'lady," Quinn said. "I'm certain he'll be very interested to hear why a lady would come alone to converse with a red savage."

With a final anguished glance at Cain, Elizabeth followed the irate officer out of the hold toward what she was certain would be an extremely unpleasant interview with Captain Douglas.

Chapter 13

Sommersett House, London
August 1664

Elizabeth rose from her high-backed settle in
the orangery, moved to one of the tall windows, and stared out over her father's formal garden. The symmetrical design of dwarf boxwood
and topiary pyramids extending to the river was
maintained as flawlessly as she remembered. The
brick paths were swept spotless by the gardeners;
not one stray leaf or fallen twig marred the perfection.

The Thames ran just beyond the end of the garden. If it hadn't been for the brick wall at the base
of the slope, she could have seen boatmen ferry-
ing their passengers and cargo on the river.

Elizabeth had never cared for the rigid formal-
ity of a parterre garden. Even as a child, she had
preferred the lush profusion of herbs and trees at
Longview, the family's country house. In the
country garden were fountains and thick hedges
and a holly maze where a child could hide for
hours from stern guardians. She sighed, remembering the pristine beach and clean forest smells
she had left behind in the Colonies.

A slight sound made her turn quickly toward the doorway, but no one appeared. Instead, there was the muffled sound of footsteps retreating down the long hall. Elizabeth brushed nervously at the folds in her skirt and glanced back out the window.

No, she decided, the garden was not quite the same as it had seemed when she walked there last winter; it looked smaller, hemmed in by the river wall. And the cages of white sparrows that hung from the ceiling of the orangery were poor comparisons to the wide variety of colorful birds she had seen in the Virginia Colony.

Still, the garden at Sommersett House was the first bit of green she had seen since the *Lady Jane* docked in London. How could she have forgotten how narrow the streets were—how dark and dirty. The stench of the city was always frightful in August. Elizabeth had rarely been in London in the heat of summer. Cities stank. How could it be otherwise, when sewage ran in open ditches along the streets and any butcher was free to dump his offal into the common ditch?

No, London hasn't changed, she assured herself. I have. When did I become so squeamish? Dirt and squalor were as much a part of London as the glitter of Whitehall, or the excitement of the theater.

She returned to the doorway and looked up and down the hall. There was no sign of her father. Elizabeth sighed impatiently. I suppose I should have been glad to find that he was here in London, instead of in the country, or gone off to Bath with my stepmother.

Sommersett House was nearly deserted. Only a skeleton crew remained to staff the large house while the family was away. Many of the rooms had been closed off. Of the servants she'd seen when she'd arrived last night, she'd known only two.

Elizabeth wandered aimlessly back to the settle and sank onto the horsehair seat. Although she had convinced Captain Douglas that she'd taken the wine and meat to his prisoner on a foolish woman's whim, she had remained under suspicion for the rest of the voyage. Mistress Wright had lost no time in spreading the story of Elizabeth's shipwreck and rescue by the Indians. Doubtless the captain believed her wanton or simply a little mad.

That was of no consequence; what did matter was that there had been no opportunity to see Cain again until she had watched him being dragged away from the docks yesterday. The fact that he believed she had betrayed him to the English soldiers preyed on her mind until she could think of nothing else.

He's alive, she reminded herself—alive and strong. It had taken four men to wrestle him, chained, into a coach. Naturally, no one had bothered to tell her where Cain was being taken, or who had purchased him.

Never mind, she thought. Father will be able to learn the truth soon enough. There is little that happens in London that he doesn't have a finger in. Wasn't it common gossip that he maintained a network of thieves and beggars as spies?

"Elizabeth. Let me look at you."

She turned toward the sound of her father's voice, stood, and sank into a deep curtsy. "Father."

Roger Sommersett regarded his daughter with shrewd eyes. A thickset man of medium height with a large nose and prematurely gray hair, he was dressed in a fashionable scarlet short-waisted doublet with slashed sleeves and matching breeches. The velvet breeches were decorated with ribbons and cut narrow to show off his shapely calves.

"Turn around," he instructed. "You look well enough to me. I was told you had suffered great hardships."

"Are you certain you were not told I was mad?"

Sommersett's green eyes, the exact shade of Elizabeth's, lit with good humor, and he extended a broad ringed hand.

Elizabeth raised it to her lips. "Father. I'm so happy to see you. I was afraid you would be in the country."

He smiled and patted the top of her head fondly. "You have caused quite a stir, girl. But then you always did take after those godforsaken Scots on your grandmother's side of the family." His expression hardened. "Are you still fit for marriage?"

"Sir?" She blushed and stepped back, feeling foolish for allowing her father's blunt manner to disturb her. *What if my family had believed me lost at sea? I'm here now, and that's all that matters to Father. Sommersett interests come first— isn't that the first rule he ever taught me?*

"Damn me, girl, have you gone soft in the head? Is your maidenhead intact? Will Dunmore find legal reason to reject you as a bride?"

"I don't want to marry him."

"What?"

"Don't be angry with me . . . please."

Sommersett swore an oath so foul that Elizabeth began to tremble. Her father had never struck her with a closed fist, but she had seen him knock her older brother halfway across the stable when he was enraged. Sensibly, she sidled away to put the settle between them. Vile curses continued to roll off his tongue until his face turned an angry purple and he ran out of breath.

At last, he ceased his blaspheming and fixed his daughter with a thoughtful gaze. "No need to hide from me, chit," he said gruffly. "Your sister Alice had not your virtue, yet we sent her to her marriage bed with the Sommersett honor upheld." He shook his head. "Never fear, I'll not blame you for what a heathen stole. You're not with child, are you?"

"No, Father, but—"

"Then nothing's torn that cannot be mended. Dunmore will demand that you be examined by midwives, naturally. It won't be the—"

"You must listen to me," Elizabeth exclaimed. "I have to tell you what happened."

Sommersett's hooded eyes narrowed. "The matter is ended. There is no need to discuss—"

"There is a need," she flung back. "I have a need. For once in my life, I want you to listen to me and to what I want."

His shoulders tensed and he drew back an open hand, then he began to chuckle. "You're not all your mother's child, are you, Elizabeth? She always said you had my tenacity. All right, have your say. I'll listen. But I warn you, I have a meeting with Buckingham at noon. I'll not leave the King's favorite waiting for a chit's whim." He sat down on the settle and motioned to her. "Come, sit beside me. You're in no danger, despite your sassy tongue. Think you I'd introduce you to your future husband with your face bruised and swollen?"

Cautiously, Elizabeth obeyed and began to tell

her father what had transpired after the *Speedwell* went down off the Virginia coast. Sommersett gave her his complete attention, saying nothing while she spoke.

"And so you see, Father," Elizabeth concluded nearly an hour later, "why Cain cannot remain a prisoner. We must find him and buy his freedom."

"This man is the reason why you say you cannot marry Edward Lindsey."

She nodded and looked down at her lap. The fingers on her left hand fumbled nervously with the lace decolletage of her lavender satin gown.

"Let me be absolutely certain I understand you," he said. "You believe yourself in love with this . . . this Indian, and you wish to wed him instead of Lord Dunmore."

"Yes . . . no." Tears blurred her vision. "It's not that simple." She sniffed and tried to gain control of her cracking voice. "I want you to find Cain and send him back to Virginia." Elizabeth reached for her father's hand and squeezed it.

Sommersett allowed the familiarity but did not return the pressure. "You are more disturbed by your ordeal than I believed if you think your family will permit you to marry a savage who eats raw meat and worships trees."

"Cain doesn't—" she began in protest and then broke off. There was no way she could explain Cain to a man like her father. It wasn't possible. How could she explain something she didn't understand herself? "Father, he—" She sighed. "You're right, of course. I didn't expect to be allowed to marry him. But he does deserve a reward for saving my life. Surely, it would sully the Sommersett honor to let such a debt go unpaid."

"You were intimate with this creature?"

"No!" She felt heat rise in her cheeks. "This creature, as you call him, is a man—a man of great honor. I haven't shamed you. I retained my maidenhead. I am as pure as when you sent me forth."

"Then why do you say you do not wish to marry Dunmore?" He removed his hand from her clasp. "The man to which you have been betrothed since you were nine years old."

Elizabeth rose stiffly and walked to the window. This interview was not going as she had hoped. She pressed her cheek against the cool glass and stared unseeing at the garden. Her stomach churned. Cain's future, his very life, hung in the balance. If she could not convince her father to help, she would be condemning the man she loved to certain death.

"Well?" Sommersett demanded.

She turned to face him, her face as pale as milk, and forced herself to say the words that would do most toward soothing her father's ire without surrendering. "Perhaps I will wed Edward," she said. "I don't now. I only know that I am not the same person who sailed to Virginia to wed a stranger. I have changed inside, in ways I cannot . . ."

Elizabeth paused and drew in a deep breath. "Forgive me, sire. I know that you have my best wishes at heart. I don't wish to disobey you, but I cannot wed a man I don't know. I want time to make Edward's acquaintance—to see if I can have any feeling toward him at all." Jade fire flickered behind her eyes, and her tone took on a thread of steel. "I want your promise that you will not force me to marry Edward if I decide I can't abide him."

"Has Dunmore offended you in some way?"

"Damn me, Father! You don't understand. How could the man have offended me when I haven't laid eyes on him since I was a child? That's the point! He is an unknown. I don't know if I could ever love him, or even come to respect him as a wife should respect and admire her husband.''

Sommersett scoffed. ''Love. What girlish prattle is this about love? Marriage is an alliance between families. You never complained before about the choice I made for you. Why now?''

She faced his rising rage with unyielding spirit, meeting his glare fearlessly. ''Because Cain has taught me something of the love a woman should feel for a man, I don't want to spend the rest of my life tied to—''

''Enough.'' He stood up. ''I will think on it.''

''Why can't you give me an answer now? Every hour we wait puts Cain in greater danger. We must locate him before it is too late.''

Sommersett held up his hand. ''No. No more. I told you I would consider your plea. I have ever been lenient with you, Elizabeth. Doubtless I've spoiled you and encouraged your headstrong notions. We will speak of this again tonight.''

''Can you not at least try to find out where Cain is?'' she dared. ''I know you—''

''Must I give you a taste of my hand to secure your obedience?'' he snapped. ''There is no need to search out your savage. 'Tis common gossip that Dunmore purchased the Indian. He has been bragging about Whitehall for weeks that he'd ordered one of the natives from Virginia.''

''You let me prattle on when you knew all along that Dunmore had Cain? Damn you for a cold, unfeeling bastard!''

Elizabeth didn't flinch when her father's hand smacked across her face.

* * *

Cain had tried not to look for Elizabeth when he was dragged off the English ship and thrown into a coach. He'd promised himself that he wouldn't—that he would forget she'd ever existed. But he hadn't been able to keep that promise. Elizabeth was flesh of his flesh and bone of his bone. The only way to cast her from his heart would be to tear it out and throw it onto the ground.

He'd had many weeks to mull over her denial. After she had come to the place where he was chained, his captors treated him better. He was given fresh water and food twice a day. Men with tools had come to build a platform so that he might sleep above the filthy bilge water. They had even left him blankets against the chill. The question was, had she ordered him to be well cared for out of affection or guilt? He wanted to believe in her innocence, but common sense told him that she had indeed betrayed him.

The inactivity enforced by the chains that bound Cain had tormented him. No torture could have been worse for a man who had known only the freedom of the forests and open sea. His eyes had ached for the sight of green grass and the flash of a bird wing; his ears had strained in vain for the cry of a hunting hawk.

The fetid odor of the ship's hold had sickened him, but it was nothing to the stench that enveloped him as the coach rattled and bumped along the city streets. He had been manacled hand and foot when the sailors had dumped him facedown on the floor of the coach, but he was alone inside the vehicle. It had been easy to work himself onto a seat where he could see out, despite the drawn leather curtains.

When Cain was a child, he had marveled at his

grandmother's wonderful tales of London—of trading places, called shops, where all manner of wonderful goods could be had for the asking; of brightly decked noblemen riding through the streets on magnificent horses; and of houses so tall they blocked out the sun. Of course, he hadn't believed all her stories; even a little boy knew that men couldn't build wigwams higher than trees.

Cocumtha had said that London was only one town, that England had many, and she had said that more people lived in England than there were grains of sand upon the beach. Until today, Cain had believed she was exaggerating—stretching the facts to make a good story. Now, he wondered if she had been telling the truth about how many Englishmen there actually were. He hadn't imagined so many people walked the face of the earth.

Grandmother had never seen the land of her ancestors; all she knew of England was what her own parents had told her. Cain thought that much had been lost in the telling. No wonder the English wanted to come to Lenni-Lenape land. This place was as foul and crowded as a nest of buzzard fledglings.

From the window of the coach, Cain saw a woman taking water from an open ditch beside the street, and not an arrow's shot away a man was dumping the carcass of a dog in that same stagnant stream. True, a few people were dressed in garments of fine cloth with weapons of shining steel at their waists, but even those men gave off a scent as strong as week-old fish.

Eventually, the space between the houses became father apart and the road rougher. Patches of green and an occasional tree were visible from Cain's window, and he realized they must have reached the end of the city. He tried to fix directions in his mind. He must remember the way back to London if he was ever to make his way home again.

"It will not be easy," Cain said to himself. "I am a stranger in this land." He knew that he must learn English ways if he was to defeat his captors. "I must become as one of my enemies," he murmured. The thought was bitter, but not as bitter as having his bones lie forever in this far-off land. "I will learn," he promised himself, "and I will use their own wisdom against them."

Night fell over the English countryside, and the coach traveled on. Cain stretched out on the leather seat and closed his eyes. He did not know if he could sleep, but he would try. Whatever waits ahead, he thought, I will need my strength.

Unbidden, an image of Elizabeth rose in his mind. "I will find you again," he promised softly, "and you will learn the price of betraying a warrior of the Lenni-Lenape."

Elizabeth had wasted no tears over the slap her father had given her. Instead, she'd retreated to her own chambers, then she'd sent Betty to the kitchen for cool water to bathe her smarting cheek. To her surprise, it was not Betty who returned with the pitcher but Bridget, her Irish maid who'd failed to sail on the *Speedwell* with her when they'd left for Virginia.

"Ye wanted water, m'lady."

"What are you doing here, you faithless limmer?" Elizabeth demanded. "You've nerve enough for two to show your face."

Mischief danced in Bridget's dark eyes, and she giggled shamelessly. " 'Tis awful glad I am to see ye, and that's a fact." She carried the silver ewer across the room and poured water into a painted china bowl. "Where ever did ye find that bird-boned little baggage? Too timid to say boo to a mouse. Cook put her to work turnin' the spit."

"Bridget." Elizabeth hid her delight in seeing her old companion behind a sharp tone. "I asked you a question. Why are you here at Sommersett House?"

The Irish girl's eyes widened in feigned innocence. "Here, m'lady? Where else would I be? Haven't I been in yer service since we were children?"

"Why weren't you on the *Speedwell*?"

"I truly meant to be there," Bridget avowed. She averted her eyes, and scarlet circles tinted her plump cheeks as she busied herself with the bowl of water. "Me sister Maureen was taken wi' the fever so sudden like that I had to fetch the priest for her. He gave her last rites, she was so bad. By the time she took a turn for the better, it was too late. I went to the docks, m'lady, I swear on me dear mother's soul, but the *Speedwell* was gone."

"You lie as well as ever, you shameless slut," Elizabeth accused. "You were afraid to go to Virginia with me. Admit it."

"Fearful I was," the black-haired girl allowed, "and rightly so—seein' how so many went to their doom aboard that cursed ship—but I'd never disobey ye. 'Twas Maureen's fever that's at fault. When I found I was too late, I came straight back here to Sommersett House. Mistress Wells let that lazy Maggie go and kept me on in her place. I was *that* glad when I heard ye'd not drowned in the sea. Ye'll be needin' me to do for ye again, won't ye, m'lady? Nobody else can do yer hair like I can, you've said that often enough."

"Maureen is as healthy as a pig," Elizabeth declared. "And you are a bald-faced liar." She smiled and held out her arms. "But I'm glad to see you anyway, Bridget. I've missed you."

Bridget flung herself into Elizabeth's arms and hugged her tightly. "They said ye were dead," she cried, "but I lit a candle for ye every Saturday, and I prayed to Saint Anne to bring ye safely home."

"If Saint Anne is the one who saved me, she took a peculiar form." Elizabeth stepped back and chuckled. "Wait until I tell you what happened to me. I vow, even you've never spun a tale so outlandish."

"Do tell, m'lady," the maid urged. "There are such rumors flying belowstairs, ye'd never suppose." She tilted her head to one side. "That wench Betty has sense enough to keep a still tongue in her head. She'd admit or deny nothin', though Cook tried to bribe her wi' a pork pie."

"Betty's loyal. I promised her she'd be trained as a proper maid. Since you're back, you can take her in hand yourself."

"Me, m'lady?" Bridget grimaced. "That fluttersome jade's better suited to the scullery. She's not got the looks for a lady's maid, nor ever will, I vow." She grinned at Elizabeth.

"Betty can't be blamed for her face, no more than you can take credit for yours. You'll treat her well, or I'll turn you out for good and set her in your place," Elizabeth threatened. "Now, do you wish to hear of Virginia or not? If you do, hush your chattering and listen to me."

The two of them talked all afternoon and into the evening. Bridget squealed and laughed and watched with sparkling eyes as Elizabeth related all that had happened to her since she'd left London, omitting only her personal feelings toward Cain. At dusk, Betty came up with a tray of food.

Elizabeth inquired whether the girl had eaten,
then sent her away with a few kind words. When
they were alone, Elizabeth and Bridget shared the
repast as they had done when both were children.

The great clock on the landing had just struck
ten when an unfamiliar maid came to summon
Elizabeth to her father's bedchamber.

"Wait here until I return," Elizabeth bade
Bridget. "No, go and fetch Betty. She slept in my
outer chamber last night. God knows where Cook
put her tonight. Put her on the pallet, then wait
to help me prepare for bed."

"Yes, m'lady." Bridget gave a proper cursty.

Elizabeth nodded her approval. Bridget was
canny enough to know when and where to behave more like friend than servant. For a few
hours they had scaled the walls that lay between
their stations in life. Now, that time was past.
Wordlessly, heart pounding, Elizabeth followed
the new serving woman down a long flight of
stairs and along the twisting corridors to her father's rooms in the Tudor section of the house.

They paused in the shadowy hall outside his
lordship's chamber and the maid knocked, then
opened the heavy oak door for Elizabeth when he
gave permission to enter.

Elizabeth greeted him formally. "Sire."

Sommersett was reclining on a walnut daybed
near the fireplace, wineglass in hand. This wing
of the house was always chilly, despite the time
of year, and a small fire burned on the hearth.

Elizabeth noticed that her father had changed
from his earlier stylish attire into a comfortable
old dressing gown and had removed his wig, covering his close-cropped hair with an embroidered
man's cap. He beckoned her to come closer.

"I trust your day was satisfactory, Father," she murmured.

He frowned. "You care not a damn for my day, Elizabeth. You've come to hear my decision on your request."

"I have." She stood before him, hands clasped, hiding her terror behind a calm exterior.

Sommersett drained the last of the wine and rose to his feet. "I met with Dunmore late this afternoon," he said sternly. "I find no fault with him. Your wedding will take place on Michaelmas Eve."

Elizabeth blanched and grasped the arm of the daybed to steady herself. "But, Father—"

"We will hear no more of this romantic fancy of wild men. You will wed Dunmore and—"

"I will not!"

Sommersett rose and stood over her. "You will wed where you are bid, and you will never mention that Indian again."

"Will you drag me bound and gagged to the altar?" she cried. "I tell you, I'll not have him."

He seized Elizabeth's shoulders and shook her. "You'll obey me, girl, or I'll have your Indian lover drawn and quartered, and you locked away in Bedlam for a madwoman."

Hot tears scalded her cheeks as her hair tumbled loose and fell about her shoulders. "You would take your spite out on Cain for my rebellion?"

"Stupid bitch," he roared. "Do you think you can stand against me in this?" His fingers dug into her flesh until she gasped with pain. Swearing, he thrust her away, and she fell back against the daybed.

"All my life you have prated on of Sommersett honor," she accused, finding her balance and facing him brazenly. "Where is that honor now—to so abuse a man who has done our family naught but good?"

His face grew suddenly old. "You were always my favorite, Elizabeth. I coddled you against your stepmother's good advice. But I will not let you ruin your life on a romantic whim. I swear to you, if you do not yield, you will see what's left of that savage fed to the hounds."

She turned away and let the chill of the room seep into her bones. When she spoke again, it was in a strained whisper. "And if I wed Edward Lindsey, will you send Cain home to Virginia?"

"Do you dare attempt blackmail?"

"No, Father—not blackmail but a bargain." A bargain penned in hell, she thought as she twisted to face him once more. "Compromise, if you will. Surely, compromise is a worthy Sommersett trait."

His lips thinned. "So be it."

She sank into a deep curtsy. "Then I am once more your obedient daughter, sire." *And a bride,* she cried inwardly, *whose heart lies not with her intended, but already in the grave.*

Part Two

Chapter 14

Sotterley, Essex
December 1664

Elizabeth moaned with pleasure as Cain's hand cupped her bare breast and brought his hungry mouth down to lave her love-swollen nipples. Tendrils of his blue-black hair brushed her tingling skin, and she trembled beneath him as waves of intense desire swept over her. The throbbing, incandescent heat between her thighs became an agony of yearning as she arched her hips against his hot, hard body. "Cain," she whispered, "love me. Please . . . please love me."

His mouth teased and sucked the hard, erect peaks of her breasts as his strong hands claimed her willing body, stroking . . . tormenting until she cried out with the sweet aching of wanting him. "Eliz-a-beth," he murmured huskily, "my own . . . my wife." He raised his head to stare into her eyes, and his lips crushed hers in a searing kiss of total possession.

Elizabeth wrapped her legs around his and dug her fingers into his broad shoulders as tremors of pulsating delight coursed through her. "I've wanted you," she cried softly, "by all that's holy, I've wanted you here in my bed."

"Why did you doubt me? Did not this one promise

*he would come for you?" Cain caught her face between
his hands. "Touch me," he entreated her. One hand
dropped to close over hers and move it to the turgid
source of his passion. "Touch me," he repeated in a
breathy whisper.*

*Elizabeth's fingers tightened around his engorged
shaft, and she felt him shudder with pleasure. Slowly,
she began to stroke him, letting her hand slide up and
down his silken member as he covered her breasts and
belly with scalding kisses.*

*"Eliz-a-beth," he groaned. He wound one hand in
her hair, and let the other trail down her hip to rest
on the mound of tight curls between her legs.*

The intensity of the sensation brought her upright in the great poster bed. Elizabeth stared
about her in confusion. The covers and pillows
were all awry, and Betty's sleepy face was just
appearing over the foot of the bed.

"M'lady! Are ye all right?" Betty was as naked
as the day she was born, and her hair stuck out
all over her head like an overripe cattail. "I heard
ye cry out."

"No, no, nothing's wrong," Elizabeth stammered. Breathless, she fell back against the goose-
down feather pillows and tried to reconcile reality
with the vivid memory of her dream.

"Yer fevered, m'lady," Betty insisted. "Look at
ye. Shall I fetch Bridget?"

"No," Elizabeth answered sharply. "Go back
to your pallet. It was only a bad dream." She ran
her fingers through her damp, tangled hair and
pulled the covers up to her neck. It was only a
dream, she reminded herself, only a dream.

She began to shiver and wondered if she really
was ill. Her body was drenched in sweat, and her
heart was beating in a rapid, irregular rhythm.

Her mouth and throat were as dry as chalk. She licked her lips to moisten them, then sat up and reached for the water goblet beside her bed. It was empty.

"Betty! Betty," she called. "Fetch me something to drink. I'm parched."

The girl mumbled sleepily, and Elizabeth heard the rustle of clothing as Betty fumbled for her shift.

"No need to go belowstairs. There's wine in the japanned cabinet."

Betty brought the silver chalice, filled to the brim and spilling over. Elizabeth leaned over the edge of the high bed and took a sip, unwilling to stain the rose silk sheets. She waved the child away, then retreated to the center of the curtained bed with the cup.

After several sips of the unwatered wine, Elizabeth's brain began to clear. It was the same dream, the fantasy she'd experienced over and over in the months since her marriage to Edward.

You're a fool, the voice in her head said sternly. *Cain is back in Virginia by now. He's forgotten you, and you must do the same by him.*

She sighed and took another swallow of the strong Dutch wine. *Why can't I forget him? Why must I torment myself night after night with these sinful desires?* She smiled wryly in the darkness. "If I knew that—"

"M'lady?" Betty called. "Did ye want—"

"Go to sleep. No." Elizabeth scooted to the end of the bed and parted the heavy drapes. "I wish to be alone. Take your pallet into the dressing room and sleep there."

Betty rubbed her eyes with her fists. "But m'lady, the lord bade me—"

"Sleep at the foot of my bed like a dog," Elizabeth finished. "As if you could prevent me from putting horns on him if I wished to do otherwise." She made a sound of derision. "Never mind, 'tis not your fault. At least drag your bed near the fire. 'Ods-heart! I cannot break wind without you there to hear and repeat it to Dunmore."

Betty began to sniffle as she tugged her pallet toward the fire. "I didn't mean t' get ye in trouble, m'lady, I swear. His lordship only asked me did we go t' early service, and I—"

Elizabeth sighed impatiently. "No, 'tis nothing, Bett. I'm not angry with you. You had no way of knowing I'd lied to him. You must obey Lord Dunmore, of course. Go to sleep, child." She drew the curtains closed and slid back against the heaped pillows. "None of it is your fault," she finished softly.

Two and a half months a bride, she thought, and I'm not yet a wife. No wonder Edward was eaten up with jealousy.

She and Dunmore had been wed with all pomp and splendor on last Michaelmas Eve. The simple marriage ceremony had been followed by a grand supper at Sommersett House. Both the King's brother, the duke of York, and the Lady Castlemaine had danced at her wedding, and the festivities had gone on until 'daybreak the following day.

According to custom, she and Edward had been undressed and put into bed together some time after midnight. She had been willing, if not enthusiastic, to complete this essential part of the ritual, but Dunmore had other ideas. As soon as the doors to the chamber were closed, he rose and donned a dressing robe. Ignoring her, the bridegroom spent the better part of an hour drinking beside the fireplace. Then he produced a tiny gilt flask from his pocket, threw back the sheets, and liberally splattered blood on her bare thighs and the linen.

"Say nothing of this, if you wish to live to enjoy what this marriage has brought you," he snarled. Then, without another word, Edward called for his manservant, dressed, and returned to the celebration.

After a suitable time, she followed his example. They danced and laughed and blushed in response to the general teasing. Later, they joined the guests of honor at an elaborate breakfast. When the festivities were over, she went to her own chambers and slept alone. At noon, Dunmore's man, Jim, came to tell her maids to prepare to depart for his country home in Essex.

Elizabeth stifled the urge to hurl the costly silver cup against the wall. Catching her lower lip between her teeth, she set it down on the table beside the bed and covered her face with her hands.

Day by day, her frustration had grown. How was she supposed to accept the role of wife and mistress of Dunmore's estates? How could she provide him an heir if he did not remain at her side long enough to carry out a decent conversation—let alone perform a man's duty?

The staff at Sotterley was without reproach; a capable steward, Hugh Cardiff, managed all outside the house, and his wife acted as housekeeper within. Mistress Cardiff instructed the maids, other than Elizabeth's personal servants, and supervised the kitchen. Mistress Cardiff carried the great ring of keys on a belt at her waist—the keys that unlocked the doors, the spice chests, and the money box. She paid the servants on the first day of every month, and she hired and fired staff members.

I'm nothing more than a fashion poppet, Elizabeth thought, waiting here on the shelf until some spoiled child comes to play with me.

She had seen Edward four times since their wedding in September, when he'd come to the country to hunt. They'd shared three meals, including their wedding breakfast, and he'd not spoken more than a few dozen words to her.

"At least let me come down to London with you," she'd suggested the last time he'd been at Sotterley. Autumn was a lively time at court; there were masques and balls, horse races and stage plays. In London, she could expect to be invited to private parties and elegant suppers with all manner of gaming and entertainment. Her sister Ann and her family were in residence there, as well as many of Elizabeth's friends. "I'll die of boredom here, m' lord Dunmore."

"I think not," Edward had replied coldly. "Are we not, after all, honeymooners?"

"I am not used to inactivity," she'd flung back at him. "I need something more to do than try on the new gowns you've so thoughtfully provided. At least instruct your housekeeper to give over the running of Sotterley to my care. I assure you, sir, I am not ignorant of such affairs."

"With your reputation, your time might be better spent in prayer than in the pursuit of frivolous pleasure."

She had been angry enough to slap his face, but she'd realized it would only further alienate him. Instead she'd curtsied as an obedient wife should and retreated to her own chambers. When she came down the next morning, she learned he'd returned to London.

Before leaving, he'd subjected her maids to the usual interrogation. On each visit, Edward had gone to great lengths to question all the servants on her daily routine. It had been her resentment of this petty tyranny that had caused her to lie to him about attending church services. Now she'd been caught in a foolish untruth, and she didn't know if she was angrier at her husband or at herself for stooping to such childish behavior.

Elizabeth tugged several pillows into position behind her back and curled her legs under her. Pride wouldn't allow her to shed tears of self-pity. Swallowing the hard lump in her throat, she stared at the glowing coals on the hearth and tried to reason out what had gone wrong with her marriage. Other than this latest exchange of heated words, she knew she had given Edward no reason to be dissatisfied with her.

"If he was repelled by my experience in the Colonies, why did he go through with the marriage?" she whispered. "Why?"

Edward Lindsey did not appear to be a spiteful or vindictive man. His round, freckled face, ready smile, and butter-blond hair gave him an almost boyish appearance. His eyes were a clear, pleasing shade of blue, his voice manly without sounding harsh to the ear. A thin, aristocratic nose and a full, sensual mouth added to his charm.

Elizabeth pursed her mouth. If I didn't know Edward's reputation, I might suspect that he was one who preferred his own sex to women. But Edward had kept as many mistresses as any other young man of his station, and Bridget had pointed out several by-blows of his among the flocks of servants' children that ran in and out of the courtyard. No, her husband was not a lover of men. What then could be his problem?

She had known Dunmore as a child and had not liked him very much. But then I was a brat myself, she reminded herself. She had quarreled with him—struck him in the face if she remembered correctly. She had been only nine years old; surely, he could not carry a grudge for so many years over so insignificant a matter. The details of the incident were hazy—something about a kitten. Edward had been teasing another girl, and Elizabeth had come to her rescue in a whirlwind of righteous fervor.

Elizabeth tried to remember anything she had ever heard or seen of Edward's behavior that might explain his attitude toward her. As she recalled, he had been a lazy boy, rather than malicious. He'd been good at his studies, and was an exceptional horseman. As a young man, he'd gathered a reputation as an unlucky gambler and a heavy drinker, but that was far from unusual among noblemen, especially second sons. Edward had suffered no real disgraces that she'd heard of, committed no crimes.

As far as she knew, relations between the Sommersetts and the Lindseys were good; Edward's father and hers had been companions in France. And, even though she was bitter toward her father for insisting on this marriage against her will, she was sure he'd never have knowingly given her over to a monster. Try as she might, she could not come up with an answer to the puzzle.

By morning, Elizabeth decided that she had been reasonable long enough; it was time to take drastic action. Regardless of what Edward said, she would return to London. "I'll hunt after breakfast," she informed the maids as they laced her into her blue wool riding habit. "Mary, go you down to the mews and tell the falconer I want the small merlin." When the girl was gone, Elizabeth beckoned to Betty. "Do you ride?" she asked quietly.

"A horse?"

Bridget tittered, and Elizabeth glared at her.

"Bett, have you ever ridden pillion behind a man?"

Betty's eyes widened. "No, m'lady. I never did."

"Then Bridget will go and you must remain here today. Have Mistress Cardiff instruct you in your duties." Elizabeth patted the girl's arm. "You belong to me, Betty. You needn't be afraid. I will look after you, no matter what."

Betty nodded. "Yes, m'lady. But what am I t' do?"

"Go downstairs and ask one of the cooks for bread and cheese, cold meat, and wine. Have him pack a basket to take with us. If the hawking is good, I'll stay out until late afternoon." She motioned toward the door. "Run along with you."

Betty hastened to obey, and Elizabeth turned to Bridget. "Dress warmly and pack a change of clothing. Tuck the bundle under your cloak. We ride fast and far this day."

Their eyes met meaningfully. "Then I should bring yer jewel chest," the Irish girl replied. "In case the game turns dangerous."

"As you will. But take the contents and leave the box. I'll have no wench report the loss until we're safe away."

"Leave it to me, m'lady," Bridget answered with a saucy wink. "Me darlin' mother always said I had a quick hand."

Elizabeth rode out across the frost-tipped fields of Sotterley later that morning with an entourage of two grooms, four men-at-arms, three foresters, the chief falconer, and her maid, Bridget. At first, the head groom had been reluctant to saddle the horses Elizabeth had picked out, but she had insisted.

"I'll ride the gray. Saddle that roan for my maid." She needed good horses. It was eighteen hours of hard riding to London if the roads were passable.

The man had hesitated, fear and doubt showing plainly on his weathered face "The horses be spirited, m'lady. If ye were t' come t' harm . . ."

"Are either of the animals vicious?"

"No, m'lady, but—"

She'd dismissed him with a haughty wave of her hand. "Saddle them, I say. At once! The hawk grows restless." The ladies' horses at Sotterley were well-bred and sweet-natured. Such a mount was a delight to ride on a leisurely outing, but for the excursion Elizabeth had in mind, a gentle palfrey would not do. The Sommersett women were all accomplished equestriennes, and hardy Bridget could ride like a Cossack. Elizabeth was sorry to have to leave Betty behind, but she could send for the wench later if need be. For now, Elizabeth prepared to ride hard and fast and to let no one stand in her way.

Sotterley lay north and east of London, not far from the highway that led from Colchester to the capital. Essex was heavily wooded and dotted with rivers and marshland; the old Roman roads had scarce been repaired since they were built and were in poor condition. Still, an unusually cold spell had frozen the ground, and Elizabeth knew that the highway would get worse, not better, before spring. If she intended to act, this might be her best opportunity.

Elizabeth commanded her huntsman to lead the party wide around a farmer's field of winter wheat. Then they trotted their horses through a park of ancient oaks and across a low-lying meadow beside the river. Elizabeth reined in and signaled the falconer to bring up the merlin and transfer the bird to her leather gauntlet. The other men fell back a distance, allowing the huntsman to seek out game for the lady's sport.

Speaking softly to the hawk to calm it, Elizabeth removed the hood and cast it skyward as one of the huntsmen startled a pair of ducks from the water. Like a bullet shot from a gun, the merlin rose and plunged toward the prey.

Elizabeth signaled to Bridget, and both women brought their quirts down across their horses' rumps. The animals leaped forward and galloped headlong toward the narrow bridge across the river. Elizabeth's gray thundered across the wooden bridge as the first of the men-at-arms whipped their horses into a run. Bridget's mount was a half length behind, and the women urged the horses up a bank and down the path on the far side of the water.

For nearly a mile, Elizabeth drove the gray gelding at breakneck speed along the winding trail. Once, she slowed the animal enough to allow Bridget's roan to catch up. The Irish girl's cheeks glowed red from the cold and her eyes sparkled with excitement as she leaned low over her horse's neck.

"Are you all right?" Elizabeth cried.

"Aye, but they're right behind us!"

Elizabeth laughed and touched the gray's neck with the crop again. The spirited animal quickened the pace. She had deliberately chosen what she felt were the best animals in the stable, and she and Bridget were lighter burdens than the men. She didn't expect to stay ahead of the men-at-arms indefinitely, just long enough to give them a merry chase.

Just ahead, the path split. One leg followed the edge of a woods; the left disappeared among the trees. Elizabeth chose the open way. They'd gone not more than a few hundred yards, and this trail too led into the forest. The women reined the animals to a canter and ducked their heads to avoid the low-hanging branches.

The path twisted and turned through the woods. Once, they crossed a clearing where a dirty-faced man paused, axe in hand, to watch them pass. Then, as the trees thinned, Bridget suddenly cried out. Ahead, blocking the trail, were two of Dunmore's mounted huntsmen.

Elizabeth pulled hard on the reins and tried to ride around the men. One threw himself out of the saddle and seized the gray's bridle.

"Stop!" the man cried. "God's teeth, m'lady! Have ye gone mad?"

Elizabeth slashed at the huntsman with her quirt. "Unhand my horse!" she commanded. Startled, the man let go of the bridle and stepped back, his eyes dilated with fear and anger. "Dare you lay hands on me?"

"M'lady Dunmore—" The huntsman broke off and glanced at his companion for support. The second man shrugged, clearly as distressed as the first.

"Yes!" Elizabeth cried. "I am Dunmore's wife. His wife—not his paramour, not his servant. I ride to London. Do you ride with me, or will you try to stop me by force?"

"We have no orders—" the man holding Bridget's horse began.

"I have given you orders," Elizabeth snapped. "Mount your horses and come along, or stay here like craven dogs and take full responsibility if anything happens to us on the way."

"But m'lady!" the man at her horse's head protested. "You cannot ride to London without escort. The roads are thick with highwaymen. Just last week two travelers were robbed and murdered near Brayntre."

"Then it seems it would behoove you to accompany us."

"Lord Dunmore will be angry. He—"

"Did he tell you I was to be held prisoner?"

The man's face turned the shade of old tallow. "No, m'lady, of course not, but—"

"My father is the Earl of Sommersett. It is to his house in London that we journey. If a hair on my head is harmed between here and there, you will answer not only to Lord Dunmore, but also to the wrath of Sommersett." Elizabeth twisted in the saddle and motioned to Bridget. "Come, girl. The winter's day is short, and we have far to ride." She snapped the reins, and the gray leaped ahead.

Bridget followed her mistress, and the two huntsmen scrambled into their saddles and reluctantly set off after the women.

"Lord Dunmore will be very angry if ye go to London wi'out his permission," Bridget said, guiding her horse close to Elizabeth's.

"Doubtless he will," Elizabeth replied. "But m'lord has yet to learn that a Sommersett woman is not a rush mat to rest his feet upon."

The maid shook her head. "He may beat ye, m'lady."

Elizabeth's eyes narrowed as she guided her

mount up a rise onto the London highway. "My husband may try."

Three hours later, several weary men-at-arms and a groom caught up with Elizabeth and her party on the Colchester Highway. It took only a few threats and a few forced tears on Elizabeth's part to convince the newcomers to accompany her to her father's home in London.

Chapter 15

Sommersett House, London

Elizabeth rose in her bathtub and allowed a maid to drape her with a towel. She stood placidly as one woman dried her hair and yet another rubbed her body briskly with soft, scented cloths. Bridget dropped a shift over her mistress's head and called to the serving men in the doorway to carry away the copper tub of bathwater.

Elizabeth took a seat before the fire and someone thrust silk mules on her feet. She shut her eyes as the tedious process of dressing continued.

Naturally, her father had been shocked when she had ridden into Sommersett House six days ago with only a motley retinue of foresters, men-at-arms, and a single maid.

"Not that I'm not happy to see you, chit," he'd admitted when he had finished chastising her, "but your husband needs to give you a sound thrashing." He chuckled. "Since your marriage, that chore, at least, is out of my hands."

She'd lied and told him that boredom had driven her to the city. "I shall die if I miss another season of plays and balls," she'd insisted. Blushing prettily, she'd explained that she'd come to

Sommersett House, rather than her husband's London house, because she didn't know the state of his household.

"A wise decision, my dear," Sommersett agreed. Unspoken between them was the thought that if Dunmore kept a mistress, the woman might be in residence there, and that would cause undue embarrassment for all parties concerned.

"You must send word to your husband that you are here," her father had insisted.

"My thoughts exactly," she'd replied.

A message had been sent by a footman to Dunmore's home. So far, there had been no response. Exhausted, Elizabeth had gone to bed and slept around the clock. Since then, she'd engaged in the usual activities of sophisticated women of her class; she had visited her friends and her relatives, had engaged a mantuamaker, and had set about renewing her contacts in the city.

Her concern about her husband's reaction to her departure from Sotterley was real, but Elizabeth refused to allow it to ruin her pleasure at being back in London. Sommersett and her stepmother, Sibyl, were rarely at home, but her sister Ann lived only a few blocks away. Ann, the marchioness of Dawes, was near childbed. She was so delighted to have Elizabeth come by to see her that she set aside her usual peevishness and was actually good company.

"Ouch!" Elizabeth was drawn sharply back from her musing by the heat of the curling iron on her neck.

Bridget slapped the maid's face. " 'Ads-flesh, ye nitty jade! Will ye scar m'lady's beauty wi' a hot iron? Give me that." Weeping, the girl handed over the tool and began to busy herself wiping up water spots on the floor.

"No need to make such a shrieking," Elizabeth snapped. "I'm not hurt. It just startled me."

Being careful not to muss the ringlets at the sides of Elizabeth's face, Bridget smoothly drew back the hair over her mistress's crown and began to arrange the heavy mass at the back into a chignon. The woman who had dried Elizabeth's hair brought a succession of gowns for inspection, so that her mistress might choose one for the morning. A second girl offered shoes to match.

Elizabeth frowned and waved them away. Her wardrobe had been so extensive that she'd been unable to take even half of her wedding finery with her on the ship to Virginia. She'd had new gowns sewn since she got back, but she no longer took the interest in them she used to. "I'll wear the ice blue with the lace collar," she said absently. "I've nothing special planned for—"

Someone knocked, and Bridget signaled Mary to answer the door. Mary conferred with a liveried footman, then hurried back to Elizabeth.

"M'lady, Lord Dunmore is here insisting to see you at once."

Elizabeth's hands flew to her hair. "Are you finished with this?" she asked Bridget. "Good. Go downstairs and tell m'lord that I will receive him directly." She waved to the nearest maid. "Well? My gown, quickly."

There was a gasp from the serving girl behind her, and Elizabeth glanced toward the doorway. Her husband, Edward Lindsey, was standing there glaring at her.

Elizabeth covered her surprise with a formal greeting. "M'lord." Mary draped a dressing gown over Elizabeth's thin ivory-colored shift, and Elizabeth rose to offer her husband her hand. "You are welcome."

Edward frowned. "Out. All of you," he ordered. "I wish to speak with Lady Dunmore alone." The maids took flight like a flock of frightened sparrows.

Elizabeth withdrew her hand and regarded him coolly. She was frightened of what he might do to her, but she'd not let him see it. "I trust you are not displeased with me, Edward."

"Displeased? Displeased?" His face took on a florid cast. "I am furious. You've made me the laughingstock of—"

"To the contrary, sir," she countered with spirit. "I have been the soul of propriety. I came straight to my father's house, and I have been surrounded by servants—some of your own, I might add—since I left Sotterley."

"You knew I wanted you to remain in the country," he accused hotly. "To take horse and ride across Essex like some . . . some gypsy wench . . ." He trailed off and made a sound of derision. "It is most unbecoming."

She shrugged delicately and spread her hands palm up before her. "I was bored, nothing more. I meant no disrespect," she lied brazenly. She'd not admit to him that she'd felt a prisoner at Sotterley, or that she considered his behavior since their wedding to border on the demented. "As for riding," she continued, "I've often ridden horseback from Longview to London with my father, and that requires several nights on the road."

"What you did when you were in the care of Lord Sommersett has nothing to do with this." Edward's pallid lips thinned. "I'll not have my honor besmirched by your behavior."

She stiffened. "What touches your honor, sir, touches mine." Her eyes flashed. "You've heard no gossip about our *personal* life, have you? I assure you, it was never my wish to shame you or to set our marriage up as an object of ridicule."

Edward took her hands in his. "We've not begun this well, have we?"

Elizabeth's gaze faltered and she blushed, withdrawing from his cold grasp. "I think not, and I confess I am greatly disturbed by—"

He leaned forward and kissed her cheek. "It seems the thing to do would be to start again. I apologize for my churlish behavior on our wedding night," Edward said. "I was—"

"We were both overwrought," she soothed. "Will you sit and have coffee with me?" He nodded acceptance, and Elizabeth covered her nervousness by pulling the bell cord to call her maids.

Today Edward was every inch a gentleman of fashion in his long, black, curled wig and shallow-crowned velvet hat. The forest-green coat suited his complexion well, and his slim figure showed off the elegant garments to perfection. Edward is an attractive man, she thought. Is it possible that our marriage can be set right? Her pulse quickened with excitement as she turned back to her husband with a slight smile.

"There is nothing I desire more than being your friend," she said. "If I've led you to believe otherwise, then I am truly sorry."

Edward lowered himself into an upholstered armchair, set his ivory-headed walking stick aside, and struck a courtier's pose. "I'm content to have peace between us, my dear. Actually, since you're here in London, you may as well stay for a few weeks. It's probably more convenient for you to remain at Sommersett House. My house is in shambles. I'm completely redecorating the bottom two floors. Will it be an imposition on Lady Sommersett to have you in residence?''

Elizabeth shook her head. "Not at all. I rarely see my stepmother."

"But Lord Sommersett is here?" His tone was politely inquisitive.

"Yes, of course. And my brother James lives here with his wife, Margaret. They are away now, but we expect them back within days." She seated herself nearby. "You need not fear for my reputation."

The maids reappeared, and Elizabeth gave instructions for the refreshments. Mary went to fetch them, and Bridget and the others began to set up a small table and clear away Elizabeth's clothes.

"I am thinking only of you, my dear," Edward said. "There are so many lewd women at court. Gossip runs rampant, and I'll not have my wife the subject of malicious attacks." He chuckled. "Actually, your ride to London set them back on their heels. The story was so preposterous that some were loath to believe it." He rested his hand on the gilded scabbard of his sword. "My groom Dickon came running when I got out of the coach and pleaded with me not to wreak some terrible punishment on him and his family. I fear the servants at Sotterley will never be the same."

"I knew you would not blame them for my rash behavior," Elizabeth said calmly. "You are too wise to take out your anger on the servants." Inwardly, she was pleased. Her husband was much like her own father. A few honeyed words would go far in managing him. Such a marriage wouldn't be the worst thing that could happen to a woman, even if she never felt love for him.

Edward laughed again. "Damn me, Elizabeth,

sparring with you will be a challenge. I'd not heard you had such a ready wit."

"Or sharp tongue?"

His brow furrowed. "I fear we both are apt to speak before we think." He pursed his lips indulgently. "You must come to Whitehall with me on Thursday next. I shall have a delightful surprise for you and all the court. His majesty is giving an intimate supper—no more than seventy will be invited—but naturally my wife will be welcome."

"Whitehall? I cannot possibly go with you, Edward. What would I wear?" She spread her hands expressively. "Naturally, my wardrobe here at Sommersett House is full, but there's nothing suitable for supper with their majesties."

"I think you may leave that matter to me. Lady Castlemaine's gown has been finished for days, and she engages a wonderful Flemish mantua-maker. I'll send the woman around this afternoon. Mulberry watered silk, I believe, with an underskirt of pearl. Puffed sleeves, and a tastefully low decolletage. We don't want to show too much of your gorgeous breasts. If we're borrowing Lady Castlemaine's seamstress, it's best to let Barbara outshine you. My waistcoat and breeches are in pearl and mulberry, and we will match nicely. You'll need gold brocade . . ."

Elizabeth lowered her lashes modestly and gave her husband the appearance of her full attention as he chattered on. The thought occurred to her that she had accused Cain of being vain of his appearance. The remark seemed silly in light of Edward's peacock attire and obvious concern with the details of high fashion. It was wrong to blame Edward for being exactly what he was supposed to be—a gentleman of the court—but she could not help comparing him to Cain.

Why do I torture myself by thinking of Cain? she wondered. This is my life now, and this is the man I will share it with until death parts us. I must make the best of the situation.

". . . the Dunmore pearls," Edward continued. "I shall see that they are here in plenty of time. I'll send my coach for you, and perhaps—yes, I'll have Lord and Lady Maxwell escort you there. You don't mind if we meet at Whitehall on Thursday evening, do you, my dear? The surprise, you know. I wish to make . . ." He beamed. "I wish to make an entrance."

"Of course I don't mind," she replied dutifully. "Lady Maxwell was an old friend of my mother."

"Excellent. I don't recall the time. My man can tell you when he comes with the pearls." He paused and smiled at her. "Perhaps it's for the best that you did come down from Sotterley. You really are quite beautiful, Elizabeth."

"Thank you, m'lord." Elizabeth found it more and more difficult to retain her composure. Why was Edward so amiable today? It was almost as though he were a different man than the Edward Lindsey she had married. She was puzzled and deeply concerned. Who hadn't heard of men and women who were normal one minute and taken with fits of madness the next? Was it possible that she was wife to a lunatic?

He glanced toward the door. "Send your maid to see what's happened to our coffee, and tell them to bring up a pitcher of ale as well. I'm quite parched."

"As you wish." She motioned to Bridget, then

gave Edward her genuine attention as he launched into an amusing tale about the duke of York and his latest mistress.

The splendid banqueting house at Whitehall Palace glittered with the light of thousands of candles. Lords and ladies, bedecked in silks and satins and priceless jewels, flowed in and out of noisy clusters. Like rare exotic birds, they bobbed and chattered, laughing and slyly whispering to one another, sharing all manner of scandalous gossip and subtle insinuations.

Edward's count of seventy guests for King Charles's intimate gathering had doubled, and there were more servants and musicians than Elizabeth cared to count. Between the talking and the music, the noise was nearly overwhelming.

She had accepted Lord and Lady Maxwell's escort, and they had traveled to Whitehall by river rather than coach or sedan chair. "London is far too dangerous at night," Lord Maxwell had insisted. "Footpads and scoundrels. The hanging trees at Tyburn bear heavy fruit, but it has scant effect on the crime."

The journey by boat was not without its own dangers. The tide was swift in the Thames, and the tricky run beneath London Bridge never failed to make Elizabeth's heart pound with excitement. Tonight, a heavy black, choking fog, fueled by thousands of smoking chimneys, had hung over the city. Even though the tilt-boat was canopied, the ladies had been forced to mask their faces and cover their hair to keep from becoming dirty before they reached the palace.

When they had safely disembarked at Whitehall Stairs, Elizabeth was surprised to see that

Lady Maxwell was adorned with beauty patches and a great deal of facepaint. She also wore a vermillion damask gown that revealed much more of her person than Elizabeth thought seemly for a lady of advanced years and plain countenance.

Nevertheless, Lady Maxwell was a favorite of Queen Catherine, and she and Elizabeth were soon formally presented to their majesties. Her majesty was kind enough to ask after Elizabeth's health and to inquire about the climate in the New World. The King had murmured only a few gracious words, but the expression in his eyes let Elizabeth know that the hours spent in fittings for her mulberry watered-silk gown had been well spent.

Left to her own devices, Elizabeth was soon surrounded by soft-spoken, dazzling young courtiers paying her extravagantly false compliments. Although she laughed and made the correct responses, she was shocked to discover that the pageantry of the opulent Stuart court no longer held the same fascination for her that it had before she left for Virginia. The glittering gentlemen with their gilt swords, false curls, and beribboned, high-heeled shoes seemed oddly effeminate, and she found herself giving acid replies to their overtures.

The King disliked sit-down suppers. Instead of being served in the normal manner, the guests wandered about and selected tidbits from small gilt tables set at intervals around the magnificent banquet hall. Forwarned, Elizabeth had eaten before she left Sommersett House. She had no intention of spilling a sauce of hummingbird tongues down the front of her new gown. It was enough to seem to sample the dozens of highly spiced meats and dainty pastries without soiling one's fingers or lips.

All eyes this evening were on his majesty's former mistress, Lady Castlemaine. Rumor was that she had quarreled bitterly with the King. He had danced two contrantos with the Queen, and one with the beautiful Louise de Keroualle. "She is surely the cause of Barbara's pique," Lord Darcey whispered into Elizabeth's ear. "No amount of paint can cover the fact that Lady Castlemaine is showing her age."

Elizabeth gave a noncommittal answer. Barbara had been in and out of favor with King Charles so many times that a wise person took no satisfaction in her adverse fortune. Lady Castlemaine never forgave an enemy, and she had a long memory.

Bored by her companion's court gossip, Elizabeth glanced around the room for her husband. Edward had promised to meet her here, and so far she had seen or heard nothing of him or his promised surprise.

Her father caught her eye and smiled. She nodded, and he resumed his conversation with the lord steward of the household, James Butler. Sommersett had come directly to the palace from an earlier appointment, which was why Elizabeth had come with Lord and Lady Maxwell. He beckoned to her, and she excused herself to Lord Darcey and moved to join her father across the crowded room.

There was a stir near the door that led to the privy gallery, and Elizabeth turned to see her husband enter the room. She caught a glimpse of two liveried footmen behind Edward before the astonished crowd surged around him.

"What is it?" a woman near her demanded.

Lady Godwin-Wills stood on tiptoe and strained her neck to see. "Someone said Dunmore has an islander."

An old man's voice boomed above the clamor. "God's bowels! The man's mother-naked!"

Lady Dixon gave a startled yip and pressed forward, trodding on the toes of her partner. A lady-in-waiting fainted, and Elizabeth was jostled aside by Lady Castlemaine. Caught up in the rush of the curious, Elizabeth was pushed toward the doorway. Then her father appeared at her side and took her arm firmly in his.

"Come, my dear. Edward won't want you to miss his moment of glory." Sommersett's massive bulk plowed a path through the onlookers.

"How dare he?" an angry gentleman cried.

"With her majesty present!"

"Disgusting."

"Lady Castlemaine doesn't seem to mind the exhibition. She's—"

The crowd grew suddenly silent.

The towering black-haired man in front of Elizabeth could only be King Charles. Even seen from the back, his majesty's unusual height and regal stance proclaimed his identity as clearly as the deep plum coat and gold-headed cane. Sommersett stopped short as both he and Elizabeth realized at the same time who was ahead of them.

"Did you bring him back with you from America, Dunmore?" a man beside the King asked. Elizabeth knew that the voice belonged to the Duke of York.

"Yes, your grace."

The duke whispered something to his brother, and the King began to laugh. Immediately, the others in the excited crowd began to speak again, but this time the comments were favorable. King Charles turned away to say something to the lady next to him, and Elizabeth got a clear view of the man behind her husband.

Her eyes widened in shock. She swayed and would have fallen without her father's strong arm to support her. Elizabeth clenched her eyes shut and tried to hold back the blackness that threatened to overwhelm her. "Cain," she whispered, almost inaudibly.

Sommersett's fingers dug into her arm cruelly. "Remember where you are," he hissed.

Taking a deep breath, she opened her eyes and stared full into the dark eyes she'd believed she would never see again. It was Cain. Cain, naked but for a scant breechcloth, his copper-hued skin oiled until it shone, his only ornaments feathered earrings and a collar of gold around his neck.

"Father? What have you done?" she whispered.

"Dunmore," he called out, ignoring her agony. "Well done. Are you certain he's tame enough to ensure the ladies' safety?" He stepped forward, pulling Elizabeth after him. "A prize, wouldn't you say, daughter?" He smiled at his son-in-law.

"He's gentle as a lamb," Edward assured them proudly. "I've had him in training for months. What do you think?" He looked pointedly at Elizabeth.

She stared past him, her eyes still locked with Cain's. Intense rage and hatred shone in that ebony gaze. "I'm sorry," she said. "I didn't know. Believe me, I . . ."

"I didn't expect you to," Dunmore continued. "If you knew, it wouldn't have been a surprise—would it?"

"*Ili kleheleche, dah-quel-e-mah,*" Cain said coldly. My love, do you still draw breath?

Elizabeth paled to the color of old marble and lost her battle with the smothering blackness.

Chapter 16

Elizabeth was being carried in a man's arms. She opened her eyes and struggled to free herself, but waves of dizziness assailed her. Dimly, from a distance, she heard her father's gruff voice.

"Doubtless the chit is breeding."

"The maids will see to her. Don't trouble yourself further, Lord Sommersett." Edward looked down into Elizabeth's face. "Lie still. You're not an easy bundle to carry, you know."

The raw odor of whiskey assailed her nostrils. Edward swayed beneath her weight. "Put me down," she protested weakly. "I'm all right."

He lowered her to the floor. "Are you certain?"

"Yes, I'm fine." She wasn't fine. She felt sick. All she could see in her mind was Cain. Staring into her face . . . hating her. And he had every right. How dare Edward exhibit him like a wild animal? "How could you?" she murmured.

"Could I what?" Edward supported her with his shoulder and half lifted, half impelled her down the privy gallery. His breath reeked of liquor, and his hands were sweaty.

"Bring that man here to make a show."

"He is magnificent, isn't he? My Indian. I've

decided to call him Savage. It fits him well, don't you think?''

"He's a man, not an animal."

Edward scoffed. "He's hardly a man. He doesn't even speak a civilized language. We haven't been able to teach him a word of English in three months. All he does is grunt and gabble in his own tongue—if it is a language at all. I suspect he may be weak-witted. Not that it matters. It's not his tongue that Lady Castlemaine was gaping at. I could make a fortune if I wanted to let him out by the hour." He checked his rush of words and caught her chin in his hand. "Why are you so concerned with this native?''

She pushed his hand away and stepped back. "He came over on the same ship with me from Virginia." Edward doesn't know who Cain is, she reasoned. If Edward discovers the truth, he'll kill him. "I . . . I felt sorry for him," she said quickly. "Didn't my father ask to purchase the Indian from you?''

"He did." Edward blinked as though trying to clear his head. "But I told him the beast was not for sale." His high forehead wrinkled. "I hope you are not too enamored of his muscular charms, madame," he said sarcastically. "I'll tolerate no slut in my household."

"Don't insult me," she retorted. "It was Indians who saved me from the shipwreck and cared for me until I could find my way to Jamestown. I merely feel Christian gratitude for—''

"Savage is no Christian. Bishop Wyndmere doubts the creatures have souls. Save your tender feelings for me, wife." He jerked open the door to an apartment off the hall and dragged her inside.

"What do we do here?" Elizabeth asked. This

was some court lady's chambers. The tiny room contained a curtained poster bed, a fireplace, and a few pieces of furniture. Articles of feminine attire were strewn carelessly around, and a multicolored lapdog yapped at them from a basket by the hearth. "Surely we can't—"

Edward closed the door and locked it, threw off his coat, and began to fumble with his velvet doublet. "But we can," he said, enunciating each word precisely. "The apartments belong to a dear friend. She'll not mind if we borrow them for a short time."

The dog continued to bark as Elizabeth's mouth went dry, and she backed away from Edward. "What are you doing?"

"I think it is time that you did your wifely duty by me, don't you?" His breathing quickened as he loosened the front of his breeches.

Her knees went weak. "Not here," she protested. "Not like this." She dodged behind a walnut farthingale chair. "I'm no kitchen slut that you can tumble without so much as a by-your-leave."

"I am your husband." His doublet slid to the floor. "I have waited long enough for what should have been mine." The dog rushed at him, and he gave the animal a sharp kick. Yipping, the animal retreated under the bed.

Elizabeth scanned the room frantically for a way to escape, but the chamber was small, and Edward was between her and the door. Tears welled up in her eyes, and she took another step backward. "Please . . ."

"You liked my Indian, didn't you? Did you see how I controlled him? How he obeys my every command? Unlike you, Elizabeth. You'd do well to emulate his behavior."

Her heart thudded wildly as she kept backing away. "No," she whispered. From the corner of her eye she spied a door on the far side of the bed and dashed toward it.

The door was locked from the other side.

Edward seized her by the shoulders and twisted her around to face him. With a groan, he closed his wet mouth over hers. She shut her eyes, trying to keep from gagging as his tongue stabbed into her mouth and she tasted the fiery alcohol. He ran a groping hand down the front of her dress and roughly squeezed her breast. "Elizabeth, I want you!"

Panic drove reason from her brain and she struggled to break away from him. "No! Let me go!" she cried. "I won't let you—"

"Won't let me? Won't let me? We'll see what you won't let me do." With surprising strength, he shoved her back against the bed, flung himself on top of her, and began to paw at her skirts.

Balling up her fist, Elizabeth drove it with all her might into his face. Edward cried out in pain and rolled off her.

"Bitch!" he accused. "See what you've done to me." Blood was streaming from his nose onto his white shirt.

Shocked by her own actions, she drew her legs up under her and retreated to the far end of the curtained bed. "If you come near me, I'll hit you again," she threatened in a quavering voice. "I'll not be raped—not even by my lawful husband."

"My God," he whimpered. "What have you done? You've ruined my shirt. How can I show myself? I'll be a laughingstock." He bent over and started to choke. When she heard him begin to vomit, she climbed out of the bed, unlocked the door, and ran from the room.

"Elizabeth! Elizabeth, come back here!"

Heedless of passing couples, she fled down the privy gallery. A knot of people were gathered just ahead, and she heard her father's laughter. A dark hallway led off to the left. She ducked into it and felt her way along the wall until she came to another door. Beyond that barrier lay the privy garden.

The night air was cold on her bare shoulders, but she didn't care. She stumbled into the holly maze and followed the winding path, taking first one direction and then another. Deeper and deeper into the maze she wandered. She knew she had ruined whatever chance there had been of making a new start with Edward.

"Damn his soul," Elizabeth cried bitterly as a holly branch snagged her skirt and she heard the sound of silk ripping. "Damn his drunken, demon-ridden soul."

Across the garden, men's harsh voices were raised. She caught fragments carried on the breeze. ". . . ran this way . . . must find before . . ."

Could they already be searching for her? She picked up her skirts and began to run again. The path split and she hesitated. Both ways were equally dark; either route could lead her to the heart of the maze or back into the open garden and certain discovery. Instinctively, she chose the right passage.

Overhead, the clouds parted, allowing faint rays of moonlight to penetrate the holly tunnels. Elizabeth caught a glimpse of a pale crescent moon, framed against a cold, starless sky.

"So distant," she murmured, shivering in the penetrating dampness. "So heartless." Nothing like the shimmering silver disk that had hung over the beach where she had lived with Cain. That moon had seemed close enough to touch. To hang a bowstring on, Cain had said. *"Nibeeshu,"* she whispered.

Without warning, a powerful hand closed over her mouth. Elizabeth struck out at her assailant and tried to scream, but she could make no more than a muffled squeak.

"Hush, Eliz-a-beth," Cain said softly into her ear. "Promise to be still, and I will let you go."

Tears of fear and joy spilled down her cheeks as she nodded her agreement. When he released the pressure on her mouth, she didn't shrink back. Instead she flung herself against him, kissing his arms, his shoulders, his chin. Frantically, she pressed herself to his naked body, seeking his mouth with her own.

"Cain, Cain," she sobbed. His lips were hard and unyielding, but she was beyond reason. Her arms tightened around his neck as she tasted his mouth, smelled the clean, woodsy scent of his skin and hair. "Darling," she murmured. "Oh, my darling, how I've missed you."

The feel of his warm body next to her blotted out the shame and repulsion she'd felt at her husband's touch. It didn't matter how Cain had found her. It didn't matter if the world ended in the next minute. Now—this instant—she was in his arms and safe.

Cain moaned as her willing mouth opened like a flower for his caress. Their tongues touched . . . retreated . . . touched again. She wound her fingers in his unbound hair, pulling his face down to rest against the tops of her breasts.

"Hold me . . . hold me," she begged. His hands burned like fire where they touched her skin, but she welcomed the burning. Tremors of exquisite pain shook her body. She wanted him

. . . wanted him beside her, over her . . . wanted something . . . "Cain," she repeated.

"*Hokkuaa.*" His voice was deep and throaty. Elizabeth could read the pain in that strained whisper and longed to comfort him.

"I didn't betray you," she murmured between hot, passionate kisses. "I didn't. I didn't." Her hand rubbed circles on his chest, slid down his waist and across his hip. He groaned again as her fingers brushed the source of his torment.

A horn blew, and the sound of running feet reached Elizabeth's ears. They're coming for me, she thought in a distant part of her mind. Still, she clung to Cain, letting her hand explore his hard, pulsing shaft through the thin breechcloth. "I love you," she said. "Do you understand? I love you."

"*Nindau saugeau,*" he replied. "This one can love a person."

"Yes . . . yes." She was consumed by the fire that raged in her blood . . . by the bittersweet ache that tormented her breasts and loins. "I need you."

She guided his hand to the hem of her skirts, then trembled like a leaf in a storm when he caressed her bare leg and inner thigh.

"Does this feel good?" he asked her, "and this?" His fingers brushed the quivering lips of her most secret spot, and she cried out with pleasure and sank her teeth into his arm.

"*Mishkwe tusca,*" he murmured huskily. "You were made for love."

"Be careful!" a man called only yards away from where they embraced. "He could be dangerous." Other voices came from the far side of the garden.

"They may find us, Eliz-a-beth," Cain whispered.

"I don't care," she cried. "I don't care about anything but you." She arched against him as waves of warm desire suffused her body.

He was kissing her again, so possessively that she gasped with delight at the exquisite sensations that demanded total surrender. His hand clasped the back of her neck; his strong fingers tangled in her curls as he slipped to the ground, pulling her on top of him.

She laid her face against his chest, feeling his smooth copper skin. Satin over steel, she thought. Her tongue flicked out teasingly. He tasted of salt and pine forests. "Cain," she whimpered, then took the nub of his nipple between her teeth and nipped it gently.

"*Meshepeshe*," he crooned, crushing her against him as he struggled with her petticoats. His hand found soft flesh, and she whimpered as shivers of excitement brought an unfamiliar wetness to her maidenhood. His gentle fingers stroked and probed until suddenly her entire body was shattered by tremors of intense joy.

For seconds, or minutes, she was unaware of anything else as her mind seemed to leave her body. Then she was floating back to earth, and she felt Cain stir beneath her. "Oh," she murmured. "I didn't know it would be like that."

He chuckled softly. "You be yet a maiden, *weeshob-izzi*." He raised her chin and kissed her. "You do not share a mat with your English husband."

"How did you know?"

He laughed again, so low that it could have been the wind through the holly. "I know."

She was suddenly shy. "Then you didn't . . ."

"Mata."

He rose to his feet and drew her up with him, smoothing down her dress. "This one will have you, Eliz-a-beth. This be not the time."

"I want to be with you," she protested. "I don't care what they do to us."

"I have care."

A new thought filled Elizabeth's mind. "Then you believe me? You know I didn't betray you to the soldiers when you were captured in Jamestown?"

He made a noncommittal sound. "This one does not know what he believe. Come." He pulled her after him down the path. They'd gone only a few yards when the footway opened to a clearing. In the center was a covered bench. "Stay," he ordered her. "Wait the time it takes to light a fire—then scream loudly."

"And you? What will you do?"

Without answering, he turned and left the clearing. Elizabeth stood staring after him until he disappeared in the shadows, then slowly realized her teeth were chattering from the cold. Not knowing what else to do, she did as he bade her.

The minutes passed like hours. What would she say to whoever came in answer to her screams? Her dress was torn and wrinkled, her hair tumbled about her shoulders like a dairymaid's. Even if no one linked her with Cain, her reputation would be ruined. And Edward . . . She bit her lower lip to keep from weeping. Edward would be enraged. It wasn't enough that she had struck him, had prevented him from exercising his marital right. Now she would make him an object of public humiliation. He would kill her. He would kill them both.

She plucked a holly leaf from her hair and

crushed it in her hand. The thorns pricked her flesh, and she felt a warm trickle of blood run down her hand. I'll never see holly again without remembering tonight, she thought. But the pain cleared her mind.

"I love Cain," she whispered. "I love him desperately." Even as the words dropped from her lips, she knew the hopelessness of that love. "I can't be with him . . . but maybe, somehow, I can find a way to send him home to his wilderness."

She gripped the crumbled holly leaf again. I must think of a way to block Dunmore's anger. Edward will never forgive me. Unless . . . With a smile of triumph, she threw back her head and began to scream.

Her cries brought two of the palace guards crashing through the maze and into the clearing.

"Help me! Please! I'm Lady Elizabeth Dunmore! You must help!" She pointed to a path leading into the maze in the opposite direction from the one Cain had taken. "My husband, Lord Dunmore, chased two footpads that way."

"Thieves in the privy garden?" the nearest guard demanded. "We were hunting Lord Dunmore's Indian. His servants said he'd escaped."

"Indian? We saw no Indian. There were robbers—two of them. They tried to steal my pearls." Her hand flew to the string around her neck. "My husband fought them off, but I fear for his life."

"Are ye all right, m'lady?" the second guard demanded in a thick Northumberland burr.

"Yes . . . no. If you could just escort me out of the maze." She rose and took a weak step toward the man. "You must find Lord Dunmore before he comes to harm. Oh!" She gave a little cry of what she hoped sounded like pain. "I'm so cold," she said. "If I could have your coat . . . and . . ."

She stumbled deliberately in the dry grass and dropped to her knees.

The guard ran to catch her. "Are ye hurt?"

"My husband," she repeated with an edge of hysteria. The first guard started toward the path she had indicated, and she gasped and clutched her throat. "But they might come back. Don't leave me unprotected."

"I know the way oot. Ye'll be safe enough wi' me," the Northumbrian said as he removed his coat and put it around her shoulders.

"Oh, thank you," she cried. "Thank you."

By the time they'd reached the outer perimeter of the maze, a crowd of curious lords and ladies had edged into the garden. Elizabeth shrugged off the borrowed coat and ducked into the knot of onlookers. Clouds had covered the moon again, and it was too dark for anyone to see her face.

Hands reached out to catch her, but she dodged away and found the same doorway she had used before. The privy gallery was lit with candles, but all eyes were on Lord Buckingham and Lady Castlemaine arguing loudly at the far end of the room. It was a simple matter for Elizabeth to find the apartments where she'd left Edward.

As she opened the door, the little dog began to bark again. "Shhh," she soothed the animal. "I won't hurt you." Edward's coat lay where it had fallen, and the sound of snoring came from the far side of the bed. With an audible sigh of relief, she retrieved his coat and doublet from the floor and went to his side.

"M'lord," she called, shaking him. "M'lord, you must wake up."

"Whaaat . . ." Bleary eyes rolled up at her. "What do you want, bitch?"

"You must get up and dressed," she said matter-of-factly.

"I . . . I must . . . do nothing. Just . . . sleep."

She laid his clothing on the bed and poured water from a pitcher into a washbowl on the table. Using a woman's shift for a cloth, she dipped it in the water and rung it out. "Let me clean your face, m'lord," she said. "And you must listen closely, so that you can repeat the same tale as I have done."

"Blllaaah!" He sputtered, then winced as she scrubbed the blood off his nose. "What are you talkin' about?"

"You must—" The door opened behind her, and Elizabeth turned toward the surprised serving maid. "Come in," she ordered the girl.

The maid curtsied. "This be m'lady—"

"I know whose apartments these are," Elizabeth lied. "But your lady will not mind. This is Lord Dunmore and I am his wife. We were set upon by footpads in the privy garden. M'lord fought the scoundrels off, but he was injured in the process. You must find my cloak and Lord Dunmore's servants. We will require the coach at once."

Edward pulled himself to his feet and leaned against the bedpost. He blinked and stared at Elizabeth as though she had sprouted a second head. "Footpads? In the garden?"

"You gave them such a sound drubbing that they will doubtless never show their faces here again," Elizabeth proclaimed. She smiled at the girl. "M'lord is a friend of your mistress, and he knew she would want him to recover in the safety of her rooms."

"Have you gone mad?" Edward demanded

when the girl was gone. "What is this nonsense about footpads?"

She lowered her eyes modestly. "You said you did not wish to be shamed by . . . by your accident. I made up the tale to keep you from being a laughingstock."

He swore a foul oath. "You lying slut."

"If I have lied, it is only to protect your name. Now that the deed is done, will you dress and go home, or will you bring the King himself to take part in our disagreement?"

He cursed again, but he reached for his doublet and began to struggle into it. In a short time the girl returned with Elizabeth's cloak and mask.

"Yer servants are waiting, m'lord," the girl said. "And that heathen Injun be wi' 'em. Yer footmen was all astir. They thought he'd gotten away from them, but they found him sleeping in yer lordship's coach."

He's safe, Elizabeth thought as she allowed the maid to drape the cloak around her shoulders and cover her tangled hair with the hood. She'd been terrified that the palace guards would capture him. "If you would be so kind as to drop me at Sommersett House, m'lord," she murmured.

"I shall. But tomorrow you move your belongings to my house. It is more seemly that you reside there."

Elizabeth licked her bottom lip nervously. "I thought that having me there would inconvenience you."

"Perhaps," he growled. "But it may inconvenience *you* more."

Chapter 17

London
January 1665

Elizabeth signaled her maids to draw the curtains of her mule-drawn litter and sank back onto the hard seat, pulling her fur wrap closer around her shoulders. It was bitterly cold, and wind whipped through the narrow streets of Cheapside, muffling the cries of street vendors hawking their wares on the icy cobblestones.

Bridget balanced a covered blanket in her lap. Inside was a velvet-lined box containing a pair of gold earrings that provided Elizabeth's excuse to visit Cheapside and the goldsmith's this afternoon.

Two days earlier, Sommersett had sent a servant to instruct his daughter to come to Michah Levinson's shop at this hour. Elizabeth had no idea what her father wanted or why he had taken this method to summon her. She only knew that she must obey and she must be discreet. The fact that Sommersett hadn't invited her to Sommersett House or come to see her himself told her that there was danger. She had lied to Edward, telling him that she needed to have a pair of ruby earrings repaired. He wanted her to send a servant on the errand, but she'd insisted that the jewelry was too valuable to be entrusted to any servant, and he'd reluctantly given permission for the outing.

Edward had been ill and peevish since the night they'd returned from Whitehall. Three times, the physician had come to Edward's house, and each time Dr. Hartgrove had departed with dire warnings.

"Your husband is not a well man," he'd told Elizabeth as he spread dill seed salve on an ulcer that plagued Edward's left foot. "Lord Dunmore suffers from dropsy and a weakness of the kidneys. He must refrain from strong spirits and adhere to the diet I've provided. No spices, no rich sauces, and no fish. I've bled him repeatedly without improvement. He must have absolute rest and quiet."

Elizabeth had not bothered to explain to Dr. Hartgrove that she had no influence with her husband. Edward continued to suffer from sores on his feet and toes that would not heal, and from a frequent need to empty his bladder. Ignoring the doctor's advice, Lord Dunmore drank himself into a stupor each night. And he and his new bride remained in their separate bedchambers at opposite ends of the palatial house.

Edward had been so angry with her over what had happened between them that night at Whitehall that he had barely spoken to her for weeks. Christmas had come and gone with very little celebration or merriment. He had turned down all invitations to attend dinners and masques, pleading ill health. He had even prevented Elizabeth from visiting her family.

"What would people think," Edward had whined, "if my wife frolicked at playhouses and parties when her lord lay ill? What would you go for if not to ogle other gentleman? I would guard you from the temptations of the flesh, Elizabeth—best you remain at my side.''

Worst of all, although Elizabeth could not stop thinking about Cain, she had seen him only in her husband's presence or in the company of a room full of servants. The only proof she had that she'd not dreamed their meeting in the maze was a sprig of holly she'd found one morning on the snow-covered sill outside her bedroom window.

An inner voice had told her that Cain had left the holly for her, in memory of their time together. How he'd reached her high window, she couldn't guess, but she half believed him capable of any physical feat. She'd placed the holly sprig in her jewel box, where it shriveled and dried among the cold, glittering gems.

Night after night, she'd tossed and turned, wetting her pillows with her silent tears. Why didn't I stay in the wilderness with him? she'd asked herself over and over. Why? She'd tasted the fruit of paradise and traded it for a tarnished dream. She'd exchanged a man like Cain for Edward Lindsey and a hollow existence in his artificial world where glittering jewels held precedence over simple human needs.

Her only triumph over her husband had been her success in bringing her maid Betty to the London house. When Edward ignored her request, she'd ordered two of the grooms and a gardener to go and fetch the girl from Sotterley. She'd threatened to have them hanged if the maid bore the slightest scratch, and Betty had arrived with only a case of the sniffles.

The child was at home this afternoon because there was no room for her in the mule-drawn conveyance. The litter was meant for two, but Edward had insisted Jane come, and Elizabeth wanted Bridget. The two women were squeezed into the front seat, riding backward.

Jane was a sullen wench with a large, hairy mole on her chin, and small, muddy-brown eyes. Elizabeth had disliked her the first time she laid eyes on her, Betty was terrified of her, and Bridget had come close to exchanging blows with the woman on more than one occasion.

"The shrew's naught but a spy for Lord Dunmore, Bridget had reported soon after she and Elizabeth had moved into Dunmore's London house. "He's jealous o' ye, m'lady, and he's set this baggage to watch yer every move. I caught the sly slut listenin' at the keyhole yesterday. I'd sooner drink me mornin' cup from the Thames as trust her for a minute. Bad cess to her, I say."

Bridget had brought more valuable information than the knowledge that Jane was an informer for Edward. With her Irish charm and ready tongue, Bridget had won the approval of the cook and most of the staff. Edward's footman Robert seemed particularly smitten with her.

"Robert says Jane was hired to replace Maggie," Bridget had confided to her mistress. "Maggie was here seven years and loyal to the family. A good maid, Robert said, even though the lord used to take her to his bed. He gave her ribbons and trinkets, but she did it as much for the fun as the pay. Wee Maggie liked a tumble as well as anyone, Robert said." Bridget had giggled. "I'd say the lad knew Maggie well enough."

"Is there more to this," Elizabeth had demanded, "or am I going to have to listen to a detailed account of the slut's activities with every male in the household?"

Bridget had been undaunted by the gentle chiding. "Robert says that Maggie told him Lord Dunmore was a cocksman o' the first degree. But then everythin' changed. Maggie said the master couldn't do *it* anymore. She told Robert that the master's man-thing just laid there like a dead rat, no matter how she tried to tempt it."

"I'm glad to know the servants in this house speak so respectfully of Lord Dunmore."

Bridget ignored Elizabeth's sarcasm. "Lord Dunmore packed Maggie off back to the village she come from. Gave her six months' wages and told her she'd better not show her face in London again. Robert said she married a drover."

Elizabeth had considered carefully what Bridget had related. If Edward's illness had caused him to lose his potency, that might well be the reason he was behaving so strangely toward her. It was possible that he knew he couldn't perform as a husband should and was too ashamed to admit it. She'd felt a surge of unwished-for pity toward Edward. Perhaps he wasn't as bad as he seemed. What man wouldn't be in agony over such a development?

A small, dirty hand clutched at the leather curtain of the litter. "A ha'penny, lady," a child begged. "For Jesus' sake. A ha' penny. I ain't ate in two days."

Jane smacked the child's bony hand. "Away with ye! I'll call the watch!"

The child continued to run beside the litter. "Alms fer the poor," the thin wail persisted. "Fer the sake o'—"

A mulewhip cracked, and Elizabeth heard a child scream. "What's amiss?" Elizabeth cried. Drawing back the curtain, she ordered the head

groom to halt the mules and leaned out of the
litter to see what had happened.

A short distance behind the second mule, the
ragged urchin lay heels over head on the dirt- and
manure-encrusted cobblestones, emitting a series
of bloodcurdling shrieks.

"What did you do to that child?" Elizabeth demanded of the startled groom. "Go and see if he's
seriously hurt."

"Nothin' to fret yerself about, lady," Jane said.
"Jest another beggar. They's fierce in the winter." She turned sharp eyes on the groom. "Are
ye daft, man?" she accused. "That ye'd let such
filth put her hand on Lord Dunmore's litter. The
master will ha' yer hide, he will."

Meanwhile, the object of the commotion noticed the groom advancing with the whip still in
his hand, picked himself up from the mud, and
vanished into the nearest alley.

"Wait," Elizabeth called after the child. "Come
back." Immediately, three more equally dirty
children gathered around the litter begging for
pennies.

"Fer me baby sister!" one shouted.

"Me mam! Me mam's wi' chile and dyin' fer
want o' bread!"

They shoved and scratched at each other like
feral cats, and Elizabeth realized with horror that
she could not tell the age or sex of the children.
Had there always been so many of them running
wild on the streets of London? Their pale, pinched
faces reminded her of old men, and the filthy rags
they wore left more flesh exposed than covered.

"Alms, alms, lady," they cried. One dodged a
hoof from the lead mule and ducked under the
animal's belly, coming around the far side of the

litter to grab at Bridget's basket. "A penny! A penny fer bread!"

Elizabeth gagged as a stench like ten-day-old chicken hit her, and she recoiled, realizing that the sickening odor came from the children. Tears sprang from her eyes as she drew away from the scabbed faces and clawing, chilblained hands.

"I'm nay t' blame if yer crawling with lice, lady," Jane warned.

"Bridget, give them money, they're starving," Elizabeth said.

"I've nothin' smaller'n pennies, m'lady."

More waifs were dashing from the alleys and crowding around the litter. They pushed and shoved, knocking the smaller children to the cobblestones.

"Give them whatever you have!" Elizabeth insisted. "Quickly, before anyone else is hurt."

Frowning with disapproval, the Irish maid pulled back her curtain and threw the coins over the beggars' heads. Silver coins hit and rolled across the cobblestones, and the screaming children scattered to retrieve them.

One runny-nosed moppet sat on the ground and cried. Out of pity, Elizabeth fumbled for the ring on her finger.

"No, m'lady!" Bridget cried. "Ye'll ha' the wretch hanged for thievery!"

"Move on," Jane shouted at the grooms. Dunmore's hard-faced men-at-arms closed in around the litter. "We'll be pestered no end now, madame," Jane chided. "Word'll spread, and ye'll not be able t' set foot out o' yer house. They're like rats in a pantry. Show 'em a few crumbs, and they'll steal ye blind."

Elizabeth shut her eyes and tried to block out the shriveled face of the smallest child. She shuddered. The poor abandoned their children when they could no longer feed them; there were hundreds of strays . . . thousands. A few were taken in by kindly people; more were used for thievery, prostitution, and all manner of evil.

The Sommersetts gave to the poor as a matter of course; charity toward the unfortunate was a duty of the upper classes. But as the mule litter moved along the noisy, crowded street, Elizabeth questioned for the first time a world in which some should have so much and others so little.

The groom called to the lead mule and the conveyance came to a stop. "The Jew's shop, lady."

Inside, Elizabeth was greeted warmly by Micah Levinson himself. "It is always a pleasure to receive you, Lady Dunmore," he said. "My family shared the joy of knowing you were not lost at sea."

Elizabeth smiled. The Levinsons had been staunch allies to the Sommersetts since the days of the terrible massacre at York. John Sommersett, called John the Ready, had taken eight members of Micah's family into his home and protected them during the riots. In turn, the Levinsons had informed Harry Sommersett of his impending arrest before Queen Elizabeth could have him thrown in the Tower for high treason. Harry had escaped to France until good Levinson gold could buy his pardon two years later. The tradition of friendship and loyalty between the families had remained firm despite the turmoil of Cromwell's reign and King Charles's return to the throne.

"It is good to see you too, Master Levinson," Elizabeth murmured. "I trust that Mistress Ruth is well in mind and body."

"Thank God," he affirmed. "How may I help you today, lady?"

Elizabeth glanced at Bridget. "A ruby has come loose from its setting. I thought perhaps you might repair it for me. I know you rarely do the work yourself anymore, but—"

Micah nodded. "I'm happy to be of service. If you would just step into my back room."

Elizabeth took the basket containing the earrings from Bridget. "The workroom is cramped. You two remain here," she instructed the maids and the two footmen."

"But m'lady," Jane protested.

"Remain here," Elizabeth repeated sternly. "I will be only a few steps away and perfectly safe." She handed Micah the basket and followed him into the back room, letting the heavy curtain fall closed behind her.

"I have a beautiful sapphire bracelet that you may be interested in," he said, revealing a carved ivory case. "The light is better by the window, if you wish to examine the gems."

Elizabeth moved to the window and opened the box. Inside was a note, unsigned.

Be careful. There are rumors circulating that a certain lord's brother and father may not have perished by accident, but by the hand of one who stood to gain all. Do not despair. The murderer, if murderer he be, suffers mortal illness. Guard yourself against him and secure your claims with an heir before it is too late.

She swallowed the lump in her throat and sank into the nearest chair. Her heart raced and her fingers grew icy as she read the message once more.

"What do you think of the quality, Lady Dunmore?"

Micah's deep bass was reassuring. The chilling fear receded, and Elizabeth found her voice. "Too gaudy," she said. "This color's not true."

"The gems are genuine, m'lady," Micah replied smoothly. "Your father would never condone my passing on to you anything not of the highest quality."

She moistened her lips with the tip of her tongue and forced herself to take slow, steady breaths. *Micah is telling me that Father sent the message. Sommersett would never make such accusations against Edward if he didn't have proof that Edward murdered his father and brother. Father's married me to a murderer, and now he tells me to bear Dunmore's child.*

"The earring is fixed, m'lady," Michah said. "Would you care to think further on the bracelet?" She shook her head, and he took the note and held it to a candle flame until the paper blackened and burned.

"I will consider it," she said. "If I'm interested, I'll return next week. Do you think you'll still have the bracelet then?"

He shrugged. "I am not a fortune teller, m'lady. I cannot see into the future. But I often come into possession of rare items. If I see something I believe you would like, may I have your permission to send word to your home?"

"Please do. And thank you for repairing the earring. You've done a good job, as always. It's impossible to see where it was broken."

Edward's shouting was the first thing Elizabeth heard when she entered the house. As she looked about, trying to decide where the disruption was coming from, Betty hurled herself from the nearest doorway into Elizabeth's skirts.

"Oh, m'lady," she cried. "Lord Dunmore is lookin' fer ye. He come into yer chamber and started throwin' things around. He broke a chair and . . ." She bit off her words and backed away, realizing that she had just clutched her mistress's silk damask gown with soot-covered hands. "I'm sorry," she wailed, breaking into tears.

There was another outburst of swearing from the second floor, and Elizabeth motioned to Bridget to tend to Betty and hurried up the stairs.

When she'd left the house earlier, renovation had begun on the long gallery. The furnishings had been removed, and oil paintings by Rubens and Correggio had been taken down and carried away for safe storage. Carpenters had been noisily sawing and hammering, covering the elaborately painted walls with dark wood paneling.

Now, the workmen stood staring at one end of the gallery as Lord Dunmore, still clad in a silk nightshirt and cravat, scarlet bedsocks, and satin nightcap, tore the last of the tapestries depicting Daniel in the Lion's Den from the untouched west wall. At his feet, the other four tapestries were heaped carelessly on the sawdust-covered floor.

Elizabeth's temper flared. It was all she could do to speak to her husband in a civil tone as she knelt beside a crumpled tapestry and fingered the embroidered velvet. "These arras hangings are priceless. The gold thread alone—"

"Old-fashioned tripe! I'll not have it in my house," he shrieked. "Where have you been?"

"You know where I've been," she snapped. "I went to the goldsmith to have my earrings repaired."

He glowered. "I never gave you permission to leave the house."

"You did. We discussed my going at breakfast."

"So you say. Your place was here, overseeing these lazy bastards." He glared at the master carpenter. "I'll have these walls covered by nightfall or you're all fired," he threatened. "You'll not work again in London, I vow. Thieving dogs, the lot of you."

"It may be that they could work faster if you left them to their task," she suggested. "If you don't want the tapestries, may I have your leave to dispose of them?"

"Burn them. Throw them into the Thames. I don't care what you do with them," he said. "I never want to see them again."

Elizabeth heard a slight sound behind her and turned, shocked, to see Cain standing in the doorway. He wore green servant's livery and a pair of knee-high black leather boots. His hair was drawn neatly into a club at the back of his neck and secured with a velvet bow. He nodded respectfully as their eyes met and cast his gaze to the floor.

Edward twisted to see what she was looking at. "You! Savage!" he commanded. "Gather up these arras hangings and carry them out of the house for Lady Dunmore."

"No, not him," she protested. "I'll have Robert do it."

Edward laughed. "You're afraid of him, aren't you? There's no need." He motioned to Cain. "Come here, Savage."

Cain obeyed him, his face as smooth and expressionless as marble, his movements slow and graceful as a cat's.

"He's too ignorant to learn English, but he understands well enough, don't you?" Edward stepped back nervously as the Indian came to within arm's reach of him. "The livery fits him well, doesn't it? I had it sewn especially. I mean to have Savage ride on my coach and follow me about like a page. Lord Clarion will be green with envy; he's been sporting that African with the ridiculous turban on his head. He takes him everywhere." He glanced from Elizabeth to Cain and back again. "I thought to have a turban made for Savage, but I think I'll just have him wear feathers instead. Feathers are a nice touch, don't you think?"

"I don't want a servant who can't speak," Elizabeth hedged. "I really would prefer Robert."

Edward's eyes narrowed slyly. "You'll do as I say, wife. Everyone in this house does as I say—I am lord here, am I not?"

Icy rain was beginning to fall as Cain followed Elizabeth across the cobblestone courtyard into the shadowy coach house. As soon as the outer door closed behind him, Cain let the heavy tapestry fall to the floor and pulled her into his arms.

"Darling," she whispered. Her heart pounded wildly as he crushed her against him and held her so tightly that she could hardly draw breath. "What are we to do?"

His mouth descended on hers, and she tasted again the sweetness of his caress. Her tongue darted out to ignite the smoldering coals of his passion, as his hands slipped beneath her fur-lined cloak to lay claim to her naked throat and heaving bosom.

"Eliz-a-beth," he murmured, and the single word made her knees go weak. She sagged against him as his lips brushed her throat and ear with feather-light kisses.

"I can't live like this," she agonized. "Oh, Cain . . . Cain."

He kissed her again, and the thrill flowed through her veins to turn her blood to molten lava. Her head fell back, and the cloak dropped away to pool around her ankles. The ache in the pit of her stomach was a grinding force, driving away all thoughts of danger, of discovery.

"He be not your true husband." Cain's soft, slurred English took her breath away. "I be your *uikiimuk*, your husband. You pledged your love of me on a faraway sand. Honor that pledge to-night, Eliz-a-beth, lest death rob us." He lifted her in his sinewy arms and carried her toward the coach.

"Lady Elizabeth! Lady Elizabeth!" Betty's shrill voice broke through the spell Cain had woven around her.

"Wait," Elizabeth cried. "Betty—"

Cain whirled around with her still in his arms. The young maid was standing in the open door-way, eyes huge with fright.

"Oh, m'lady!" she wailed. "I—"

"Betty!" Elizabeth repeated as she slid from Cain's arms. "Come here. Close the door, lock it, and come here."

Betty began to cry.

Cain sighed. "Do not be afraid," he said softly. "This one will not hurt you."

Betty stepped inside the coach house and pulled the door tightly closed. She was still weeping and trembling as she dropped the iron bolt into place. "I . . . I kin understand him, m'lady," she whim-pered. "I . . . I kin understand his heathen talk."

"Nonsense," Elizabeth said firmly. "Cain speaks English. It's English you hear."

Betty's pale face wagged back and forth in the semidarkness. "I speak English. He don't speak no English."

Elizabeth held out her hands to the girl. "Come here, child. You're safe. Cain won't harm you."

Betty stood rooted to the floor, gazing at Cain as though he were the Grim Reaper incarnate. "I don't know no Cain," she managed. "It's him I'm afeared of."

"His name is Cain," Elizabeth said. She glanced sideways at Cain, willing him to remain motionless as she tried to soothe the terrified maid. "He's just a man, Bett, just a good man."

"He's a savage." Betty took a step back and flattened her skinny body against the door. "He's the same'n what tried t' carry ye off in Jamestown. I saved ye then, lady, and I kin save ye again. I'll hold him back while ye run."

Cain's chuckle was like the rustle of satin. "You lock the door, Bettee. Will Eliz-a-beth run through door like ghost?"

Betty chewed at her lower lip.

"What do you mean, you saved me before?" Elizabeth asked. "How did you save me?"

The little maidservant shrank farther into her skin. "I . . . I tole Master Baldwin and the missus. I thought t' save ye from the heathen when ye was out o' yer head wi' the fever." She sniffed loudly and wiped her nose on the back of her sleeve. "I did it t' save ye, m'lady, not fer t' hurt nobody. Did I do wrong?"

Elizabeth exhaled and looked at Cain meaningfully.

He nodded. "I hear truth spoken," he admitted huskily. "This one was wrong not to believe you."

"Why do you think Cain is the same Indian that came to my bedchamber in Jamestown?" Elizabeth asked the girl.

"I heard 'em talkin' on the ship. They said ye went belowdecks and took food t' the Injun. Ye wouldn't o' done that if he weren't the same'n."

"You be right, little one," Cain said, folding his arms across his chest. "I am this man, but I never bring hurt to your lady. She be my lady too."

Elizabeth beckoned, and Betty flew sobbing into her arms. "I never meant no harm," she cried. "I never did."

Elizabeth hugged the girl. "Can I trust you?"

Betty's head bobbed. "Wi' me life, lady, wi' me life."

Elizabeth gripped the girl's shoulders and held her at arm's length. "If you tell anyone what you saw here, Lord Dunmore will kill all three of us."

A squeak of terror escaped Betty's clenched lips.

"We will die," Elizabeth repeated slowly. "He will cut you into tiny pieces and throw you down the well."

Betty moaned as her breath became irregular.

"No," Elizabeth said, shaking her. "You won't faint. You'll listen to every word I tell you. Do you understand?" Betty gave a small sound of assent. "Good. Nothing will happen to you if you do exactly as I say. I'll protect you from Dunmore."

"The savage will scalp me."

Cain chuckled again. "This one promises he will not."

The door rattled. "Lady Elizabeth? Are you in

there?'' It was the footman Robert. ''I have another tapestry.''

''Say nothing,'' Elizabeth whispered urgently. ''I will explain everything to you later. Open the door for Robert, and act as though nothing has gone wrong.''

''He will not believe,'' Cain said. ''The child is crying.''

''Say I slapped you for carelessness.'' Elizabeth pushed Betty toward the door as Cain wrapped the cloak around Elizabeth's shoulders and brought his lips close to her ear.

''Tonight?'' he whispered in Lenape.

''Yes,'' she answered in the same tongue. God help my soul, but I have waited long enough to become a woman, she thought. ''Tonight. But where?''

''Send your women away and I will come to your bed.''

She lapsed into English. ''My chamber windows are barred.''

''*La kella*,'' he murmured. ''This one will find a way.'' He knelt to gather up the fallen tapestry, and when Robert entered, Cain was standing a proper distance from Lady Elizabeth with his eyes obediently cast down.

Chapter 18

When night fell over London, Elizabeth bathed and scented her hair and body, donned her azure nightrobe of the finest silk, and sent her maids to sleep in the outer chamber. All the while, she silently argued with herself that Cain would not come to her tonight—could not.

But you know he will find a way, her heart cried. *This will be the wedding night you never had.*

Thoughts of Cain—the man she loved more than life itself—drove back the fears that threatened to numb her mind. She had not forgotten her father's message; in her heart, she'd judged Edward and found him guilty of a crime no one had dared openly accuse him of committing.

How like Sommersett to warn her. It followed as naturally that Elizabeth knew she could expect little further protection from her family. *Secure your claims with an heir,* her father had advised. Elizabeth shuddered. Did Sommersett believe she would want Edward's child? How could any woman be expected to seek the babe of one so foul that he would murder his own brother and father?

The family comes first, her grandfather, the old earl, had said. How many times had Elizabeth heard those words? They had been repeated by her uncles, her father, even her mother. *Sommersett interests are more important than the happiness or even the life of a single member of the family.* Even as a child, Elizabeth had understood that some Sommersetts were more valuable than others and that a female came very low on the list.

"Father would sacrifice me for the chance to control the Dunmore lands and money," she murmured. "He loves me in his own way, and he would suffer if I died, but it changes nothing." I cannot leave Dunmore and go to my father's house for protection. Pray God that Edward does not realize that.

Edward had been in Virginia when his older brother, the heir to the earldom, had met an untimely death. The official word was that Richard Lindsey was killed in a coach accident. Such things happened all the time. The fact that Richard's father was also killed made the incident a double tragedy. Who could blame Edward for something that happened when he was half a world away? Was it not fortunate for the Lindsey family that there was a second son to inherit the title and fortune?

Edward and Richard had been enemies since they were children. Richard had been an overlarge, overbearing bully. Elizabeth had seen him taunt Edward, pushing him into contests that a slight boy, six years younger, had no chance of winning.

"Soft Sword," Elizabeth whispered into the still room. That was what Richard had called his twelve-year-old brother that Christmas they had all been guests at Lord Sneldon's country house. Other boys had taken up the cry, shaming Edward, and sending him weeping to hide in the stables. "Edward Soft Sword." Could that bitter insult have come true so many years later?

She tried to remember snatches of gossip she had overheard from her mother's friends. Richard Lindsey had destroyed his magnificent stallion because it had lost a race he had bet heavily on; Richard Lindsey had abused maidservants at Sotterley until one, reportedly pregnant with his child, had committed suicide.

Now this same Richard Lindsey was dead and his brother Edward ruled in his place. Did Edward carry the same seeds of madness? Had he murdered Richard to become earl? And if he had, why was it necessary to destroy their old father at the same time? The aging earl of Dunmore had been ill for many years. He'd been carried about in a chair at the time of Elizabeth's betrothal.

"My father believes that Edward had them both killed." Elizabeth stared into the flickering coals on the hearth. Sommersett was a cautious, rational man with a network of spies and informers. "He would not suggest such a terrible thing to me unless he had proof."

She buried her face in her hands and rocked to and fro in despair. Her life was in danger, yet she was expected to play the part of a doting, obedient wife. Did no one care what she wanted?

Someone did. A small sensation of joy bubbled up from deep within. Cain cared nothing for the Sommersett family or for wealth and power. He had professed his love when she was no more than a ragged castaway, a bit of flotsam washed up on the waves.

A smile lifted the corners of her mouth as she traced the curves of her lips with two fingertips, lips she had pressed so boldly against Cain's. "Cain loves me."

And I love him. She breathed in deeply, letting the heady thrill wash through her trembling body. He is no more than a slave. He has nothing . . . but he has everything.

"If I must play this twisted game of power for my father, is it too much to ask a little happiness for myself?"

Outside the window, the wind howled around the corners of the house. Elizabeth folded her hands in her lap, sat quietly, and waited.

Bridget's voice startled her as the Irish girl's candlelit face appeared in the doorway. "M'lady. Lord Dunmore bids ye come to his chambers."

"What does he want?" Elizabeth asked.

Bridget's hand, holding the candlestick, wavered. "Don't know."

"Tell my husband that I am indisposed, and that I will wait on him in the morning." Elizabeth pressed her lips tightly together as she noticed the raised palm print on the maid's face.

"I tried, m'lady. I said 'twas yer woman's time, but Jane made me the liar." Bridget's eyes were red-rimmed. "He asked Betty first, and she swore ye were bleedin' sore."

Elizabeth rose to her feet. "Where is Betty?"

"That slut Jane gave her a bloody nose. I sent her to the kitchen to clean her face and shift."

"Did Jane strike you?"

Bridget shook her head. "The lord. He threatened to send me away, m'lady, if I didn't fetch ye."

Elizabeth sighed and turned away. I'll not let him bed me this night, she swore, not if it means my life.

"Lord Dunmore said ye would make excuse. He said ye must come, or he would send his savage to carry ye like a slab of beef."

* * *

Edward was propped up on a daybed in his bedchamber, the remains of his late supper on a walnut gate-legged table before him. "M'lady wife," he greeted her mockingly as he raised a glass in salute. "How kind of you to join me. Are you hungry?"

Elizabeth glanced at the half-eaten eel pie and the large blood sausage with distaste. Bits of sugar cakes and marzipan littered Edward's napkin; at his beringed right hand lay a gnawed ham bone with fat and gristle still clinging to it. Her gaze lingered on his hand. His fingers were puffy, like some pig's bladder a child had blown up for sport.

"You are ill?" she asked, keeping her voice level despite her wildly thudding heart.

"On the contrary, my dear, I feel much better. My appetite has returned." He indicated the decanter on the table. "Don't just stand there like a stick. Sit down. Will you have a glass of Canary wine? It is quite good."

She shook her head. "You know that the physician has forbidden you any strong spirits." From the smell of the room, her husband had indulged in more than wine. She wrinkled her nose as she caught the sour odor of urine. Edward's chamber pot was obviously in need of emptying.

"God's wounds! The man is a despot, damn his greedy bowels! He knows nothing." Edward sucked a lump of eel out of a rotting back tooth and chewed it. "I'll not have him at me again with his leeches and his bleeding cups." He drained the wineglass and belched.

"You're drunk," Elizabeth accused, taking the offensive. Nothing would make her accept this swine as her husband, and nothing would make her reveal the fear that threatened to cause her to lose her own supper.

"What if I am?"

She caught the inside of her mouth between her teeth and bit down until she tasted blood. "Do you think you can summon me like some kitchen drozel?" she demanded regally. "You forget who I am."

His face reddened as he came to his feet, fists clenched. "And you, madame, forget who I am. I am your rightful lord. I may summon you at any hour of the day, strip you naked, and futter you in the courtyard before all the servants, if it please me."

"You are welcome to try."

"Bitch!"

Elizabeth allowed herself a faint smile. "Your futtering seems less effective than it once was, m'lord. Before you attempt to degrade me, be certain that you can complete the performance."

Edward shrieked with fury, ripped the wig from his head, and flung the empty wineglass at her face. It missed by three feet.

She laughed.

"I'll lock you away," he threatened. "I'll—"

"You'll do nothing to me. Have you forgotten that I am Sommersett's favorite child? My father holds a letter from me, to be opened in case of my disappearance or death. In that letter, m'lord Dunmore, I accuse you of being unable to fulfill a husband's duties and of threatening my life."

Purple veins stood out on Edward's new-shaven head, and his eyes bulged from their sockets. "You lying slut! You're mad as a March hare. I'll have you confined in Bedlam."

"You're not the first to suggest such a solution, but—" Cursing, he lunged toward her. She seized a two-pronged fork from his table and held it before her. "Threaten me at your own risk," she warned. "I know more of your affairs than you realize. It was not fate that made you earl, but human intervention."

Edward's face went slack and paled to the color of lard. Grasping his throat, he fell back against the bedpost and clung to it for support. "What . . . what do you mean?" he squeaked.

She let the hand holding the fork fall to her waist. Her gaze met his, and she read the naked truth in his eyes. *He's guilty. He killed them both.* "I am Lady Dunmore," she said smoothly. "Whatever touches your honor touches mine. I would not be permitted to bring witness against you in court if I wished. Isn't it better for us to live separately in peace?"

He sagged onto the bed. "What are you saying? I have done nothing."

"Nothing, m'lord?" She smiled slyly. "Of course not. Unless . . ." She hesitated, then forced herself to cross to the table and pour herself a glass of the Canary wine. She took a sip, then turned back toward her husband. "My father knows the truth."

His chin quivered. "What truth?"

Elizabeth sighed and nibbled a slice of cheese. "It is enough that you are Lord Dunmore. You need have no fear. Your secret is safe with me." She yawned daintily and covered her mouth with her palm. "I had no wish to be married to the *second* son of an earl. I am accustomed to better things."

Edward licked his lips. "I could kill you as easily."

"I think not," she replied. "It is to your advantage and mine for us to remain good friends. I will interfere with nothing in your life if you will give me the same respect. I will choose my own servants and come and go as I please."

"And my rights as your husband?"

"Naturally," she continued, "friends need not share a bed. Take a mistress and put it about that I am barren. It should gain you a measure of sympathy among your friends."

"While you make a dung heap of my family honor?"

"I have no interest in fleshly pleasures," she lied. "Leave me to my innocent pursuits and I will behave in all ways befitting a modest matron."

"You dare to try and blackmail me into such an agreement?"

"Not blackmail, m'lord. I would never stoop to such disgusting behavior." She spread her hands prettily before him. "But I am, after all, a Sommersett. We are known for bargaining, are we not?"

"I admit nothing."

She raised her chin a notch. "And I accuse you of nothing."

"So be it, woman," he rasped. "But if you swell with another man's child, I'll drown it like a stray bitch's whelp. And if you shame me—by word or deed—I'll have you poisoned. Sommersett be damned!"

"Agreed." Elizabeth dipped into a graceful curtsy. "Good night, m'lord. Sleep well, and do mind your health. For if you die, your title will pass to another, and I'll no longer be Lady Dunmore, but simply another marriageable daughter for my father's house."

She was halfway to her own chambers before she let the tears slide down her cheeks.

* * *

Elizabeth would have sworn that she never slept, yet suddenly he was standing beside her bed. She put out her hand to touch him, fearful that Cain would dissolve as all her dreams of him had done before.

"*N'tschutti*," he whispered huskily. "Dear, beloved one." He caught her hand in his, and she felt his warm reality.

"Is it you?" She blinked back tears of joy, afraid to hope that it was so. "Are you here, or are you a dream?"

"You be the vision, Eliz-a-beth." Flickering firelight played across his chiseled features as he pulled aside the covers and stared down at her unclothed body with smoldering eyes. "My vision, that I am come so far to possess."

She trembled, not knowing if it was from the damp night air or the intensity of his penetrating gaze. "I'm cold," she murmured, holding up her arms to him. "Warm me."

Her pulse quickened as Cain stripped away his servant's jacket and breeches. He jerked at the ribbon behind his neck, and his dark hair fell free to cascade around his shoulders. "I will warm you, *nihounshan*," he promised, leaning over her to press a lingering kiss against her willing lips.

Icy rain pattered against the diamond-shaped windowpanes as he removed his leather shoes and knit stockings. Elizabeth moistened her lips and drew in a long, shuddering breath while a warm, heavy-limbed aching seeped through her.

"You smell like mint," she murmured.

He chuckled deep in his throat. "And wet wool

and tree bark. This one must climb tree to reach your window. Is not easy to climb tree in English shoes.''

Outside, an oak branch scraped against the window, and Elizabeth's eyes widened in fear. ''What's that?''

''Shhh,'' he soothed, sliding in beside her and taking her in his arms. ''Be not afraid of the storm, Eliz-a-beth. The storm is our friend.''

She moaned with pleasure as he pulled her against him and wrapped his arms and legs around her. ''Cain . . . oh, Cain. I wish I'd never come back to England. I've wanted you . . . needed you so.''

''Shhh, I am here.'' His mouth felt hers, and he took her lower lip between his and sucked gently.

''Ohhh.'' She sighed as a fluttering sensation began in the pit of her stomach and curled upward. Her nipples hardened to erect peaks as they brushed against the satin-smooth surface of his chest, and the warm sweetness between her thighs intensified.

Cain's tongue touched hers, and she opened like a spring blossom to his kiss. His mouth was as soft as velvet and sweeter than honey.

''K'daholel,'' he whispered, trailing hot, wet kisses down her throat. ''I love you.'' His hand cupped a love-swollen breast. ''Sweet wife.''

The burning in her loins became a throbbing, incandescent heat, and she groaned in ecstasy, thrusting her hips closer to his, pulling his seeking mouth down to kiss and lick her aching nipples. ''Cain . . . Cain.'' Her voice was low and throaty. ''I've wanted you to kiss me like this . . . to touch me.''

"This one has wanted you, my Eliz-a-beth, longer than you can know."

His cheek was smooth against her naked breast, his breath warm and moist as he stroked her belly and let his strong, lean hands explore her rounded hips and the nest of curls between her thighs.

"Tell me that we do no wrong," she pleaded with him as the insistent hunger grew within her. "You are my true husband, aren't you, Cain?"

He answered with a searing kiss, pushing her urgently back among the heaped feather pillows and covering her with his hard, muscular body. All conscious thoughts slipped from her mind as Cain lowered his weight onto her trembling form, and she felt the force of his pulsating shaft against her bare thigh.

"Touch me, Eliz-a-beth," he urged. His hair brushed across her cheek, and he claimed her eager mouth with fiery, consuming kisses until her head whirled.

Unable to refuse him, she closed her shaking hand around the source of his arousal. His loins tightened, and he groaned as her fingers caressed the tumescent length of his impassioned manhood.

"I want you," she cried. "Love me."

"Eliz-a-beth." His eyes reflected the flames dancing on the hearth, and she was drawn into those flames.

"Please." She writhed beneath him. Her skin burned where it pressed against his; her breath came in heaving sobs. "Cain," she moaned. The aching in her blood had become a fierce wanting, a desire that must be fulfilled or she would die.

He entered her slowly, tenderly, with agonizingly provocative thrusts, letting the swollen tip of his engorged rod caress and tease her willing flesh as she strained against him, intent on release. The brief flash of pain was gone before she could do more than gasp, and then the ancient rhythm seized them and hurled them together toward a mutual, soul-shattering rapture.

Waves of joy washed over Elizabeth as she lay in the safety of his arms and wept bittersweet tears. "Darling . . . darling," she murmured. "My darling husband."

He kissed her hair, winding the love-dampened tendrils around his fingers and tasting them with the tip of his tongue. He cupped her face in his hands and kissed her cheeks, her eyelids, her nose, and her chin.

"Did I please you?" she asked shyly, when the tears ceased to flow. "I never—"

He chuckled softly. "You learn quickly for an English *equiwa*."

She smiled up at him and tugged sharply at a lock of his hair. "And how many Englishwomen have you instructed in the arts of love?"

"Aiiee." He groaned in mock pain. "Only one."

"Good. For I am a jealous *nahanuun*."

Cain laughed. "Your Lenape is very bad."

"I am not your *nahanuun*?"

"You be my *nihounshan*, my wife. *Nahanuun* is the masked animal who washes his food before he eats—the raccoon."

She giggled, content in the circle of his arms. "If my Lenape is bad, it is your fault. All I know I learned from you, husband."

He lowered his head and kissed her full on the lips. "That is *tuun*," he said solemnly. "Mouth."

He touched the tip of her chin. "And this be *uiitshe*."

She caught his hand in hers and guided it to her breast. "And what is this called?"

"*Nunukuun*." He brushed his lips against her nipple and Elizabeth squirmed with delight.

"Show me more," she urged.

His hand slipped lower to rest on her stomach. "*Uoote*," he said.

"And this?" She brushed his swelling manhood with her fingertips.

"*Oslahiila*."

"Liar," she accused. "*Oslahiila* is lightning."

He chuckled. "You know more than you pretend, woman. Perhaps it is not. Perhaps it be *assuun hittuuk*."

"Stone tree?" She giggled. "I think not."

"This one thinks you have enough of word lesson and not enough lesson to make husband's blood run hot."

He buried his face in the hollow between her breasts, and she ran her fingers through his long, dark hair. She moved against him, feeling the warm, sweet sensations begin again. "If you could just show me once more," she teased, "then perhaps I might—"

"A man must be made of stone to satisfy you," he whispered. "But let it not be said a warrior of the *munsee* clan did not give his best."

Desire kindled once more as they whispered words of love to each other and touched and kissed. This time, Elizabeth felt no pain when they came together. Instead, there was a lingering rapture that filled her heart with happiness.

"I love you," she told him when they lay exhausted from their repeated lovemaking. "I love you more than I have ever loved anyone."

"Did this one not tell you," he replied lazily. "On the shores of the great salt sea, I promised you would come to me by your own will."

She sealed his lips with a gentle kiss. "An English gentleman would never remind a lady of her error."

He nibbled at her fingers. "A savage shows no mercy."

She laughed and curled against him. "If only we could stay like this forever," she murmured sleepily. Suddenly she sat up and thumped his shoulder. "How did you get into my chamber?"

"I tell you. I come by window."

"But there are bars on the window. Some relative of Edward's was crazy, and they locked her away in these rooms. Are you a ghost that you can come through iron bars?"

"Did the bars protect this woman who was sick in the head?"

"No. Bridget said she jumped from another window to her death."

"Hmmph. Iron can not hold back flesh. Flesh is stronger." He pushed back the blankets and rose from the bed to stand before the fire. He held his broad hands out to the heat and turned to smile at her. "For many nights I come to your window," he explained. "With my knife, I cut at the wood beneath the iron. Now these bars come and go as easily as an arrow comes from my quiver."

"You were there—at my window? Many nights? But I never heard—"

He nodded. "Good. This one was afraid the English make him clumsy. I go now, but I will come again."

In an instant she was beside him, clinging to

him with all her strength. "Don't go," she begged him. "Don't leave me. God only knows when we can be together again."

He kissed her once more, then pushed her firmly away and began to dress. "There is danger to you if this one stay too long. Let not your heart be sad. I will find a way, Eliz-a-beth. I will take you home to my own land, and we will not be apart again."

"If only we could," she whispered. "But it's not possible. You, perhaps . . . you alone. There might be a way to send you back to the Colonies."

"I do not go alone," he said. "A Lenni-Lenape does not desert his wife."

Tears filled her eyes. "Then our love is doomed."

He moved to the window in three quick strides, then turned back to stare into her eyes. "This *doom* I do not know," he admitted. "But I will take you home, Eliz-a-beth, or my life blood will run out on English soil."

"You don't understand. There's no way for us to escape Edward. Even if he—"

"I will find a way."

"Bold words!" she flared. "From a man who wears Dunmore's livery. You're no more than his slave. How can you let him shame you—treat you like a wild beast on display? Where is your Lenape pride in that?"

"No man can shame another," Cain retorted angrily. "Shame comes from within a man's heart—not from outside. I wear Dunmore's clothes and eat his bread while I learn English ways to take us back across the sea. If you do not see that Dunmore shames himself by what he does, then it may be that there is no hope for us."

"Wait," she pleaded. "I don't—"

There was a gust of wind and driving rain as Cain flung open the window, and Elizabeth was left to weep alone.

Chapter 19

London
April 1665

Passersby scattered as Elizabeth's coach rumbled over London Bridge. She hated the bridge; tall wooden buildings were crammed close together, hanging over the narrow, ill-maintained roadway. She never crossed without having the feeling that the whole top-heavy structure might collapse at any moment and tumble willy-nilly into the Thames.

Betty and Edward's spy, Jane, sat across from her; both maids had accompanied her to the afternoon performance at the Bear Garden, a popular playhouse on the south side of the river. Her husband had joined them at the comedy and then had remained with friends for the cockfights and presumably an evening of gambling and merriment.

Edward had barely spoken to her, but their appearance together would be enough to silence gossip that Lord Dunmore and his new bride were at odds. What others thought meant little to Elizabeth, but it meant a great deal to Edward. Spending an afternoon in public with him was small enough price to pay for her relative freedom.

After they'd left the Bear Garden, Elizabeth had ordered the coachman to stop at a small church. Leaving Jane in the coach, she'd taken Betty and gone into the chapel to pray. Although the interior of the church had been quiet and peaceful, Elizabeth had found no release from her growing unease.

I am not cut out to live a life of deceit and immorality, she thought as the coach bounced from side to side, rattling her teeth and sending up showers of dust and cinders. Regardless of the rampant promiscuity at King Charles's court, cuckolding Dunmore was not an easy thing to live with.

It didn't matter that half her friends' husbands kept mistresses openly, or that the King himself slept with most of her friends—including her sister Ann. The pomp and glitter that radiated around Charles and his restoration court seemed to Elizabeth to be more dross than gold. The endless balls, the fortunes won and lost at dice and dull, repetitive card games were all meaningless. The only hours that mattered were those she spent in Cain's strong arms.

We play a dangerous game, she thought. *Despite* Edward's deteriorating health, he is still capable of having Cain and me put to death if he learns what is happening between us under his very roof.

Her plans to send Cain back to the Colonies had come to nothing. When she had approached her father about making the travel arrangements, he had only scoffed.

"God's heart, Lizbet!" Sommersett had boomed. "Remember who you are! Think ye I'd

risk theft and transportation of Dunmore's valuable slave for a chit's lust? I warned you about
that creature before you married Dunmore. You'll
be in mourning for your lord soon enough. Can
you not see the flesh melting off him like wax off
a candle? When he's decently beneath the sod,
you can play as you like with his pets." He'd
frowned and stared hard at her middle. "Your
mother was with child a month after we wed.
What's wrong with you that you've not produced
an heir? Even a wench would be better than nothing. Hie thee to your husband's bed and stay
there until you swell with babe."

"Think you I fancy going to a murderer's bed?"
she'd flung back in anger.

"Edward paid to have the wheel of his brother's coach loosened. That hardly makes him chief
executioner at the Tower, does it? I've no doubt
he wanted Richard dead, but the old man's death
was probably an accident." Her father had
laughed then and patted her head. "No need for
you to worry. You don't stand between him and
a title. If he hasn't done away with you by now,
he won't." He'd eyed her suspiciously. "Unless
you're putting horns on him with that savage?"

"There's no need to insult me," she'd retorted.

"Well, then," he soothed. "Once you're with
child, Dunmore will treat you like spun glass. Just
be certain his heir has the proper color skin."

"It will."

"Then we've no problem, have we? When
Dunmore dies, I will control all that is his." Pac-
ified, Sommersett had given her a rare embrace
and sent her on her way. "Stop worrying about
men's affairs and put your mind to breeding,"
he'd advised. "I'd never have told you what I'd

learned about Edward if I'd thought you'd be so emotional about the whole affair."

The coach slowed suddenly, and Elizabeth was thrown against the side. She shoved away a curtain and stared out. Ahead, blocking the street, was a funeral procession. From the size of the coffin, the deceased appeared to be a child. Behind the mourning family walked a gloved physician in the customary long, full-skirted leather coat with an obscene birdlike headcovering complete with glass eyepiece and perfume-stuffed beak.

Elizabeth let the curtain drop and sank back against the seat. "Another plague death," she said.

"I saw a woman drop in the street at the market yesterday, m'lady," Jane said. " 'Tis said the deaths are heavy in the poorer sections o' the city."

"That family was not poor," Elizabeth replied. "I've seen that man carrying the coffin before. He's a spice merchant."

Betty's pupils dilated until they seemed to fill her blotchy face. "Cover yer mouth, m'lady," she cried. "The plague is carried on the air."

Betty had shot up three inches since Christmas, and Elizabeth had ordered her two new dresses of good wool with matching aprons and white linen collars, and stout leather shoes. For today's special outing, Betty had worn her new hooded cape of blue Flanders wool. A pity, Elizabeth thought, that her new clothes do little to improve her appearance. *I fear she will always look like a starving robin chick washed out of its nest in a rainstorm.*

"Ye should never ha' let Bridget go t' her sister's weddin' at St. Giles," Jane whined. "She'll bring the plague home and be the death o' us all.''

"Maureen is Bridget's only living sister," Elizabeth said. "Maureen and her new husband, Sean, are moving to Bristol. If Bridget didn't see her today, God knows when they could visit with each other again.''

"Irish rabble," Jane mumbled.

"No more," Elizabeth snapped. "When I need your help to instruct my maids, I'll ask for it.''

"Yes, m'lady." Jane twisted her thin mouth into a lazy smirk.

Elizabeth fumed. Both women knew that Elizabeth was powerless to dismiss her from her post, and Jane never failed to display some trace of impudence when chastised.

In truth, Elizabeth was concerned about Bridget's safety. She had asked for and been given two days off to attend Maureen's wedding. Elizabeth had sent her away wearing a new dress and carrying a gift of silver coin for the young couple. Robert, the footman, had gone along to carry a hamper of meat, cheese, and pastries to contribute to the wedding supper. Robert had come back on time, his breath smelling of ale, but so far, Elizabeth had seen nothing of Bridget. She'd promised to return last night, and it was not like the girl to be undependable.

Elizabeth made two more stops on the way home, first at an apothecary to refill her store of medicinals, and again at Micah's shop to leave a necklace for him to convert to coin. If and when it was possible to send Cain back to America, she would need access to a large sum of money. She could trust Micah to keep the money safe, and to do so without informing her husband or her father.

When they reached the house at dusk, they found total confusion. Servants were running back and forth carrying bundles and trunks, and the large traveling coach pulled by four horses was standing ready at the west entrance. Edward's barking hounds ran circles around the horses, and one of the cooks was swearing loudly at a pot boy.

"What's amiss?" Elizabeth demanded of the nearest serving woman.

"Lord Dunmore has been askin' fer ye, lady," the red-faced wench replied, setting down her overflowing basket of linens. "He's give orders that we're t' leave fer the country at once."

"There you are." Edward swore a foul oath as he ran down the back steps, wig and feathered hat askew. "Have your maids pack your things. We're going to Sotterley." Edward's face was red and puffy, and his usually immaculate attire was the worse for wear. His brown velvet coat was wrinkled, and an oyster-gray stocking sagged around his left ankle.

"But you agreed to attend the masque at Lord Wilton's tomorrow night. I thought—"

"Damn Wilton and his silly affair. Phillip Malsey's cook died of the plague this morning. They say Phillip's senile old mother is taken with hideous buboes of the neck. I played cards with Phillip just last night."

"But surely—"

"We're away to Sotterley, I say." Edward covered his mouth with a perfumed handkerchief. "Take only what is absolutely necessary. The servants can follow with anything else you need."

"Is Bridget back?"

Edward shook his head. "I've not seen the slut. If she's run off, we're well rid of her. Jane can—"

"I'll not have Jane in my bedchamber."

"Then you must make do with Betty and some wench at Sotterley. God knows there's enough lazy mawks in my employ. We'll not risk dying of the plague for a maggot-brained bawd."

"As you will, m'lord," she answered dutifully. "But I must have time to change. I cannot ride all night in these clothes." Edward muttered something in reply, and Elizabeth hurried up to her chamber.

"Bett," she cried when the girl followed her into the room, "lock the door and help me into a riding habit. I can't leave until I find Bridget."

"What if the plague's got her?"

"Then I must know. You stay here and pack my things. Tell anyone who asks for me that I've gone downstairs or upstairs. Tell them anything, but stall them."

In the courtyard, grooms were leading horses from the stable. The smaller coach Elizabeth had just used was pulled behind the big one, and a stableboy was slipping feed bags over the team's noses. Elizabeth glanced toward the coachhouse and saw Cain standing in the doorway.

"Robert," she called to the footman. "Come with me." He followed her into the shadowy coach house, empty now except for the mule litter. That conveyance had been covered with canvas for storage. Cain was standing motionless a few feet from the door. He stared at Elizabeth without speaking.

"Savage, Robert," she said, addressing the two men, "Bridget hasn't returned. We must go and fetch her. We'll need horses, Robert. Have them saddled at once. You can show me where you took Bridget to meet her sister."

"The Indian can't ride, m'lady," Robert said.

"The head groom has been trying to teach him, but I doubt he can manage a horse on the city streets."

Elizabeth looked at Cain, and he shook his head. "He can ride behind you, then," she said. "We'll take Star and one of the geldings. Bridget can ride behind me on the way back. You can ride, can't you, Robert?"

"Aye, lady. I was raised on a farm." He shifted his feet nervously. "I'm more 'n willing to go for Bridget, but it's getting dark. The streets are no place for a lady without a proper escort. You'd best—"

"Fetch the animals. I'll answer to Lord Dunmore when Bridget's safely home."

As darkness fell over the courtyard, it was easy for Elizabeth and her party to slip from the stables unnoticed. The only servant who questioned Robert's appropriation of the riding horses was Tom, the groom, and Robert quickly enlisted him to join the expedition.

Elizabeth took pains not to look at Cain as they rode through the narrow city streets to the tenements near St. Giles. So far, none of the servants except Betty and Bridget knew of their involvement. Both maids were loyal, but she knew it would be only a matter of time before someone else on the staff discovered her secret. Until then, she must pretend to ignore Cain, and he must do the same to her.

Without incident, they reached the house where Maureen and Sean had been living. Sean answered Robert's urgent knock, and to Elizabeth's relief, Bridget came out immediately.

"Oh, m'lady," Bridget cried, "I'm sorry I didn't come when I promised. Maureen was taken ill, and I've been tendin' her. I didn't dare leave her side to tell ye, and I couldn't convince Sean to go either.''

"Maureen's ill?'' Elizabeth replied. "She's not taken the plague, has she?''

"No, m'lady. To tell God's truth, we were makin' a bit merry, and she slipped a child. The bleedin's stopped and her fever's down. I can go wi' ye wi' a free heart. Sean can tend her well enough now. If ye'll just give me time to gather me things and wish her goodbye.''

"Robert.'' Elizabeth motioned to him, and the footman came to take the bundle she had tied to her saddle. "I was afraid you might have taken ill,'' she explained to Bridget. "There are clean cloths, herbs, and a bottle of chicken broth in here. Your sister may as well have them.''

"Thank ye, yer ladyship,'' Sean said. He was a tall, dark-haired Irish farm boy with big hands and feet. '' 'Tis kind o' ye to think o' Maureen. We're grateful fer yer weddin' gift too.''

"Care for her well,'' Elizabeth replied. "If she's anything like Bridget, she'll make you a good wife.''

In minutes, Bridget was mounted pillion behind Robert. "To spare the animal Savage's greater weight, m'lady,'' Robert had suggested. Cain swung up behind the groom Tom, and Elizabeth guided her own mount back the way they had come.

They had gone only a short distance when they found their path blocked by a house fire. Confusion reigned as neighbors aided the stricken family by carrying leather buckets of water to dash on the flames. Part of the burning house had fallen into the street, so there was no chance of getting the horses past the fire.

"We must back up and go around, m'lady," Robert said. "There's an alley back a bit. We can take that."

Robert led the way into the alley, the groom's horse following closely behind. Elizabeth came last. The alternate route was too narrow for a coach and so dark that Elizabeth could barely make out the tenements on either side of the street. Heavy damp fog lay thick between the houses, muffling the horses' hoofbeats and distorting what little she could see. The stench that emanated from the dwellings and the street was strong enough to make her wish she'd brought along one of Edward's perfumed handkerchiefs.

Elizabeth could hear Robert and Bridget talking, but she couldn't make out what they were saying. There were noises all around her: dogs barking, babies wailing, people cursing, and doors slamming, but the everyday sounds seemed more ominous than they did in the daytime. Elizabeth wasn't certain if it was the fog and blanketing chimney smoke or the closeness of the overhanging houses that made her so uneasy.

Footsteps passed them in the darkness, some quick and others shuffling. She heard the squeals of rodents, and once Elizabeth's mount stumbled over something heavy that gave beneath her hoof. Star snorted in fear and shied sideways. Startled, Elizabeth fell forward against the mare's neck and grabbed the mane to steady her seat.

"Are you all right, m'lady?" Robert called.

"Yes." Shaken, Elizabeth wrapped the reins around her wrist. If she fell off, she'd not want to lose her horse and be left afoot here—not even for a moment.

"We're coming to a wider street," Robert said.

"Aye, lady, I can see torch lights. It may be the King's Arms Inn," Bridget added.

Elizabeth made out the shadowy outline of Robert and Bridget as their horse started across the main street. Suddenly, there was a rumble of wheels, and a heavy wagon pulled by four horses lurched around the corner. The groom reined in his horse, and Elizabeth's mare stopped short to avoid running into them.

Without warning, several figures leaped from the darkness. Rough hands closed around Elizabeth's arm and ankle. She screamed and struck out at her attackers, pulling back sharply on the reins to make her mare rear. Something was thrown over her head, and she was dragged from the saddle. Gasping for breath, she fell heavily against a man's chest. He stumbled back under her weight and cried out in pain as her knee struck his face.

"Whorin' bitch!" he swore.

Elizabeth ripped the blanket off her head and drove the palm of her hand into her assailant's nose. He lost his grip, and she rolled onto the cobblestones and scrambled under her horse's belly.

"Get her!" another voice cried.

Something heavy struck her shoulder and the mare's hind leg. Star threw herself forward onto her front legs and lashed out with her back hooves. Elizabeth heard a thud and a shriek.

"Jesus! Harry's down!"

The mare's reins were still wrapped around Elizabeth's wrist. As the terrified animal thrashed and threw her head about, Elizabeth thought her arm would be ripped from her socket. "Cain!" she screamed. "Help me!"

Bridget was shouting for the watch. "Robbers! she cried shrilly. "Call the watch! Murder!"

A hand caught hold of Elizabeth's hair and yanked hard, trying to drag her out from under the horse. She twisted her head and sank her teeth into bare flesh. There was another yell and then her hair was free. Elizabeth grabbed the saddle and tried to pull herself up. Her legs tangled in her skirts, and she fell, then ducked under the mare's neck and put her back against the wall. She pulled Star tightly against her, so that the animal was between her and the scuffling figures.

Someone seized the mare's bridle, and the animal bared her teeth and snaked her head out viciously at the newcomer. He shrank back, then moaned and crumbled to the ground.

"Eliz-a-beth?"

"I'm here!"

Men were running with torches. Elizabeth caught sight of Robert with a cudgel in his hand standing over a fallen man. Tom, the groom, had blood streaming down his face. Bodies lay strewn about like dead rats after a terrier's attack. One man crawled toward the nearest open door.

"M'lady," Bridget called. "Are ye safe?"

"Yes, I'm all right." She sagged against Cain, and for an instant their eyes locked. Then he lifted her into the saddle and leaped up behind her. She leaned back against him, heart pounding. The attack had come so quickly that she'd not had time to be afraid. Now her knees seemed made of jelly.

"We should go before the watch arrives," Robert said.

Elizabeth looked down at the still forms in the street as the terror receded. "But they will want to—"

"Better we go," Cain murmured into Elizabeth's ear.

She slapped the reins against Star's neck, and the mare lunged forward. Elizabeth guided her onto the main thoroughfare and urged her into a canter. Robert, Bridget, and Tom followed.

When the horses clattered across the cobblestone courtyard, Betty came running from Lord Dunmore's house. The large traveling coach was gone, and only a few servants were in evidence.

"Oh, m'lady," Betty called. "His lordship's gone and left ye. He were frightful angry." Elizabeth noticed that Betty's lip was swollen and cracked, and her eyes red from crying.

Cain slid down from the horse without speaking and helped Elizabeth to dismount. Then he took the mare's bridle and waited, head down, seeming not to listen to what was being said around him.

Grizzled John Hay came from the kitchen. "We're t' go at oncet, Lady Dunmore," he explained nervously. Hay was a whip-thin groom recently promoted to coachman. He doffed his cap and glared sideways at his cousin Tom. "Lord Dunmore swore he'd have our hides if we left wi'out ye, lady. We must take the Colchester Highway. His lordship is driving straight through t' Sotterley wi'out stopping. He gave orders that we're t' do the same. God grant the plague don't ride wi' us."

Betty spied Bridget and ran to throw her arms around her. "I was afeared the black death had kilt ye," she said.

John Hay cleared his throat. "We've no time t' waste, yer ladyship. Best ye—"

"We'll leave first thing in the morning," Elizabeth said. "See that these horses are stabled and cared for."

Betty whirled around. "But m'lady, Lord Dunmore said—"

"We are less likely to be swallowed up by the plague tonight than to be murdered by highwaymen. I for one have no intention of being jarred along all night on the road when I could sleep in my own bed." She turned to Robert. "You are in charge here. See that all is ready for our departure on the morrow." She motioned toward Cain with her finger. "The savage conducted himself bravely. See that he receives meat with his supper." With a wink at Cain, she gathered her skirts and swept regally toward the house, then paused in the entranceway. "Betty will assist me this evening," she proclaimed. "You may eat and retire, Bridget. I'm certain you are wearied from the day."

"You heard her ladyship," Robert shouted. "See all these animals stabled until morning."

Elizabeth ordered supper from the remaining kitchen girls and made her way up the grand staircase to her rooms on the second floor. She should just have time to bathe before Cain arrived at her window. For once, they should be able to enjoy a leisurely meal together and the entire night in each other's arms.

She sighed and allowed a faint smile to curve her lips. *A pity I have to follow Edward to Sotterley at all. London would be much more interesting without him.*

Elizabeth leaned forward in her bath and sighed with pleasure as Cain rinsed her hair with warm, rose-scented water. "That feels wonderful," she said. He emptied the pitcher over her head, then

handed her a clean linen cloth to wrap her hair
in. As she stepped from the tub, he enveloped
her in a blanket he'd heated before the fire.
"Ohhh, I love it. I'd trade you for Bridget any
day," she teased.

Cain laughed softly as he seated her on a stool
and towel-dried her hair. Then he took an ivory-
handled brush and gently began to remove the
tangles. "If this one knows you would have hot
water, he does not wash in rain barrel."

She clasped his hand and raised it to her lips.
"Are we mad, Cain? To joke and play when the
black death rages through London? Should we
have followed Edward at once, as he ordered?"

He drew the brush through the length of her
honey-colored hair. "Among my people it is
thought that demons bring disease. It may be that
our laughter and the brightness of your eyes will
keep the demons away this night." He shrugged.
"Who can say? If we race out of the city like
frightened rabbits, it may be that the demons cling
to the back of your coach and creep down our
throats as we run." He raised a handful of hair
and kissed her damp neck. "If I die tomorrow, I
would have this night beside you, my Eliz-a-
beth."

She twisted to look up into his intense gaze.
"You are unlike any man I have ever known."

His dark eyes reflected the firelight. "You know
only Englishmen."

"Here," she continued, "with me, you are as
gentle as a nursemaid. Yet back there on the street
you were . . ." She swallowed, overcome with
confused emotions. "Who are you, Cain?"

He laid aside the brush and knelt beside her.
"Have not fear of me, Eliz-a-beth. Never I harm
you." The angled planes of his face hardened. "I

do not like to kill. I have killed and it may be that I must again—but I find no joy in spilling the blood of man or beast." His chin jutted out defiantly. "Those men in the street were worse than beasts. They would hurt you to steal what is not theirs. Waste no heart's tears on such men." Cain made a quick motion of dismissal with the flat of his hand. "They are nothing."

Elizabeth blinked back tears. "I would not spoil our evening together with dark memories." She laid her hand on the shining crown of his hair. "Sometimes I wonder what it would be like living with you in a wigwam on the shores of America. Are you never lonely?"

He rose to his feet and caught her hand, pulling her up and over to the curtained poster bed. Color stained her cheeks as he whisked away the blanket and tucked her between the sheets with only her hair to cover her rosy breasts. "You would be happy, Eliz-a-beth. I know you would." She scooted up to rest against the heaped pillows, and he settled cross-legged in the center of the bed.

"The Lenni-Lenape are one family," he explained. "We have many clans, but we consider ourselves brothers and sisters. When you came to me, I was alone, but we would not live alone in my land—unless you wished it. In the winter, my people move to a village deep in the forests. There, we spend the cold time feasting, dancing, telling stories, and visiting with our friends and relatives."

"But you must hunt in the winter, or how do you eat?" she asked.

"This be true. Early winter is the time to hunt the bear. His meat feeds us. His fat keeps the winter wind from burning our faces. His skin gives a warrior and his woman a soft, warm spot to make love." He laughed. "I would lie with you on a bearskin, Eliz-a-beth. The old women say it makes boy children."

"And in the spring? What then?"

"When the ice breaks in river, we take . . ." His brow furrowed as he sought the right English word. "*Onsikaamme*, the maple tree gives us . . ." He tapped his forehead with a lean finger. "The words be there, Eliz-a-beth, but they do not always come. The juice of this tree makes a sweet like sugar. Always is time of joy among my people. There be weddings and dancing. Much fun for children. Games. All the time, stories and laughter. The *cocumthas* make . . . They pour the cooked sweet into shapes in the snow for children. When *ake* the earth warms, we plant our gardens."

"You farm?"

"Corn, squash, pumpkin, and beans, we grow. The time of planting is a happy time. Much dancing and laughter. The time of new life. Many babies born." His restless eyes scanned the room and focused on Elizabeth's dressing table. "What be this?" he demanded. He left the bed and examined the box of cosmetics beneath her silver-framed mirror. "This be fine paint, Eliz-a-beth." He returned to the bed with the box. "I like this paint."

Elizabeth giggled. "A gentleman does not pick through a lady's personal belongings," she admonished teasingly. "Be careful. You'll spill the—"

"Hush," he said. He edged forward on the mattress, wet his finger with the tip of his tongue, and touched a bit of powdered color in the case. "I be the story-teller. You be the listener. It has not good manners for a Lenape to interrupt when a teller of tales speaks."

She giggled again as he sketched lines on her forehead with the lip powder. "What are you doing?"

"I tell of spring planting," he said. "This mark means to the young bucks to seek elsewhere for a woman. It says that your eye falls on a mighty warrior." He removed a silver beauty patch in the shape of a crescent moon from a tiny crystal box. "What is this?"

"It's a patch, to cover smallpox scars or warts, or just for fashion. Women wear them."

"Edward wears them. This one has seen. And other men—at the house of your King." He moistened the patch and stuck it on her left cheekbone.

"What are you doing?"

"Shhh. I make medicine. This mark will keep sickness from our lodge and cause your breasts to grow."

"My breasts? What's wrong with my breasts?"

Laughing, he dove at her, nuzzling his face in the softness of her breasts. The cosmetic box tumbled to the floor unnoticed as he savored the sweetness of her lips. Elizabeth tangled her fingers in his hair and pulled him close.

"I do love you," she whispered. "I must be as mad as a bedlamite, but I love you more than life itself." She relaxed her grip on the sheet, and her eyes sought his.

"This one think it grows warm in here," Cain murmured huskily in his own tongue.

"Then take off your clothes," she replied in the same language.

"Do you invite me?" he asked in English.

She moistened her lips with her tongue and raised the corner of the sheet. "It's not cold under here." His clothes followed the cosmetic box, and he climbed in beside her, wrapping her in his strong arms.

Their lips met, and Elizabeth trembled. "And in summer," she murmured. "What will we do in summer?"

"In summer," he whispered, "I will hold you like this . . . and kiss you here . . . and here."

She moaned and pressed against him, thrilling to the rising heat of his swollen manhood. "In summer," she prompted.

Cain cupped her breast in his hand. "In summer, we leave our winter camp and go to the sea. There we fish, and swim, and lie in each other's arms in the moonlight." His tongue teased her nipple to an erect peak.

"And in autumn?"

He covered her with his body. "In autumn, we return to the winter camp, laden with dried fish and clams. We harvest our fields and call our loved ones to join us in thanksgiving. We dance, and sing, and pull dark-eyed maidens into the forest to share promises of joy."

Elizabeth arched provocatively against him. "And what of green-eyed maidens?" she teased. "Is there no hope for them?"

"Ask me in the morning," he murmured, and fire leaped between them as his eager mouth sought hers.

Chapter 20

Sotterley, Essex

The riders galloped past the tiny hamlet of timber-framed houses, over a hand-hewn wooden bridge, and across a lush green meadow where fluffy white sheep grazed under the watchful eyes of two young shepherds. Tails streaming behind them, the finely bred horses stretched their long necks and raced through a carefully manicured section of oak woodland and onto a wide, brilliantly verdant field interspersed with yew hedges.

Elizabeth, two lengths ahead of the nearest rider, urged her mount over the low hedge that blocked her path. The mare took the jump smoothly and responded to the light pressure on the reins as Elizabeth guided her into a tight circle and brought her to a halt. She leaned forward and patted the mare's neck, praising her with soft words. Then Elizabeth looked back across the hedge and laughed. Cain's sorrel stood just beyond the jump with pricked ears and rolling eyes. Cain was picking himself up off the wet grass.

"You're supposed to stay on the horse when he goes over a jump," she teased. Cain's reply was a badly pronounced English oath that brought tears of laughter from Elizabeth.

In the two weeks since they had come to Sotterley, Cain had been learning to ride. It was Edward's wish that his Indian servant be trained as a groom and huntsman so that he could accompany Edward on hunting parties. Tom had been ordered to teach Savage, and so far, progress was proceeding by abrupt starts and stops.

Tom reined in his gray hunter and brought the crop-maned animal back to stand near Elizabeth's. "I'm afraid Savage's ridin' ain't much, m'lady," the groom observed with a wide grin, "but I do fink we're teachin' 'im a bit o' proper talk."

On the third attempt, Cain remained technically in the saddle as the gelding cleared the hedge, and the three riders continued across the flat parkland. Ahead, just inside a grove of towering oaks, Bridget and Robert waited with the noon meal. When they reached the spot where Bridget was spreading delicacies on a clean linen cloth, Elizabeth allowed Tom to assist her in dismounting, then instructed him to return to the manor.

"Yes, m'lady." Tom tugged at his forelock and nodded toward the Indian. "I'll take 'im back wi' me."

Elizabeth shook her head. "That won't be necessary. Robert and Bridget are here with me, and the savage may as well stay too. I intend to ride on to Druid's Well this afternoon. It's not far. He can accompany us. God knows the man needs the practice."

Getting rid of Bridget and Robert after the meal was simple; Elizabeth had only to lay her head on a blanket and pretend she was napping. She heard the two whispering, and then their careful footsteps fading away into the forest. Bridget and Robert had been unable to hide their growing attachment to each other, and Elizabeth was certain she knew the purpose for their abandonment.

Lying on the blanket under the trees was so relaxing that she nearly did drift off to sleep. The April day was warm, and the air smelled of wildflowers and ancient peat. Overhead, birds sang and squirrels chattered, and a soft wind played music through the treetops.

Her dreamlike trance was shattered by a Lenape war cry as Cain swooped down on her, seized her wrists in an iron grip, and pinned her to the ground.

"Oh!" she gasped.

He crouched over her and stared into her eyes. Cain's cheekbones bore stripes of blue and red paint, and his features gave no hint of a smile.

Excitement tinged with fear bubbled up in Elizabeth's throat, and she attempted a giggle. "Where did you find the paint?"

"Silence woman," he ordered. "You are my prisoner. I tell you when you can speak."

Elizabeth swallowed and moistened her lips. He's teasing me, she thought, to get back at me for laughing at him. But an inner voice cautioned, *Are you certain?* She wiggled in his grasp, and he tightened the pressure on her wrists.

"Lie still."

"I would have thought you were too sore to move so fast," she ventured. His nearness was both frightening and intoxicating. Her mouth felt dry, and her heart was hammering as though she'd been running. She could feel the heat of his body through her clothing. "Let me up before you wrinkle my riding habit."

"If Wishemenetoo had wanted his children to ride on the backs of beasts, he would have made horses that did not come away from the rider," Cain answered huskily. His eyes narrowed. "And I am certain he did not mean for *keequa* to make joke at husband's pain."

"Cain," she persisted, fighting her own rising desire, "let me go. Someone may see us."

"Robert and your woman go into the forest. This one does not think they will return soon."

A shiver passed through her. Wasn't this what I had in mind when they wandered off? Didn't I intend for us to . . . "It's not safe," she said. "Edward might—"

"He will do nothing. He will lie in his room and drink the fire liquid until his body dies. Can a man who cannot walk alone ride a horse?"

"He has spies to watch me. He could—"

Cain silenced her with his lips. "I like the taste of you, English *equiwa*," he murmured. "I think I keep you." He kissed her again, and she was unable to resist the singing in her blood. She returned his kiss ardently. He released her wrists, and her arms went around his neck. She hugged him tightly to her, arching against the hard length of his muscular body.

"Cain . . . no." She sighed with pleasure as he lifted her hair to kiss the soft places of her neck. "We can't . . . it's too dangerous."

"I hear you, woman." His hand slipped beneath her skirt and moved slowly, caressingly up her leg and inner thigh. "This one hear your words, but he hears your heart speak louder."

Her breath came in ragged gulps as their kisses intensified, and his hands continued to touch and fondle her. Somehow her skirts were bunched around her waist, and Cain was on top of her, whispering Lenape love words into her ear.

"Are you mad?" she protested weakly. "Not here in the open where anyone could see us. We can't . . ."

"Cannot," he whispered in his soft, lilting way. "Cannot what? This? Or this?" His mouth claimed her again, kissed her in places that he had never done before.

"Oh. Oh." Her body trembled beneath his. Against her will her hands found their way into his clothing to touch and tease him. And before she could gain control of her wayward body, they were locked in the throes of passionate lovemaking.

Later, they lay in each others' arms and gazed up into the spreading canopy of green leaves above. "I want to stay with you like this forever," she murmured.

"This is good land, but too many English. I see why they come to take Lenape land."

"You're right, you know. Many people here are starving."

"How starve? We see many sheep in meadow, and I read here the tracks of deer and game birds."

"The common people may not hunt the deer," she explained gently. "The King claims all deer, or rather the old kings did. Now many lords pay for the right to hunt them."

"How can a man claim deer? Does he feed these deer and bring them into his home at night like dogs? It is another sign that the English are soft in the head. No Lenape brave would let his wife and children have hunger when fat deer walked the forest."

"Such a man here would be called a poacher.

He would be hanged or have his hands cut off as a warning to others.''

''Let me take you into the forest, Eliz-a-beth. We could live there. No man would catch Shaa-khan Kihittuun and cut off his hands. A man who tried would leave weeping women.''

Elizabeth laughed. ''We could build a bower of oak leaves and live like Robin Hood and Maid Marian. In summer it would be a lark—but what would we do when snow fell?''

''Then this one would dress you in fur robes of rabbit and keep you warm in my arms.'' He kissed the tip of her nose. ''There be fish in those rivers and ducks in the sky. We could live as the true people do.''

She sighed. ''It's a wonderful fantasy, but not very practical.'' She lifted his hand and brushed his rough fingertips with her lips. ''I love you, Cain, but how can I make you understand? We can't run off to live like outlaws in the forest. They would hunt us down like beasts and murder us. I was wrong when I didn't stay with you in America. Even then, I wanted to, but I was afraid to follow my own instincts. I believed we were too different to ever know happiness together.''

''And now?'' He cupped her chin in his hand. ''What do you believe now?''

She sighed again and covered his hand with her own. ''I think our love is greater than the differences. But it's too late for us, Cain. If I hadn't been such a fool, you wouldn't be a prisoner to-day.''

He traced the outline of her lips with a forefinger. ''Those days be past. My *cocumtha* say it gains nothing to shed tears over what be past. We must think of tomorrow, Eliz-a-beth. Our children cannot live like this.''

He touched a raw nerve within her. "I don't want to think about children," she said abruptly. *I'm not with child. I can't be. There are a dozen reasons why a woman's courses might be late.* "I want your children someday, but not now. If I had your babe, Edward would not let it live."

"He will die before an *apetotho* of ours."

Elizabeth shivered at Cain's ominous words. She had missed her flow last month, and she was two days late again, but she hadn't been sick. She'd been as hungry as a stableboy for weeks. All the old wives' tales said a breeding woman was sick.

She raised her eyes to meet his. "You can't understand his power," she argued. "Edward is an earl. He can call up many armed soldiers to—" She broke off, at a loss for words. "Imagine a great chief of your people—a man who could lead hundreds of warriors."

"No Lenape warrior would follow a man who seeks to war on children."

"Then the English are different from your people," she said sadly. "You must find a way to escape . . . to go home. There is nothing ahead but heartbreak for us here."

"This one say before, Eliz-a-beth. He does not go alone across the sea."

When Robert and Bridget returned, Elizabeth was still dozing on the blanket and Cain was riding his horse in slow, easy circles in the meadow. Every trace of his Lenape facepaint had been lovingly washed away by Elizabeth.

Before Bridget could pack away the remains of the meal, Tom came galloping across the field. "M'lady!" he shouted. "M'lady! Ye mun come

at oncet. They's evil news from London. Lord
Dunmore bids ye 'urry.''

Minutes later, still dusty from her wild ride,
Elizabeth ascended the wide marble stairs and
joined her husband in the great hall. The ceiling
was arched with dark oak beams, and the dusty
heads of long-dead boars and stag antlers lined
the walls. An open fireplace large enough to roast
a whole steer dominated one end of the room,
and the floor was covered with rush matting.

Elizabeth's nose wrinkled. The rushes were
long overdue to be changed, and the half dozen
hounds lying about the hall did nothing to improve the air. ''Tom said there was ill news from
London,'' she began. ''I—''

Edward set aside the book he was reading and
reached for his wineglass. One bandaged foot was
propped up on a stool, and his eyes looked too
large for his face. ''Steel yourself, Elizabeth,'' he
said. His words were compassionate, but the tone
was as brittle as frost.

Her heart leaped in her throat. She had outrid-
den the others, lashing the mare to get here. Now,
suddenly, she didn't want to hear what Edward
had to say. She had the most dreadful premoni-
tion that the bad news concerned her father.
''What is it? What's wrong?'' she forced herself
to ask.

Edward sipped his wine slowly, smacking his
lips. A trickle ran down from the corner of his
mouth to drip from his chin. Elizabeth watched
the drop in numb fascination. ''God has laid His
hand upon your house,'' he said finally. ''Your
stepmother has died of the plague.''

''No.'' Elizabeth shook her head. They had
never been friends, but still . . . for plague to
come so close to—

"And your brother James and his wife, Margaret."

She stared at him in disbelief. *The bastard! He's enjoying this.* "James?"

"Dead and buried in the garden at Sommersett House."

"And my father?" She clutched the back of an oak settle until a fingernail snapped. The finger began to bleed, but she didn't notice. "What of my father?"

Edward smiled grimly. "God has taken him to His bosom."

Elizabeth felt as though the floor swayed under her feet. "Father's dead?"

Edward motioned for his valet-de-chambre to pour another goblet of wine. "A pity. I understand the title must pass to your brother Charles. He's on the grand tour with his tutor, isn't he? Hardly more than a child, and not robust, I hear."

Black spots whirled in her brain, and she fought back tears. "I must return to London at once for Father's funeral."

Edward leaned over to pat a hound's head. "There is no funeral. He was buried in the vegetable garden in the middle of the night by a gardener and a cook. Danger of spreading the contagion, you know. It's happening everywhere. Dreadful loss, isn't it?"

Fury drove the faintness back. Elizabeth rushed to the table, seized the wineglass from Edward's hand, and hurled it against the fireplace. The precious glass shattered and shards flew in all directions. Yipping, the dogs scattered.

"How dare you?" Elizabeth cried. "You foul whoreson! How dare you sit there grinning while Sommersett's body lies in a row of cabbages?

Even dead, he's more of a man than you'll ever be!"

Edward grabbed his ivory-headed walking stick and raised it defensively.

"You don't have to be afraid that I'm going to hit you," she hissed. "I wouldn't dirty my hands." She whirled and started from the room.

"I will excuse your hysterical behavior due to the sudden shock of your bereavement," Edward called after her. "You may remain in your chambers until tomorrow evening."

She turned back to face him. "I'm not a child to be sent to bed without supper."

Edward's face hardened. "You will do as I say, Elizabeth. Your father is carrion. We both know that that puling child of a brother, Charles, is no threat to me. I am your master now. It would be wise for you to remember that and to make an effort to curb your shrew's tongue."

Elizabeth's eyes flashed. "And if I do not?" she dared.

"Then I would begin ridding myself of those useless maids you keep about." He licked his lower lip. "And I would forbid you the use of the stables."

"You bastard."

"That, my dear wife, will cost you an extra day. Remain in your room until Friday night, when—you will remember—we are expected to attend Lord Bittner and his guests for an evening of entertainment at Bittner Hall."

"I won't go. You can't expect me to accompany you—"

"Oh, but you will, Elizabeth. And I'll not have you in mourning. No dreary black—wear the gold and coral satin, the one with the puffed sleeves and the very daring decolletage. I'm certain Lord Bittner will appreciate your charms."

Her face blanched. "I'll wear the ruby watered silk," she flung back. "If I'm going with you, I need to chose something that won't show wine stains."

Three days later, Lord Dunmore's coachman guided his team cautiously off the Colchester Highway and onto the rutted track that led past Bittner Hall. A misty rain had been falling since morning, and the dirt road was already treacherous. The six horses threw their chests against the harness and sank to their hocks in the mire as they struggled for solid footing.

Inside the coach, an elegantly gowned Elizabeth sat beside Edward and tried to keep from touching him as the clumsy vehicle swayed from side to side. Betty sat across from her mistress, holding Elizabeth's fan and personal effects. Edward's bad leg rested on the far seat, cushioned by a folded blanket.

" 'Twill do you no good to sulk, Elizabeth," Edward said, opening his gold snuffbox and placing a pinch in his nose. He sneezed and repeated the process with the other nostril.

"It is barbarous of you to refuse me time to mourn my father," she replied. "Making small talk with you seems pointless."

"I'll not have you embarrassing me in front of my friends," he repeated for the third time. "Bittner is the world's worst gossip."

"Then he'll have something to spread about, won't he?" Elizabeth said. " 'Sommersett's daughter seems to care little for her father's passing,' " she mocked. "Have you thought of that, m'lord?"

"Nonsense. London is a pesthole. Those of us who have escaped must carry on as bravely as we can. Lady Bittner will play the virginals and that wretched daughter of theirs will bore us with her atrocious harp. Then we'll enjoy hazard or whist—hardly a bacchanalian evening."

"The plague can strike anywhere."

"Miasma spreads the plague. I'd not expect a woman to understand the principles of science, but—"

Edward's words were cut off by a musket shot.

"Stand and deliver!"

Horses whinnied as the coach stopped short and slid off the road. Betty screamed, and Elizabeth leaned from the coach window to see three men on horseback blocking the road ahead.

"What's amiss?" Edward demanded.

"Your money or your life!"

"Highwaymen!" the coachman shouted.

There was a scuffle in the boot of the coach, and another shot rang out. Elizabeth heard a low moan and the thud of a body falling into the mud. Before she could react, the far door was wrenched open and a masked man shoved a pistol through the opening.

Edward struck at the highwayman with his cane, and the pistol went off. Betty gave a startled gasp and tumbled into Elizabeth's lap with blood running from her mouth.

"She's been shot," Elizabeth cried, gathering the girl into her arms.

Betty's eyes widened and she uttered a low whimper. "M'lady," she whispered. "It . . . it hurts. I . . . I . . . can't . . ." She sighed once, and her body went limp.

The masked man yanked Edward from the coach just as another opened Elizabeth's door.

"Out!" the man commanded.

"Murderers!" Elizabeth accused. "You've killed a helpless girl!"

"You'll be next if ye don't do as yer told. Get out, me foine lydy." The outlaw thrust the muzzle of a flintlock into her face.

Badly shaken, Elizabeth laid Betty's still form against the seat and climbed from the coach onto the muddy road. She kept her eyes fixed on the robber's face and tried not to think about the dead girl's blood soaking the front of her gown.

The masked man dragged a limping Edward around the back of the coach and tied him against a tree. "Do you know who I am?" Edward cried. "I'm Lord Dunmore. You can't treat me like this!"

Elizabeth caught sight of the footman's body. The second footman, Robert, and the coachman stood shivering near the lead horses' heads.

"Please," the coachman begged, "I've a wife and four younguns. Don't shoot me."

The man with the mask wore a military coat of faded blue with tarnished buttons. He glanced at the coachman, then at Robert. "I s'pose ye got a sad story, too."

"Don't wan' no trouble," Robert said. His speech was slow and slurred, and he tilted his head to one side.

Elizabeth's brow furrowed, and then she realized what game the footman was playing. "Robert will give you no problem," she said. "He's slow-witted."

The masked man laughed. "What? A big laddie like ye? Clod-skulled, is 'e?" He gave Robert a shove. The footman staggered backward and looked frightened.

"He has the mind of a child," Elizabeth insisted.

"Leave him alone." The third man, still on horseback, spoke with authority. "We've no time for your games."

Elizabeth turned her attention to the speaker. Her gaze traveled swiftly up the high military boots, over the full breeches, black wool coat, and broad leather baldric. His hands were expensively gloved, and a plain serviceable sword hung from his left hip. He wore a starched, white linen cravat, damp now with rain. The upper part of his face was covered by a black silk mask, and on his head was a wide cocked hat.

He smiled and swept off his hat, revealing long yellow curls. "Captain Thomas, at your service, m'lady."

Elizabeth knew the name. Bridget had come home from the market singing a song about the rogue. *Captain Thomas, the scourge of the highway*, flashed through her memory. She raised her chin and stared back at Thomas bravely. "I don't know you," she replied, "but your occupation is obvious. You're a common murderer and a thief."

"Your maid's death was a regrettable accident, and more *his* fault"—he waved toward Edward—"than mine."

"Betty was hardly more than a child. She never hurt anyone in her life. Her blood rests on your soul and that of your cowardly accomplices."

"Shut yer gob," ordered the blue-coated man who had taunted Robert. "Ye'll get nowhere wi' that high-nosed talk."

"Yes," Edward agreed. "Hold your tongue, for God's sake. Would you see us both as dead as your maid?" He looked back at Thomas. "I've little money on me, but you're welcome to what I have. Take it. Take it all."

The third man, the only one not wearing a mask, searched through Edward's pockets and came up with his snuffbox and some silver coins. "They's little enough 'ere, cap'n," he said. "Shall I strip 'im?"

Elizabeth pulled off her rings and her ruby necklace and earrings. "You'll want these," she said, holding them out. The horseman nodded to the blue-coated man, who snatched them greedily from her hand.

"Now you have everything," Edward insisted. "Take your ill-gotten gains and go."

Captain Thomas reined his black horse closer to Elizabeth. "This bold young woman, Lord Dunmore, is she your sister?"

"She is my wife," Edward replied.

"Good. Then you should be willing to pay a handsome ransom for her safe return. Have a thousand pounds English ready. I'll send a messenger to tell you where and when to have it delivered. If you report this to the authorities, you'll not see her again alive." The highwayman leaned from the saddle and caught Elizabeth around the waist.

"No!" She struck at him with her fist, and he twisted her about to sit sideways in front of him. "Put me down." She kicked and squirmed, but her legs were hopelessly tangled in her cloak and wet skirts.

"Cease your caterwauling, woman," Thomas threatened, "before I knock you senseless."

Certain that he meant what he said, Elizabeth stopped her struggling and caught hold of the horse's mane. The captain's arm tightened around her waist, and he pulled hard on the reins. The animal reared, pawing the air. The highwayman set his spurs into the horse's sides, and they galloped off down the road with the other bandits close behind them.

Elizabeth clamped her eyes tightly shut. The last glimpse she'd had of Edward's face in the lantern light caused her greater fear than the roadway rushing past beneath the horse's flying hooves.

Edward looks relieved, she thought. *He's not* going to pay the ransom.

Chapter 21

Elizabeth was soaked through to the skin by
the time the highwaymen reached their destination. When Captain Thomas reined up his
horse in the courtyard of a tumbled-down manor
house and released his hold on her, she slid to
the ground and lay there like a broken doll. The
steady rain against her face no longer felt cold;
she was too numb to feel anything but terror.

Betty's dying face came back to haunt her.
Again and again Elizabeth's mind replayed the
awful picture of her little maid lying in her arms
with blood seeping over them both. For nearly a
year now, Betty had been a constant presence in
her life. The girl had driven her to tears with her
whining, her irrational fears, and her lack of common sense, but Betty had remained doggedly
faithful. Elizabeth had loved her despite all her
faults, and now she was dead.

I should have left her in Jamestown, Elizabeth
thought. I saved her from drowning in the shipwreck to cause her violent death here in England.

Someone grabbed Elizabeth roughly by the
shoulder and yanked her to her feet. "Get on wi'
ye," a man ordered. Her weary mind didn't know

who was speaking to her and she didn't care. She took a step and stumbled.

"Easy there," Captain Thomas said, lifting her off her feet. His mask was gone. "You'll feel better after we get these wet things off and something hot into your belly."

A pretty dark-haired young woman held a lantern high. "Jackie?"

"Aye, Tess," Thomas replied. "We've company for you."

"God's bowels! What have ye done now?" the woman demanded shrilly. She led the way ahead of them, her light bobbing to and fro as they threaded their way through fallen timbers and piles of litter.

Down a flight of stairs and through another doorway Thomas strode, carrying Elizabeth as though she were a small child. At last they came into a firelit room, and he lowered her gently to a high-backed oak settle near the hearth.

"Have ye lost whatever wits ye ever claimed?" Tess fussed. "To bring *her kind* here?"

"Enough," Thomas rumbled. "Where's your manners? The lady's wet and cold. Find her a blanket and something dry to put on." He turned to Elizabeth. "Would you care for a sip of brandy?"

Elizabeth held out her hands to the fire. Nothing had ever felt as good as the warmth of those flames. Her teeth began to chatter, and she was seized with tremors. Thomas thrust a flask into her shaking hands, and she drank without thinking. The strong liquid burned a fiery path down her throat, and in a few seconds, she felt warmer.

"Here." The woman threw a blanket at Elizabeth. "Put this around ye and strip off that fancy gown. God's bowels, Jackie, look at all the blood.

Ye might have pulled the gown off her before ye tried to murder her. What a waste of good silk. The dress won't fetch a quid in that condition.''

"Leave off, wench, before I slap some manners into you,'' Thomas said. "The blood's not hers. Her maid was killed in the game.''

Elizabeth tried to speak, but her teeth were chattering so hard she couldn't get the words out clearly. "I . . . I can . . . can't take off the—''

Tess swore a sailor's oath and sliced the lacing at the back of Elizabeth's gown with an eating knife. The gown fell forward, baring Elizabeth's shoulders, and she stood to step out of the ruined garment. Vaguely, she was aware that Thomas was still in the room and staring at her, but she didn't care. The petticoat strings were so wet that they had to be cut away too. Next, Elizabeth removed her shoes and stockings and stood before the fire clad only in a thin linen shift.

"The rest of it,'' Tess ordered. "Must I undress ye like a babe?''

Elizabeth turned to look at the highwayman. "Sir, if you please,'' she managed, exhausted and near tears.

"Madame.'' He gave a half bow. "I will give you the courtesy of my back.''

Quickly, Elizabeth shed the rest of her wet clothes and pulled a coarse linsey-woolsey shift and gown over her head. Tess bundled Elizabeth's garments into a ball and carried them away.

Elizabeth gazed at Captain Thomas. He was a rather handsome man, younger than she had first supposed, with a large nose, a squarish chin, and laughing blue eyes. "What are you going to do with me?''

He approached the hearth and took the opposite chair. "You heard what I told your husband, m'lady. I intend to hold you here until he pays the ransom. Then you will be returned to your family unharmed.''

"I don't believe you."

He took another drink of brandy. ''I'm not a cruel man. Have you ever heard that Captain Thomas was cruel?''

"I put little faith in the honor of a highwayman.''

"Aye, put yer faith in steel, I say.'' The other two outlaws entered the room with a great stomping of boots and flinging of wet cloaks. The man who had shot Betty was speaking. Without the mask, Elizabeth saw he had thinning brown hair with streaks of gray and a scar puckering the left side of his mouth.

''Or lead and black powder," the other added.

''You have met me, but you've not been properly introduced to my companions,'' Captain Thomas said to Elizabeth. ''This is Will.'' He indicated Betty's killer. ''And Shiner.'' Shiner grinned, exposing two missing front teeth.

Tess returned with several mugs of ale and a great platter of roast pork and bread. ''Thought ye might be hungry,'' she said. ''It bein' such a nasty night out.''

''There's my good girl,'' Thomas replied. She set the food and drink down on a stretcher table, and Thomas pulled her into his lap. ''Give us a buss, Tess.'' She giggled and kissed him on the mouth.

The men began to eat, and Tess offered Elizabeth a portion. She shook her head. ''No, I couldn't.''

''Suit yourself,'' Tess said. ''Starve fer all I care.'' She returned to sit on Thomas's lap again,

sharing sips from his ale and trading small talk
with the men.

Elizabeth pulled her chair closer to the hearth
and wrapped herself tightly in the blanket. She
was warmer now, but still miserable. Her eyelids
felt heavy, and her whole body ached. I must not
sleep, she thought, but the more she concentrated on staying awake, the more difficult it became.

Captain Thomas's gentlemanly behavior did
nothing to alleviate her fears. What if Edward
doesn't pay the ransom? What then? She had seen
the faces of the highwaymen and she knew their
names. Could they afford to let her live, even if
Edward produced the thousand pounds?

The penalty for highway robbery was death by
hanging. Elizabeth knew it, and she knew well
that her captors knew it. *They'll kill me. No matter
what happens, I'm going to die.*

And worse than the thought of death was the
sure knowledge that she would never see Cain
again.

It was two hours before dawn, and the chief
huntsman at Sotterley lay snoring beside his wife
in their sturdy plank bed. The fire on the hearth
had burned down to dying coals, and the single
room of the timber-framed cottage was dark.

The floorboards creaked, and one hound stirred
in his sleep, then settled back down, its nose
touching the still-warm hearth. A shadow detached itself from the blackness and moved silently across the room to the wall where the
huntsman's bow and quiver of steel-tipped arrows hung on a rack of deer antlers.

Cain took down the great English longbow and
balanced it in his right hand, gauging the weight

and the strength of the cast. Then he slung the quiver over his shoulder and removed a steel hunting knife, sheath, and belt from the hook. He glanced over at the sleeping couple and smiled, then crept from the room as quietly as he had come.

The first rays of dawn filtering through the oaks found the Lenape warrior, clad only in moccasins and breechcloth, crouched over the spot where the robbery had occurred the night before. The man called Robert had told him what had happened and that Lord Dunmore seemed little concerned by his wife's kidnapping.

"It ain't natural, I tell you," Robert had protested vehemently. "The Lady Elizabeth be worth every penny of a thousand quid. Were she mine, I'd give the whole shooting match for her, I tell you." Robert had sunk down on his bed in the servants' quarters and buried his face in his hands. "My Bridget will have my hide that I let those outlaws away with her mistress, not to mention the killing of the little one."

Cain had listened to every word, keeping his features immobile, hiding the pain that threatened to rip him in two. "Where happen?" he had asked the footman. "How far?"

Robert's detailed reply had led Cain to this place. The fresh mud told the story clearer than the white man's paper-that-talks could ever do. Here was where the coach slid from the road. Cain put his fingertips into the prints left by Elizabeth's shoes. She had taken only a few steps, and then her trail vanished. Yet the tracks of a mounted horse sank deeper into the roadway here. Clearly, this man had taken Elizabeth up on the animal with him, as Robert had said.

Cain's lips thinned as he studied the hoof-

prints. The animal had shifted from side to side
and reared, proving that something or someone
had startled it. Elizabeth had fought her captor.
There were three horses, but only the one carrying his woman concerned him. A horse, like a
man, had a print different from all others of his
kind. The horse would lead him to the warrior
who had taken his wife, and that man would give
her back before he died.

"Eliz-a-beth," Cain whispered in the Lenape
tongue, "I know you carry our child, even if you
do not." He had been a father before, and he had
witnessed the changes in a woman's body when
she conceives. He had felt Elizabeth's swollen
breasts and seen the hint of deep rose around her
nipples when they made love in the forest. "I
should have spoken."

He paused for a moment in the shadows of an
ancient oak, dropped to his knees, and offered a
prayer to the Great Ones.

"Give me strength," he prayed. "Give me
courage to do what I must do. And if I am far
from my own land, the distance should be as the
width of a bee's wing to you who knows all and
created all. Give me back what is mine or let me
die with honor."

Only then did Shaakhan Kihittuun take the tiny
paint pot from the medicine bag he had recon-
structed so meticulously over many nights. With
the skill of an artist, he performed the ritual of
donning full war paint. At each step, with each
change of color, he repeated the ancient chants,
handed down from warrior to warrior among his
people for time out of time.

When the ceremony was finished, Shaakhan
Kihittuun rose and began to follow the highwaymen's trail. Behind him he left marks of his pass-

ing so plain that a blind man could follow them. If he was killed before he rescued Elizabeth, he must be certain that Edward's people would find her.

Elizabeth lay on a pallet on the floor in the dark. She had slept since Captain Thomas had brought her here in the late hours of the night, awakened, and slept again. She had no idea what time it was, or even if another day and night had passed.

She'd been frightened when he'd risen from his chair and taken her arm. "Come, m'lady, 'tis time you were abed."

"No. Leave me be," she'd protested, knowing all the time that she was at his mercy, knowing that she might face rape or worse.

"The *lydy* thinks ye mean t' tumble 'er," Will scoffed.

"I've never 'ad a gentlewoman," Shiner said.

"No," Tess said, "and ye never will. *Ladies* such as 'er fancies their men wi' full sets o' chompers, even if they're made o' wood."

"Hold your foul tongues, the lot of you!" the captain ordered. "There's no need to frighten the lass. Come along, Lady Dunmore, your honor's safe enough with me. I fancy my women willing."

"Willin' or not," Tess said, "keep yer hands to yerself, Jackie me boy. If ye've any energy left tonight—it's fer me."

Captain Thomas had taken a candle and led the way to a small room that must have once been a buttery, a storeroom for provisions and bottles. There were shelves, a built-in table along one wall, and even a fireplace. The shelves were bare now, except for a few empty bottles and a broken cask. There was one door and no window, and the floor was relatively free of debris. Rolled up in one corner was a pallet and a blanket.

He'd handed Elizabeth the candle. "I'm sorry I can't offer you finer accommodations, but this is the only room I can lock you in and be certain you'll still be here when I come for you. You'll be safe enough from Will and Shiner. Pay no heed to their talk. You can slip the bolt on the inside of the door if you please. Just don't try and lock it on me. It ruins my disposition for the day if I have to break down doors in the morning."

"When can I go home?"

"We'll give your lord a day or two to stew in his own juices, then I'll send a messenger to ask for delivery of the money. You'll go home as soon as I get it."

The candle had burned out during the night. Elizabeth had risen once and felt her way around the room. She'd thrown her weight against the two-inch-thick oaken door, but it had only creaked. The bolt on the far side held firm.

No one had come with food or water, but that didn't matter to her. She wasn't hungry. In fact, she was sick to her stomach; she hoped she wasn't getting ill from the wet ride and the cold. Her head didn't feel hot to the touch, but she was nauseated. Even the thought of food was enough to make the room spin.

The darkness was unnerving. *What if they leave me here to die?* If she had to die, she hoped they would have the decency to shoot her. Even the air here was stuffy. Would it get worse and worse? She wondered how long it took a woman to die of thirst. After the time in the open boat, she'd never wanted to experience that feeling again. *I'll take my own life before I die that way.*

But she knew she wouldn't. She would fight death as she'd always fought the injustices of life. *Suppose I'm with child? Cain's babe?*

She got up again and went to the door. "Is anyone out there?" she cried. "Let me out!" She pounded on the door with her fist. "Let me out of here!"

Upstairs, Thomas heard the banging and turned over in bed. Tess lay facedown beside him, her nude buttocks only partially concealed by a blanket. "Wake up," he said. "Our guest seems to want her breakfast."

"The hell, I will," Tess mumbled into her pillow. "Ye so worried about her *highness*, ye can get up and wait on her."

Thomas slapped her bottom playfully. "Up, wench, and do as I say. You're in this as much as I am, and I have to do all the work."

Tess pushed a tangled lock of black hair out of her face and stared at him with bloodshot eyes. "Taken a fancy to her, ye have, I believe. Ain't gettin' cold feet, are ye?"

"No, pet," Thomas replied lazily. "Unfortunately, the beautiful lady must die as soon as we get our hands on the gold. This is the last hand of my game, and I intend to play it well to the end. She's seen our faces, and she could testify against us in court. It's regrettable, but I'll have to shoot her."

"See us swing, she would. No more pity fer the likes o' us than a Christmas goose. Not to mention that she'd soon say ye weren't—"

"The *real* Captain Thomas," he finished for her. "No, this way is much cleaner. We get the thousand pounds, and Captain Thomas, the dashing highwayman, gets the noose for the murder of Lady Dunmore."

"David Thomas will shit hisself when he finds out what ye done. But he deserves it, the sot. He never did treat ye right, Jackie. Never give ye an honest share when ye were ridin' with him."

Jackie Moore, alias Captain Thomas, reached for the blond wig and settled it on his close-cropped head. "I make a handsomer Captain Thomas than he ever did, and I can shoot straighter than the wily bastard."

Tess rolled out of bed and retrieved her crumpled shift from the floor. "Don't know why I got to fetch and carry fer her when she's gonna end up crow bait." She dropped the shift on the mattress and began to pull on a stocking. "What o' Will and Shiner? That thousand quid would look bigger with only ye and me to share it, Jackie me boy."

He lay back on the bed and crossed his arms behind his head. "That mind of yours is always thinking, isn't it? That's what I love about you. Bee-stung lips, curves in all the right places, and a head on you a bishop would envy. You touched on a weak point in our plan, girl, but not one I haven't been considering. Thomas, the blackguard, was greedy. Once he had his hands on Lord Dunmore's money, he turned on his companions and murdered them too."

"David?"

He laughed. "No, Tess. David doesn't kill them. We do. It only looks like David Thomas did the foul deed."

She giggled. "No end to his evil, is there?"

"Oh, there will be. Rest assured. The King himself will be incensed at this ruthless kidnapping and murder. Captain David Thomas will be hunted down like the dog he is and swung from a Tyburn tree. And that"—he grinned—"will be the end of his life of crime."

An hour later, Tess unlocked the door to Elizabeth's prison. In one hand she balanced a bowl of porridge and a mug of ale, and in the other she carried a half loaf of bread. "I'm comin'," she shouted. "I'm comin'. No need to make such a racket. Ye'll wake the dead." When she opened the door a crack, Elizabeth hit it with the full force of her shoulder.

The door flew open and struck Tess. The food went flying, and Tess fell backward. She opened her mouth to scream, and Elizabeth hit her over the head with a bottle.

Elizabeth dashed down the shadowy corridor and up the flight of steps. The door was missing at the top of the stairs, so she pressed her body against the wall and listened. Nothing. Heart racing, she retraced her steps of the night before to the room with the fireplace. It, too, was empty. She was halfway across the chamber when Tess screamed.

Elizabeth made a break for the far entrance as Captain Thomas entered the room. "What's this?" he said. "Tired of our company so soon?"

She tried to dodge past him as he lunged for her, but he was too quick. He grabbed her wrist, and she swung the bottle at his head.

"None of that now," he cautioned, capturing the other wrist. He tightened his grip until she gasped with pain and dropped the bottle.

"Let me go!" she screamed futilely. "Let me go!"

"All in good time, puss." He twisted her arm behind her back until she stopped struggling. Tears of anger ran down her cheeks.

Tess staggered into the room, a trickle of blood running down from her hairline. "Kill the bitch," she screamed. "Yer gonna kill her anyways—ye might as well do it now!" She rushed at Elizabeth, and Thomas turned to block her with his body. "Yer dead!" Tess taunted. "Dead as a butcher's dinner."

Elizabeth snapped her head to stare into Thomas's eyes. He flushed. "It's true, isn't it?" she cried. "You do mean to murder me?"

"Come along, m'lady. You're much too noisy," Thomas said, ignoring her question. "First thing you know, you'll have Will and Shiner all upset." He shoved her back to the stairs and then down to the buttery.

Elizabeth choked back sobs of terror as he pushed her inside the dark room again.

"You'd best stay put," he threatened. "As mad as Tess is over her split head, she'd be apt to slit your throat. And there's no sense in leaving us before your appointed time."

He slammed the door, and she was left alone with the knowledge that each hour that passed might be her last.

At Sotterley, a rescue party was being organized. The earl had sent a rider for the sheriff and other messengers to summon men from the neighboring estates. He had also given orders that a search was to be conducted for his runaway slave, the Virginia savage.

"I want the Indian alive," Dunmore insisted. "Be certain he is not maimed."

"Yes, m'lord," the master-at-arms replied. " 'E'll not get far. The dogs will scent 'im."

"Naturally, your primary mission is to recover

Lady Dunmore and to capture the outlaws. The sheriff tells me that there is a bounty on Captain Thomas's head. Is that not true, sheriff?''

"Aye, sir, it is," the sheriff agreed. "A hundred pounds, dead or alive."

"And to that sum, I will add another hundred," Dunmore said. "This fiend shall not escape to prey on the innocent again."

"Amen to that, your lordship," the sheriff said. "God willing, we shall find your lady unharmed."

Before the searchers left the manor house, Dunmore sent for Tom the groom. The earl met him in the long gallery.

"Leave us," Dunmore instructed his valet-de-chambre.

Red-faced, Tom clutched his shapeless cap and stared at the floor.

Dunmore glanced up and down the room to be certain they were alone. "I have a special task for you, Tom."

"What be that, m'lord?"

"Remember the job you did for me before?" Tom mumbled assent. "You did it well, and you were well rewarded. I was so pleased that I've chosen you to—"

"Ain't gonna kill nobody else," Tom said. "Wouldn't ha' done it before iffen I'd knowed the old lord would be kilt. 'E was a good man, 'e was. Always 'membered us belowstairs at Christmas."

"How dare you interrupt me when I'm speaking?"

"Ain't gonna kill nobody else, 'cept maybe them 'ighwaymen."

"You will kill who and when I tell you to."

Tom backed away a few steps and blinked. "I liked the old earl! Never meant t' 'urt 'im."

"You altered the wheel on my father's coach, Tom. My father was angry with you because you were careless with one of his horses. You were afraid that he was going to give you the sack, and so you deliberately caused the accident that killed him and my brother."

" 'Tweren't like that, and ye know it, m'lord. Ye told me t' do it. Ye paid me afore ye went to America, and . . . and ye said wait and do it when ye was far away."

"No one will believe your word over mine, Tom. I will find proof—witnesses. You'll hang if you don't do exactly as I tell you. This time, and every time." Dunmore unwrapped a pistol from a roll of cloth. "Take this, Tom. You know how to shoot it, don't you?"

"I were a soldier under Cromwell. Ye know it, well as me. I kin shoot."

"Good. Take the pistol and one of my fastest horses. Be certain that you are at the head of the rescue party. And if my wife is found alive, be certain that she is killed in the fracas."

Tom shook his head and backed away. "Ye wants me t' kill 'er ladyship? No. I won't do it. I likes 'er, I does. She be good t' us. I don't want no part o' killin 'er."

"I'm not asking you, Tom, I'm telling you. You'll kill her if you get the chance. If you don't, and she comes home to Sotterley, we'll think of another way. But you will dispose of the lady for me or you will hang. Do you understand?"

"I ain't no murderer."

"Would you rather hang?"

"Course not, m'lord, but—"

"No buts. Do as you are told. I will protect you, no matter what happens." Dunmore smiled and sipped from his glass of wine. "Believe me, Tom. It will be much easier the second time."

Chapter 22

Lord Dunmore watched from a diamond-paned window until the rescue party galloped away with the packs of dogs running eagerly beside them. He waited until the sounds of hoofbeats, baying hounds, and hunting horns had faded on the wind, and then he sent his valet-de-chambre for Elizabeth's maid, Bridget.

Edward settled into a comfortable chair and propped his bad foot on a rush stool. Nothing had gone as he had expected since he'd returned home to England . . . nothing. "I never meant to kill you, Father," he murmured softly. "Richard, yes. I loathed him, but never you. All I ever wanted was to come first in your eyes."

He squirmed on the embroidered seat as the pressure in his bladder increased. *God's bones, but I cannot go as long as a six-month babe without pissing.* He sighed deeply and took another sip of the sweet Dutch wine. *It's my health that's failed me, not my mind.* If it weren't for the sickness that plagued him, everything would have been different.

Even Elizabeth . . .

She was beautiful, spirited, intelligent. She was well read, she was a flawless rider, and she danced as lightly as any woman at Whitehall. "A perfect match," he said, staring absently into space. "A woman I would have chosen if I'd been given a choice."

If the dropsy hadn't taken his manhood, all would have been well with his new bride. She would have given him sons to be proud of and perhaps daughters as beautiful as herself. "We could have been happy together, Elizabeth, as happy as any married couple can expect."

He'd been unfair to her; he knew it. The shame had been more than he could bear, and he'd tried to drown it in strong spirits. The drink had only made things worse between them—but it helped ease his troubled mind. It padded the ugly corners of the night and dulled the guilt he felt over his father's death.

Now, he and Elizabeth were enemies. He could no longer trust her. She could start rumors against him—not only gossip about his father's and brother's accident, but vicious tales about his inability to act the part of a man.

And Sommersett had conveniently died of the black death. Powerful, vengeful Roger Sommersett . . . Edward chuckled and drained the gem-studded goblet. Sommersett lay in a hasty grave, unshriven and unchurched, while he, Edward, still lived—after a fashion.

Edward's eyes narrowed and his irises paled to the color of opal. As long as Sommersett was alive, I dared not harm his daughter, he thought. Now I will have her dower, her jewels, and a new wife—a meek, biddable creature who knows nothing of my past mistakes.

"And to be certain there are not too many questions about my dear wife's passing," he murmured, "her maid must go." He smiled,

pleased with his decision, and reached for a piece
of candied rose petal. The silly wench who had
died in the robbery had made his task easier.
Now, there was only the Irish slut to deal with.

"Lord Dunmore says to come at once and bring
her ladyship's jewels." Edward's valet-de-
chambre stood in the doorway of Elizabeth's bedroom and instructed the weeping Irishwoman
sternly. "He says you're to step lively."

"He wants me?" Bridget stalled. "Is there word
of m'lady? Is she safe?" She had busied herself
all afternoon in shaking out Eizabeth's summer
gowns and sorting what must be discarded or
mended.

"Are you deaf, girl? Gather your mistress's
jewelry and report to the long gallery immediately."

"Aye, sir. But . . ." She trailed off as the valet
dismissed her with a haughty glare and went his
way. "Why?" she whispered faintly. "What can
he want wi' her things?" With a shrug, she took
Elizabeth's jewel case from an imposing lacquer
cabinet near the window. She started for the door,
then hesitated.

On impulse, she unlocked the box with the tiny
silver key that hung on a cord around her neck
and removed a string of pearls. She knelt beside
a chest, lifted the heavy lid, and slid the necklace
into the secret pocket in Elizabeth's second-best
cloak. Then she refolded the garment and carefully replaced it in the chest before hurrying from
the room.

When she reached the gallery, Bridget curtsied
and held out the jewelry chest. "Ye wanted this,
yer lordship."

Dunmore took the box and frowned. "The

key." She handed it over with trembling hands, and he unlocked the box and glanced over the glittering array of gold and precious jewels. "This is everything?"

Bridget nodded. "Aye, m'lord."

He dipped into the velvet-lined case and held up a handful of necklaces and earrings. A blood-red gem fell from his grasp and skittered across the floor. "There are items of value missing," he said. "The jewelry was your responsibility."

Her face blanched. "No, m'lord. Nothin' is missin'. I swear it. Lady Elizabeth wore the—"

"Silence. You'll speak when you're told and not before. I'll harbor no thieves at Sotterley. Get out of this house and off my land." He shook a grossly swollen finger in her face. "If I lay eyes upon you again—ever—I'll have you hanged."

Tears rolled down Bridget's cheeks. "But m'lord," she protested, "I ain't—"

"Out." His voice was cold and low. "Before I change my mind and forget m'lady wife's affection for you."

Bridget turned and fled, Elizabeth's emerald and gold pendant wound securely in her hair beneath her starched linen cap.

Chuckling, Dunmore retrieved the fallen ruby and began to spread Elizabeth's jewelry out on a card table before him. "Much more than I expected," he murmured, "much, much more."

At twilight, Cain crouched behind a tree and watched as a man left the old manor house and crossed to the well with a bucket. The man tied the bucket to a rope and lowered it, then drew it up brimming with water. When he turned toward the dilapidated stables, Cain slipped toward the back of the building.

Shiner spoke quietly to the four horses as he entered the clear area where they were tied. Most of the stable was crumbling, but two stalls remained intact. He'd offered water to the nearest animal, a bay, then started toward the next one when he heard a rustling behind him.

He dropped the water bucket and turned toward the sound, peering into the shadows of the ruined barn. Captain Thomas's black horse snorted and shifted from side to side, pushing against the tie rope. "Who's there?" Shiner demanded. "Will? Is that you?"

Silence.

The outlaw pulled the pistol from his belt and wound the ancient wheel-lock mechanism to ready the weapon. Then he took the lantern in one hand and the pistol in the other and ventured cautiously into the tumbled-down section of the building. Something stirred beneath a moldy pile of leaves, and he kicked at it.

There was a squeal, and a thin brown rat scurried into the darkness. "Bloody bugger!" Shiner hawked up a gob of phlegm and spat after the rodent. "Keep away a' me. I'll blow yer trotters off." He grimaced and returned to the horses. "Shiner, feed up them horses," he grumbled. "Shiner, see t' the fire. Where in 'ell's that bumfiddle, Will, I wants t' know? Shiner ain't nobody's muck-worm."

He hung the lantern on an oak peg and picked up the overturned bucket. He took two steps, and the black horse pricked up his ears and rolled his eyes. Then Shiner found himself lying flat on his back with a naked devil perched on his chest. The devil's face was streaked with blood and the ashes of hell, and he was pressing cold steel against Shiner's exposed throat.

"Do not speak," the devil warned.

Shiner's adam's apple bulged, and the knife blade bit into his skin. He gasped as warm blood trickled down his neck.

"Listen," the devil hissed.

Shiner groaned assent.

"You have a captive," the devil said softly. "A woman. Release her or you all die."

He brought his red face down close to Shiner's, and the bandit groaned again as he stared into the devil's coal-black eyes.

"Do you understand?"

"Yes. Yes."

The knife blade flashed in the yellow lantern light, and a powerful blow rocked Shiner's jaw. The devil and the stable dissolved into soft blackness.

When Shiner regained consciousness, the devil, Shiner's wheel-lock pistol, and the four horses were gone. He staggered to his feet and ran to tell Captain Thomas what had happened.

"You drunken sot!" Thomas rose from his half-eaten supper and slammed a clenched fist into Shiner's chest, knocking him halfway across the room. "How dare you come in here babbling about devils? I'll devil you! Where the hell are my horses?"

"I tole ye! He near cut me throat. See?"

"God's wounds! Am I to do everything myself?" Thomas seized a pair of pistols from the table and started out the door. "Tess! See to the woman. Take a gun and shoot anything that moves. Will! Will! On your feet, you lazy snaffle-biter. Go out the back way and circle around. Be certain you don't fire on me or Shiner."

Tess began to load a pistol. "Be careful, Jackie,"

she warned. "Could be gypsies if they stole the horses. They's quick ones wi' a blade."

" 'Twere a devil, I tell ye!" Shiner rubbed his aching chest. " 'E took me pistol."

"Take another," Thomas ordered. "You'd better hope we can recover those horses, or I'll string you up by your nuts and leave you for the ravens."

Quickly, Thomas led the way to the front entrance. He pushed open the heavy wooden door and scanned the courtyard from the protection of the doorway. All was dark and still. The moon had not yet risen above the trees, and there was no wind. Ghostly clouds drifted high over the manor house. Thomas took a half dozen steps from the house, then let out a yell and leaped for safety as a flaming arrow arched over his head and buried into the timbered wall.

"Let her go!" a man's voice shouted. "I do not warn you again. Let her go, or die."

A musket shot reverberated through the courtyard, followed by a man's scream. Then there was only quiet.

"Will?" Thomas called. "Did you get him?" A minute passed. "Will!"

They found Will a few yards from the stable with two feet of feathered shaft protruding from his chest and a look of surprise on his frozen features. His pistol and knife were missing, and his hair had been sawed off at the base of his skull.

"What'd I tell ye?" Shiner shrieked. "The devil done it." He sniffed the air and looked uneasily over his shoulder. "I kin even smell fire and brimstone."

"Back to the house," Thomas said.

"What of Will?"

"Leave him. He's not going anywhere."

"I don't like it, cap'n. Why'd 'e take Will's 'air, I wants t' know? I ain't a coward—you know that—but devils . . . I never agreed t' no truck wi' devils. 'E wants the woman, let 'im 'ave 'er, I say."

"You've a rat's arse for a brain. No devil pulled the bow that sent that arrow through Will. 'Twas a man—a forester or another outlaw—but a man. And he'll be a dead man when I get him in my gun sights."

Shiner followed close on Thomas's heels as they ducked back into the house. "A man ye say, a devil I say. Who seed 'im? Who 'ad 'is 'ot breath in 'is face?"

"Tess?" Thomas burst into the room where they'd shared the meal. The roast chicken cooled on the wooden platter. "Tess?" There was no answer. "He's done something to Tess," Thomas warned Shiner. "Watch my back."

Warily, they made their way down the narrow corridor. There was a thumping noise, and they turned the corner to find Tess bound and gagged. Thomas knelt beside her and ripped away the cloth that covered her mouth.

"Where is he? Did he find the woman?"

Tess took a gulp of air and shook her head. "I don't think so. He asked me where she was, but I didn't tell him nothin'. He's a wild man, Jackie. No devil but one o' them blackamoors from Africky."

"The devil I seed weren't no blackamoor," Shiner protested. "They must be two o' 'em."

"Did he hurt you?" Thomas asked Tess.

She shook her head again as Shiner fumbled with the leather thongs holding her wrists and ankles together. "He grabbed me from behind. He come out o' the dark like a wolf. I never seen or heard a thing 'til he had his hand over me mouth.'' She stood up and leaned against Thomas. ''I'm scared, Jackie. I never seen such as him.''

''Did you see more than one man?''

''No.''

''Then 'e weren't no blackamoor,'' Shiner said. ''A devil, I say, 'til I'm proved elsewise.''

The captain shoved a pistol into Tess's hand. ''Hold on to this gun, if you can. I'll get the pretty lady. If it's her he wants, she's our best bait to trap him. Wait here, both of you, and for God's sake, don't shoot me when I come back with the woman.''

As Thomas threw open the door to her cell, Elizabeth woke with a start. ''What?'' she cried. ''What do you want?''

''You're coming with me.'' Thomas grabbed her arm and pushed her ahead of him out of the buttery and up the steep stairs. ''Shiner,'' he called. '' 'Ere.''

Tess and Shiner joined them in the main room. Elizabeth glanced from one to another. ''Has . . . has my . . . Has Lord Dunmore paid my ransom?''

Thomas caught her wrists, twisted them behind her back, and tied them together. ''Find something to bind her mouth,'' he ordered Tess.

''No. Don't,'' she pleaded. Were they going to kill her now? ''Please. I won't make any noise.'' Elizabeth's protests were muffled as Tess gagged her with a length of torn petticoat.

''You've a friend come calling,'' Thomas said, ''an ill-mannered friend.'' He yanked Elizabeth hard against his chest and brought a pistol barrel close to her head.

Thomas dragged Elizabeth to the front entrance. ''You!'' he shouted. ''I have the woman here. I'll kill her if you don't come out with your hands up.''

From somewhere off, an owl hooted. No one noticed Elizabeth's sudden intake of breath or the widening of her eyes. It's Cain, she thought, I know it is. Fear knotted her throat and made her light-headed. *Be careful*, she cried inwardly. *Please, be careful.*

''I have a pistol at her head,'' Thomas said. ''I'll blow her brains out if you don't surrender.''

Elizabeth swallowed hard and shut her eyes.

''What's it going to be?'' Thomas demanded. He caught hold of Elizabeth's hair, and she winced with pain.

They waited, not speaking, and the sound of their breathing was loud in the darkness. Tess was the first to smell the smoke. ''Fire!'' she cried. ''The manor's on fire.''

''The place is dry as tinder,'' Shiner said. ''It'll go up like an 'ay rick.''

''Fetch the box, Tess,'' Thomas said.

''No.''

He whirled on her. ''What did you say?''

''I'll not go back there and risk fryin' fer yer gold. Fetch it yerself, if ye want it so bad.'' Thomas slapped her across the face, and she backed away, crying. ''No, I ain't goin' back alone,'' she repeated. ''Smack me all ye want, but I ain't that stupid.''

''Wait here then,'' he said, shoving Elizabeth down to the floor. ''Don't move, and don't let loose of the wench. If he means to take her, he'll not risk killing her.''

Elizabeth laid her head against a fallen beam and tried not to panic. The cloth cut into the sides of her mouth and made it difficult to breathe. I could die here, she thought. She blinked away tears and bit her lower lip to hold back the over-whelming fear. *And what of the child you carry?* an inner voice cried. *If you die, your unborn child dies with you. Are you a Sommersett, or a puling goose girl?*

Our child—Cain's and mine. Suddenly, she was absolutely certain that she carried Cain's babe, and the knowledge gave her strength to battle the terror. Her forehead creased with determination, and she straightened her bowed shoulders. I won't let you die, she promised the tiny spark of life in her womb. I'll do whatever I have to, but I won't let you die.

"I say let the devil 'ave 'er," Shiner said.

"Hold yer tongue," Tess cautioned. "Ye heard what the captain said. We're safe as long as we have her."

Elizabeth heard the owl hoot again, and her failing courage rose. I'll jump up and run, she thought. Maybe they won't shoot. If I'm dead, they can't get the ransom.

Minutes passed. Slowly, Elizabeth stood up, gauging the distance to the door. If she was quick enough, perhaps they wouldn't be able to stop . . . Her spirits plunged as the sound of a man's harsh breathing signaled Captain Thomas's return.

He was panting as he lowered a heavy metal box to the floor. "The far end of the house is on fire," he said hoarsely. "Smoke's pretty thick in there already."

"Let 'er go," Shiner urged. " 'E's waitin' out there in the dark, I kin feel it. 'E'll put an arrow through us jest like 'e did poor Will."

Thomas moved forward to grab Elizabeth's arm. "Who is it?" he demanded, pulling the gag away. "Who's out there?"

"I don't know."

He took her by the shoulders and shook her until she feared her neck would snap. "Don't lie to me! Who is it?"

"I don't know."

Thomas cuffed her across the face. "Lying slut. I'll teach you to—"

"Leave off!" Tess cried. "That's doin' no good. We gotta get out o' here before the roof burns over our heads. Push her out first. If he wants t' shoot, let him shoot her."

Thomas pulled Elizabeth in front of him and shoved her toward the open door. "We're coming out!" he shouted. "Shoot and you kill the woman." He glanced back at Shiner. "Bring the box. If you drop it, I'll kill you."

Tess and Shiner pressed closely at the captain's back as the four stepped into the firelit courtyard. Tess held her weapon ready as Shiner staggered under the weight of the money box.

Sparks from the roof of the manor house had ignited the stable, and Elizabeth gasped as the heat of the fire hit her full in the face. Choking, she closed her eyes against the smoke and stumbled. Thomas caught her.

"Make a move and I'll kill her," he threatened. Once more, he took hold of her hair and pressed the pistol against her head. "I mean what I say. They'll hang me no longer for two women than for one."

Cain wiggled backward through the grass as they moved away from the house. It would be child's play to kill the little man and the woman, but the big man was the leader. Cain couldn't kill him without taking the chance of hitting Elizabeth, or of having the highwayman shoot her if

Cain's arrow only wounded him. As hard as it was to wait, he knew he must.

Firing the house had been a risk, but it would bring other Englishmen. If Edward's men followed the trail he had left, the flames in the sky would bring them quickly. Without horses, the bandits who held Elizabeth prisoner could not get away. Either he would kill them, or the earl's men would.

The outlaw's woman, the one he'd heard them call Tess, carried a gun too. He had surprised her in the house when he was searching for Elizabeth and had taken a weapon from her then. Now this Tess had another pistol, and he knew instinctively that she was as dangerous as either of the men. She was a woman who could kill as easily as a shark kills, and with as little regret. He had seen the ruthlessness in her eyes. A wiser man would have finished her when he had the chance. Cain sighed. Have I put Elizabeth's life at risk because I would not cut a woman's throat?

Cain glanced up at the cloud-strewn sky. The moon played tricks tonight, now giving light, now plunging the earth into total darkness. It was a bad night for an archer. But a good night for wolves, he thought. The trace of a smile creased his lips. What would these English *manake* think of a Lenape wolf?

Shiner's nerves were raw as they entered the all-encompassing gloom of the forest. A twig snapped under Tess's foot, and he jumped, nearly dropping the heavy box. He stared hard at the darker outlines of the tree trunks. Then something rustled in the dry leaves and he let go of the box and fired his pistol wildly into the darkness.

"What the hell are you shooting at?" Thomas spun around, wrenching Elizabeth's arm cruelly.

"I 'eard somethin'. Over there." Frantically, Shiner began to reload his pistol.

"Fool!" Tess spat. She knelt beside the money box and began to scoop up the gold and silver coins that had scattered on the ground, dumping them back in the container. "That's all I kin see, Jackie."

"Pick up that box and keep walking," Thomas ordered Shiner.

Overhead, the clouds parted and moonlight filtered through the branches. Elizabeth stifled a cry of fright as the bloodcurdling howl of a hunting wolf echoed through the trees, followed by a second, and then a third.

Tess shivered and moved closer to Thomas. "Mother of God," she whispered. "What's that?"

"Wolves," Thomas whispered harshly. "But that's crazy. There haven't been any wolves in Essex in a hundred years."

A ray of hope bubbled up in Elizabeth's mind. I know of one wolf that could be out there, she thought with rising excitement. A wolf with bronze skin and hair as black as a crow's wing.

"It's that devil," Shiner said. "Devils and witches kin turn themselves into anythin'. I seed one burned in Cornwall what would turn 'erself into a black pig."

"Shut yer gob 'bout witches and such," Tess said. "I don't like that talk."

"Let me go," Elizabeth said. "You've lost your horses, and my husband's men are out there in the woods waiting for you. If you want to save your lives, you'll take your stolen goods and run."

"Aye," Shiner said. "She's talkin' sense. Let's go while we kin."

Thomas turned the pistol on the little man. "I told you to pick up the box."

Shiner took a step backward. "Split it up now, cap'n. I want no more o' this. It smacks o' 'ellfire. Jest give me what's rightfully mine."

"You'll have your fair share," Thomas promised.

"Will I?" Shiner raised his pistol, and Tess leaped at him from behind, bringing her pistol down across his wrist. With a cry of pain, he dropped his gun and turned and ran, tripping and crashing through the woods like a madman.

"Come back here!" Thomas shouted.

Tess raised her pistol and fired at the little man's back. Shiner screamed once and toppled, thrashing into the underbrush. Thomas released Elizabeth, and she darted away, running for her life.

"Jackie!" Tess yelled. "The woman."

Thomas whirled just as Elizabeth's foot tangled in a tree root and she fell headlong to the ground. His pistol clutched in his hand, Thomas ran toward the spot where she lay.

"Cain!" Elizabeth struggled to get up as the highwayman closed the distance between them, but her bound wrists kept her off balance and she fell once more.

Thomas loomed over her, breathing hard. "A pity you have to die, pretty lady," he said softly, "but as you said, you're of no more use to us." He lowered the pistol and took careful aim at Elizabeth's head.

Watching from his hiding place among the trees, Cain dropped to one knee and notched an arrow in the bowstring. For a heartbeat, he held the arched bow, waiting, praying. Then a single ray of moonlight pierced the darkness and he released the arrow. It flew like a hawk to the kill.

"Damn me." Thomas sounded almost surprised as the arrow plunged through his chest. He dropped to his knees and fell forward on top of Elizabeth, and Cain hurled himself toward them. Elizabeth tried to roll free, but the weight of the highwayman's body pinned her to the ground.

"Jackie!" Tess's scream echoed through the trees.

"Cain!" Elizabeth cried. "Watch out for—"

Cain leaped toward Thomas as Tess raised Shiner's pistol and fired point-blank at him. The explosion deafened Elizabeth momentarily, but her eyes were wide open. In horror, she watched as the force of the bullet struck Cain in the head and threw him backward into the deep grass.

Chapter 23

"**J**ackie!" Tess wailed. She dropped Shiner's empty weapon and crouched beside Thomas. "Ah, Jackie me boy, ye've gone and done fer yerself, now." She tugged at his upper body, cradling him against her, and Elizabeth, soaked with his blood, wiggled out from under him.

A pale shaft of moonlight illuminated the black-haired woman's grief-contorted features as the two stared at each other. Sweat broke out on Elizabeth's face as she fought to loosen the bindings that cut into her wrists.

"Whore!" Tess's tears fell onto the dead highwayman's face. " 'Tis yer fault, all o' it. Jackie shoulda killed ye straight off." Her gaze fell on the pistol still gripped in her man's right hand. "I can't bring him back, but I can finish ye." Tess lunged for the pistol as Elizabeth's hands came free.

Before Tess could raise the gun to fire at her, Elizabeth charged Tess and knocked her down. Over and over they rolled, kicking and scratching, each struggling fiercely for possession of the pistol. Tess held on to the heavy wheel-lock with a death grip, but Elizabeth's right-hand fingers

318

dug into Tess's wrist, and she struck at Tess with her left fist. Tess yanked Elizabeth's hair and tried to gouge her eyes with her fingernails.

Tess bit down on Elizabeth's forearm. Elizabeth cried out in pain and butted her head against Tess's exposed chin. The pistol fell from Tess's grasp. Elizabeth straddled her and delivered two hard blows to Tess's face with her right fist. Then Elizabeth grabbed handfuls of Tess's tangled hair and pounded her head against the ground.

Tess's hands closed around Elizabeth's throat, and Elizabeth punched her in the nose. As Tess's nose began to spout blood, the fight went out of her. Sobbing, she tried to protect her injured face with her hands. Elizabeth seized the pistol and scrambled to her feet, aiming the weapon at her opponent.

The sound of baying hounds and a hunting horn rang through the forest. "That's Lord Dunmore's men," Elizabeth warned. "Stay where you are, or I'll save them the trouble of hanging you." She backed away slowly, then dropped to her knees beside Cain.

Despite the feeble light, she could see that his face was covered in blood. "Cain," she whispered. "Cain?" She laid down the gun and touched his face with a trembling hand. To her relief, his skin was warm to the touch. "Cain, can you hear me?"

He lay motionless, his arms sprawled over his head, eyes closed.

"No use to call the dead," Tess said. "He's as stiff as me poor Jackie."

Elizabeth laid her cheek against Cain's chest and listened. She was certain she heard a faint heartbeat. "You're alive." Cautiously, her fingers probed his hair for the bullet wound and found a ragged path across the crown of his head. The laceration was bleeding badly. Pulling up her skirts, Elizabeth tore the hem of her shift with her teeth and ripped off a length of cloth to staunch the flow of blood.

Quickly, she wadded up a section and pressed that against the gash. Then she wrapped a makeshift bandage tightly around Cain's head. When she glanced back toward Tess, the woman was gone, but Elizabeth didn't care. All that mattered to her was keeping Cain from bleeding to death.

"Darling, don't die on me. Please don't die." She took his face between her hands and kissed his lips. "You can't leave me . . . not now," she murmured.

Elizabeth's chest tightened until she could scarcely draw breath; her eyes stung with unshed tears as she covered his face with kisses. *I can't lose him now! Not after all that's happened.* She lifted his hand and clasped it against her breast. "If you live, I'll never leave you again," she promised. "As God is my witness. If you live, we'll go home to America together—the three of us."

"Truly?" Cain's voice was barely audible.

"Cain?" Joy rushed through her body. "Cain?"

His eyelids flickered. *"Ili kleheleche, n'tschutti?"* Do you yet draw breath, my beloved?

"N'leheleche," she replied. "I live, my husband." She laid her head against his bare chest again, and this time his heartbeat was strong and regular.

He struggled to sit up but had not the strength.

"Lie still," she begged. "You've lost so much blood. Lie still until help comes."

His fingers found her hair and stroked it. "Did you mean what you have spoken? Will you go home with me?"

"Yes . . . yes."

"Will you build my lodge fire and listen to my tales until we be old together?"

"I will."

"*N'wiquihilla*. I am weary."

Fear blossomed in Elizabeth's heart. "Hold my hand," she said. "Hold tight, darling."

"The . . . the bandit woman," he mumbled. "I . . . I should have . . . should have . . ."

"Shhh. Don't worry, love. She won't hurt us anymore."

"I come . . ." His breathing was harsh. "I come to save you, wife. Now, you must . . ." Cain's eyes closed, then snapped open. "I am the *tumme*, the wolf. Did you know?"

"I knew," she answered softly. "I knew you would come to save me."

"Eliz-a-beth." His head lolled to one side, and she gave a cry of anguish. "No," he said. "Have not tears. This one . . . does not die so easy. Let me sleep . . . just a little . . . and we will . . ."

A dog barked, and then the first rider galloped up through the trees. Elizabeth stood and called out to him. "Over here. We're here."

The groom reined in his horse and leaped from the saddle, pistol in hand. "We found a dead man back there near the stables." He pointed with the muzzle of the gun. "Be ye safe, lady?"

Elizabeth recognized his voice. "Tom?"

"Aye, 'tis me." He took a few steps toward her. "We saw the fire. Are the outlaws—"

"All dead but one, a woman. She ran off into the woods." Elizabeth knelt and took Cain's head in her lap. "He saved my life, but he's been shot."

Tom drew closer, pistol ready. He kicked at

Thomas's still form. "Yer well, m'lady? They've not 'armed ye?"

"Please help me with him." Already blood had soaked through Cain's bandage. "The wound will have to be stitched up." She put her fingertips against his lips to reassure herself that he was still breathing.

Tom raised the pistol until it was level with her chest. "Lady?" His voice cracked, and the gun wavered.

"Tom? What's wrong with you? I told you that the highwaymen are all dead. Put that gun down and help me get him to your horse."

"Aye, lady," he said softly. "I reckon that's best."

In minutes they were surrounded by the sheriff and his retinue. Whining dogs milled in circles and sniffed at Captain Thomas's body as the men with torches gathered in tight knots. Robert dismounted, handed his reins to another man, and hurried toward Elizabeth. "M'lady, are you all right?"

"Well enough," she replied. "But Savage's hurt badly."

Robert bent to examine the Indian. "What happened to him?"

"He was shot. The ball only creased his head, but he's lost a terrible amount of blood."

Robert's eyes met Tom's. "His head may be broken. 'Tis more fittin' if you let us care for him, m'lady."

Elizabeth clung tightly to Cain's limp hand. "No. He's my responsibility. He was hurt trying to save me."

The sheriff called for light, and someone thrust a torch into the dead highwayman's face. "Anyone know his name?" the sheriff asked.

Elizabeth looked up. "That's Captain Thomas," she said. "There's another one over there in the woods. The woman shot him."

The sheriff stared hard at the dead outlaw. "I don't know who he is," he said, "but he's not Captain Thomas. I saw the real Captain Thomas tried in London two years ago . . . got a good look at his face. They sentenced him to hang, but he escaped from Newgate. He's still active, but this isn't him."

"This man told me told me he was Captain Thomas."

"Then he lied to you. Thomas is a smaller—" The sheriff broke off as a green-garbed forester dragged the struggling, cursing Tess into the circle of torchlight.

"That's the woman," Elizabeth cried. "She murdered one of her own companions and tried to kill my husband's servant."

"She's a liar!" Tess screamed. "I'm an honest—"

"Silence, woman," the sheriff admonished, "unless you'd have us string you up here and save the court the cost of your trial."

Tess began to weep. "They'll not hang me," she protested between sobs. "I'll plead me belly."

Elizabeth followed Robert and Tom as they carried the unconscious Cain to a horse. "I'll hold him before me, lady," Robert said. "It's bad to move him, but worse to let him lay here with the blood running so."

"Tom?" Elizabeth extended her hand. "I'll ride with you. We must get him to the nearest house."

"No need for that, Lady Dunmore," the sheriff said. "We've brought an extra mount. Are you strong enough to ride?"

"I am."

"Then we'll return to Sotterley at once. Lord Dunmore was most emphatic that there be no delay." The sheriff waved to a huntsman, and the man led the sheriff's horse to him.

"We can't! This man is badly wounded," Elizabeth insisted, distraught. "He must have medical care at once, or he may die."

"Lord Dunmore entrusted you to me," the sheriff said firmly. "The man's a savage. If he lives or dies, it makes little difference."

But it does to me, Elizabeth thought passionately, as she gathered up the reins of her horse. It makes all the difference to me.

By the time they reached Sotterley, it was long past midnight and the skies resounded with the earth-shaking boom of thunder. Lightning zigzagged across the far horizon, and heavy rain clouds threatened to deluge the riders. A messenger had galloped ahead to tell Lord Dunmore that the sheriff's posse had been successful and the gang of marauders all killed or taken prisoner. The earl came out to the courtyard in nightrobe and cap to greet the triumphant party.

Ignoring Dunmore, Elizabeth guided her exhausted mount close to the entrance to the servants' quarters and instructed Tom and Robert to carry Cain in to bed. He had regained consciousness during the journey, and the bleeding had slowed, but he was still too weak to walk unaided. "He risked his life to save mine," she said loudly, for the benefit of the onlookers. "It behooves us to give Savage the best of care." She waved to a staring kitchen boy. "Go into the house and fetch my maid, Bridget. She has some knowledge of healing, and she can sew up his wound."

The pimply-faced youth tugged at his forelock.
"Can't, lady. Bridget's gone."

"Gone? Gone where?" Elizabeth brushed back
her disheveled hair and tossed the reins of her
horse to a groom. "Be easy with Savage," she
said sharply as the men lifted Cain from the saddle. "If you start his head bleeding again, I'll have
the skin from your back."

Lord Dunmore dismissed the sheriff and stalked
across the yard toward Elizabeth. "What do you
do here, lady?" he demanded. "Have you taken
leave of your wits? Look at you! Dressed in rags
and as gore-stained as a butcher's apprentice."
He scowled at her. "Get you to your chambers
and summon the maids to bring you water to
wash. I fear your experience with the highwaymen has left you daft."

Elizabeth stared into Edward's tumid face with
such contempt that he unconsciously shrank back.
"You would let him die?" she snapped. "Is this
how you reward your faithful servants?"

"Speak not to me of faithful servants," he said
peevishly. "You have been deceived by one you
trusted." His features softened and he smiled indulgently. "But we shall not quarrel when we
have so much to be grateful for. Come, wife. It's
starting to rain. Come into the house."

Dunmore took her dirty, bloodstained hands in
his cold, pallid ones, and it was all she could do
to keep from shuddering in distaste. Suddenly,
the hours of exhaustion and anxiety drained her
spirit, and she wanted nothing more than to lie
on a soft, warm bed. "What is this about Bridget
being gone?" she asked flatly.

" 'Tis a disgusting matter, and not one I would
spread about. The slut has fled with most of your
jewelry."

"I don't believe it!"

"Nevertheless, it is true." He tugged at her hands. "Come in and let your women put you to bed. I will send my barber to tend Savage. Doubtless, he is not hurt as badly as you fear."

"Bridget has been with me for years. She would never—"

"Inside, lady. If you must act the shrew, let it be in private, not for all the world to hear."

She pulled her hands free. "When? When did this happen?" The rain was beginning to fall harder, and she shivered. Her stomach churned, and a ribbon of fear wound upward from the base of her spine. *What if my babe has been harmed?* Her gorge rose in her throat, and she put a hand over her mouth. "I . . ." she began.

"Go to your chambers and have the maids bathe you and put you to bed," Edward ordered. "When you are presentable, I will come and explain exactly what happened in your absence."

Elizabeth swallowed, trying to maintain her tenuous composure. Too much, she thought. Too much has happened. I can't think. "If you send the barber surgeon to the Indian, I will do as you say," she murmured dutifully. "I could not rest if I thought he was untended."

"Good." Edward's mouth lips curled upward in a mocking smile. "Regardless of how little concern you have for me, m'lady, know that I have been in anguish over your violent abduction. I've had long hours to consider the wretched condition of our marriage with regret. You have my pledge that all will be different between us from this night on." He patted her cheek. "I do love you, Elizabeth, in my own fashion. I think I always have."

Once those words might have meant something to me, she thought ironically. Now they mean less than nothing. There was no room in her life for Edward or his false promises. All that mattered was Cain and the child she carried beneath her heart. *I'm leaving you, Edward. I'm going home with the man I love.* She turned away from him without speaking and made her way wearily toward her apartments.

Elizabeth was halfway down the second-floor gallery when she heard hurried footsteps on the servants' staircase, and a man came around the corner.

"M'lady, I must speak with you."

"Robert? Is something wrong with Cain—I mean Savage? Has his bleeding—"

The tall footman shook his head. "No, m'lady. He sleeps soundly. There is something wrong, but it's not with the Indian. It's Bridget."

"Yes . . . Bridget." Elizabeth looked up and down the gallery and stepped close to Robert. "M'lord says she stole from me and fled, but I don't believe it."

" 'Tis a foul lie," he protested hotly. "She's no thief. Lord Dunmore accused her and threw her off Sotterley without recommendation. She'll never be able to find another place as lady's maid, or even as house servant."

"Who told you what happened?"

"A friend in the stables." Robert's jaw tightened. "I'm leaving, m'lady. I'll not stay here without her. I'll not serve a lord who treats his people so unfairly. Bridget and I had plans to marry. I have to find her, but I don't know where she's gone. Would you have any idea at all?"

"Her sister Maureen's gone to Bristol with her new husband. I hear the plague is not so bad in Bristol. Mayhap Bridget went to Maureen."

"Aye, it makes sense. She was close to her sister. But Bristol is a big place, m'lady. I know not where to search them out."

"Sean's cousin works at a tavern called the Sea Cook's Locker. Bridget said Sean was hoping to find work as an ostler there."

"Thank you, m'lady. I'll not forget you."

"If you find her . . . when you find her, tell her . . ." Elizabeth bit her lip to keep from weeping. "Tell her that I know that Dunmore lies. I'll help her if I can."

" 'Tis goodbye then, m'lady. I'll leave at first light. I've a bit of wages saved, and I'd not see his lordship again."

"God go with you, Robert." She watched as his broad shoulders disappeared around the corner. Father, Betty, and now Bridget. One by one, I'm losing everyone that means anything to me. Everyone but Cain. "And I won't lose you," she whispered into the still room. "I won't."

"Come in and close the door, idiot," Dunmore said. "Is there naught but straw beneath that pate?" Thunder rattled the windows of his bedchamber, and driving rain beat against the thick glass panes. Dunmore lay propped up with piles of pillows in his poster bed; the only light in the room came from the fireplace and a single candle.

Tom wrung his hat between his callused hands and shuffled his feet. "M'lord," he mumbled.

"Closer, damn you. I can't hear a word you're saying above this abominable storm." Edward licked a bit of jam from his fingers and wiped them on the bedspread. Crumbs littered the front of his gown.

Head down, Tom approached the bed with slow, hesitant steps.

"You failed me, Tom," Dunmore said. "You were the first to reach the lady. The sheriff told me. You found her, and you let her live."

The groom shook his head. "Weren't no chance t' do fer 'er. The savage were there. 'E'd a' kilt me, did I try and 'arm 'er ladyship."

The earl frowned. "Where's the pistol I gave you?"

"Stable."

"I want it back. Bring it here at once."

Tom turned to go.

"Not yet! I haven't dismissed you, lack-wit. There's something else for you to do first."

"Aye, m'lord." Tom's eyes were dumb as a beast's in the flickering candlelight.

"You will go to Lady Dunmore's chambers in the tower. She is greatly distraught, due to her . . . ravishment by the outlaws. They did unspeakable things to her, you know—vile things."

"She didn't say nothin' 'bout—"

"Would she, Tom? Would a lady speak to a groom about her defilement? Her loss of honor?" Edward's hands tightened on the silk bedcovering. "A tragedy for Sotterley, Tom, but not the first. A grandmother of mine threw herself from a window in the tower when her only daughter died in childbirth. She was mad, you see. As mad as m'lady."

" 'Er ladyship din't seem mad t' me. Tough she were, not crazy."

"You're wrong, Tom. Very wrong. That's why I am lord here, and you are fit only to shovel out horse dung. You will go to m'lady's chambers and throw her from the window. With the storm, no one will hear her cries. No one will know she's dead until morning."

The groom's eyes took on a flicker of cunning.

"Ye wants me t' murder 'er. I'm t' throw 'er from the tower window."

"Excellent. You comprehend a simple command in your native tongue." Dunmore smiled. "Keep working at it, and you may yet achieve the intelligence of one of my hounds."

"I'm t' murder the lady, and then t' fetch ye the pistol."

"Exactly."

"Nobody will know I did it."

"How could they?"

"Ladies got maids and such."

"Not tonight, Tom. Once she was put to bed, I gave orders that she was to be alone in her chambers. Do it now, before the storm abates. When it's done, you'll be paid in silver."

Tom exhaled sharply and nodded. "Aye, m'lord." He left the earl's quarters and hurried down the dark corridors to the far end of the house. He met no one. He heard nothing but the wind, and the rain, and the crash of rolling thunder.

Elizabeth groaned and buried her head deeper in the pillows. The knock at her door came again, incessantly. "Who's there?" she asked sleepily. It was still dark, and the fire on her hearth had burned to orange coals. "Who is it?" Then she thought of Cain and rose from her bed.

She flung open the door. "What's amiss?"

The man had no candle.

"You're not . . ."

" 'Tis Tom, m'lady. Tom the groom."

"Tom? What are you doing here? Is the Indian—"

He pushed past her into the room and closed the door behind him. "Don't be afeared o' me," he said gently. "I'd not 'arm ye, lady. But Lord Dunmore, 'e wants ye dead."

"What?"

"Nay. Listen, quick. There's no time." Tom gripped his cap in desperation. "Ye mun flee, lady. Flee fer yer life."

Elizabeth began to shiver uncontrollably. "How do you know?" she begged him.

"He bid me come and throw ye t' yer death in the stones below. From that window, the lord said, like 'is grandmum afore. Say yer mad, 'e would. Say ye took yer own life."

"But why do you tell me?"

"I'm a 'ard man, m'lady. Born in a ditch, wi' no sire and little brain. But I can't murder no woman." He cleared his throat. "I'll saddle ye the fastest 'orse in 'is lordship's stable, that much I kin do. But ye mun save yer own skin, lady. Fer when one as powerful as 'im sets 'is mind t' a thing, 'e'll find a way. If not me, another, fer 'e's set a price o' siller on yer 'ead."

Elizabeth's senses reeled as beads of perspiration broke out on her forehead. "Edward sent you to murder me?" she said in disbelief.

"Aye."

"He offered you silver to throw me from my window?"

"Aye. Ye mun flee," he repeated. "Whist the storm lasts ye may get away." Tom shook his head. "After that . . . Ye've nay time fer women's weakness, do ye wish t' live."

She took a deep breath and swallowed hard. "Yes," she replied, "I must get away." Not only me, she thought. I must save Cain as well. "I'll not bide here to be slaughtered like a spring lamb." She took another breath, and the acrid taste of fear in her mouth began to recede. "Edward will not get the best of me,'' she murmured, more for her own sake than for the groom's.

In the recesses of her mind, she heard her father's words. *Never forget, Elizabeth—you were born a Sommersett.*

''Nay,'' Elizabeth said, ''I'd not have Dunmore think he'd won out over a Sommersett.''

Chapter 24

"You must saddle three horses to ride," Elizabeth said softly, "and fetch three more to lead behind us. Summon Robert from his bed and tell him to make Savage ready to travel as best he can. They must both dress in plain groom's clothing—not Lord Dunmore's livery."

"Aye," Tom agreed. " 'Tis canny t' take extra mounts. 'Is lordship could do no more t' ye, did ye empty 'is stables of fine 'orseflesh. Robert is steady, 'e'll guard ye well. But why do ye risk the wild man? Ye may as well carry Lord Dunmore's banner as ride wi' 'is redskin. Be noticed, 'e will, wherever ye go."

"We must chance it, Tom, for I cannot go without him." She laid a hand on his sleeve. "You've been a friend to me, but I've naught to reward you with. My jewel box is gone, and I've not a single coin to offer you."

The groom shook his shaggy head. "Din't want no silver, lady. Wants ye safe away from the earl. A bad one, is 'e, not like 'is father, the old lord."

"Go now, and do as I bid you." She squeezed his arm. "I'll not forget your help."

When he was gone, Elizabeth lit a candle and hurriedly dressed in sturdy, sensible clothing. She pulled on her riding boots and rolled a few other items of clothing into a bundle and tucked them into a basket, along with the remains of her supper and a bottle of wine. Removing her second-best cloak from the chest, she started for the door, then hesitated when she spied Bridget's scissors lying on a table.

I'll cut his hair, she thought. Cain would probably object, but it would be easier to pass him off as an Englishman without his long hair. Pray God, he would be strong enough to ride so soon after his injury. But there's no choice, is there? For better or worse, the decision had been made for her. If there was any hope for Cain and their child, they had to make an escape now.

When she reached the stable, Robert and Cain were waiting for her. Tom was just saddling the last of the three animals. Cain was sitting on the floor, leaning against the wall. His head was bandaged, and he wore a pair of plain baggy breeches and a dark homespun shirt.

Elizabeth knelt beside him and took his hand in hers. "Are you all right?" He nodded. "Fetch him a hat," she said to Robert. "I'll cut his hair."

Cain grimaced as she removed the scissors from her basket and set about trimming his flowing locks in a servingman's style. "Iroquois," he accused.

"I'd shave you bald if it would help us get away," she said, covering the discarded hair with loose hay.

"I chose dark 'orses, lady," Tom said. "Grays show up too good agin' the forest."

Robert's face was strained. "Do you know what you do, lady?" the footman asked.

"The lord seeks 'er life," Tom said.

"Then I'm your man," Robert pledged.

"Can you ride?" Elizabeth asked Cain. His chiseled features were washed free of blood, but nothing could hide the dark circles beneath his eyes or his raspy breathing.

"I ride," he answered harshly.

Tom assisted Elizabeth into the man's saddle. " 'Tis best fer a long 'ard ride, lady," he apologized. "A sidesaddle—"

"I can ride astride," she assured him. "My brothers taught me when I was a child." She motioned to Robert. "Put him up behind me."

"He may not be able to hold on," the footman cautioned. "He's too heavy for you to—"

"He rides with me," Elizabeth said firmly. "Take a length of rope and tie us together."

"Put me on my own horse," Cain said, steadying himself against the animal's side. "I can ride."

"I've seen you ride when you had a *whole* head," Elizabeth said. "Put him on my horse." Swiftly, Robert obeyed, securing Cain with a rope.

" 'Ave ye a safe place t' go t', lady?" Tom asked.

"We'll go to Longview, to my family's country house," she said. "My brother's retainers will give us shelter."

Minutes later, the three rode out into the pouring rain and turned their horses toward the London highway. The storm showed no signs of abating, and the rain soaked their garments and beat at their faces.

"Do you really mean to go to your family's country house?" Robert leaned toward Elizabeth and shouted above the rain. "This is not the—"

"We're going to Bristol!" she cried. "Bristol is on the sea."

"Then why did you—"

"Dunmore will send men after us. If Tom relents and tells him where we rode, let them seek us anywhere but where we really are."

Lightning struck on the far side of the meadow, and Elizabeth shut her eyes against the sudden flash of light. Her horse shied and broke into a gallop, despite the burden of two riders on its back. "Hold tight," she warned Cain. "We ride fast and hard this night and into tomorrow."

He laid his head against her back and tightened his hold around her waist. "Take me where you will," he said, "so long as our trail leads home."

The kitchen boys had just crawled from their pallets and started to build the charcoal fires in the great hearth when Tom returned to the master's chamber. No trace of light showed in the east, and rain still pounded against the glass windows. The tall marquetry clock on the hall landing had just struck five-thirty.

Lord Dunmore lay awake. His head had pained him through the early hours of the morning, and twice he'd had to leave his bed and seek the chamber pot. He'd gone to the windows repeatedly, knowing there was no way he could see Elizabeth's tower window from his room. He'd listened in vain for a woman's screams, knowing just as well that the storm would muffle any outcry she made.

He jumped when Tom tapped at the door. "Who is it?"

"Tom the groom, yer lordship."

"Come in." Dunmore peered at the man's face, trying to decide if his mission had been a success. "Damn you," he snapped, "you're dripping water all over my floor. What have you been doing—swimming?"

" 'Tis rainin' out, m'lord." He pulled the pistol out from beneath his rain-drenched cloak. " 'Ere be yer gun, yer lordship." He laid it gingerly on a low table.

Dunmore swore a foul curse as he rose from his bed. "I know it's raining, dolt. Do you think me deaf, I cannot hear the rain and thunder?" He hobbled toward the groom. "Well? Did you do it or not? Is she dead?"

"No m'lord, I couldn't throw the lady from the tower window as ye asked. I'm done wi' killin'."

"You fool!" Purple veins bulged on Dunmore's forehead. "Again!" he screamed. "You dare to come here and tell me you failed me again?" He walked to within an arm's length of Tom, raised his walking stick, and slashed him viciously across the face.

Blood welled up on the groom's face as he ducked out of reach of Dunmore's fury. Tom's features hardened. "Lord or not, ye've nay right t' strike me like a dumb beast."

"Strike you! Strike you, you dog's vomit! I'll kill you!" Dunmore staggered toward him and lashed out with his stick again.

Tom caught the end of the cane and twisted it out of his master's hand. He snapped it across his knee. "No more," he threatened.

Dunmore swore and lunged toward the pistol on the table. Tom sprang as the lord's hand closed around the weapon's grip. Dunmore fought with surprising strength, and the two fell to the floor, struggling, and rolled over and over, each striving for posession of the gun.

Thunder muffled the sound of the explosion. Dunmore cried out once and then fell back, his eyes wide and unblinking.

Shaken, Tom rose to his feet and stood with the

smoking pistol in his hand until Dunmore's body ceased to twitch, then he stepped over the spreading pool of blood and put the weapon into his lordship's hand.

"Ye got it wrong, m'lord," Tom said. " 'Tweren't 'er ladyship what killed 'erself out o' shame. 'Twas ye. Ye couldn't bear the shame o' another man beddin' yer lady when ye could nay mount 'er yerself. Poor ailin' lord. Yer sickness musta touched yer mind."

Smiling in the darkness, Tom backed from the dead earl's chambers and closed the door tightly behind him. " 'Tis the stables and a warm bed fer old Tom," he murmured. "And I'll be as sorrowed as the next when word o' me lordship's death comes belowstairs." He sighed. "And 'twas jest as ye said, m'lord. 'Twas easier the second time."

The journey to Bristol was not one that Elizabeth would wish to repeat in her lifetime. They traveled mostly by night and slept by day in ruined churches or barns, and once even in the shelter of a great hedge. Cain's wound gave him a fever. For four days he was too sick to ride and they had to trade one of the riding horses for the privilege of camping in a farmer's stone sheep shed. They ate rabbits that Robert snared, and stale bread, and sometimes nothing at all.

They rode the horses at breakneck speed until the animals' sides ran with sweat and foam sprayed from their mouths. When the roan mare went lame, Elizabeth traded her to a tinker for two flea-ridden blankets, a kettle of hot stew, and a tin of powdered dovesfoot to curb Cain's infection and lessen the fever.

"The gypsy will hang if he's caught with one

of the earl's horses," Robert reminded Elizabeth
as they rode from the tinker's camp.

"True enough, but a man who makes such poor
stew deserves to hang."

On the eighth day, Cain was strong enough to
ride alone, and although they were down to three
horses, they made better time. They'd seen no
sign of pursuit, but none of them was willing to
relax his guard.

"Lord Dunmore will see us all in hell," Elizabeth reminded Cain and Robert. "He'll stop at
nothing to find us, and his gold will buy many
favors."

Cain's hand went to the hilt of the knife he
wore strapped on his waist. "No one will take
you while I live," he promised her in his native
tongue.

She shook her head. "We must all live."

"Amen to that," Robert agreed. "I've no wish
to meet my maker with four inches of steel in my
gut."

Refugees fleeing from London's plague clogged
the roads and made travel on the highways difficult. The villagers' fear of the black death made
all strangers suspect, and after one farmer shot at
them, the three learned to keep off the roads and
away from settled places. They sighted troops of
soldiers almost daily; once, they barely escaped a
roadblock at a ford in a river.

Cain pulled his hat low over his face and kept
his head down whenever they passed anyone on
the road. They took turns sleeping and keeping
watch, venturing to make human contact only
when hunger made them desperate. And when
they did seek food or a place to sleep, it was usually Elizabeth who did the bargaining.

"You be as sharp as a peasant wench," Robert

said admiringly as they divided a roasted hen.
"Begging your pardon, m'lady, but I'd never
have thought of giving scissors for my dinner."

"Bridget's scissors for her mistress's chicken,"
Elizabeth replied with a grin. "I'd say the bond-
woman made the best of the deal."

"Aye, there's something to that, but the farther
we go from Sotterley, the more you sound like
my own sweet Bridget and less like the grand lady
you are."

"I do what I must." Her eyes met Cain's. "We
all do what we must."

On the evening of the twelfth day, they crossed
the Avon and reached the outskirts of Bristol.
Cain and Elizabeth waited in a shadowy lane near
a small church, while Robert rode in to try and
locate Bridget's brother-in-law at the tavern. As
they grazed the horses beside the tombstones, a
wedding party came out of the church.

The young bride's laughter drifted through the
peaceful graveyard, and Elizabeth felt a pang of
regret. Her hand went unconsciously to her belly,
and she drew in a deep breath. "Are we truly
wed in the eyes of God, Cain, or is this child I
carry to be born in bastardy?" It was the first time
she had voiced the fear that had plagued her since
she'd first realized they had created a babe. It was
also the first time she had spoken to Cain about
being pregnant.

He chuckled softly, put his arms around her,
and pulled her against his chest. "This one knows
of the child to come, Eliz-a-beth. It gives me joy."

She nestled her head beneath his neck, letting
her fingers trace the line of his jaw. "How did
you know?"

"Your body tells me. Are you sorry we make
this little one?"

"No. I want your child, but . . . How can we be married? You're not even a Christian."

"No, and you be not of the true people—the Lenni-Lenape. My God cares not. He opens his arms to all children of the earth." He kissed her hair, then tilted her chin to place a gentle kiss on her lips.

The kiss was sweet, but it did not quell her concern. "To be born a bastard is a terrible thing," she said when their embrace ended. "If I've sinned, our child will carry the stain forever."

He laughed. "How can *ommamundot*, a child, have sin before he draws birth? The English are wrong. A child is good. A child belongs to Wishemenetoo. He is only . . ." Cain frowned as he searched for the right word. ". . . loan to parents. A gift of joy. This word you say—*bastard*—this one does not understand. Wishemenetoo's gift can only bring honor. If there is bad, it rests on head of mother and father, never *ommamundot*."

Elizabeth looked up into his face. "Would you speak the marriage vows before a clergyman of my faith?"

"No English shaman would say the words for us."

"But if he would?" she persisted.

"If the words will make you easy in your heart, I will say them but, for this one, we are man and wife until the forests grow beneath the salt sea and the dolphins swim upon the land."

Her eyes gleamed. "Wait here, then. If this good minister can perform one ceremony, perhaps I can prevail upon him to do another."

Ten minutes later, Cain and Elizabeth stood hand in hand in the bare, whitewashed church and repeated the vows that wed them according to English custom. The cold-eyed cleric made clear his disapproval of their hasty marriage far from home and family.

"We are going to the Colonies," Elizabeth had told him blithely. "I am with child, and we would be married according to law."

When he'd protested that they were strangers to him, no banns had been cried, and he had no way of knowing if they were close kin or already bound in wedlock, Elizabeth had bribed him with Dunmore's bay gelding.

"Where did such as you get so fine a horse?" the minister had demanded. "Is it stolen?"

But Elizabeth had murmured denials, shrugged, and fluttered her hands, and the greedy churchman had consented.

"God bless you, sir," she said meekly. "I'll want a copy of our marriage lines, as well as those to be entered in your parish book."

She signed the page boldly, *Elizabeth Anne Sommersett,* and offered the book and quill to Cain. "Make your mark here," she instructed. To her surprise, he took the quill and wrote his own name in flowing script. *Cain Dare.*

Startled, she stared up into his twinkling eyes. "My *cocumtha.*"

The parson puckered his thin face into a sour expression. "What heathen talk is that? Be this man Irish? I wed no papists in this church."

"No, good reverend, let your mind be at rest," Elizabeth soothed as she held out her hand for the proof of her marriage. "The Dares have been honest Englishmen since the time of Good King Richard. I can assure you that neither of us is Catholic."

The minister peered at Cain suspiciously. "He's dark enough to be an Irishman."

"His mother was Welsh," Elizabeth lied.

"I'll have the saddle with the beast," the cleric said.

"Nothing was said of a saddle," she retorted.

"Would you rather I called the sheriff, Mistress Dare?" he threatened.

"Let him have the saddle," Cain said. "He be welcome to it."

"Irish or Welsh, 'tis little difference," the minister grumbled. "Pagans, the lot of them."

Robert and Bridget were waiting outside in the lane. Bridget gave a cry of delight and threw herself into Elizabeth's arms. "I never thought to see ye again."

Elizabeth hugged her tight. "Or I you. Leave the bay, Robert. 'Twas payment to the minister for our marriage." She produced the precious paper. "It's true, we're wed. Here are our marriage lines."

Bridget drew back. "But m'lady, ye are still wed to—"

"Shhh," Elizabeth laid a finger over her lips. "Let's away from here, and I'll try to explain. Are you well, Bridget? How did you come to Bristol without harm? The roads are thick with travelers."

The four walked down the lane away from the churchyard, leading the two horses, Robert's sorrel and the remaining chestnut. Cain walked close to Elizabeth's shoulder, saying nothing, but she felt his eyes on her in the darkness.

"First," Elizabeth said, "there must be no more of 'm'lady. 'Twill mean our lives if we are captured by Lord Dunmore's people. We are Cain and Elizabeth."

"Aye," Bridget answered thoughtfully. "But Elizabeth is too dangerous—best we call ye Lizzy.

Few would look for an earl's lady behind such a milkmaid's name.''

"Good enough." Elizabeth sighed and caught hold of Cain's hand. It tightened around hers and gave her courage. "We came here because we didn't knew where else to go. We need your help, Bridget. We must get back to Cain's home, to the Colonies. I'm to bear his child. If Dunmore captures us, our babe will die also.''

"He's a wicked man, Lord Dunmore." Bridget smiled up at Robert. "Ye'll not know how happy I was when Sean brought Robbie to the house.''

"You should have realized I'd not be so easy to get rid of," Robert said. "I was leaving service before the lady bid me ride with her. Dunmore accused you of stealing from her ladyship.''

Bridget stopped and stared at Elizabeth. "Ye didna believe me a thief, did ye?''

"No. I'd believe nothing Dunmore told me.''

"He took yer jewels, ye know. He ordered me to bring them to him, and he took them all himself. He had no right—what's yers is yers. Husband or not . . .'' Bridget's eyes narrowed suspiciously. "Does the lord still live?''

"Aye,'' Robert said.

"Then this marriage to . . . to *him* . . .'' Bridget motioned to Cain. '' 'Tis no real marriage at all.''

"No,'' Cain said in his softly accented English. "Eliz-a-beth be my wife.''

"We were handfasted in America,'' Elizabeth explained. "I gave my pledge to him before witnesses. 'Tis my marriage to Lord Dunmore that means nothing.''

"Then why this second exchange o' vows here at Bristol?'' Bridget asked.

"I had no paper before, no words spoken in a church. Now I do.'' She handed the folded parchment to the Irish girl. "I'm entrusting my marriage lines to you. Keep them safe for me, and when you can, put them into the hands of Micah Levinson or one of his sons."

"But London is a pesthole. Any that remain there are—"

"In time the plague will pass. Micah Levinson is too wise to be caught in the city. When London is safe again, he'll return, or his sons will. If I knew where Micah was now, I would go to him for money." She spread her hands. "I have nothing, Bridget. We fled with what we have on our backs."

Bridget laughed as she tucked the parchment inside her wrap. "What ye ha' on yer back is more than ye know, m'la—" She corrected herself. "Lizzy." She knelt beside Elizabeth in the road and ran her fingers down the inner lining of Elizabeth's cloak. "Hah! Feel this." She guided Elizabeth's fingers to a hard lump in the bottom hem. "Open the seam, and ye'll find a string o' pearls, each one worth a workin' man's fortune."

"But how? Why?" With the aid of Cain's knife, Elizabeth freed the precious pearls and cupped them in her hand. "You put them there," she said to her friend.

"Aye, for just such a time. You've led a sheltered life, m'lady, and I've not. When Lord Dunmore asked for yer jewels, I saved that out . . . just in case."

"Thank God, you did. I thought to come to you a beggar." She squeezed the pearls tightly. "These may buy us passage to Jamestown," Elizabeth told Cain.

They were entering the town, and the street was crowded despite the hour. Men and women hurried past, some on horseback and others on foot, some driving livestock before them or pushing heavily laden wheelbarrows. One stout woman led a cow with two baskets of codfish strapped to the animal's back. Cursing drovers maneuvered two-wheeled carts and horse-drawn sleds along the narrow streets, and everywhere were barking dogs and filthy, ragged children. They ran crying beside the passersby with outstretched hands and slept, like piles of stray puppies, in the doorways.

Cain took the pearls from Elizabeth and weighed them in his hand. "They are pretty beads," he said, "but is hard for this one to understand why the English value stones from the sea and not children."

Bridget shrugged. "'Tis plain to see why he canna remain here. 'Twill be hard to pass him off as English."

Elizabeth chuckled. "I told the minister his mother was Welsh."

"Fooling the clergy is one thing," Robert said, "but the trick will nay work long. No insult meant to you, Cain, but savage you are, and savage you look."

Bridget led the way through the twisting streets to an old stone tavern. "Maureen and Sean have a room beyond the inn bakehouse. 'Tis warm enough, and ye'll be welcome, but 'twill be snug for six of us. The town is packed with those who have fled from London, and families come from the country seeking work. I'm sorry there's no better place to offer ye, m'lady."

"Any place with a roof over it will seem like Whitehall," Elizabeth replied. "We've been sleeping on the ground for so long I—"

"Be there no place we can sleep alone?" Cain asked.

"None that I know o'," Bridget answered, "but I'll ask Sean. I was lucky to find them still here. They are bound for the Virginia Colony too. But they have taken the only way poor people can to better themselves; they've signed on as indentured servants for passage across the sea. They will work wi'out wages for four years in America. After that, they'll be free to take up land o' their own."

Leaving Robert to watch the animals, Bridget took Cain and Elizabeth to her sister's quarters. Maureen greeted them shyly, offering them food and drink and the only stools in the cramped room.

"My Sean is workin' in the stables," she said when Bridget had explained why her former mistress was in Bristol. "He doesn't get off until late, but I know Sean will help ye, if he can. He has no love for English lords, beggin' yer pardon, yer ladyship." She blushed and stared at Cain from under thick, dark lashes.

Bridget whispered into her sister's ear. ". . . newly wed," Elizabeth heard her say. ". . . someplace to be alone."

Maureen looked from Elizabeth to Cain in disbelief. "He . . . he is an Indian?" she ventured timidly. "Ye are truly wed this day?"

Elizabeth nodded. "Truly."

Maureen whispered something to Bridget, then tied on her apron and threw a shawl over her head. "I'll be right back," she said and ducked out the door.

"Ye can trust her, lady," Bridget assured Elizabeth. "She'd cut off her right arm before she'd betray me."

Elizabeth cast a longing glance at the only bed in the room. I'd give a manor in Yorkshire for a soft place to sleep right now, she thought. But that's Maureen and Sean's bed. We'll be lucky if they find us a spot on the floor.

Before Elizabeth could finish the bread and cheese Maureen had given them, the younger girl was back. She flung open the door and grinned broadly. "Sean says if ye dinna mind sleepin' in the hayloft, yer welcome to take clean blankets and go there. 'Tis not what a lady's used to, I'm certain, but 'tis private. None will bother ye . . . and on yer weddin' night . . ." She trailed off, blushing furiously. " 'Twas only a thought. If ye'd rather ha' our bed, we—"

"We will take the loft gratefully," Elizabeth assured her. She smiled at Cain. "If it suits you, husband." She offered him her outstretched hand. "Would you spend our wedding night in a hayloft?"

Chapter 25

For a long time, Cain and Elizabeth lay wrapped in each other's arms on the sweet-smelling hay in the loft above the tavern stables. Elizabeth had believed herself exhausted, but now that they were alone, with a fresh linen sheet beneath them and a wool blanket above, she found she could not sleep.

Below, in the barn, horses stamped and whinnied, and a cow lowed softly. The sounds were restful ones; they took Elizabeth back to her childhood in the country. The stable was clean, the hard-packed floors swept, and the stalls knee-deep in bright straw. The odors drifting upward to the loft were earthy scents of grain, horses, and oiled leather.

"This one takes you from a king's palace to a shelter for beasts," Cain murmured as his warm, wet tongue tasted the contours of her throat. "Be you sorry you chose to follow my path?"

"Ummm." Elizabeth sighed and snuggled closer, letting the warmth of his heavy, muscled body permeate her tired limbs. "I don't think so," she teased, pulling the thick homespun blanket tighter around her naked shoulders.

"Think? You do not know?" He stopped nib-

bling her ear and propped himself up on one el-
bow to gaze down at her with almond-shaped
eyes. "Look at me, Eliz-a-beth," he commanded
in his own soft language.

The eddies of warmth that coursed through her
veins intensified as she rolled onto her back and
smiled up at him. Moonlight spilled through the
cracks around the loft window and pooled around
them, illuminating his craggy, hawklike features,
making his heavy-lidded eyes look as dark as glittering obsidian blades. *"K'daholel,"* she whispered. "I love you."

The corners of his mouth turned up in a smile
sweet enough to charm the birds from the trees,
and Elizabeth laughed.

"Why do you laugh?" he asked. He lowered
his head until she felt the heat of his lips against
her own. Her mouth opened slightly and their
tongues caressed, retreated, and touched again.

Tremors of pleasure shot through Elizabeth.
"Come here," she ordered.

"I be here."

"No . . . closer." She put her arms around his
neck and pulled him down until her mind reeled
with the musky, virile scent of him. "God, but I
love you," she admitted.

Cain had bathed in the cold waters of the River
Avon; even now his thick hair was damp. His
body was always clean and free of sweat, more
so than any Englishman Elizabeth had ever
known. But there was a scent about him that was
his alone—a wild, strong odor that never ceased
to excite her.

Their lips met again and they kissed, gently at
first and then with smoldering passion. Elizabeth
moaned as the heat from Cain's thrusting tongue

surged through her to ignite a throbbing flame of longing. "Cain," she murmured. "Darling."

His left hand slipped between them to cup her softly rounding belly. "Be you well?" he asked tenderly. "This one would not harm our child with our love."

Elizabeth trembled at the force of his hard, bulging loin against her bare leg. "You will not hurt us," she said throatily. "This child is strong. If what has happened in the last weeks didn't hurt it, our love cannot." She arched her body against his and flicked her tongue along the line of his lower lip. "I want you, Cain . . . I need you."

"Ah." His breath was warm and sweet against her face. "My heart sings to hear your words." He brushed her cheek with his callused right palm. "*Wanishish-eyun*, Eliz-a-beth."

"I don't know those words," she whispered.

He sighed and ran his left hand possessively along her curving hip, then up across her midriff to cup a breast. "You must say the same to me," he instructed as his fingertips teased her nipple to a swollen bud. "*Wanishish-eyun*, Cain. *Nindau sauqeau.*"

"*Winishish-eyun*, Cain," she repeated. "*Nindau sauqeau*. Oh!" She cried out with joy at the exquisite sensations he was creating within her. "Oh . . . that's nice." He chuckled, lowering his head to take her nipple between his lips. "Ohhh."

"*Wanishish-eyun*—you are fair," he murmured. "*Nindau sauqeau*—this one can love a person." He raised his head and gazed at her again, taking both hands and spreading her hair around her face and down to cover part of her breasts. "Englishwoman with hair like autumn grass, you are fair," he said. "Most fair of any this warrior has seen.'' He lifted a silky lock of her hair and kissed it.

Elizabeth lay against the heaped hay with one knee flexed and one arm thrown above her head. ''And when I am not fair?'' she teased. ''When my body is as swollen as a whale, what then? Will you love me still, Lenape warrior? Or will you seek out a slim, dark-haired maiden with black eyes and a gentle tongue?''

He lowered his head to kiss her belly. ''This one will seek no other woman so long as you live.'' He kissed her again. ''You worry too many. Our child will make you beautiful. And you will be fair to this man when your hair is white as wind-driven sand upon a beach, and your teeth have worn away from chewing deer hides.''

''Deer hides? You expect me to chew deer hides?''

''Of truth, all good wives do. Makes hide soft.''

''Then you'll have to learn to like stiff hides,'' she protested. They both laughed as he threw himself upon her, entangling her legs in his and kissing her willing mouth again and again. They rolled over until she lay on top of him. His hand brushed against their folded clothing and his fingers closed around Elizabeth's string of pearls.

Still chuckling, Cain took the pearls and draped them in her hair. ''Pretty,'' he said. ''They glow like stars in the moonlight.'' With a single quick movement, he pinned her to the hay again. ''Now,'' he declared, ''you be this one's prisoner. I am Iroquois brave, and I take great *delust* in torturing prisoner.''

She giggled. ''*Delust*? What is *delust*?''

''I am showing you.'' He coiled the pearls into a circle and rubbed them across her cheek, lightly touching her skin. Then he lifted the necklace and kissed her where he'd rubbed the pearls.

She giggled again. "That's not torture."

His dark eyes sparkled with mischief. "It will be," he promised. "Wait." He brushed the pearls along the hollow of her throat, then kissed her.

Elizabeth's pulse quickened, and she twined her fingers in his hair. "I think I like this kind of torture."

Slowly, tantalizingly, he stroked her body in small, lazy circles. His touch was soothing, and a sweet languor spread through her. First, she was aware of the cool, smooth sensation of the pearls, then his moist tongue heated her skin. "Ummm." she sighed. "That's nice too."

A sheen of perspiration broke out over her body as Cain moved down to her breasts, over her navel, to caress her belly and loins. Her own hands would not be still. They moved over his broad shoulders and down the rippling muscles of his chest. Her breath came in ragged gasps, and she whimpered softly when his exquisite torture reached the apex of her thighs.

"Do you have surrender?" he said huskily. His face was taut, his eyes heavy-lidded with passion.

" 'Tis you who will surrender," she replied, snatching the pearls from his hand. They dropped from her fingers into the hay as she arched provocatively against him, exploring his lean buttocks with a wandering hand and catching his nipple between her teeth to suck gently. Her body flushed with desire as she writhed beneath him. She moaned deep in her throat, rubbing her love-swollen breasts against his chest, fanning the flames of her own desire, until Cain rolled onto his back and pulled her on top of him again.

"Love me like this," he urged, lifting her hips

until she settled astride him and felt the impassioned thrust of his throbbing manhood. "Come to me, wife," he murmured hoarsely. "Join with me."

The flame that burned within her had become a fierce aching. She gasped as he filled her with love . . . as they sought a mutual rhythm of giving and taking. She clung to him, crying out with joy as the intensity of their white-hot desire rose to fever pitch. Elizabeth felt as though they were caught in some great cresting wave, reaching higher and higher . . . until at last they tumbled together into the depths of the cool, dark sea.

For what seemed forever, she floated, unaware of time or place. Then she felt Cain's lips against her own, and she sighed contentedly. "Will it always be like that for us?" she asked him.

He chuckled. "Perhaps. Perhaps it be better."

She laughed and laid her head against his chest. "Hold me," she whispered. "Hold me."

They slept and woke to love again. And as the first rays of dawn tinged the loft with red and gold, Cain rose from his place beside her and searched the hay for the string of pearls.

"What are you doing?" Elizabeth asked sleepily.

"Looking for your beads."

She rubbed her eyes and sat up. "My pearls?"

"Here they be." He held them up before her. "You say the English treasure these beads."

"Yes, but—"

"Do the tribe called Irish value them too?"

"Of course, but why—"

"This man Sean and his wife, they go across the sea. This is true?"

"Yes. You heard Bridget. They have signed on as indentured servants. A ship will take them to

Virginia, and they will work for Englishmen there
until their time is up.''

''Their names be written down in an English
book?''

''Yes.''

''If we try to go on ship, men will write down
our names and Edward's men will capture us—
true?''

Elizabeth nodded. ''Of course, but—''

''Hah.'' Cain sat back on his heels and grinned.
''The English never look at the faces of servants.
They be servants, like some would say, 'They be
horses.' ''

Elizabeth pulled the blanket around her breasts,
blushing as she remembered what had passed between them in the night. ''I don't understand
what—''

''Listen, woman. Always you talk, talk and do
not listen. This Sean and his woman Maureen,
they go to Virginia because they are poor. Yes?''

''Yes. Sean has no real trade and there are
many men seeking each job.''

He pulled a full-sleeved shirt over his head.
''Then we give them your beads, and we take
their places on this ship that sails west to my land.
No one looks at our faces when we go aboard.
We be Irish servants, yes?''

Elizabeth dropped the blanket and stared at him
in surprise. ''It might work. Yes! It might—at least
it's a chance.'' She threw her arms around his
neck, and they rolled over and over in the prickly
hay.

''You think I make good Irishman?'' Cain asked
as he covered her face with kisses.

She laughed. ''No. But you might pass as one
if I can keep you from talking.'' She ruffled his

short hair. "And until this grows out, you'll be safe from Iroquois war parties."

"Hmmm." He grimaced. "A warrior must make sacrifices."

She hugged him tightly, and her expression grew serious. "If we get to America, we'll still be in danger," she murmured. "We'll be bond servants—prisoners. They'll expect us to work for many years at the hardest kind of labor."

Cain's dark eyes gleamed. "Show me the shores of my own land," he said softly, "and this one will find a way to deal with the English. Our child must be born free. I will wrap her in a bearskin and carry her down to the sea at the sun's dawning."

"A daughter? And if it's a boy?"

Cain laughed. "A bearskin will do for a Lenni-Lenape warrior. But do not pick a name. That honor goes to *Cocumtha*. She will ask a blessing for our child. She will choose what the little one is to be called."

Elizabeth grew thoughtful. "If she's still alive. But she's old, Cain. She may have died while we were gone."

He shook his head. "No, *Cocumtha* lives. She lives to cradle our child—yours and mine." He sighed. "One thing I have worry of."

Elizabeth's green eyes grew large. "What's that?"

"Suppose my child has green eyes like cat instead of proper color brown eyes? It make great disgrace."

"You!" Grabbing a handful of hay, she stuffed it down the front of his shirt. Cain had to remove both the shirt and his breeches to get rid of the hay, and in the process, Elizabeth lost her blanket.

The sun was high overhead when they returned to Sean's room to meet the others.

It was midmorning before Elizabeth could explain their plan to Sean and Maureen and Robert and Bridget. "I will give you a letter of ownership," Elizabeth said to Sean. "If you take the pearls to my agent, Micah Levinson, in London, he will sell them and give you a fair price. Then if you still want to go to the New World, you can go as landowners, not servants."

" 'Twould mean us breakin' the law," Sean answered slowly. He looked at his wife. "But 'twould also mean the difference between poverty and riches. What say ye, Maureen?"

"Me, I'd rather go home to Connaugh and live like squires than cross the sea to be eaten by wild beasts and carry out chamber pots for the English." Timidly, she reached for Sean's hand. "Take the necklace, mon. I'd see my old grandsir again before I die."

"Ye know what yer doin', lady?" Bridget asked. "If ye take Maureen's place, 'tis no turnin' back. Ye leave yer place here and all it means to become common folk."

"Among the people, the Lenni-Lenape, there be no common folk," Cain said. "Eliz-a-beth will be a free woman."

"You'd forsake all fer the wilderness, lady?" Bridget continued. "Be certain, is all I say."

"What's certain is that Lord Dunmore will have them murdered if they stay in England," Robert put in. "If they try to buy passage, someone will mark their names and report them to Lord Dunmore for the reward. They'll not live to sail as paying passengers, I vow."

Robert had sold the remaining two horses and

had offered the money to Elizabeth. She'd refused, saying the silver was little enough reward for what he'd done to help them. "I've no means to buy passage, other than the pearls," Elizabeth said. "If I try to sell them in Bristol, we'll be discovered, and there's no time for me to try and find Micah."

"Ye have other means," Bridget said. She went to a shelf and took down a tiny blackened tin. "This is yers, m'lady." She dumped the contents into Elizabeth's hands. " 'Tis your emerald necklace, as ye well know. I stole it when his lordship asked for yer jewels." She blushed to the roots of her dark hair. "I thought ye were dead, lady, and I was afraid of bein' turned out wi' nothin' for my years o' service. I'd never steal from ye alive, but—" Her shoulders quivered, and she began to weep.

Cain took the necklace from Elizabeth's hand and held it in the sunlight that streamed through an open window. "This is great value too?"

Elizabeth nodded.

"Of use to English, but little among my people. Better we have brass fishhooks."

"I agree," Elizabeth said. She met Cain's steady gaze, then glanced meaningfully at Bridget.

Cain put the gold and emerald necklace into Bridget's hands. "We will trade," he said. "We want good English fishhooks and needles and thread." He grinned at Robert. "Is enough, this necklace, to buy a bakery?"

Elizabeth looked puzzled. "Bakery?"

"Robert tells me he take Bridget as wife," Cain explained. "He says he will not be footman again. He wants to make bread and sell to others."

"But I can't take it," Bridget wailed. "I stole
. . . and . . . and . . ."

"I'd say my necklace will buy a bakery, and a
mill to grind the flour," Elizabeth said. She rose
and went to stand beside Cain. "You have served
me faithfully for many years, Bridget, and—"

"And I lied to ye too!" She sniffed loudly.
"Maureen were never sick when I didn't come to
the *Speedwell* afore. I didn't come because I was
afraid to sail across to the Colonies." She rubbed
her nose with the back of her hand. "I don't deserve—"

"You probably don't," Elizabeth agreed, "but
since I am your lady and you are my maid, you'll
have to accept my gift. Take the emerald and buy
Robert the bakery he wants. He's a good man,
Bridget. I can think of no two people I'd rather
see happy."

"Ye could come wi' us," Sean suggested,
"back to Ireland. It's a fair land, Robert. Not too
many Englishmen."

"Are ye forgettin' he's English?" Maureen
asked.

"I try to overlook it," Sean replied with a grin.

"Then you'll do as we ask?" Elizabeth laid her
hand on Sean's arm. "You'll let us take your
places on the ship?"

"Aye," Sean said. "We will. The *Portsmouth
Maid* sails in a week with a cargo of indentured
servants fer the Virginia Colony. A friend o' mine,
Johnny Dooley, and his sister are sailin' on it. Me-
thinks they'd help ye out a little if they could.
And God go wi' ye, yer ladyship. Ye'll need His
blessing to make a safe journey wi'out being discovered."

"Ye'll have our prayers, m'lady," Bridget assured her. "I'll never forget you." She began to weep again.

"Don't cry for me," Elizabeth said as she took hold of Cain's hand. "I'm leaving nothing behind that I care for except my friends."

"But it's a wilderness," Bridget said. "Full o' savages and bears."

Elizabeth squeezed Cain's hand. "True enough," she agreed, "but I've come to favor savages more and more."

The Virginia Coast
August 1665

The sailing ship, the *Portsmouth Maid*, ninety-two days out of Bristol, lay off the Virginia capes waiting for an easterly wind to carry her safely into the Chesapeake Bay. Despite unseasonable calms and a severe storm off Hatteras, the ship had made what her captain considered a fortunate voyage. Only twenty-one of their one hundred and ten passengers had died of illness and misadventure, all but two of those indentured servants.

For days, the captain had waited only a few leagues from land for the prevailing westerlies to change. The August heat was oppressive below-decks, and he feared that more of the cargo of bondmen and women would sicken and die if they couldn't reach land soon. In desperation, he had ordered that the servants be allowed up on deck for a few hours to bathe in buckets of sea water and to benefit from the slight movement of air.

Among those who climbed the ladders out of the hold were a small group of Irishmen and women, including a man and wife on the ship's list as Sean and Maureen Cleary. Maureen Cleary was swelling with child, as were several of the other women servants aboard ship, and her husband was especially protective of her as they came on deck. He paused for a moment by the railing and stared east at the faint line of trees.

"Aye," a sailor cried. "There's Virginia Colony o'er there. Pray God we kin ever get t' it."

The Irishmen kept away from the English indentured servants. They gathered together in a knot at the stern of the vessel and spoke among themselves in their native Gaelic. The Clearys did not speak at all, but no one appeared to notice, and no one saw the small eelskin bundle that Sean Cleary hid inside a coil of rope.

After a few hours, the captain ordered the indentured servants returned to their quarters belowdecks. The wind was beginning to shift, and he had hopes of making the mouth of the bay before midnight.

Two hours before midnight, Cain and Elizabeth crept silently up the ladder toward the deck. "Are you certain it's safe to try now?" she whispered.

"No, but it be not safe to wait longer." He took her arm and helped her the last few steps. "The Irish have hid us aboard ship, but in the English town I would be seen. No man will put irons on Shaakhan Kihittuun again."

A crescent moon lit the deck in fitful patterns. Clouds hung low over the land, which was too far away for Elizabeth to see in the dark. The air was hot and humid; far off to the south, she heard thunder rumble. "Are you certain you know which way the shore is?" she asked.

Cain held her hand tightly as they made their way to the stern of the ship where he had left the small bundle containing their supplies of fish-hooks, needles and thread, and his knife. They halted and stood motionless in the shadows of the mast as a sailor passed by close enough for Elizabeth to smell the rum on his breath.

"I'm afraid," she admitted.

"Do you want to go back?"

"No."

"Good." They reached the coil of rope, and Cain stripped off his clothing and tied the eelskin bundle around his neck. "Now you," he urged. "Quick."

Her teeth chattering from fright, Elizabeth unfastened her skirt and stepped out of it. Next came her blouse, her shoes and stockings, and her stays. When she was clad only in a thin linen shift, Cain motioned her to the railing and threw all of their clothing over the side.

"Why?" she whispered.

"We leave no trail for the English captain to follow." He pulled her into his arms and kissed her. "Hold your breath," he warned. Then, before she could protest, he lifted her high over the rail and tossed her into the sea.

Elizabeth struck the warm water with a splash and went under. She bobbed up and began to swim as Cain surfaced beside her.

"Be you all right?" he demanded.

"Yes, yes, I'm fine."

"Then hold my back, and let us swim." Moonlight shone on his laughing face. "I wish to get the smell of this English ship off my skin forever."

Elizabeth clung to Cain as he swam with powerful strokes away from the slowly moving ship. She kept glancing back over her shoulder to see if anyone had heard the splashes and discovered their escape, but she saw no sign of any movement other than the sailors at their normal tasks.

Gradually, the ship grew smaller in the distance, and to the east, she could make out a dark line she knew was beach. "I must be mad," she said to Cain. "I've nothing, not even a shoe for my foot or a cradle for our babe."

He laughed. "The woman who wants little is happier than the one who has much. Be you happy, Eliz-a-beth?"

"Yes." And she laughed with him. "Very, very happy."

Cain turned in the water and took her in his arms again. "I will make moccasins for your feet, *ki-te-hi*, and a cradleboard for our little one to sleep in."

"But who will chew the hides to make his blanket?"

"That, my *keequa*, we must bargain over." He kissed her again, and they turned east toward home and a new beginning.

Epilogue

July 1672

Elizabeth sat on the sand with her bare feet in the cool, foamy surf and watched as Cain speared fish in chest-deep water. Behind her, in the shade of the pine and oak trees, copper-skinned children ran and laughed beside a half dozen summer wigwams. A few feet away, a saucy black-capped tern perched on the bow of Cain's unfinished dugout and regarded her quizzically.

Up the beach, Elizabeth's friend, Dame Equiwa, Corn Woman, waded out of the blue-green water with a basket of clams. Wearing only a short woven grass skirt, she paused with the container balanced on her hip and called an affectionate greeting.

Elizabeth smiled and waved. "Good catch."

"Join us for the evening meal," Corn Woman shouted. She pushed a heavy wet braid back off her heart-shaped face. "I'll make berry cakes to go with the clam soup."

Elizabeth nodded and rose, plunging into the gently swirling water up to her knees. Cain came

364

toward her with a large trout squirming on the
end of his fish spear. Drops of sea water sparkled like diamonds against the fish's iridescent
scales.

"Will two be enough?" Cain called.

"What? I can't hear you?" Elizabeth shaded
her eyes against the bright sun with a tanned
hand. Her heart thrilled like that of an adoles-
cent girl as she gazed at him, taking in the corded
muscles rippling beneath the bronze surface of
his skin, the flat, hard belly above the short
leather loincloth, the sleek sinewy thighs. He's
my husband, she chided herself mentally. What
decent wedded woman gets butterflies in her
stomach whenever she looks at the father of her
children?

Yards behind Cain the surf broke, and the
waves rushed toward the beach only to ebb and
break again. Seagulls wheeled and dove overhead, adding their raucous cries to the voices of
the children and the crashing waves.

He waded closer. "Will two fish be enough?
This one's smaller than—" He broke off as Elizabeth turned her attention to the child in the tiny
dugout, paddling an arrow's shot beyond the
breakers.

Cain put a comforting arm around Elizabeth's
shoulder. "Have not worry," he said in English.
"Look at her. She's as much at home in the sea
as they are." He laughed as the fairy-sprite stood,
balanced herself gracefully in the child-sized dugout, then flung her lithe, honey-colored body onto
the back of a dolphin. The heads and fins of two
more dolphins appeared on the far side the dugout—a huge male and an infant.

Elizabeth gasped. No matter how many times

she'd seen her daughter ride the female dolphin, Elizabeth had never lost her fear for the child.

"Shhh," Cain soothed. "Look at her."

Laughing, the child clung to the dolphin's dorsal fin as the majestic creature rose out of the water and skittered across the top of the waves. The dolphin gave one final bounce and dove gently. The girl's head disappeared beneath the water, and Elizabeth's heart missed a beat. Then her daughter's dark crown appeared, followed by an ecstatic little face. Her laughter drifted across the water to her proud parents as she swam back to the dugout with sure, effortless strokes.

The larger male dolphin nosed her gently as she climbed back into the boat. Giggling, the child scooped a fish from the bottom of the craft and tossed it to her "rescuer."

"Mar'ee!" Cain called. He waved to the girl. "Enough play. Time to come in and help your mother."

"*Nukuaa*," she pleaded. "Please, Father. Just a little while longer. The baby dolphin nearly ate from my hand."

"Now, Mary!" Elizabeth insisted.

Reluctantly, the child waved a paddle in assent. "All right, I'm coming."

"You spoil her frightfully," Elizabeth said to Cain as they returned to the beach. "No English child would dare be so familiar with her father."

"No child is spoiled by love," he replied. "Our people have always raised children so. They are a gift of the Maker." Removing the trout from his long barbed spear, he carefully washed the blood from the haft.

A naked four-year-old boy, Dame Equiwa's

oldest, ran toward them eagerly. "I'll carry your fish spear, uncle," he lisped in Algonquian. "I'll be careful, I promise."

"In English?" Elizabeth asked. "Can you say it in English?" She had long since given up trying to sort out Cain's relatives and clan members, and accepted the fact that most of the children of the tribe would call them uncle and aunt out of respect if not blood kinship.

Konueek's round face twisted with effort. "Me car-ray arrow of fish. Pl-eashe!"

Cain and Elizabeth laughed. "Very good," Elizabeth said as Cain handed the boy his spear. "Keep the point away from you, and walk—don't run."

"Your lessons be having effect," Cain said as the child trudged manfully ahead of them bearing the long wooden spear like a trophy. "Soon, children of our tribe speak English almost as good as me."

She cut her eyes to him. "It's what I love most about you, Cain, your modesty. I hope they learn to speak better than you. Then I'll teach them all to read and to write. We can't let Mary and her brother grow up ignorant, can we?"

"You would make Englishmen and women out of them all," he teased in his own tongue. Other children came to carry the fish to Elizabeth and Cain's wigwam, and Cain took his wife's hand and drew her into the shade of a spreading oak. "It is well you teach them. Some people do not want their children to learn strange English ways, but knowledge is good. It makes us strong. The time is coming fast when our way of life will be challenged by the coming of the white man. We must change, or we will be no more."

Elizabeth looked back toward the beach where her daughter was bringing her dugout through the surf onto the sand. Her hair, as black and glossy as a crow's wing, hung loose in a silken curtain to her narrow waist. Mary's petite body was as slim and muscular as a boy's, her sturdy legs beneath her woven skirt were strong from running and climbing. Her tiny hands were equally skilled in drawing a bowstring or skinning a rabbit. But no boy ever had such beautiful eyes, large and expressive beneath perfect dark brows, eyes as green as the sea off Dover—Sommersett eyes, she thought.

Elizabeth blinked back the moisture that gathered in her own eyes as she gazed at Mary. "What will the world be for her?" she murmured, as much to herself as to Cain. "Where does she belong?"

"Wherever she wants to," he answered. "I will teach her our ways, and you will teach her of her English heritage. Mar'ee will find her own path . . . and she will run over it as lightly as the mist skims over the sea." He pulled Elizabeth close against him. "Are you sorry? Did you make the wrong choice when you followed me back to this land?"

She whirled in his arms and hugged him tightly. "Never!" she cried. "Never. You . . . your people have given me a happiness . . . a peace I never knew existed. I—"

"Eliz-a-beth! Eliz-a-beth!" Dame Equiwa came toward them with a brightly decorated cradleboard in her arms. "Your small warrior is awake," she explained good-naturedly, "and he's fussing for what only you can give him."

Elizabeth took the baby and began to whisper calming endearments as she unlaced him from the softly padded cradleboard. "All right, all right, sweetness," she murmured. "I believe his hair is going to be much lighter than Mary's," she said to Cain, "but these eyes are getting browner every day."

Cain took his two-week-old son from her gently and cuddled him against his chest. "Proper color eyes for a man," he teased, "human eyes."

The baby cooed and stared wide-eyed at his mother's face. Then one corner of the tiny mouth turned up in a smile.

"It's time you had a name," Elizabeth said. "I don't know why—"

"*Cocumtha!*" Mary shrieked with joy. "She comes! *Cocumtha* comes!"

Elizabeth stepped around Cain's bulk to look down the beach. Mary was already leading a group of shouting children toward the approaching procession of men and women. Swinging from a stout pole between two bearers was the leather sack-chair that could only contain Cain's indomitable grandmother, Mistress Virginia Dare.

"I told you *Cocumtha* could smell a feast days away," Cain said. "She's come to share our joy of this little son and to give him a name."

"Well, she'd better not decide to call him Walter Raleigh, or Ananias, after her father."

Cain laughed. "Would you prefer Mikoppokinaakun or Kuikuenkuikiilat?"

"Frog? You would, wouldn't you? You'd name your firstborn son Frog just to annoy me," she teased back. She knew that their son would have an Indian baby name, a secret name, and later a name that he would earn and live by as an adult. She was certain that Mistress Dare would chose a proper English name for the baby to please her granddaughter by marriage. "I was thinking more of Henry, or perhaps Arthur. Henry Dare—that has a solid ring to it.''

''Aiiee. But what do they mean, these English names? They sound like bare feet slapping against mud.'' He kissed the top of the infant's head and handed him to his mother. The bright-eyed baby was sucking hungrily at his fingers. ''Feed him,'' Cain said. ''He needs his strength for a name day.''

''I don't suppose you suggested any names to your grandmother the last time we saw her,'' Elizabeth said. She nestled the baby against her and pulled a full breast from her soft doeskin gown. Everyone in the village had run down the beach to meet their guests, and she and Cain and the baby were alone. ''Pretty names?''

''Pretty,'' he scoffed. ''Pretty for a warrior?'' He looked down at them with loving eyes. ''Perhaps I did mention that your father's name was Roger.''

Her eyes sought his. ''I loved him dearly, but I'd not name our son for that hard man. If I had a choice, he would be called Adam.''

''What means this . . . this Adam?''

''He was the first man my God created.''

''He was a good man?''

''I believe that all men and women spring from his loins.''

''Adam. Adam Dare.'' Cain pursed his lips and nodded slowly. ''Yes, it sounds like an arrow hitting a mark. A good name. It may be that *Cocumtha* will chose this Adam name.'' He smiled at her and his son. ''In fact, Eliz-a-beth mine, I will wager you a new copper cooking pot on it.''

''And where would you get a copper pot?''

''Ah hah!'' He grinned. ''Always does a woman question, question a man when he brings her presents. A woman should say 'Thank you' to her lord, and be properly grateful. Like so.'' Quickly, he removed a leather pouch from the cradleboard and took out a beautiful necklace of silver beads and turquoise. His hands trembled as he fastened it around her neck.

"Oh, Cain," she cried. "It's beautiful. But where . . .''

He stepped back to see how the necklace graced her smooth throat. "You traded your jewelry to bring us home," he said huskily in Algonquian. "Tonight, you receive many gifts from our friends and relatives in honor of your new son. There will be feasting and dancing—all will share in our joy. But this one is selfish. He wants to see your eyes alone when I give this to you.''

Elizabeth touched the brilliant blue stones one after another. "I've never seen anything like this. But our tribe doesn't—''

"No, not our people. The necklace comes from far away to the south in the land of the setting sun. These stones"—he fingered one of the turquoises—"are said to be pieces of the sky.''

"But how? What did you have to trade for such a lovely thing?''

"Wampum. The shell beads of my people. In the land of west, our things are precious. From hand to hand they are traded. When I saw this, I knew it must be for my wife.''

The baby gurgled, and Elizabeth shifted him to the other breast. She raised her eyes to Cain. "I love you," she whispered, "and I love your gift. I'll wear it always.''

He bent and brushed her lips tenderly with his. "This one has love for you, Eliz-a-beth," he murmured. "Since I took you from the sea, we were bound together.'' He pulled back, and his eyes sought hers. ''Be you content, *ki-te-hi*, truly?''

She laughed up at him, and the glow in her eyes told him all his heart demanded to know.

Avon Romances—
the best in exceptional authors and unforgettable novels!

The Timeless Romances
of New York Times Bestselling Author

JOHANNA
LINDSEY